Praise for the novels of Mon

"The Jewel of the Blues is a gem... Monica Chenault-____ jazz in Jim Crow America to vivid life, gritty and unfo_____

—**Kate Quinn, *New York Times* bestselling author**

"The Jewel of the Blues is a dazzling Jazz-Age novel that propels the reader onstage alongside Lucille Love as she sets her sights on stardom. Vivid detail and page-turning drama make this a fascinating read."

—**Chanel Cleeton, *New York Times* and *USA TODAY* bestselling author of *The House on Biscayne Bay***

"Chenault-Kilgore brings to life a rich and soulful tale of ambition, vengeance, and yearning. At the book's heart is a rhythmic portrayal of love, family, and friendship. A sparkling jewel, indeed."

—**Diane Marie Brown, author of *Black Candle Women*, on *The Jewel of the Blues***

"The Jewel of the Blues is a jewel of a novel! I thoroughly enjoyed traveling right beside the melodic Loves in this story of music, family, love, loss, redemption, and dreams."

—**Eliza Knight, *USA TODAY* and internationally bestselling author of *Starring Adele Astaire***

"Chenault-Kilgore's latest is an ode to the Black musicians of the Jazz Age who risked everything to follow their dreams, as well as a taut drama bursting with intrigue. In Lucille, she's conjured up a heroine who practically leaps off the page with her passion and spark. Enthralling, fearless, and joyful."

—**Fiona Davis, *New York Times* bestselling author of *The Spectacular*, on *The Jewel of the Blues***

"A vivid and captivating tale of the glamorous Lucille Love, as she navigates the Jazz era with courage and dignity, in spite of a family secret that threatens to unravel the brilliant career she's created."

—**Joshunda Saunders, author of *Women of the Post*, on *The Jewel of the Blues***

THE
JEWEL
OF THE
BLUES

MONICA
CHENAULT-KILGORE

GRAYDON
HOUSE

**GRAYDON
HOUSE®**

ISBN-13: 978-1-525-80506-6

The Jewel of the Blues

Graydon House
22 Adelaide St. West, 41st Floor
Toronto, Ontario M5H 4E3, Canada
www.GraydonHouseBooks.com

Printed in U.S.A.

Recycling programs
for this product may
not exist in your area.

Also by Monica Chenault-Kilgore

Long Gone, Come Home

Visit the author at monicachenaultkilgore.com.

For John, with love

THE FRUIT MAN'S BLUES

There once was a man who sold me sweet, sweet berries
A helluva good man was he
He loved his wife
And he loved his life
But what he loved most was me
You see I was his child born from the seeds of cherries
With a voice as luscious as fresh strawberries
He gave me the sky
And taught me to fly
On all the gold coins he could carry
I don't have time to give him all his praise
I got to work, work, work, work so I can get a raise
But just one little slice
Of fruit so juicy and ripe
Sends me back to see him no matter the price
Oh, how I wish
I could get me a dish
Of that fine chocolate man's blackberries

PART I

THE LOVES

Hank and Evelyn Love

1

Evansville, Indiana
1906

"Straaaw-ber-ries... Fresh pa-lumms... Suc-cu-lent fresh fruits and vegetables! Cuu-cumbers!" Hank Love swiped the back of his hand across his sweaty forehead before singing out the next verse. "Get your nice, plump straaaw-ber-ries here!"

Caught in the rapture of the heat and white streaks of baking sunlight, the sweet perfume rolled off the peaches, plums and strawberries. To get Caesar, his steadfast silent partner for the day, to take a couple steps forward, Hank patted the horse's hind parts. Caesar bobbed his head in compliance and pulled the fruit cart deeper into the cooler alley and out of the sun. The handmade sign advertising Fresh Fruit and Produce posted at the alley's entryway, along with the wafting fresh fragrance of the fruits and vegetables, would be enough to entice buyers to his makeshift stall. It wasn't quite noon, and the city streets were filled. But, unfortunately, only a few passersby took the steps off the sidewalk to inspect Hank's display.

Hank took a rag out of his pocket to wipe his forehead that was now peppered with beads of sweat. The heat wasn't the only cause for Hank's perspiration—it was also worry. He had to sell as much as he could today because he desperately needed money to pay for his tenancy. So far, it didn't look promising. He had never missed a payment, but he couldn't count on any leniency from the landlord—not here in Evansville, Indiana. The landlord made no bones about wanting him off the property that Hank and his family had worked for all the years they'd stomped their feet across the dirt. He, his wife, Evelyn, their baby girl, Lucille, as well as the rest of their blood and extended family that lived under the same roof, never lacked for food; they ate what they grew. But coming up with the money to keep the little family on the plot of land had become increasingly tough. Most times Hank was able to put aside his worry and leave it in God's hands. Month after month, He never failed him. But this month was promising to be a test of faith because the money just wasn't there.

Evansville had become a sundown town. There was a law on the books that colored folks had to be off the road before dusk or risk going to jail—or worse. So Hank needed to sell what he had while the sun was still in the sky, and in enough time to be home by sunset to avoid trouble. There had been racial skirmishes in nearby cities as of late. He, along with his neighbors, raised their voices to protest, but city leaders refused to hear their case. They also included the threat of coming to every Negro's home within the city limits to discuss the law in detail. Despite the veiled intimidation, the protests continued. Until the law was overturned, Hank didn't want to take any chances of being a victim of repercussions.

A stray black cat shot through the alleyway. Startled, both Hank and Caesar jumped. Then Hank froze in his tracks. Following the cat's trajectory was the progressive padding sound of boots striking cobblestone coming from the street. Hank turned slowly, intending to chase off a random kid who sometimes tried to steal from him, but the sharp click of metal told him he needed to take a different course of action.

The top of his head went cold when he caught sight of a shotgun barrel pointed directly at him.

At the other end of the gun were the steady gray eyes of a grimy white man leaning against the back of the wagon. Caesar danced from side to side from the unexpected weight of the stranger.

"Whoa, boy," Hank whispered as he gently patted the horse and kept his eyes on the shotgun. The horse's muscles vibrated, and Hank could tell Caesar's nervousness matched his own.

The man pushed away a bushel of cucumbers that went rolling across the ground. "Boy, you better do exactly what I say or today is gonna be your last day." He hopped in the back of the wagon, kicking aside a box of peaches. A few tumbled over and their rose-colored bottoms hit the stones.

Caesar threw back his head, gave a deep-throated whinny and jerked the wagon forward.

The man wriggled his way between the boxes and bushels and lay down flat against the wagon bottom. From clenched teeth, the man squeezed out, "Now, let's get going—and just 'member I've got this gun aimed right at the back of your head."

Hank saw the man was bleeding. A growing red stain spread across the front of his jacket, but the man made no effort to conceal his wound. He kept both hands on his shotgun and held tightly to a large sack tucked under his arm. A piercing staccato of gunshots suddenly rang out from the main street and reverberated against the brick walls of the surrounding buildings. Hank whipped his head toward the entrance of the alley and saw the silhouettes of men in long coats with long guns and bags in their arms, whizzing past. In their wake was a chaotic commotion of gunfire, shattering glass and people screaming and shouting. Even from where he stood, Hank could see that the men who raced by looked just like the man who was now hidden from sight, wrapped around bushels and boxes of produce, tucked away in the back of his wagon.

Caesar suddenly bolted, grapevining his hooves from one side of the alley to the other, tugging on his reins with the intent of escaping the noise. The frightened horse lunged against his reins in every direction, and each time the wagon tipped from one side to the other, sending heads of lettuce and tomatoes flying to the ground. The wagon swayed deeply until it finally flipped over—along with its passenger—crashing against the cobblestones. Spooked even more, Caesar dragged the overturned wagon farther into the alleyway, which dead-ended into the back of another building.

Hank peered through the capsized wagon's splintered planks. The man, buried in a rubble of produce, grunted and wheezed. "Get me out of here, nigga! Help me…"

Hank could see the man's eyes rolling back into his head. The corner of a broken wagon slat was embedded squarely in the man's chest. His pleas for help faded against a cloud of footsteps and the grinding sound of vehicles from the street. Hank looked up from the recesses of the alley to see people running in one direction—toward whatever happened—or seeming to chase the new motorized police wagon that had barreled past. Hank couldn't imagine what possibly occurred to draw such a stream of curious people, but he knew his bleeding passenger had a hand in it.

Hank peeled back broken wood to try to free the man. It was then the sack that the man had held firmly pressed against his body caught Hank's eye. It was partially hidden under pieces of fruit and splintered wood. He wasn't sure what drove him to do it, but Hank slowly reached into the mass of rubble and tugged at the corner of the sack. It was heavy. When he received no resistance—an assurance that the man was dead or close to it—he yanked the bag to release it from between sharp edges of broken slats. Property of Second National Bank and Trust appeared across the bloodstained cloth. Hank looked toward the street. Still, no one came to his rescue or even seemed to notice him. He managed to stuff the sack under his arm inside his jacket. Watching the wagon for any movement, he moved slowly toward Caesar, who calmed at his touch but bucked to give the wagon a final hard kick.

A shotgun blast exploded from the wagon. Hank fell backward. A spray of splintered wood and pulpy fruit flesh splattered his face. Hank felt searing pain rip through his skin leaving a trail from his cheek to the top of his head. From that point, all Hank heard were the muted sounds of Caesar's hooves stomping at the ground and screams coming from somewhere in the far distance. All he could see was a blur of purple, orange and red until it faded to black.

When Hank regained consciousness, searing pain shot from the top of his skull and a hot stream of blood stung his eyes. He winced as each of Caesar's four legs hit the ground. He held his head, which felt like a heavy sack filled with cotton. He couldn't recall how he unhitched and mounted the horse or when he left the remnants of his wagon along with the dead man in the alley. He couldn't remember how he ended up on the silent road leading away from town. Although the road in front of him was a blur, he knew the horse would find his way back home. When he could no longer focus, Hank let Caesar make his way down the roadway at his own pace, allowing the pain to take over and send him back to unconsciousness.

When he opened his eyes again, through a gauzy haze Hank saw the small white clapboard church he called home in front of him. He took a deep breath and fell against the horse's neck, relieved. Through a peephole of light, Hank could barely make out a neat dirt path leading to a prim white two-story house with four windows. White sheets pinned to a clothesline whipped in the light breeze. He slid to the ground, leaning against the side of the building. Hank's heavy limbs seemed plastered to the spot. The grass was cool and wet beneath him. The bag had fallen open and gold coins spilled out over his legs and the grass that he now saw was tinged red with blood.

His head rang with a hymn that climbed octaves, piercing through the bright blue sky. It was the beautiful soprano voice of his wife, Evelyn, accompanied on the piano by her father, Reverend John Pike. Her operatic high notes stung, or maybe it was the big black rowdy bees that were buzzing around the windowsill above his head.

Am I in heaven? Hank thought.

As if to answer his question, Hank patted the hard ground before digging his fingers into the earth. Pushing hard against the ground, he lifted his body, attempting to stand. He succeeded only a few inches until his knees gave way and he collapsed.

"Daddy!" A barefoot little girl ran up to him but stopped short a few feet away at the edge of the building. A rustling of skirts followed closely behind the child.

"Hank! Hank!" Evelyn knelt beside him, delicately touching his face to examine the extent of his injuries. "What happened, Hank? Where's the wagon?"

Jumbled thoughts spilled out in a collage of sentences. "I… I gotta go back… Evelyn, they be looking me…them fruit is gonna spoil… They're gonna hang me for sure…"

"Hank, you're talking gibberish. What's all this?" Evelyn picked up the bag and a shower of coins fell to the ground. "Where did you get this money?"

The little girl, sensing fear and confusion, started to cry.

Hank mumbled, "Is that my baby…my little angel? C'mere, Lucille." He weakly waved his hand, motioning the child to come closer. "C'mon over and hug yo' daddy."

The child hesitated at first, but then bounced over, flung her body into her father's lap and proceeded to pick up a handful of gold coins. "Daddy, are you hurt?"

Hank winced, gritted his teeth and sucked in his breath before responding in an even tone. "I'm all right, girl. I ain't hurt."

"Good. But what happened to you? You look hurt. Are you sure? I love you, Daddy."

"Ah, now that's the sweetest sound I'd ever wanted to hear."

"Get out the way, Evelyn. Let me get this man to the house." Reverend Pike rounded the corner. The reverend was a commanding figure both in stature and voice. When he spoke, anyone in earshot did exactly as they were instructed. Evelyn stepped aside.

Reverand Pike bellowed, "Can you stand, Hank?"

Evelyn instructed the child to go to the kitchen to help the cook. She then joined her father and wrapped Hank's arm over her shoulder to help lift her husband up the stairs. They reached the stairs to the house, and Hank could no longer lift his leg. His head throbbed and his sight was fading.

Hank, having passed out again, awoke in a gray fog. Wrapped tightly in starched sheets and under a pile of quilts, Hank wrestled with the covers until he freed his arms and torso enough to sit up. He touched the damp, sticky, blood-spotted bandages that were wrapped around his head and half of his face. The slow-moving mechanism in his head ground gears trying to piece together the previous events. Through the haze of cotton gauze, Evelyn's face came into view. Her knitted brows and lined forehead told him all he needed to know—that he must look like he was on death's doorstep. Hank shifted his body, swiveled out from underneath the stiff sheets and blankets, but the pain held him locked in his spot on the bed.

"Don't even try to move, Hank. Rest. You need to rest. We can talk about what happened later."

"Evie, wipe them frown lines from your face. Don't worry.

I'm all right." He took a deep breath, puffed out his cheeks to blow away a wave of dizziness. "Ooo, it feels like you pulled a shade down over my eye." He hovered his hand over his left eye. "It feels like sharp knives are poking me in this eye, but I can still see pretty good out of this one." He gently patted the right side of his face to lightly rub tears running from his good eye. "Yep, I can see my sweet angel." He tried to give her a smile, hoping it would ease his wife's fears. "How long have I been out?"

"Hank, you haven't been laying here long at all. It's only been about a half hour or so since we brought you in here and cleaned you up. Now, please lay still till we can get a doctor over here to have a look at you."

"Ain't gonna be no doctor. No need." Grimacing, a thunderbolt of pain shot through Hank's head and he plopped back against the headboard.

"How you doing, Hank?" The reverend's deep voice cut through the conversation.

"I'm trying my best to keep him still, Father. Did you find anything out?"

Before answering his daughter, Reverend Pike leaned in close to whisper into Hank's ear. "They gonna be looking for that money, Hank."

Hank nodded feebly. "But they don't know I have it. Wasn't nobody in that alley but me, Caesar and a dead man that's buried underneath the wagon."

"That dead man was one of them bank robbers. Right before we found you, Zeke came running up here saying that the police are looking for three men who took all of Second National's money. They shot up Main Street and killed some innocent folks as they escaped."

Evelyn jumped in. "Robbers? Dead man? Hank, what have you gotten into?"

Hank stayed silent. Reverend Pike continued, "I don't want

anyone to pin nothing on you. In this town they'll kill you. Just like that, no questions asked. For safekeeping, we'll give that money to the freed spirits for now."

The reverend was referring to a crawl space under the third pew where only decades before many a black family hid, lying flat on their backs until they were safe from slave owners who ventured north of the Mason–Dixon line in search of their escaped property.

"In the meanwhile, you and Evelyn can go visit her sister in Kentucky. Eliza Beth and Harper will take good care of all of you."

Hank said softly, "No, Rev. I'm not going back that way."

"Think about it, Hank. You and Evelyn will be safer going down there than staying here."

Hank held a hand to his head. "Evelyn, can you go get me some cool water, please? Rev, I need to talk to you for a minute."

"Hank, there's a pitcher of water right by your bed. There's no need for me to leave."

Hank grimaced as he squeezed out, "Woman, please."

Evelyn sniffed, turned and marched out of the room. As she retreated, Hank, having regained some of his strength, recounted the course of events that occurred downtown in the side alley.

Reverend Pike stayed silent, hovering over Hank as he listened. "Hank, you've always been such a determined man. I knew you would break down barriers to get what you wanted. That's one of the reasons I allowed Evelyn to marry you, even though you didn't have a penny in your pocket. Her mother, on the other hand, would've wanted her to marry into high society—God rest my sweet Delilah. But my Evelyn chose you to love, so I let her. I did that because I believed your ingenuity, devotion to hard work and to the Lord would keep my daughter living a comfortable and safe life."

Hank nodded slowly. "Rev, I'm doing the best I can."

When Evelyn returned with a new pitcher and a mason jar filled with water, she found the two men nodding their heads in agreement as if there was nothing left to do but execute a plan. A plan that started with packing up the wagon and heading south, and staying with relatives until things died down. The immediate flight would be framed as a trip to visit family and a mission to spread the gospel to the small churches along the trail.

Reverend Pike hugged his daughter and left the room, leaving the explanations to her husband.

"You mean we're running away? But you didn't do anything. Why can't we just return the money and explain to them how it came into your possession? You can say you found it, that is, if someone asks."

"You know exactly why, Evelyn. This ain't the time or place to think that them folks are going to be rational. Besides, no matter what happened, it will be an excuse for them to kick us off the property, endangering your father and the church we built here. I can't put you and Lucille in danger like that."

She quickly spit out, "Well, you already done that, haven't you? I overheard something about a dead man, a bank robbery and…and just look at you! I don't appreciate being kept in the dark. You and my father have got it all wrong, keeping things from me. I deserve to know—and have a say in what we do and where we go."

After a beat, Evelyn began snatching up the family's belongings, jamming them into suitcases and carpet bags. She marched from one side of the room to the other, turned and stomped to the dresser, then over to the closet. Her heels dug sharply into the wood floors as if intending to leave a mark. The swish of her apron, skirt and petticoats accented the staccato drumbeat of her steps. "Well, for how long, Hank? And why can't we just take the train like civilized people?"

The reverend wanted them to take the train but Hank, being cautious, knew that the family traveling by train down south would make them an easy target to spot if someone just happened to be looking for them. The safest bet to go unseen would be by wagon. Reverend Pike reluctantly offered Jupiter, the dapple-gray workhorse, when Hank insisted Caesar stay behind.

"No time for that, Evie. Now get some things together so we can head down to your sister's. We don't need a lot, just a few things to tide us over for a few weeks." He knew as he said it that he was lying.

"Why? What's the rush? First, you need to see a doctor about your eye and that gash in your head. What about the farm? What about—"

Hank stopped her midsentence. "Enough with the questions! Get Lucille and let's go. You got to trust me here, Evie."

"I do, husband. I really do. I don't want to argue. Before God and everyone who loves me, I said my vows to honor our marriage. I'll go with you anywhere. But Hank, this has gone too far."

Peering between strips of gauze, Hank watched the tall, robust woman he'd been married to for over ten years pace back and forth in front of him. She was taller than him, even when she was barefoot. From the view of the bed, she looked even taller. Like her father, she cut a commanding figure. The tight bindings of her apron could barely contain her. The thick, wavy hair piled on top of her head could hardly be restrained by her movements, and spindles of curls dropped around her face. The woman's smooth walnut brown skin bore a tinge of red across her freckled cheeks. He knew it wouldn't be easy, and he understood her anger, but he needed his wife to just go along with him. When she finally stopped pacing, a sure sign that the peak of her anger had passed, Hank dropped his head as if it was too heavy to carry.

Evelyn softened when she saw her husband's hands pressed

against the sides of his face. Still, not quite ready to give up the fight, she continued her protests. "But what about Father? He's gonna be left here by himself. He's not going to have a wagon, or a horse or anyone to help with the farm."

"The church folk will take care of that. We'll take Jupiter and leave Caesar so your daddy will have a plow horse. Rev will be okay. Going to your sister's was your father's idea anyway. I didn't agree with him at first, but now I do…one hundred percent."

She asked quizzically, "My father told you that we needed to go back down south? I can't believe that. If it wasn't for the church and my sister, Daddy said he would never go down south ever again. Besides, sis don't even know that we're coming."

"She will soon. Your daddy will take care of that. He'll get word to her in his own way. You know we know how to send messages faster than the government."

Hank was now sitting up and pushing himself off the side of the bed. He stiffened and slowly turned his head from one side to the other, wobbling slightly as he adjusted to the darkness and heaviness on the left side of his head. Evelyn rushed to his side to help him stand but he brushed her off. "We'll take the unpaved roads down to the river. We'll rest a bit at the Quaker house, then take the ferry over to Kentucky. You know the route."

"I haven't been that way since I was a child. A whole lot of things have changed since then," she grumbled.

"Evelyn, my dear wife, please just trust me," Hank begged. "Both you and Lucille need to come with me. This is important. I'm doing this to keep you and Lucille safe. The Rev too, but I know hell will freeze before your daddy leaves this place. Someone is going to be coming soon. Maybe it's the sheriff or some other crackers, but they're going to be looking for me. They know money is missing and they know that one of the men who had a hand in taking it is dead in my wagon. They're going to have a lot of questions and no matter how I answer them, they won't be satisfied. I know it. You don't want to know what they might do if they find me."

Evelyn stopped. Her eyebrows rose and her large brown eyes widened. "If you're so set on going and not telling me the whole story, then maybe you should go by yourself!"

"Evelyn, I got caught up in some bad action and I did something on impulse. You have to believe that what I did, I did for you and Lucille. On the way down to the Ohio River, I'll explain everything. You'll see why. We'll come back after a while, and we'll have everything we ever wanted after that."

Deep down, Hank knew not a soul would believe the pieces of the story he could remember, but many would understand his motivation. Even his wife would be hard-pressed to believe he took part in a plan to break the law. Apart from his participation in the demonstrations about Evansville's sundown laws, he had traveled a straight and narrow path to stay alive.

So when it came time for questions from his closest kin, the police and a group of county sons, Hank and his family were already gone.

2

The Loves left early enough to take an uncommon route in an uncommon fashion. The wagon rhythmically rolled along the uneven dirt road. Hank and Evelyn let the sway and spurts jostle them about as they teetered on the edge of the buckboard with their little Lucille nestled between them. The child's head bobbed up and down but the steady clip of the wagon never woke her. The family traveled a path following a crude map, drawn by Reverend Pike, of personal contacts and a belt of small churches that catered to congregations of folks who kept their noses close to the land and their eyes watching for change in the stars.

"We'll stop at Sister Jo's along the way so we can all refresh—Jupiter too. She'll want us to stay but we got to keep going till we get to Eliza Beth and Harper's place outside of Bowling Green. Right now, the less time we spend in any one place the better for all involved," Hank instructed.

As Jupiter plodded along, birds screamed out warnings from the high branches overhead echoing from one side of the road to the other. Or maybe the birds screeched out that a predator was in their midst? Hank felt that too. Between each pulsating throb at his temples, he couldn't escape the feeling that someone was following them. He concentrated on shaking off the chill that ran down his back. Determined not to let fear defeat him, Hank told himself their music was merely welcoming the three travelers to a new world. He only began to relax once the birds ceased their collage of sounds and the road was quiet.

Despite the circumstances, he loved the sense of freedom he got from being out in fresh air. He believed he could hear his open wounds closing, his skin rejuvenating, weaving over his cuts, and the dried patches of blood disappearing under his bruised skin. He was a deep-colored man and the full spectrum of red, blue, green and purple undertones returned to his skin, radiating in the light. His muscles swelled and settled against his bones as the wagon's wheels randomly jutted one way and then the other as it fought to command the road. His buttocks were numb from sitting on the hard wood seat and taking on the dips and divots of the road, but he welcomed the sensation. It made him harden his resolve to protect his family and more determined to drive forward with a sense of purpose.

Evelyn stopped talking about a mile earlier. She rattled pages of a worn copy of *The Colored American Magazine* to make sure her husband knew of her displeasure without having to say a word. She pretended to be rereading stories written by the magazine's editor, Pauline Hopkins. It was a perfect way to get back at her husband as Pauline Hopkins, whom she claimed to be a distant relative, was a woman who had taken charge of a major newspaper, written organized lectures on race and made a name for herself in the art world. A woman who did not seem to take to being led around the countryside on the whims of a man, regardless of necessity.

Hank got the message and turned his attention back to the carefree songs of the singing birds. He knew Evelyn was angry for having to leave so abruptly and was irritated by Lucille's wails of wanting to go home. Hank wished he could do something to comfort his wife but knew it would take time. Having explained what happened, he didn't blame Evelyn for staying silent. She wasn't about to scold him too harshly with their daughter sitting between them.

He wrapped an arm around his little girl so she could feel like she was driving the wagon to keep her occupied until she dozed off. Every now and then, little Lucille would snap awake and begin humming. He knew his little cherub-faced girl would eventually start singing a song of her own making. At least, he hoped so. It would mean his daughter wasn't fretting over their sudden departure anymore. That would be a welcome distraction for Evelyn, who cut her eyes over in his direction to show either concern for his wounds and pains, or disgust with his decision-making.

Hank thought their daughter was the sweetest thing that ever happened to him and Evelyn. She was pure joy the moment she came into the world. The moment he saw black curls pasted against her head as the newborn slipped into the light of this world, he knew from the swell of his heart that dared him to breathe he would do anything to protect her, her mama and his family. Lucille came out as a blinding starburst of light. A bright star he and his wife created.

When she awoke, Lucille asked, "Daddy, where are we going? Are we going to go back to Paw-paw?" At five years old she still possessed round chubby cheeks. She had bright hazel eyes, a shade brighter than her mother's.

"Princess Lucille Arnetta Love, you, me and your mama are going on an adventure. We're going to see your aunt and uncle in Shake Rag. You remember Aunt Eliza Beth and Uncle Harper? We're gonna stay with them for a little bit. They are going be so happy to see you as big as you are. Hey, Princess Lucille Arnetta Love, you know what I seen?"

The little girl burst out in a wide grin. Whenever her daddy asked that question, she knew he was going to sing her a story. Hank wiped his mouth and cleared his throat.

"'I seen a man, his name was Sol. He was as skinny as a long beanpole. I seen a man, his name was Sam. He was as wide as twenty-four hams. I seen a man, his name was...' Now tell me who you seen."

Lucille laughed out, "'I seen a man, his name was Rabbit.'"

"You did, Princess? Hmm... Let me see. 'That man was the size of a big old bad habit.'"

Lucille, giggled. "No, Daddy, that doesn't work. 'I saw a man, his name was Mouse.'"

"Oh, that's easy. 'He was as big and wide as a house.'"

Both father and daughter squeezed out chuckles that tumbled through the air until Lucille nestled herself and again fell asleep in the crook of her daddy's arm.

"Evelyn," Hank said through the comfort of the moment, "that girl of ours can sing just about anything."

"Yep." She smiled. "I do believe that voice of hers is going to be her fortune. I'm going to teach her all I learned about music and the vocal instrument. So, we'll see. You just remember she got her voice from me and her ability to create a song from you."

When the sun began to head toward the long stretch of horizon, the air became moist and heavy with the scent of rolling water. They were moving perpendicular to a swelling creek that raced to intermingle with the Ohio River. Evelyn and Lucille stretched out in the back of the wagon between covered mounds of all the clothing and foodstuffs they had hastily snatched up from the place they called home for all the years Hank and Evelyn had been married. Hank pulled out the last bit of tobacco from his pouch and stuffed it in his cheek. Chewing helped take his mind off the pain and contemplate his next move.

Taking that money was an impulse, but at the source of that

impulse were years and years of feeling pulverized by the narrow-minded views of others who kept him not only hemmed into being a farmer on a shrinking plot of land, but also crafted odious laws that made it harder to eke out a living. During the very best months, he barely made enough to provide for his family's basic needs, let alone save a little something for their future. He had seen so much that tested his resolve. The things most people held dear—family, good neighbors, loved ones and hard-fought land—were snatched away by arbitrary laws that benefited only those who wanted to fill their own pockets and coffers from the sweat of others. But with each hurdle, Hank still managed to scrape by, put a pittance away for a rainy day and invest what he could back into the land that nourished them.

They made it to the crook in the bend of the Ohio River at sundown and could barely see the path off the main road marked by parallel tracks made from years of wagon wheels. Buried behind row after row of tall pine trees, at the end of the long trail, sat Sister Jo's house. The tiny clapboard was held together with what looked like hopes and dreams or by the wall of tall sunflowers that grew on each side.

As the Loves approached, two figures appeared on the porch, one wringing their hands and the other, a stockier figure standing wide legged with hands on hips. Both stood squinting with cautious curiosity, not expecting strangers on their doorstep on the eve of dusk.

A shrill voice cut through the light blue. "Is that Evelyn Love? Hank Love, is that you? Well, I'll be damned! Y'all all right?" Sister Jo waved, greeting the Loves with a wide, almost toothless grin. She clapped her hands and jumped up and down like a child on Christmas Day. Her smile faded when her eyes landed on the strained look on Evelyn's face, the loopy manner of the little girl and, most worrisome, Hank's dusty and rust-stained bandages and swollen face. Sister Jo couldn't hide her concern for the state of the worn and weary Loves.

Grabbing hold of the porch railing, Sister Jo took the steps one at a time and made her way toward the wagon. "What brings y'all down this way? You know what? Never mind that now. No time for explanations. Just get in here. Let me get some food into you and let you settle a bit."

The short, heavyset, light-skinned woman looked around, then lowered her voice. Signaling to her husband in almost a whisper, she said, "Carl, help Hank with that horse. Put that wagon in the barn so nobody can see it."

Sister Jo ushered the Loves inside the small house warmed by an iron stove and lit by a flickering fireplace and a gas lamp. A table was set with two place settings. Sister Jo quickly pulled a rocking chair from the corner and a small stool from what looked like a storage room. She pointed the Loves to a seat, reached for dainty porcelain cups hanging from hooks and poured Hank and Evelyn a cup of coffee each. She gave Lucille a bit of buttermilk along with a biscuit to keep her busy. By the time they were settled, Carl returned from tending to Jupiter.

"Let's eat first. Then you can tell me and Carl what brings you here. I don't want you eating my food with a mouth full of worry."

Hank and Evelyn glanced at each other. Hank replied, "Well, I thank you for such a warm reception. Especially with us showing up so unexpected and all."

While pouring water from a pitcher into a basin and dipping in his hands, Carl shouted from over his shoulder, "Please, brother, y'all family. You're always welcome. Now let's sit down, bless the food and eat."

It was the sips of cool water, the generous plates of fried chicken, okra and tomatoes that unknotted their stomachs, released their taut muscles and allowed contentment to seep into their bone-tired bodies. It was a relief to sit by the fire with kin, magnetizing the blood in their veins with stories that lessened pains and reminded them of the deep love that connected them. For a brief moment it felt like the familial atmosphere of a holiday supper. Hank and Evelyn relaxed and forgot about the dead man, and the gold coins and dollars that set them on this trajectory.

After dinner, while Evelyn cleaned up the dishes, Hank, Sister Jo and Carl sat with feet outstretched and faces glowing from the fire. They spoke in whispers. Hank didn't want to put these hospitable elders at risk in case someone was tracking him for money or revenge. The less they knew the better. He skirted around the details stating only that his fruit and produce wagon were destroyed when his pull horse went wild and overturned the wagon, explaining how his face got messed up in the accident.

To put Sister Jo and Carl at ease, Hank chuckled. "Since there was nothing to salvage, of the wagon or my good looks, Reverend Pike suggested the family make a clean start down south to be near Evelyn's sister."

Hank's explanation was sufficient to pacify Sister Jo and Carl. Sister Jo's response was only to fret over Hank's wounds. She fetched salves and pastes made from shoots, stalks and leaves of things that grew near trees to cut down on infection. She also gave Evelyn fresh bandages.

"Y'all can go on upstairs," Sister Jo directed. "It's only one bed. I'll put some water out for you."

Under the steep slant of the roof where neither Hank nor Evelyn could stand up straight without touching a beam, Hank found a mirror and gazed at his reflection. He knew from the time he saw the monstrous gash carved across his face that he would never be the same. The rest of his body wasn't much better. The accumulation of jagged tracks across his body—the ugly gash that tore his face in two, and the scars on Hank's limbs—were keepsakes of black men's experiences of living in parts of the South. His story was in the scars on his ankles, his crooked smile that hid the hitch in his bent jaw and the indentations on his neck from a noose he was lucky enough to talk himself out of. Even embedded under the bush of thick hair, now streaked with gray, were jagged valleys from the handle of a whip.

Hank knew he would never regain his sight in his left eye. Even though the thought of being partially blind made him grab his chest to hold his heart in, he was grateful he made it out alive. Most of all, he was thankful that he had Evelyn by his side. His family meant so much to him that he would stop breathing at the thought of leaving them in a world without protection.

At least he had one good eye that gave him all the sight he needed to move his family to safety and, hopefully—with the new money he now possessed—prosperity. What he could see was a spectrum of possibilities beyond their current situation. So Hank remained cheerful with each sharp pain that shot through his body. He partially lost his sight, but not the hope that he could build a life for himself and his family on a small plot of land where he could control his destiny, out of the reaches of men who only wanted to cheat him. He'd wait a spell like he promised his father-in-law before going back to claim the money he left in the freed spirits space back in Evansville. He was satisfied with the money he carried on him and what he had secretly tucked away. The few coins he had hidden deep in his pockets gave him a sense of security despite their origin. He would find a way to use the coins to save his family—if they truly needed saving. It was blood money, but he thought after all the misery dealt to him, this was his payback. It was fate that brought the money to him, and it was now in the hands of fate how the money would benefit him.

Although they had taken their hosts by surprise, by now Reverend Pike would have gotten the message to several churches to expect his daughter and son-in-law as they made their way down south to Evelyn's sister's house. It was surprising how quickly word of mouth and cryptic letters traveled across county and state lines. Hank trusted that the information on their travels would faithfully fall into good hands and ears. If the feeling of being followed continued, maybe they'd head down to Tennessee, skirt around Nashville with the aim of reaching Chattanooga or even on to points in Alabama.

Hank, Evelyn and Lucille, well rested and nourished, left Sister Jo's and Carl's early the next day. Sister Jo tried her very best to convince them to stay a while longer, from inviting them to attend church service, to relaying the ancestors' direct instructions that had come to her in a dream, to tears. It was tempting, but they had to get moving to put distance between what had already happened and what could possibly happen.

Filled with Sister Jo's chicken, corn and broad beans, and loaded up with tomato sandwiches and sweet tea cakes, Hank kept moving south to reach the point where they would have to ferry across the Ohio River and at least two tributaries to get to Bowling Green before reaching Shake Rag. He knew he was heading in the right direction as the air grew thick and heavy with moisture and the bright green grass turned from emerald to almost deep royal violet under the shade of hickory, white oak, sourwood and tall beech trees. Every inch of the family's clothing was plastered against their bodies. They were drenched in sweat. Crickets began strumming their legs to accompany their evening songs and complement the sound of tumbling, rushing water from a nearby stream.

They reached a Quaker House where the family fed them and the horse, gave them dried meats and fruits and helped secure a ferry across the river. Initially, the Loves would have had to wait until all the farmers loaded up their grains, fruits, vegetables, horses and cattle for transport before gaining passage. Once the family landed in Kentucky, they had to travel twenty miles southeast on rambling roads that wound around markers of boulders and hand-painted signs announcing the names of landowners, their tenants, nearby towns and, for those who remembered, tribes and gods and instructions for seeking refuge. They shared the road with only an occasional truck or beast of burden pulling wagons stuffed with grains and tobacco. For long stretches, the lush earth and air was fresh and silent. The sky took a different route than expected. The sunny morning quickly changed to a parade of dark clouds. A steady rain fell, tapping out a stream of music across the tarp covering Evelyn and Lucille as they huddled together in the back of the wagon.

Hank held steady as the rain fell. He sat, staring ahead, chewing on a piece of straw while water poured from the broken rim of his hat into the bandanna tied diagonally across his face to hold his bandages in place. Between the rain and Hank's one eye, it was a miracle the wagon held to the path.

Evelyn shouted from underneath the tarp, "Pull over, Hank. You're soaking wet. Thank goodness for Jupiter or else we'd be in a ditch. Let him rest. We can sit a spell under them trees and wait out the rain."

They had been traveling all morning. Although Hank wanted to continue, he knew that the wait was warranted given the downpour, but if they sat, they could get stuck in the mud and lose valuable travel daylight. He had no choice but to give in to Mother Nature and make the best of it. They had plenty of provisions to stay the night in this spot if necessary. They were hidden from the road, and Hank promised to stay up all night to watch over his family as they slept.

Despite his plans, Hank woke to streaks of the early-morning sun spreading slowly across the landscape. He eased his body upward and rubbed a rough hand across his face grazing his bandages. His deep sleep made him forget and suddenly he was reminded of why his head was wrapped in gauze. He turned toward the back of the wagon. Lucille was curled up like a baby fawn sleeping blissfully. Her skin was smooth and brown like soft velvet. Hank knew the sudden change and confusion was becoming hard on her, but thought that since she was so young, she might not even remember this time. He wanted desperately to reach out and kiss her cheek but stopped short as it finally dawned on him his wife was gone.

He strained to search in the distance beyond the gathering of trees until Evelyn's voice drifted along the breeze. He spotted his wife's shapely profile in a narrow clearing, sitting underneath the wide trunk of a tree that had set itself apart from the rest. She sat with her back to him, facing the rising sun brushing her hair and singing what he knew was the aria "Ocean! Thou Mighty Monster." It had been sung by Sissieretta Jones at a concert stop in Indianapolis before heading to the World's Columbian Exposition in Chicago. It was a little highfalutin for him; Hank was just happy hearing a few strums of a guitar, but his wife passionately admired the much-lauded colored opera star who had sung for President Harrison at the White House. Like Sissieretta, Evelyn's soprano voice rang out, strong and deep as the earth and bright as the sun, across the open landscape. She delicately held the silver-handled brush, a prized possession that had been passed down from only a few generations, as she pulled it from the crown of her head down long strands that shone red or brown in the sunlight.

Hank watched. Her fingers deftly twisted and pinned her hair around the nape of her neck. He was hesitant to break the spell of seeing a lovely woman bathed in the light of the morning sun. When she returned to the wagon, her hair was neatly pinned, her face glowing as if she had just awoken from a nap.

"It's so beautiful this morning. I had to get out and speak with God this morning. I prayed on it and... Hank, I'm worried. I've gotta speak my mind and put my foot down. We can't be traveling around here like a lost tribe."

Spellbound by the sight of his wife's beauty and forthrightness, Hank stuttered out, "Please, Evelyn. Just know this. I love you more that I can say." He jumped down from the wagon, grasped her hands and pulled her close. "I know it's tough to swallow but believe me we're going to be all right. I promise you. We'll be coming up on Eliza Beth and Harper's house soon. They should be expecting us. We need to stick to the plan: stay with them for a bit then make a real plan to find a place to settle. Then, after a while, we can get the money from the freed spirits and buy us some property. We'll give the Rev some for the church of course. I don't regret what I did, taking that money and all, but in retrospect, I'm sorry that I put you and Luce in such a—what do you say?—a pre-car-ious position. I'm certain that this newfound money will not only serve the church but also assure our little girl can get all the education she needs. We just got to let the trail get cold. I can't lie to you, it might take a while. Anyone could've taken that robber's sack and they ain't gonna worry so much about one missing Negro. They been trying to get rid of us anyways."

"We could have just taken the money with us then! I told you I'd go anywhere with you, with our baby," Evelyn pointed out.

Hank nodded. "Maybe we should have taken all the money with us. But the Rev was right. If I had that sack on me they would hang me as one of the robbers for sure. The Rev knows how to work 'em to throw off our scent. Trust me, Evelyn. We'll be all right and back on track. We'll stay close to the roads till we get to the church folks' homes."

"Hank, I just don't know how much longer we can be on the run. It's not good for Lucille. I didn't pack any Chamberlain's remedy. After yesterday's rainfall, I was sure all of us would wind up sick and coughing, or worse."

"We're almost there, Evie. We'll get out from underneath this cloud when we reach the Harpers. I don't mind the rain. Besides, I need to feel like I've been forgiven and the rain washes away our sins, as they say."

3

Shake Rag, Kentucky

The Loves planned to stay in Bowling Green, Kentucky, with Theodore and Eliza Beth Harper for at least the next six months. The Harpers lived in a comfortable bungalow on the last street in a section called Shake Rag. The few short blocks that made up the thriving area were a salve to Hank and Evelyn's wounds. It was a town within a town, solely a little slice of businesses, schools and churches where the black population of Bowling Green felt safe.

They worshipped and sang at State Street church almost every night and generally all day on Sundays. Evelyn adapted to a routine of helping her sister Eliza Beth in the gardens, canning and cooking. Harper and his wife had no children, so they doted on Lucille. They gave her a doll that Eliza Beth made with spun yarn. Dyed dark red strands were twisted into hair and the brown fabric was embroidered with bright eyes and a smile. Once again, being around family, the Loves began to relax. Hank's wounds healed to a shiny pink, and his bruises faded, leaving only remnants of that horrid day in Evansville.

Evelyn appeared to stop worrying and Lucille happily found playmates among the other children. However, the peace was short-lived.

Hank pushed his hat back on his head and let the sunshine fall on his face as he sat on the front steps. The sun was high in the sky and his skin burned with the piercing rays. He took the slight pain from the heat as penitence, a reminder that he was but a servant to unalterable nature. Evelyn sat behind him in a rocking chair that was violently beating the floorboards. He knew the blissful time had waned and something sparked her resentment. Maybe it was the events at church making her homesick, or the passing conversation about the children graduating from State Street High School or Bowling Green Academy who were planning to go off to Fisk or Howard Universities. Or maybe it was the normalcy of successful businesses being run by enterprising black men and women in the neighborhood, like Nancy's Tea House and the Southern Queen Hotel, that offered a safe haven to black travelers as they traversed the Dixie Highway. Maybe the brief interlude of calm, watching Lucille flourish and grow taller, playing with other children who attended church, caused her to reflect instead of celebrate. Hank was convinced something had nicked her skin and caused her to dig up reasons to blame him for all they had to leave behind.

Evelyn was a church farmer's daughter, accustomed to a neat, streamlined life of hard work and the social refinements of pretty dresses and educated sensibilities. In response to their now spartan life, Evelyn held on even tighter to Lucille. Hank could see his daughter gasping for air under the weight of her mother's restrictions. He had to do something to make his wife happy for the sake of his daughter. He couldn't lose Evelyn. If he lost her, he'd have lost everything.

To break the silence, Hank blandly shouted out, "What time is the service?"

The wind kicked up and the tree limbs waved their branches

in the hurried breeze before Evelyn snapped, "You know exactly what time, Hank. I've told you many times already. What
we need to talk about is where we're going after this. Harper
and Eliza Beth are family, but we can't impose on them forever."

"Calm down, woman. You know God's got a plan for us.
Harp done got us invited to his brother's church in the next
town. They got a jubilee service next Sunday and we can be
their guests on the program. They're always open to new members and, on top of that, Harper says they're looking for a choir
master. Maybe we can see how it feels." He rubbed his chin to
stop himself from saying anything about the nervous feeling
clawing at the back of his neck.

"Hank, how long we gonna keep doing this? Can we just
settle down? When we left Evansville, I thought we would
find a spot and work to call it home. What's wrong with right
here? We've been here long enough to know. The people are
nice enough. We can stay here. You can find a job on one of
the farms. It ain't far from home. We can do short trips to go
back and see my father."

"That's the problem. Something tells me this ain't far
enough."

"You can't outrun the devil, Hank. You got to stand up and
fight him with force."

They received a series of letters from Reverend Pike cryp-
tically stating no one beyond the police stopped by the church
to inquire about the mess in the alley. Apparently, the reverend
convincingly relayed the story that Hank simply left his wagon
in town because the horse had a problem with its leg, making
it impossible for him to pull the wagon. He told them his son-
in-law planned to go back later, but decided to send one of the
younger parishioners to fetch it since Hank had to get things
set for a planned family trip. Rumor was that the man found
underneath the fruit wagon was shot in the street by an offi-
cer when attempting to flee. There was no mention of missing

money. In as few words as possible, the reverend stated that he hadn't heard a thing about a dead man until Clarence, the parishioner who retrieved the wagon, told him of the commotion and the mess. In one of his letters, the reverend wrote:

It was two of the sheriff's boys who came asking, and I think at least one of them believed me. And that one asked about you when he saw me in town about two weeks later. I just told him you were still out of town because you found work on some farm. I didn't give no details and he didn't ask for any. No one has returned yet. We just gonna keep praying and going on like nothing ever happened. Everyone here is safe and healthy. The church is selling fruits and vegetables by the side of the road, and not in town except for Saturdays.

Even with the reverend's reassurance, it wasn't long until the itching that irritated the back of Hank's neck was gnawing at his stomach. He thought attending church service would calm his nerves, but the sight of a thin white man with a ragged, stained brown hat pulled over his head standing by the crowd of trees that surrounded the church only compounded Hank's worries. He swallowed hard. The man's faded shirt was tucked loosely into sagging worn pants. The sleeves of his shirt were rolled up to reveal a dirty and tattered undershirt. Maybe he was down on his luck and needed the help of prayer. Maybe he found his way to the side of town that wouldn't judge him, but instead lead him on the path of forgiveness. Maybe.

It was the beginning of spring but already hot and heavy with humidity. The doors of the church were wide open to adjust to the rising heat inside, but also as an invitation to all those who sinned. Hank spotted the man when he lifted his head up from prayer. As the congregation stood with eyes closed and palms open, Hank turned his head to stare straight through the church's open doors. Beyond the bare dirt pathway right across the street was a man leaning against a tree. His presence sent a shock wave through Hank's body. His mind skipped back to a clear picture of men running past his cart in the alleyway and the stone-gray eyes of the man who jumped in the back of his wagon.

The man didn't appear to see Hank, now leaning far out into the aisle, craning his neck to get a better look. The man just seemed to be waiting. *But for whom?* A sharp elbow jabbed his side.

"What are you looking at?" Evelyn whispered.

"It's nothing," he said unconvincingly. To close her queries, he delved into the second verse of hymns with feigned enthusiasm.

After church the man was gone, but Hank was left with a nagging feeling that lingered just out of reach, pulling at everything inside of him. Hank had to do something he knew wouldn't sit well with his wife. They had to keep moving. They'd made it through the winter in Shake Rag, feeling safe enough in the little town. But Hank needed insurance. He couldn't believe the strange man's appearance was just chance. Hank needed to sever the ties connecting him and whatever forces that might be out there working against him and his family. He still held out hope that the Loves would be in the clear once sufficient time passed and then he'd find a stretch of land where he could build a house. His wife and family deserved that.

In a small leather pouch that been his granddaddy's, Hank carried ten gold coins and a small roll of twenty-dollar bills. Hank retrieved the pouch from the wagon, counted the money to make sure it was all there, pulled the leather cord tight and put it in his pocket. It was his secret stash—not even his wife knew about it. He was lucky to have kept it from her for this length of time. She didn't know that the coins he carried with him were related to the bag now resting in the dark under Reverend Pike's church's floorboards. To keep his secret, Hank had pushed the pouch deep inside a mason jar filled with dried beans and wrapped the jar in an old oil cloth which he kept under the seat in their wagon. Every now and then he'd check the pouch. When his granddaddy traveled from the South to the North, he carried that same pouch filled with seeds along with the dreams of a good life. Hank felt the pouch provided the protective spirit for his current treasures.

"Take this, Harp." Hank pressed a coin into Harper's palm. "You took us in. You and this town treated us like family. This is for all you and your neighbors have done for us."

Harper's eyes widened at the sight of the coin that appeared to have been rubbed to a glistening aura, resting in the middle of the lines zigzagging across his palm.

"Where'd you get this from, Hank? This has got to be—"

Hank cut him off. "Don't worry. That money found its way into my hands and now I'm passing it along to you. Listen here, don't spend it until long after I'm gone—I mean I'm try'n to meet the Lord but I don't plan on doing that for a while. Just hold on to it until me and my family have moved on, when you absolutely need it."

"If anyone is lookin' for you, Hank, this would be the first place they'd go. A black man spendin' money…passin' around some gold coins like this, well it won't be long before someone starts makin' connections between these coins and whatever trouble you're in."

Hank took a beat and rubbed his thumb into his palm. He had taken a big risk by telling Harper more than he should have about Evansville. He only hoped Harper's knowledge wouldn't put him or his family in danger. "Oh come on, Harp. How they really gonna know it was me who gave you that coin?"

"Hank Love, you can't be that stupid. There's talk that there was a dead white man found underneath your broken-down wagon full of fruit and vegetables. It don't take too much for a person to think you know somethin'. Yeah, they gonna be looking for you. They gonna start with the Rev and work their way down to us."

Hank made a feeble attempt to wave off his friend, trying his best not to show any concern or concede there were possible holes in his logic. Blinking slowly to clear up the cloudiness forming in his eye, he focused directly on Harper. There were unspoken rules from the time he first opened his eyes to the world, that there was no need to give voice to the depth and breadth of their experiences. There was always more to what was said and no need to give it additional weight.

Harper could probably guess there was more to the story of this shiny coin—maybe even that Hank was hiding something more treacherous than what Harper imagined. From the hard stare he gave his brother-in-law when he finally looked up from the coin, Hank had to guess that Harper's imagination and the grizzled rumors were close enough to the truth.

Hank began to think. *Have I been too careless? Am I being naive thinking folks will readily accept the story of a simple fresh start away from Indiana or that word won't run rampant this far away from home?* Still Hank stood resolute. "Don't you worry about that coin. It's yours now and that's it."

"Naw, man…you done put us in jeopardy if what I suspect is right. I don't think you realize how much danger we all in."

Hank rubbed the long, jagged line that ran down his face and shifted the toothpick he had been chewing from one side of his mouth to the other. His head hurt more than ever. As much as he didn't want to believe it, he knew what Harper said was true. Simply having the money was dangerous. But he couldn't turn the money in to the bank. They'd find some way to blame, jail or even hang him. He knew that for sure.

And if the robbers were to find him, they'd kill him for sure, no matter what the answers were to the questions they'd ask.

Hank sighed. Every time he thought he'd finally be able to go back to Evansville to make things right, he realized he wasn't safe at all. Maybe he'd never be safe. The only way out was to keep moving farther and farther away from Indiana. That meant focusing on not being found.

Harper patted Hank on the shoulder. "No matter what, though, you know we're behind you, brother. Hank, you know you can stay. You, Evelyn and Lucille, that little angel, can stay right here with us. At least until you get something of your own. It ain't safe on that road."

"It's safer than where I've come from, brother."

"Hank, where will you even go? In another town, you have to build more trust. You don't have that much family beyond here."

Hank thought for a minute. Perhaps he was being too hasty again. He had packed up Evelyn and Lucille and left Evansville before he had too much time to think. But Harper was right—there weren't many other places that took kindly to a new rootless family passing through. And maybe blowing in and out of these small towns was more suspicious than staying put. The strange man who showed up at the church made him nervous, but Hank had only seen him once. For all Hank knew, the man was no more than a local hobo.

"All right, Harp. Maybe a little while longer won't hurt."

Over the next few weeks Hank stayed in a perpetual state of high alert. His muscles tensed, his spine steeled against foreign shadows, whistling wind and the scurry of creatures that reminded him of footsteps. He immersed himself in work and church, keeping busy enough so as not to alert Evelyn, but also as a distraction.

Hank sat in the hard church pew rocking from side to side,

back and forth, his knees lifted by the tapping of his feet. Evelyn had lent her voice to the choir, and he let the music take him. He closed his eyes to let the sermon and hymns work. A loose tear rolled down his face. He wiped it away, hoping to wipe away many other things. Yet behind closed lids he could see a shadow passing over his face. He opened his eyes. In front of him was a flurry of flapping fans and mothers' hankies waving away the heat. He turned around to see if someone had passed by and sat behind him.

It was the same man that he had seen before; he was turning up again and again. He stood framed in the light of dusk after Bible study, at the start of the last few church services as parishioners greeted each other and when they shook the minister's hand after mass. He even appeared at the other churches the Loves visited. Sometimes Hank watched as he leaned against a tree or sat on a nearby stump. But each time he saw him, Hank was sure the man was watching him.

Today the man stood just off to the side of the front steps of the church. He was dressed the same each time. His pants fitted loosely and were caked with grime. Hank surmised he needed a few meals. The brim of his hat barely supported the layer of dirt covering it. From what Hank could see of his face, the man had piercing blue eyes and sported a light-colored beard that covered his deeply lined face. His expression never changed.

As the family left church, again the man was nowhere to be seen. However, Hank sensed he was lurking about, watching. He tried to shake off his feelings. They had been gone for over eight months now and were over a hundred miles away from Evansville. Nobody outside their tight-knit family circle even knew the Loves were here in Shake Rag.

After that Sunday's service, even though Harper insisted they stay longer, Hank thought it best that they pack up the wagon and move on. The minister sent word to Miss Garnetta Opal, a woman who ran a rooming house about fifty miles away in

Gallatin, Tennessee. Gallatin had seen its fair share of misfortune—fires, floods and illness had spirited away many residents. Only the stalwart remained to keep the city on the map. There, the Loves would be received as guests and given a place to stay and fellowship. Everyone knew Miss Opal as a botanist and teacher who led a ministry of educating girls in the sciences in a classroom in her home—perfect for young Lucille, who was meant to be starting school.

Gallatin might be the perfect place, Hank thought. *And, most importantly, it's farther away from Evansville.* Who would even think of looking for them in Tennessee?

4

Once again, Jupiter's head bobbed before Hank. Lucille, seemingly happy to be on another adventure, hummed a song to her doll while braiding and unbraiding its hair of yarn. Evelyn pretended to be deeply engrossed in her book—*Contending Forces* by Pauline Elizabeth Hopkins—about Negro romances in the North and South. She told him it was a tale of heroes, heroines and villains, and shocking interracial blood lines before the Civil War. Evelyn said she mostly wanted to read the story because it was written by the talented, smart woman who was pushed out of her position as editor of *The Colored American Magazine* by men.

The Loves traveled in a lazy cadence down the quiet road where they were the only travelers. It was late Sunday afternoon. Most families were sitting down for a meal, praying over platters of food before diving in to eat. Lucille finally drifted off to sleep. They were only a few miles from town when the spaces between houses stretched out into wide fields that separated neighbors. In the distance, sun-beaten roofs of barns, lean-tos or structures constructed to hold farm tools or livestock could be seen. By the time they reached an old wooden and stone trestle bridge that covered a thin passage over a strolling creek, the sky had grown gray and dark clouds raced across the sky. Hank held his head down trying to ignore the impending downpour. He focused on getting to the next town, where there would be a hotel or boardinghouse where they could spend the night. But out of the corner of his eye, in a clump of trees, he caught a glimpse of movement. Hank snapped to attention.

At first, it was a shadowy form, a small darting figure that flickered in the distance. When Hank pulled the wagon under a cluster of trees to escape the rain that now fell in sheets, the figure appeared again, this time clearly visible and standing firm. When Hank saw clear blue eyes peering from beneath a tattered hat, a bolt of fear carved its way down Hank's face following the jagged trail of his scar.

Hank shouted, "Hey! Hey, you there! What do you want?" He jumped down from the wagon, landing in squishy mud. Hank quickly retrieved his balance and ran toward the blue-eyed man, who had disappeared again. Hank had had enough of the cat-and-mouse game. He aimed to confront the man once and for all to set him straight. He'd deny everything and convince this man that they had nothing, no money—stolen or otherwise.

Hank ran deeper into the woods. Evelyn's frantic shouts evaporated behind him. Low-hanging branches whipped him across his face and arms. He tripped over roots, rocks and mounds of wet earth that were hidden from him in the dark left side of his vision. He recovered from his stumbles and kept moving, determined to find the man that haunted him and now seemed to be hunting him. But each way he turned there was no shadowy figure, no piercing blue eyes staring back at him. Hank finally stopped and spun around, giving up. Soaking wet, he walked slowly back to the wagon.

"Hank, what on earth is wrong with you? Who are you yelling at? Tell me! You jumped off here like you saw a ghost. You had us scared to the bone. What's got you so riled up?"

Hank turned a full circle scanning the area. "Evie, we've got to go now!"

"You saw somebody, didn't you? Someone from Evansville, right?"

Hank didn't want to cause alarm so he shook his head and mumbled out a stream of words that could be taken as no.

"It's raining cats and dogs. Get under the tarp with me and Lucy. We can wait it out before moving on. There's a barn over there. If we're lucky we can just wait there until it stops."

"Naw, we've got to get going now. You and Luce stay in the back. I'll get us moving until we can find a better place to hang our hat."

"But Hank, you're soaked through and through. You'll catch your death from pneumonia…"

Ignoring his wife's pleas, Hank patted the horse on his flank and pulled himself up onto the buckboard. The old farm wagon pulled out from the sanctuary of the trees and back onto the road. Luckily, the sky brightened and the rain lessened. Evelyn and Lucille came out from underneath the tarp to sit next to him. The passing of the fast-moving rain cloud left the dirt road soft but not too sluggish, and the horse was able to keep a steady pace.

"We'll be close to Franklin soon. We'll be all right then as long as the road holds out. We'll find our people. There will be a place for us to stay along the outskirts of town."

As they headed around a bend, rainwater crystals captured the light from a remorseful sun and dripped from every leaf and sprinkled the grasses with beads of twinkling light. They passed the open mouth of an empty barn that was missing a good portion of its roof when a voice shouted out from the shadows, shattering the silence.

"You're Hank Love, ain't you?"

Hank's hands tightened on the reins, slowing down his horse's gait. Hank lifted up a hand, signaling Evelyn not to speak. She sat next to him breathing hard enough to hear. She pulled Lucille close and tightly clasped a hand over her daughter's ears. Lucille seemed to recognize her mother's fear and sat unmoving in the crook of her mother's arm.

Hank squinted hard, searching beyond the barn door before a man emerged from the darkness. It was the same white man that had been spying on them from outside the church and who'd been hiding in the trees just up the road. Hank, not accustomed to being asked who he was—particularly from some filthy white man—wasn't about to start answering that question now.

Hank shouted back, "What do you want? Money? We don't have any."

"Oh, I think you do." The man's voice was clear and sturdy, belying his physical appearance. "I think you have plenty. You see, I know you from Evansville and I think you know where's the rest of my money." The man drew in a long breath before blaring out, "And I want it now!"

"I don't know what you're talking about, sir."

"Don't play stupid with me! You took something from my brother. I know it was you 'cause you left town as soon as they found him, all shot up under some apples and pears. You took off. That says guilty to me. So where is my money, nigger!"

"Whoa, sir. We don't have any money. I don't know what you're talking about." Hank looked the man straight in his eye, but he was also trying to see if there were any other men behind him, or if the man carried a gun. Not seeing either, Hank placed the reins in Evelyn's hand then slowly eased himself down from the wagon, whispering, "Get out of here if things go wrong." He thought he might have a chance if he could disarm the man.

"We're just carrying a few things to take to relatives." Hank held his hands to show flat palms. Even though there were no visible signs of a weapon, that didn't mean there wasn't one nearby—or other men for that matter. Hank had to do what he could to distract the man. "You can come on over and check," Hank offered.

"Or I can just shoot you dead right here."

"Please, sir, not in front of my wife and child." Hank slowly took a few steps toward the barn. "Now, I'm willing to talk about it…"

Jupiter tapped his hooves into the dirt, sending plumes of dust swirling. Lucille began to squirm and squeal to get her mother to let go. But Evelyn held firm while mouthing *Let's go* to Hank. Hank, with his hands up, ducked between the crooked fence posts that surrounded the barn while keeping his eyes on the man.

Hank toe-heeled closer to the man, getting a full view inside the barn. It was empty. He hadn't seen a house for some time before this point. Their voices carried out across the field.

The man stepped forward so that he was only a few feet away from Hank. Pointing a finger, he yelled out, "I know'd it was you who took that money from my brother. When they told me you left town, I knew something was wrong. I don't care what that preacher said. Wouldn't no man leave his only source of income in the street like that."

"Okay. Yes, I do remember that day." Hank was close enough to lower his voice. He tried to speak calmly. "My horse was spooked by some gunfire and dragged me and my vegetables all along that alleyway. I really don't know anything about your brother. Honest."

"I don't believe you." He pumped up his chest and crossed his arms. "My brother is dead and all I want to know is what happened to the money he was carrying. I lost—"

Hank lunged at the man before he could finish his sentence.

The man kicked Hank in the stomach, causing Hank to fall back, his head hitting the barn doorframe. Hank sunk to the ground. He tried to scramble back up. Then the man punched Hank in the jaw. This time Hank fell sideways and landed on the floor.

At that moment, Lucille ran to the barn reaching out for her father. "Daddy... Daddy... Mother says to..."

Lucille stopped mid-sentence as the man took a step forward and scooped her up by her waist. As fast as he grabbed her, he took a few steps back and held her up in front of him like a half-filled bag of flour.

"AAAEEEEE...!" Lucille kicked wildly and gave a long wailing scream.

The man bucked her up with his knee until he had the little girl in his outstretched arm, held up high in the air by her ankle. The little girl's dress and petticoat fell open, covering her mouth and revealing her brown legs, one kicking aimlessly in the air.

"Mama!" she screamed.

Battered and bloodied, Hank kept his sight on Lucille, determined to use every ounce of his strength to reach the man. Lucille kicked and flailed but the man's grip withstood all the little girl's efforts to free herself. Hank realized he had misjudged the man, thinking he wouldn't be as strong as he was. But the man stood over him, holding Hank's daughter high in the air and threatening to kill her.

Hank crawled, grunting each time he dug his hands into the hard clay floor to pull himself toward the man. Blood dripped from the deep cuts across his cheeks. Fat red drops plopped on the back of his hand and rolled down his knuckles. Despite his shortness of breath and loss of focus, Hank kept moving. His baby girl needed him, and he summoned up all his energy to move faster. He dug in even more.

"Gimme that money, nigga, or I'll drop her. I'll smash her head in. I'm going to do it right—"

Hank swiftly pulled a knife from his pocket and plunged it into the man's foot, knowing he made his mark. The knife pierced the thin leather of his shoe and sank into the flesh and grizzled bone in the middle of his foot.

The man let out a yelp. He dropped Lucille to the ground but still held her ankle. He attempted to lift the child back up as if she were a ham on display.

"DADDEE… DADDEE!" Lucille's pleas cut through the air as she twisted upside down in the man's grip.

"DAMN YOU, NIGGA!" The man's face turned red and he reached for Lucille's neck.

A shotgun blast roared from behind Hank. Startled, Hank jerked his head around and raised himself on his elbows. Behind him, Evelyn stood, her chest heaving as she tossed the gun to the side. In front of him, Lucille lay in a heap.

Hank fell back to the ground and stretched his arm out toward his daughter. "Lucille!" he screamed out. He was on his knees when the edge of his fingertips touched the soft curl of her hair. Her small body quivered.

Evelyn raced toward them screaming, "Hank! Lucy! Are you okay?"

At her mother's touch, Lucille gulped in a lungful of air and began to wail. Hank fell back into his wife's chest. He surveyed their surroundings from her tight embrace. The man lay against sacks of grain, his arms and legs spread wide as if his body had flown backward. Blood splattered his face and poured through a perfect round hole in his chest.

Hank pulled himself away from his wife. He brushed his hand against Evelyn's cheek, then covered Lucille's eyes. He needed to feel his flesh and blood. "Ev'lyn, get her out of here." As he stood up and balanced, he directed, "I'll take care of this. Evelyn, get her outta here! Get back to the wagon and get outta here now!"

Evelyn wrapped her arms tightly around Lucille's chest, locking her daughter's arms to her sides as she pulled her backward. Lucille's little heels dragged crooked lines into the dirt.

Heaving greatly, Hank retrieved the gun, ran to the wagon to deposit it and returned to the barn drawing a box of matches from his pocket.

The fire grew brighter and higher as golden flames and black smoke sucked up the man until his limbs were no longer in sight.

"DA-DEEE!" Lucille howled.

Lucille pushed against the stone wall of her mother's arms, trying to wriggle out from her grasp. Before her eyes, the remaining roof of the barn collapsed, feeding the hungry fire that belched sparks and smoke that rose to the dark sky. Her mother only tightened her grip.

Lucille screamed out through a veil of tears, just as the remaining walls of the barn fell into each other. "DADDY! DADDY!"

No one ran through the darkness of the woods as the blaze crackled and popped. Even if they had, no one was there to tell the story of what happened. When the Loves looked behind them, only a trail of black smoke could be seen high above the silhouettes of treetops. They were far away from the burning barn but not close enough to city lights to secure a hotel or rooming house to spend the night. Evelyn pulled the wagon deep into the trees for the oncoming night. It wouldn't be the first time they slept in the wagon, but she hoped it would be their very last. She pitched a tent over the back of the wagon and secured it so that no one could see its inhabitants.

Under the tarp, Lucille was wrapped tightly under a quilt. The little girl bolted upright when, through a rapid succession of short breaths and the loud thumping of her heart, she heard her mother's voice. Was she praying or reading from her Bible? Lucille, still in a haze of sleep, heard her father's voice speaking in whispers. His pain was evident as she heard him shift his body from one side to the other.

Her mother whispered, "Ever since you took that money and decided we had to leave Indiana, we've lost so much. Hank, look at you. That money has left you near blind and your leg looks almost burnt to the bone. What more can we afford to lose? Does someone in this family have to die?"

"Where'd you get the gun, Evelyn?"

"Eliza Beth gave it to me for protection."

"You kept it hidden from me?"

"Hank, you've kept your secrets. A woman must have her secrets and that gun was mine. You don't need to know everything that I do. You just need to know that I will do anything to protect my family."

"But my job is to protect you."

"It's my job to help you deliver on that promise and make sure you've got backup."

Hank raised his arm and gently touched his wife's cheek. "Listen, I didn't have much choice back there. I don't have any remorse. That man was trying to take our baby away from us... to hold her hostage or kill her to get what he claimed was his money. He wasn't going to hurt my little girl."

"Well, he can't hurt anyone now." Evelyn tightened her grip on her husband's arm.

Lucille rubbed her face, blinking her eyes to adjust to her surroundings. She wrestled out from under the tight covers. She scrambled out of the tent to find her father lying under the wagon on a mattress of soft grass. Except for a long stretch of bandaged leg, he was covered with several blankets. Between the three of them the pungent smell of smoke permeated the usually sweet green smell of a summer's night. It burned her nostrils and the back of her throat, leaving a bitter taste in her mouth as if she was still back at the blazing barn.

Her mother broke the silence. "Are you sure we're safe here tonight, Hank?"

"Lucy, go'n back up in the wagon and go to sleep. See, baby, I'm all right now. Climb on up into bed, little girl." Her father made an attempt to smile, but it was easy to see, even in the dark, how much effort it took him.

Lucille slid under the wagon and moved in closer to her father.

"Be careful, Lucille, your father is hurt."

"Daddy, I love you. I love you. I love you. I'm so glad you're all right. I was so scared."

Lucille didn't want to leave her father but, comforted by his presence and satisfied with giving him a hug, she did as instructed. She lay in her makeshift bed and listened to the sound of rustling grass and the soft sounds of her mother's and father's bodies close together below her.

"Yeah, we're good if we stay quiet," her father said in a gravelly but soothing tone. "Tomorrow we'll keep heading southwest toward Gallatin. There, we can stay at the church or Miss Opal's for a few days. We'll keep moving until we can find a safe place to put down roots. I promise we'll get settled soon."

PART II

THE TRAVELING LOVES

5

Miss Opal's House
Gallatin, Tennessee
1909

Somewhere in the distance, floorboards rhythmically creaked and moaned. Either a rocking chair was busy soothing away worries or the devil was filing his hooves so he could wake the dead. The salty-sweet smell of baked ham and biscuits scented the air. Lucille's stomach rumbled and growled, waking her just enough to find the room and everything in it swimming around her. Lucille closed her eyes tight to still the churning currents swallowing her up, drowning her with images that slid beyond her grasp. She was burning hot. Fire spit out through her pores. Lucille threw off her covers and pulled her knees to her chest to protect herself from the growing flames and heat that crawled up from her feet and were now lapping at her thighs. The fire flickered from yellow to white. Climbing black smoke seared her cheeks. She wanted to scream but her world suddenly turned upside down. And in the center, where down was up, she was surrounded by fire. Her father stood with both arms outstretched, glazed in fiery orange, his brown skin covered in an oily slickness. No patch covered his eye; both eyes were bright and wide. No scar dissected his face. His lips parted, closed and parted again, trying unsuccessfully to shout, *Gimme back my...*

Lucille woke shivering and breathing heavily. She screamed out to finish her father's sentence. "Daughter! Gimme back my daughter!"

"Lucille! Lucille, my baby, wake up!" The soft stroke of her mother's hand on her cheeks and her comforting voice pierced through the dream. Her face came into focus.

Lucille reached out for her mother and held her tight. "Where's Daddy? I was dreaming about Daddy."

"Your father? He's fine. He's just fine."

As if to confirm her mother's claim, Hank Love stepped through the door, pulling up his suspenders. "Evelyn, what's going on? I can hear Lucille screaming all the way from the barn."

"Just another one of her dreams, Hank. See, sweet girl, your daddy's all right. You're all right. In fact, we're all right." Evelyn held her daughter close, patting her arm with one hand while she signaled to her husband with the other to join them.

"Lemme talk to the girl, Evie," Hank said as he sat down on the bed.

Evelyn scooted over to let her husband wrap his arms around Lucille. Lucille sniffed back tears, comforted by the smell of cloves and cinnamon that rose from her father's skin. The fire slowly faded out of her mind's eye.

"Don't be 'fraid. Don't you ever have no fear. Those flickering flames are just the flutter of angel wings. Dreams are just clearing your mind so you can get a fresh start in the morning. Trust me. All the answers you need will come after a bad dream when the sun rises."

Rocking Lucille back and forth, he hummed a tune she had heard for as long as she could remember. Lucille sat tucked under his chin, soothed by the vibrations emanating from his throat and chest as her father started to sing:

"Your mama and your daddy got you by the hand
Leading you onward to a promised land
So sing, sweet child, sing loud and clear
'Cause them bad times ain't nothing to fear
Keep a'walking right and the night's gonna pass
Sleep little girl, good times comin' fast"

The melody was always the same. The words changed to suit the moment, but the sentiment remained—through good times and bad, your family, before and after, is always with you to keep you safe. It was the melody Lucille hummed or sung to herself when she needed assurance that whatever caused her worry would shortly go away.

Aside from Lucille's occasional dreams, the family was able to put distance and time between them and the spectacular events that left two dead men in their wake. Miss Garnetta Opal's boardinghouse was a hidden treasure located in a tiny town in Tennessee at the end of a foot trail on the northern side of the waning Appalachian Mountains. If someone was look-ing for the Loves, they would have to use a treasure map. One road went through the town, but if anyone traveled down that road they would have to squint and turn their head sideways to catch a glimpse of an outline of the large house, grain bin or laundry waving in the breeze.

The temporary stay stretched out to three years. The Loves found the house and its proprietor to be their anchor. It was far enough from Evansville, but close enough so that the promises Hank made to one day return to his wife's family home didn't seem out of reach. It put enough distance between them and the fire that scorched and squelched the threat from the past. Hank's lost eye and burns were assumed to be what most black men thought they were: a map of survival from injustices. Like the bagful of money that sparked their trek, Hank and Evelyn never spoke of it—not even to each other, and especially not in front of Lucille. Both were afraid that any words on the subject would open the universe and lead someone to their door demanding answers—or worse, demanding an eye for an eye. Hank could only hope that Lucille's occasional night terrors would diminish and she would leave whatever she might remember behind as she got older.

Miss Opal's was the only home Lucille had come to know—and she loved it. There was something about the short, round woman with heavy breasts that met her waistband. Miss Opal was always in motion. She spoke with pointing fingers as if she was constructing the path before planting her feet in front of her. She walked leaning forward, as though she had no other option but to get to her destination. There was a place she needed to be, and nothing and no one was going to stop her from getting there. Lucille felt drawn to Miss Opal and ran to her to get a hug, where she would hide in the warm little cave of Miss Opal's breasts and the generous folds of her apron.

In Gallatin, the Loves fell into a routine of work outside and inside the house in exchange for attic space, which was two large rooms with windows at both ends that had views of the front lawn and expansive fields in the back of the property. Whatever the vantage point, they could see someone coming or going for almost a half a mile. Evelyn played piano for the only church in town and gave music lessons. Hank found work in the neighboring fields. They retired the dedicated Jupiter to a wide pasture next to the boardinghouse, where he grazed freely. He was only pressed into service when they went to church or to haul fresh vegetables to town.

What also made life at Miss Opal's fascinating was the other guests of the house. They came and went in every direction along the Dixie Highway. There were travelers en route from

Canada to America's most southern points to solve a mystery of a lost brother. Another house guest was traveling from Florida to Chicago to find fame or simply steady employment. One guest from Louisiana was making his way to New York to go to school. Whoever stopped through, Lucille loved listening to stories of their travels. She marveled at their worldly experiences in what appeared as daring fantasies. They spoke of music, theaters, dances, women in the latest fashions and whether either candidate running for president as Roosevelt's successor—Ohioan William Howard Taft or Democrat William Jennings Bryan from Nebraska—would make any changes to better the race situation. Even at her young age, Lucille came to realize the stories always carried the same theme: experiences of near death, the fall or morality of people who succeeded against all odds in their search for justice, riches or notoriety.

Her mother shooed and swatted her away when adults were present and the lively debates got raucous. "You are too little to be listening to grown folks' conversation."

But Lucille found a way. She hid underneath the windowsill and wrapped herself within the lace curtains so she could listen to the storytellers. She favored one man in particular, a fellow they called Buster who was a frequent guest during the Loves' stay. Buster seemed to love to entertain anyone who shook his hand and even those few who kept their distance. Not only did he frequently tell stories about all the things he witnessed, he also acted them out in such an animated fashion that made her laugh.

Buster was on what he called a personal expedition; her father said it meant he was going around looking for work that wasn't too hard wherever he could find it. Buster had family in Africville, in Halifax, Nova Scotia. Lucille wasn't sure where Africville, Halifax or Nova Scotia were. When she asked Miss Opal, the teacher not only pointed it out on a map but also made a lesson of it by providing the girls of the rooming house

with a history of the little town that was founded by the enslaved loyalists to the British crown since the beginning of the
Thirteen Colonies.

Lucille heard Buster speaking with the young Sampsons, a
dancing couple who were freshly married and on their way
to Chicago with the hopes of being selected for a big musical
revue. Buster had his hands on his hips, singing and shuffling
out a few rhythmic steps to Bert Williams's song "Nobody."
The Sampsons gave him a round of polite applause, which encouraged Buster even more. Buster was more than happy to
continue his one-man act and Lucille tucked herself deeper out
of sight so she could catch every bit of his antics.

"I sneaked in and saw Bert Williams and George Walker at
Procter's Twenty-Third Street theater up in New York City.
The show was a spectacular musical comedy revue that had me
laughing 'til I thought my sides would burst. At the end they
performed a parade number that rivaled no other. I think it
was George Walker's wife, the lithe and limber Aida Walker,
who shined in the cakewalk finale."

Something stirred within her when the visitors sat around
the table to tell stories of musical shows, bands, marches and
cinemas. Buster talked about watching nimble dancers, Joe and
Sadie Britton, and read their glorious reviews that appeared
in the *New York Age* saying that the colored dancing team's
feet—particularly Joe Britton's—had never gone to his head.
"'There may be feet in those hard-soled shoes of his, but they
tap wood as if they carried cargoes of radium,'" Buster quoted
from the newspaper.

Many of Miss Opal's guests had passed through big cities
that clamored with workmen. Carpenters, bricklayers and steel
workers pounded out their trades as the cities grew. They spoke
about searching for work and dodging ladders, buckets, nails
and tarps that lined the wide streets, and finding no openings
for them in the boom of expansion. Lucille heard stories of men

being chased off work sites or told to go to the Mammy University to learn to be of value as a domestic. Buster said the cities were dressed in signs everywhere you could look. Signs with laws and ordinances, announcing new businesses and products, and who could enter and who was prohibited. Guests spoke in hushed and somber tones about the catastrophes of injustice that befell many colored men or women where lines were still drawn despite modern city life.

For the most part, the Loves only traveled the back roads, avoiding thoroughfares where wildly speeding motorcars, buses and trucks competed with horse-drawn vehicles. Sitting in their buckboard wagon for what felt like a trek around the earth, Lucille couldn't quite imagine the life as she heard it from the disappointed and enlightened boarders. They traversed the big cities like New York and Chicago, even on ships sailing across the Atlantic to all sorts of foreign ports.

No matter the topic, Lucille sat quietly—either under the windowsill or a nearby covered table so her mother wouldn't snatch her up by the ear.

Miss Garnetta Opal held a makeshift class consisting of five little girls. There had been a school nearby, but ever since the incident where bricks crashed through the windows, the classes were moved to Miss Opal's home. Miss Opal told Hank and Evelyn that in exchange for their room and board Lucille could attend her classes.

"I can't allow no little colored girl in my house go untaught. She's old enough to start reading, writing and arithmetic right now. Evelyn, you know the importance of a good education. It's what gonna keep us all alive."

Lucille had never been to a formal school. Her mother and father had many an argument about finding a place where she could begin to attend school on a regular basis. Her father would disappear into the woods when the subject was brought up. Her mother threatened to have Lucille sent back to Indiana to be raised by her grandpappy, but Daddy wouldn't have it.

"Patience, Evie!" Hank would shout to Evelyn's frosty anger. "We ain't, under no circumstances, separating this family! We gonna settle soon and in time to get that girl in school."

A thaw of sorts occurred when Miss Opal whisked Lucille off to her classes.

Miss Opal was big on math and wanted every girl to be an expert at applying math to every problem. Miss Opal lectured, "Mathematics is a way to solve everything. It's older than any of us. It's the pattern of life. It's order smoothing over all the chaos in this world. You know what? God was the greatest mathematician." Miss Opal looked Lucille squarely in the eye. "Master math, and you can calculate a resolution to any problem."

She returned her attention to all the girls. "Disappearing progress…that's what I fear the most. Our advances since Reconstruction, just up and disappearing at the snap of a finger… at the whim of someone wicked."

Lucille knew better than to interrupt with a question or comment. Miss Opal's lessons always evolved from practical function to big-picture, real-world applications.

"We can't just sit idly by and watch though. That's why I got you girls here. I'll always challenge the old way of life trying to keep me and my people from disappearing in the fields. And you know what? The key is us—us women and girls. We gon' do whatever we have to do to lift up the race."

She stared at Lucille again, who turned beet red for being singled out in front of all the other girls. "And someday, you will too. You watch. Use your talents to progress."

Lucille listened to every word. *Talent?* When it came to talent, Lucille wasn't sure what she possessed. She knew that her mother was talented from all the praise she received every time she sang at church. Her mother's voice made her dream; Lucille would go into a trance when her mother sang. She'd stop whatever she was doing to listen. She watched the rise and fall of her mother's chest as she drew in air and let out the most exquisite sounds. Sometimes she would close her eyes and open her mouth wide to form oohs and aahs just like her mother.

As her limbs grew longer, Lucille spent hours seated at Evelyn's side as she played the piano and sang "O mio babbino caro." Puccini seemed to be her mother's favorite. Her mother told her Puccini's aria was a story of a young woman pleading with her father to let her marry. She pointed to certain words and translated them into English. Amazed at her mother's voice, Lucille wanted to stop, listen and watch as she demonstrated such love of the music that told a story. It was a love that had passed from hand to hand. The sheet music, cantatas of Mozart, Purcell and Wagner, yellowed and stiff from age and use, were handled gently as if precious heirlooms.

Evelyn had learned music from her mother, who learned all she knew from Miss Hattie, an enslaved woman who was the long-serving music director at Fields of Grace Church until the day it mysteriously burned down. Miss Hattie was exposed to classical music by a mistress who considered herself local nobility. Miss Hattie was plucked out from the other household children to learn how to read music so that she could turn pages of sheet music while her mistress played lyrical compositions and sang arias for their guests. Those guests thought it a novelty to have a colored girl reading music as if she was part of the performance. The young Miss Hattie was given a white wig and an elaborate dress to wear on such occasions.

Miss Hattie learned to played piano just from watching her mistress and passed along all that she learned to others who showed a spark of interest. Evelyn was a star pupil. Up until the time Miss Hattie passed away, all who sang under her direction knew classical arias along with every hymn expected to be sung at any country church service.

"Lucille Arnetta Love!"

Lucille froze. She had been resting under the windowsill, listening to lively bits of conversation that floated in from outside.

"Lucille, come sit closer to me," her mother commanded while sitting straight-backed on the piano bench. "I'm going to play 'What a Friend We Have in Jesus' and I want you to sing out. Sing it as loud as you can, okay?"

"Yes, ma'am."

Her mother's fingers hit the keys of the piano, hammering out a recognizable introduction to a familiar song. When a bolt of notes hit her, Lucille began to say the words she heard so often as the music carried her along. She spoke softly, until her mother abruptly stopped playing.

"Do you know what you're singing, little girl?"

"Yes, ma'am." She hadn't really paid much attention to the meaning of the words—she was more interested in duplicating the melody. It was all the usual stuff that she had heard almost every day in church anyway.

"I don't think you do. I'm going to repeat the words. Listen carefully. Take a quick study and tell me what you think they mean."

Lucille's cheeks grew warm. She didn't want to disappoint her mother with the wrong answer. "I think they mean love, Mommy," she said timidly. Her mother seemed pleased. Encouraged, Lucille added, "God loves you forever."

"That's right! Isn't that something? That's good news. Now let's sing it again. Sing like you're trying to tell the world something so special...because it is, you know."

Mother and daughter sang several verses of the hymn together. By the time they finished, Miss Opal and a few of the other guests were gathered around the piano.

Miss Opal clapped her hands and gave a little joyful hop. "Ooo-wee! I told you that little girl can sing. That little girl has a big, old voice. Let's have her sing a solo for church tomorrow."

"Garnetta," Evelyn said sternly. "I don't know about that. It's too soon to have her…"

Miss Opal fluttered a dish towel in the air. "Aww, Evelyn, that girl ain't shy. Are you, honey? She sounds clear as a bell for such a little one. I bet she can sing with Father Devine or any of them other traveling saint evangelists. Folks pay every time they pass the plate thinking they can buy their way into heaven."

"I'm not trying to tie my girl to a circus act. My plan is that we are going to get her formally enrolled in school, then on to college for a degree in music."

"She's learning now. I teach her the fundamentals. She's a fast learner and applies everything I teach to the things we do in real life. I bet she could take any state or college test and pass it."

Evelyn added, "Oh Garnetta, you've done a wonderful job teaching Lucille and them girls. I just mean…"

"Evelyn, I'm not talking about her being in no medicine show. I'm for sending that girl to college on the wings of her God-given talents. But for now, she can sing for the Lord, sis! Honey, from what I just heard, that girl's voice can rescue the perished. Mark my words, you got something there. Just look at this crowd! Come on, play another."

Lucille sat quietly swinging her legs. Her feet brushed against the ground, kicking at the doll that now lay against the piano leg. Its black button eyes and stitched smile laughed back at her. Lucille stuck her tongue out at the doll before catching a glimpse of her father. He squatted in the parlor doorway watching the impromptu performance and listening to the women's exchange. He gave his daughter a broad smile and Lucille returned a wide toothy grin right back.

What she didn't see was that her father had been feeling restless, anxious and unsettled. He had been sitting out on the front porch chewing on tobacco and studying the horizon. He was contemplating how to approach his wife about their next move, when a booming voice he didn't recognize beckoned him inside. It was his daughter Lucille's voice.

Sitting on his heels peering through pant legs and hems to watch his own daughter miraculously spill out notes and phrases with a mature sound of a grown woman, he beamed with pride. His little girl sang without any sign of fear or embarrassment, in front of a crowd of adults.

Hank caught his wife's attention and she stopped playing, the arch of her wrists poised in midair. Lucille took advantage of the moment to slide down from the piano bench. She stopped short and looked back at her mother to get her permission to run into her father's arms.

Miss Opal broke the brief silence. "That was beautiful, sweet girl. In fact, that was excellent! Evelyn, you had no idea your daughter could sing like this before now?"

"Did you hear me, Daddy?"

Her father chimed in over the din of accolades, "Oh yes, yes, yes… That was better'n beautiful. That sounded like a chorus of angels. Go on, ladies. Don't stop on my account."

Instead of continuing with another song, her mother waved everyone away including Lucille, who followed Miss Opal out of the parlor. Miss Opal disappeared into the kitchen, but Lucille hung back, just outside of the parlor doorway to listen to her parents speak in hushed tones.

Her mother glanced over at her father to see him rubbing his chin, his jaw working as if he was chewing on an idea and fixing to do something. Even Lucille knew this was a signal that a plan was brewing.

"Now Hank, I can see what you're doing. You're working on something. Don't get too excited," her mother said softly.

"It's too late for that, my dear, sweet Evelyn. I've got an idea."

As if reading his mind, Evelyn shot back, "Hank, I'm not going to exploit my daughter by setting her up as a medicine show or carnival show act!"

"No, Evie, we're going to give her voice over to the Lord. There's no harm in that, right? We're just going to spread His love. We're in church every Sunday and several times a week. I think if the girl wants to sing, singing in church should be about enough."

Pressed so tightly against the wall she thought the flower print of the wallpaper would rub off on her skin, Lucille felt her heart race at the idea. Singing in front of a crowd would be new to her, but just this small performance in the parlor made her feel special. She wanted to feel that way again.

Hank continued, "Maybe that's why we're out here on this road. Besides, this can be the way to get us out of here. We now have a really good reason for traveling like we've been doing. Not escaping from them unjust devils out there. We'll be spreading the gospel. Your daddy certainly would agree with me on that."

Miss Opal returned with a book in her arms, clearly having overheard everything as well. She spied a guilty Lucille in the hallway, but only tsk-tsked as she entered the parlor, muttering an apology for interrupting the discussion between husband and wife.

Lucille peeked around the doorframe to see Miss Opal place the book on a table so Hank and Evelyn could see the title, *A Guide in Voice Culture.*

"He's right, Evelyn." Miss Opal tapped a finger on the book. "This might help make up your mind. It was written by an Afro-American woman, Emma Azalia Smith Hackley. I heard her perform and give a lecture a few years ago. She's dedicated to teaching the youth about Negro composers. This can help with formal preparation. Because anything for the Lord can't be bad. Also, think about what Ida B. Wells said: 'To right wrongs is to turn the light of truth upon them.' Lucille's God-given talents can do just that."

Miss Opal received an appreciative nod from Hank as she left the room, looking quite satisfied that she made her point.

Lucille prepared to be scolded for listening in on the conversation. Instead, Miss Opal smiled at her and disappeared back down the hallway.

Hank continued, "Actually, come to think of it, it won't be just her, not our little girl. It will be mostly you. You're the musical talent, *Miss Black Patti the second*. You will be the musical center of whatever we do. I'm just a simple farmer but I can set a few things up and accompany you on my guitar. That might be nice. We can call ourselves the Traveling Loves."

"I don't know, Hank. Why can't you just focus on finding us a place? A little house with a patch for us to grow a little something. I can get a job sewing or teaching music to bring in money. Hank, I was so scared when we left Daddy and the church. I wasn't sure about it then and, even after all this time, I'm still not sure that it was the right thing to do."

"Evelyn, all I've ever known is how to see opportunity in whatever Mother Nature lets me coax from the earth. I follow her lead, respecting the give and take of the land and sky. When she feels good, she gives me what I need. This here is a sign that something good is about to spring up for us all."

Lucille's heart swelled with excitement. Something good was exactly what everyone needed.

6

There was no stage or lights in the unexpected clearing deep in the middle of Sharon Woods. There was only a wide swath of cornflower blue sky overhead where the sun shone on every uncovered forehead. Surrounded by a circle of horse-drawn wagons filled with people swinging their legs over the sides and weather-worn elders sitting in armchairs and makeshift benches, Lucille Arnetta Love sang as loud as her lungs permitted. Her only accompaniment was the rhythmic rustle of leaves, stomping feet, clapping hands and her father's deep humming while strumming his banjo. Standing on a mound of dry grass, in the center of a crowd of folks smiling and cheering her on was the best feeling Lucille ever felt in all her eight years on earth.

Since the moment the residents of Miss Opal's house gathered around the piano, there was hardly a time when Lucille wasn't singing. All she could remember was being thrust into the center of grown people after being told to sing as loud as she could. She wasn't afraid at all. Lucille felt at ease being seen and heard. Singing began to feel like waking up in the morning and catching the first wisps of cool morning air. It was like breathing.

When the Loves weren't visiting churches, they'd practiced in Miss Opal's parlor—Hank plucking on the strings of his banjo or sometimes the guitar, Evelyn singing the lead melody and occasionally sitting at the piano when it was Lucille's time to shine. The rooming house had always been a place to learn, but now it became sort of a home base for rest, recovery and rehearsal for the next performance.

Lucille couldn't remember a time when she didn't know all the words of any hymn that her mother or father wanted her to sing. Lucille never faltered, stumbled or paused. She also knew that whenever she sang, if she closed her eyes, balled up her fists and scrunched her little body down to deliver a note with all her might, someone would bounce up on their tippy toes or march around in circles waving their hands in the air. The excitement of the crowd shouting, "Praise Him… Praise the Lord… Yes, Lord!" filled her up and she'd make her voice sail out into the clouds. Her feet couldn't help but follow the crowd and tap along with the beat.

Today as she performed "Swing Low, Sweet Chariot," she did exactly that, let the crowd's energy guide her. When Lucille reached the second verse, her hands joined in. They pointed up to the sky, shaking with the lyrics pleading to the Lord for mercy and understanding. In the third verse, when the song turned toward a body joining the saints, she jumped in the air.

Lucille was so immersed in making sure the crowd knew who was "coming for to carry her home" that she grabbed the corners of her starched white church dress, held them wide and jumped up as high as possible. When she landed, she twisted the corners of her dress from side to side and marched toward her audience as she sang. It was at that moment her mother swooped in, and with a firm grip around her daughter's wrist, scooped her up. As Lucille floated up from the ground, she noticed the change in scenery. She opened her eyes to faces that had shifted from joyful grins to tight frowns and *tsk-tsk-tsk* shaking heads.

Evelyn finished the song in full operatic high soprano fashion, punctuating each note as if she herself had floated down from the choir of angels in heaven. She didn't miss a beat, twirling each word while crossing the field, carrying her daughter, now shocked into silence, behind the line of wagons. Church service resumed with a few hallelujahs as they exited, and the pastor rose up in a sermon about the sins of the flesh.

"Don't let me ever catch you dancing that way in front of the church again! Do you hear me? This is music for God, not some dance of heathens. You keep that dress down and stand exactly the way I taught you. God gave you this tremendous voice. Show some respect or else He'll take it away. Do you hear me, Lucille Arnetta Love?"

Lucille, looking down at her feet, nodded slowly. Rubbing her wrist, she thought, *How could what I did be so wrong?*

Her father slid in from behind the wagon. Rubbing his face, he shouted at his wife, "Evelyn, you leave that little girl alone. She was just filled with the spirit, that's all. Don't be so harsh."

"Spirit nothing, Hank Love. That was the devil walking up beside her, just the pure devil. We got to keep her on the right path."

Lucille looked up at her father. His dark face was etched with the scar that ran from his hairline, crossing his closed eye and down his cheek. Whether he wore his eye patch or not, Lucille thought he was the most handsome man alive. When their eyes met, he gave her a wide smile and a slight nod.

Lucille then whipped around to her mother, who was still pacing with anger. "I'm sorry, Mama, it won't happen again."

Since her parents came up with the idea of singing for their supper as the Traveling Loves, Lucille had sung almost every day at some church function or another. Lucille had grown confident and, as she sang, she began to search the audience for signs that every note had hit its mark. She got used to the broad, open-mouthed smiles, the flat palms that waved before her and the women with big bosoms who exercised every bit of their bodies as they jumped and leaped in praise during her songs. She beamed when the grannies patted her cheeks as she was constantly paraded in front of them. She yearned for the pride that radiated from her mother's eyes. Daddy tried to temper Evelyn's growing arrogance when Lucille obstinately pushed her morning oats away and demanded ham and eggs for breakfast.

"It's all your fault, Hank. You've spoiled this child with your affection on top of all the attention she gets. We've got to be sterner with her to balance it out or she'll never learn to be humble and gracious."

"Evelyn, I'll leave that to you. But you know something? It's all right that she shows a bit of spirit now. She gonna need a bit of straight spine where she's going."

Over the next five years, the Traveling Loves covered the sawdust revival trail performing at every church and outside healing crusades found along paved or unpaved roads. Lucille sang revival gems one hundred times over and it had been the same routine for the last few shows. However, a new routine emerged: after every performance, Lucille's mother and father would hide out of sight, arguing. Between performances, when the Loves returned to Miss Opal's, Evelyn complained about their hand-to-mouth existence, even though the family was very well taken care of; as guests of a church or sponsoring civic organization, the Loves stayed in the nicest hotels, were graciously fed the most bountiful meals and given an honorarium for their performances. Still, her mother argued, they didn't have a home like all the other parishioners and were living in what she called a hatbox. Lucille didn't mind—she loved Miss Opal's—but from her mother's snappy retorts to everything her father said, the lack of a home seemed to be the reason why Evelyn picked at everything she could possibly find to show her displeasure.

It was after another performance in a city where the church was a storefront with its name and service hours hand-painted across boarded-up windows. Her father had chosen the song without her mother's approval and joined in on his guitar to raise the tempo just enough to push the song over the edge of propriety, at least according to Evelyn. One half of the congregation whooped and hollered, and the other half covered their mouths in shock over Lucille's version of an old Negro spiritual—some even called it blasphemous to the point that the pot that they didn't have a stove for began to boil over. This wasn't the first time they played the song this way, but it was a Sunday service and the clapping and stomping over their joyful rendition felt more like a sinner's Saturday night. Lucille had joyfully followed her father's lead while her mother stretched out her verses, taking her time during her solo in an attempt to pull the trio into a more dirgelike pace. Lucille, giddy with their performance, completed her last note with a twirl and curtsy. She then slid into a pew to listen to the rest of the service. Her parents made their way out to the vestibule where an argument over the song choice and rendition carried through the air and mingled with the pastor's sermon, leaving the congregation with sideway glances as they strained to hear what was being said.

Turning a deep crimson, Lucille puffed out her cheeks in embarrassment. She slumped down in her seat hoping no one would say a word to her. Squeezing her eyes tight, Lucille prayed her parents would stop shouting. The minister continued without skipping a beat and most of the congregation returned to wailing and swaying like waves on a turbulent sea at the pastor's fiery words. At the height of the fervor, a rustle of fabric accompanied by a wave of increasing body heat swept in from Lucille's right. Her mother slid next to her with eyes creased tight and lips quivering as she recited an intelligible

prayer. Lucille imagined it was something about Daddy finding a place of their own and taking the Traveling Loves off the
seemingly never-ending road.

Relieved that her parents had finally ceased their display,
Lucille wiggled in her seat. Her body itched with nervous energy. She pressed a finger to her knee to discreetly rub away
the tingling sensation. She then started to scratch at the spot
and once she did, she couldn't stop. Her dress and tights had
been scrubbed washboard clean in lye soap that was intent on
annoying her skin. She pulled at the collar of her starched stiff
dress and swung her legs to keep from digging holes into her
skin. All the shouts of prayers and hallelujahs falling heavily around failed to distract from her irritated skin. Her body
now ached from the assault, and she wanted relief. Her mother
seemed to care less about Lucille's distress; she was deep in her
own trance of devotion. Evelyn rocked back and forth with her
hands folded in prayer and eyes still closed. Lucille looked to
her left beyond the last seat in the row and saw that the double
door of the church's side entrance was ajar. Glancing back at
her mother, who was in a trancelike prayer, she slowly scooted
toward the sliver of light and slipped out the door.

Outside, the deep blue of the evening fell around the tall
buildings, leaving an opening to a sky scattered with tiny stars
ready to mark their presence. She wasn't afraid to be alone in
the alleyway between two buildings. The cool air and sense of
adventure relieved her itch. She could still hear the pastor shout
as he delivered a singsong sermon. From the building in front of
her, a different kind of music wafted from inside. A steady brash
beat of a bass drum, along with a tart *blaat, blaat, blaat* of a cornet drew Lucille's attention. She moved closer to the building
opposite her. The doors were ajar and to Lucille, they seemed
to hold a mystery. She crossed the alleyway and peeked through
the crack in the doors. The bright lights and sounds from within

were as enticing as sweet cake fresh from the oven. Curiosity overtook her and she slipped inside as the music grew louder.

A tall curtain fell from the high ceiling, blocking her view of what appeared to be a stage. Men in silhouette moved silently behind the curtain, beyond the reach of the stage light, in between ropes, blocks and bags of sand. No one seemed to pay any attention to a child wandering behind stage in the dark. Lucille walked closer to a sliver of light flashing between a slit in the curtains. Drawn in like a moth to a flame, she couldn't help but carefully pull it aside to get a peek at what was going on. She gasped; it was a show unlike anything she had ever seen before.

Bathed in lights, center stage, was a practically naked white woman. Lucille had never seen a woman in such a state of undress. Her creamy white skin rippled in the light. Strips of sheer fabric and shiny glass beads fell around her thighs, flashing like twinkling lights dangling from fleshy, round hips. Lucille had also never seen a woman with a powdered face, cheeks and lips rouged so ruby red. Entranced by the woman's voluptuous body and painted face, Lucille couldn't take her eyes away from the performer.

The naked woman gave the audience a wide smile, arched her back, kicked her legs and twirled around the stage. Lucille dared to peel back the curtain a little farther so she could get a better look at each curve and dimple as the performer pranced toward the stage lights. Illuminated by the light, Lucille could see fluttering lashes and sparkling eyes surrounded by a sea of deep blue shadow, accentuated by delicate lines drawn to the top of her brow and down to the round ridge of her cheeks where they were met at a tiny star-shaped mole. Her hair was piled in cottony soft mounds on top of her head. Only a few wayward tendrils dared to escape and curl against her neck and cheek, damp with sweat.

Everything about the woman shook with each drumbeat and pop of the cornet. Her plump bosoms bounced each time she thrust her hips forward to accentuate the boom of the bass drum. Lucille could see only the tops of the audience's heads, but heard them roar when the woman rolled her fingertips up her body and placed her hands flat against her chest. She reached out to what seemed to be her adoring public, signaling her love for them.

Sharp "Har...har...hars" splashed out over loud, shrill whistles as the theatergoers hopped up from their seats to toss hats, caps and gloves on the stage at the naked woman's feet. Lucille had never seen an audience react to a performer like this before. She could only compare it to church services where the congregation would all stand and clap when filled with the Word, but Lucille mostly heard polite applause from muffled gloved hands or hollow bare-handed claps at revival meetings.

It was then the dancer, on her toes, backed up and skittered upstage so close to where Lucille stood peeping from behind the curtain. Momentarily blinded by the glare of the spotlight, Lucille whipped the curtain closed. Just as quickly, she opened it again. The woman was just within arm's length. Lucille could smell her sweet musky scent and see her muscles flex. She was close enough that Lucille could count the colored glass beads and rhinestones that adorned the woman's body, glittering like Christmas decorations. Lucille resisted the temptation to reach out and touch her, mesmerized at the woman's freedom, unrestricted by bodices or confined by stiff fabric of any kind as she strutted across the stage.

Lucille wondered, *Is this woman and her nakedness what the preachers talk about when they shout to be cautious of the wicked?* She never could understand what that meant. *It couldn't be.* The people beyond the edge of the stage seemed to love the practically naked woman. They called her by name and shouted for more.

Lucille continued to watch the woman shimmy and shake. When she dropped down into the splits at the beat of the drum, she turned to give Lucille a smile and a wink. Lucille gasped at the sight of the woman's bare legs splayed out in either direction—one in front and the other behind. Lucille quickly closed the curtain again. Lucille saw that the woman's features were much like her own; her nose, lips and hips gave her away. Lucille then knew what the rhinestones hid—the woman on the stage, passing from one bright light to the next, was as colored as she was. Maybe her mama, daddy, grandma or grandpappy gave her that one drop of blood. Lucille wondered if all the folks who were wildly screaming the dancer's name knew or even cared about the woman who gyrated before them. It was then Lucille felt she was looking into a mirror.

"LUCILLE LOVE!" The razor-sharp sound of her mother's voice and a hand yanking Lucille's hair snapped the little girl out of her stupor of admiration. "We have been looking all over for you!"

A corral of footsteps came out from behind shouting. "Hey, you two! Get outta here!"

Evelyn gripped her daughter by the collar and dragged her out of the building.

"Your daddy and the church folks were about to form a search party for fear you might have been dragged off somewhere! And I find you hiding out here watching this filth!"

Lucille stuttered out a lie, saying she had gone to look for her father and was on her way to wait in the wagon for him. Her mother cut her off between her clenched teeth, warning Lucille not to say another word.

Lucille kept her eyes downcast as her mother pinched her arm and led them away from what she supposed was the hellfire sin on earth. But she couldn't get the image of the naked dancer swinging her hips and covered with dazzling jewels out of her mind. The performer was so beautiful, brave and free. Before reentering the storefront church, Lucille noticed the marquee outside the theater building. It read, Starring the Queen of Burlesques. Lucille thought, *That colored girl was deemed royalty after all. That's why they loved her so much.*

7

Gallatin, Tennessee
1915

Lucille, who was soon to turn sixteen, had begun to feel trapped. Her parents' constant bickering about her performance methods—and even their singing, which most times was a way to escape from the everyday doldrums—only made a feeling of emptiness in the pit of her stomach grow bigger. That feeling didn't seem to want to go away. Sitting in a clearing behind the revival tent the Traveling Loves were appearing at, Lucille wrapped her arms around herself and hugged tightly as a reminder to keep her eyes shut. *If I keep my eyes closed tight, I'll only hear music.*

Eventually Lucille clasped her ears to drown out the sounds of the church and her parents. She shivered as the guilt and shame of *not* having any guilt or shame gnawed at her. She felt good when she sang. She thought about Buster and the wild stories he told on Miss Opal's porch. His audience of fellow travelers hung on to every word as he clapped, slapped his knees, stomped and posed with exaggerated smiles and frowns. They loved him and rooted for more. And Lucille wanted and needed to hear the crowds cheer her on too.

Lucille squeezed her eyes tight and held her ears even tighter. In the cloaked silence, everything before that moment disappeared. All her worries of her mother's admonishments were replaced with a shimmering gold light that pulsated before her. Music notes—halves, quarters, eighths and triplets, some sharp and some flat—swirled in her head. A voice enticed her to step lively through.

C'mon, Lucille Love, give 'em what you got, then give 'em some more. Give 'em a little something that they've never seen before!

It wasn't a big, bold voice falling around her from heaven. It was a subtle whisper in her ear coming from deep within the yellow ball of light. It was like the steady hum of birds and insects that chimed out for love, the rise and fall of crickets rattling in the morning summer breeze or the lone midnight hoot of an owl. All were sounds she came to recognize as the rhythm of her days and nights when she traveled in the horse-drawn wagon along the country roads.

Sing, girl…dig deep…dig deeper…deeper. Let it rise up…

Lucille heard it clearly and followed suit. She stood, feet firmly planted, taking a deep breath in preparation to bring whatever words came to her to life. It was like she had been called to do this all of her almost-sixteen years of life. Every ounce of her being was transfixed on pushing out every note, no matter where she was, no matter who her audience was. She saw herself in a clearing in the middle of a deep green forest surrounded by the yellow light guiding her to some unknown destination.

It was then a deeper voice broke through her thoughts and her spontaneous solo. "So you like to sing, do you?"

Shaken from her thoughts, Lucille opened her eyes to a young, clean-shaven, coffee-colored man with black hair neatly parted and slicked back with pomade. From his mud-stained shoes to the tip of his head he reminded her of all the reels she had seen where the hero and the heroine shared a kiss. He was smooth and handsome like the actors in *Something Good*. Even though the performers in the film reminded her of her parents, staring at the man in front of her only reminded her of the kisses.

"Hello, miss. My name is Marcus Williams. You like just singing to these church folks? I believe I can help you take that voice of yours to the stars."

"Ummm...hello, Mr. Williams. Mother and Daddy are over there." She pointed in the direction of a clump of trees. A trill voice sounded out.

"You always treating that girl like she one of those stage acts. Over my dead body, she is not. My girl is singing for the Lord!"

"No, Lucille...you don't mind me calling you Lucille, do you? I want to speak with you. By the way, please call me Marcus."

He stretched out his hand and Lucille limply took it, thinking it would be disrespectful if she didn't. Most of the time, Mother would be the one who made all the introductions and arrangements. Lucille had never spoken to anyone regarding where and when she sang. She was never allowed to make any decisions about anything. From what clothes she wore, to the color of ribbons in her hair, all things were selected with care by Mother.

"I'm a talent scout. You know what that is, Lucille? I search out talented people like you for some of the biggest shows across the nation. At least, I will be working with those big shows when I find the right act. And I think I've found that act—you! The Traveling Loves have been playing around these small towns for years and I've taken note. I've seen you and your folks perform a few times and, from what I can see, you've been doing everything your ma and pa have asked of you. Now, I'm asking you, what do you want to do with that great big voice of yours?"

No one had ever asked her what she wanted. *Ever.* The question struck her like a thunderbolt to the heart and she knew exactly what to say.

"Mr. Williams—I mean, Marcus—I want to stand in the

middle of a big light, performing on a big wooden stage in front of every human being in the big wide world. I want to be a sensation. You know, like that Broadway star Aida Overton Walker. She got to perform all over in Europe dressed in French silks and diamonds everywhere. People are still talking about her."

"I like that." Marcus smiled broadly. "I can make it happen. Let me talk to your parents."

"This ain't no pretty life, pretty boy." Hank stood with his arms folded across his chest, sizing Marcus up. He flipped his eye patch up and pushed it back to expose the long scar and closed eye to be more intimidating. He took a long minute just chewing on tobacco before spitting on the ground. He wiped his mouth with the back of his hand before extending it, daring Marcus to shake it. Marcus boldly reached out and firmly grasped Hank's hand. Hank abruptly retracted his hand and buried it back into his folded arm.

"I'll say that again. This ain't no pretty life, pretty boy."

"No, it's not, Mr. Love. That I think we can agree on," Marcus responded without backing down.

Evelyn stood to the side, her eyes floating up and down the length of Marcus. Her mouth turned down at the corners and she stood with the same posture as her husband. "All your big words and them fancy clothes don't tell me you won't take advantage of this little girl's potential."

"Mr. Love, I've seen you, your talented wife and immensely talented daughter, Lucille—who truly can be a star—perform several times now and I think you got something here. I'm a talent scout on the way to being a producer…or trying to be one. I've got an eye for talent, at least. I want to put on plays and theatrical performances for us black folks with legitimate contracts and getting legitimate pay. I need a group like you to get started. I've done a few gigs at home in Chicago and I'm convinced that I can do that here." Marcus reached out and unfolded his hand to reveal a one-dollar bill. "Take this. It's all I have. You take it and if I don't deliver on making the Traveling Loves a household name in every place in America, you can keep it."

"Well, if this is all you have, how you gonna eat and sleep, Mr. Williams? You from Chicago, right? You got people around here?"

"And your wife, Mr. Williams…where is your wife?" Evelyn added inquisitively.

Marcus tipped his head to give Evelyn a slight bow. "Why yes, I do have a wife. Thank you for asking. I am happily married to a wonderful woman named Rose, and she means the world to me."

"Well, if she's so wonderful, why aren't you with her?"

"With her blessing…" Marcus paused a moment before continuing, "I have taken a sabbatical of sorts to start a business. I want to start it with you, the Traveling Loves."

Hank jumped in. "You didn't answer my question. All you got is one dollar? Don't sound like a successful scout, manager or producer to me. If I was that wife of yours, I'd be looking for another husband."

Marcus laughed. "I'm being honest with you, Mr. and Mrs. Love. I'm just starting out. My wife is a seamstress and has her own business. She designs and sews garments for all the up-and-coming black folks in Chicago. She's got a good start in making money. We're hoping that we will be able to build something when both our endeavors hit pay dirt. And they will—that I can promise. I'm pretty enterprising. I know where to find a place to lay my head and get a few crumbs to eat. I ain't worried about that."

Hank walked over to stand closer to his wife. He pulled his patch back down over his eye, rubbed his chin and twisted his lips before folding the dollar in half and sliding it into his pocket. He took a deep breath.

Marcus took Hank's silence as an opening. "I'm that sure

about it. I've been looking for an act, a family-friendly act, a dynamic start to becoming a producer the likes of none other." Looking at Lucille, he said, "I think I've found it."

"You've found something, all right, and it's my baby girl. Because I can see how you've been looking at her. Yeah, I know that little girl with the big voice is the future."

"That's right, Mr. Love. She can be a star on stages across America and Europe, that is if we don't head off to war."

"I do like your enthusiasm, young man." Hank patted his chest. "And this broken-down old farming man don't have nothing to do with getting her on no stage. But believe me, that's where she belongs."

Marcus stood silent, tapping his feet. He held his head down as if deep in thought. He looked over at Evelyn. "You know, while on the road I can arrange a meeting with Mrs. Emma Azalia Smith Hackley. Won't that be nice? It might be beneficial for Lucille to meet her. She has been involved with creating music programs for colored students in Washington and Ohio. She, being a virtuoso coloratura soprano herself, has sung with much praise and reviews for her rendition of Dell'Acqua's 'Villanelle' among other things."

"I'm quite familiar with Mrs. Hackley. She and her husband have done so much to establish formal training programs at several of our colleges and universities. I would be impressed if an introduction could be made. I'm not sure about Lucille's bel canto abilities but she's so young. Arias and cadenzas are possible. But I'm not the one to convince, Mr. Williams." Evelyn smiled and shot a look at her husband. "Though I am impressed with your knowledge and attempt to sway me."

Marcus looked a bit sheepish for being caught with such a ham-fisted play. "Mrs. Love, I'm really not that knowledgeable of the specifics of that style, but I do know the entertainment business. The Fisk Jubilee Singers are traveling everywhere. They are impressive and have a following. I can see Lucille, being so young and all, as a featured soloist touring as a vocalist and winning over many hearts. She has the capability to do it all. With her big sound and range, she could even sing like Mamie, Bessie or Ma Rainey."

"Wait a minute," Hank cut in. "You not going to have my baby moaning out any blues."

"No, I promise she won't be doing nothing like that, Mr. Love. It will be tasteful and appropriate. Nothing but family-friendly entertainment."

Hank snorted and crossed his arms. "Now listen here, this is how it's gonna play out, pretty boy. You gonna manage us, the Traveling Loves, for one year. All of us. And if I don't see no changes, meaning more money in my hands and a happy smiling wife—treated royal as a queen, singing whatever she wants—then the whole deal is off. The deal is a year with us or nothing at all. I need you to show me what kind of advance man you can be in getting the Traveling Loves booked at recitals or the big festivals as a first-class act. You do that and I'll think about you managing my daughter."

8

Marcus started his year-long test run by booking the Traveling Loves into a string of revivals and seasonal festivals throughout Tennessee and Mississippi. The venues were close enough in proximity for their horse to carry them to each one. So far, only once did they have to sleep overnight in the wagon.

Quickly enough, it was apparent that Marcus had a talent for finding new places and an assortment of enterprising people along the same routes the Loves had traveled so many times before. He was able to find things that would make them feel safe traveling the Southern road when families told stories about loved ones who had gone missing while taking the same roads. He managed to find accommodations that presented the family with the finest foods and softest beds.

Although the venues didn't change much, it was the little things Marcus did that made Lucille feel there was a slight change in the wind. They'd gone from whitewashed wooden churches to cement and brick buildings. Since Marcus took over, the Loves were received differently. She didn't know what he said that wasn't said before, but whatever he was doing, Lucille began to feel a sense of excitement when they reached a destination. The Loves were treated like extraspecial guests.

But Hank remained unimpressed. "From what I can see so far, he ain't much of an advance man," Hank hummed out from between puffs of his pipe more than once. "I could have done this myself. Good thing he's working for free."

Over the course of a few months, Lucille found Marcus fascinating. It was something about his smooth skin, the color of coffee that settled in the cup after stirring in fresh thick cream; Lucille had never felt this way about anyone before. He was kind and generous. Marcus gifted her a turquoise silk caplet trimmed with a white silk cord. The sensation of the silk made her feel confident when she wore it. The first time she walked out to sing in her new caplet, along with white lace gloves he gave her, she truly felt like she had wings to fly away.

Besides her frock, Marcus bought two books which he gave to her father: Johnson's *History of the Negro Race* and *History of Negro Soldiers in the Spanish-American War*. Lucille expected they were given not only to keep her father happy but also busy while she and her mother did the singing. Marcus gave Evelyn Kinkine hair tonic, shampoo soap and a cultivator comb.

"These books cost me one dollar and twenty-five cents. And the fine hair products were a bargain at one dollar and fifty cents for the set. They came all the way from New York City!"

Silent and as if choreographed, Lucille's parents politely set their packages in their laps and tugged at the brown paper and string until her father spoke.

"No need to try and buy us, boy. Just do your job."

Though Hank and Evelyn wouldn't admit it, Marcus became a welcome distraction for all three Loves. They didn't seem to argue as much. In fact, his presence appeared to bond them closer together. They spent most of their time watching every move their new agent made or debating his every suggestion.

He kept them deep in discussion, with their heads bobbing together like a team of horses.

Then there were the placards and handbills Marcus had printed to announce the Traveling Loves appearances. Their names printed alongside Spectacular and Sensational gave Lucille goose bumps. Lucille thought the handbills and publicity were nothing less than remarkable. However, she kept her opinion to herself. When Lucille was alone, she traced the words on the placards with her finger while thinking about the near-naked performer she had seen so long ago at the theater next to the church. Lucille didn't mind being called sensational if the audience loved her as much as they seemed to have loved the bejeweled lady they awarded bursts of applause with each swing of her hips.

There was one thing Lucille wasn't happy about. As much as she loved seeing their name in large typeface, she hated her billing: The Little Girl with the Big Voice. The way her dresses began fitting her told her she wasn't a little girl anymore and Lucille wished everyone would stop treating her as such.

Her mother, however, prickled with discontent over the handbills and once she saw the ads in a local newspaper, she vociferously complained to her husband. "Look at this, Hank. We look like some vaudeville revue. What's next? Is he gonna have you telling jokes and me and Lucille dancing the seven veils?"

Lucille was afraid that her father was going to cut Marcus out completely to satisfy his wife's protests, until Marcus came up with the one booking that the elder Loves were hard-pressed to find fault with. Marcus announced with the flourish of a side show barker that the Traveling Loves were invited to be the pre-act for the Dixie Serenaders, one of the most successful all-colored musical comedy and grand opera shows.

"This is the highest-class colored entertainment in the world! Folks are paying twenty-five to fifty cents for admission. I'm telling you, this is the start of something big!"

Even Hank had to admit this was the first time they would be playing a theater where white folks would be attending in a roped-off reserved section. "How'd you get that, boy? What did you promise them?"

Marcus waved his hand toward Lucille.

"You promised them my little girl?"

"I promised them a voice like no other. They have a cast of contraltos, baritones and soprano singers, but nothing like little Lucille, or either of you Loves for that matter. I showed the theater owner and show's producer your promotional photographs, reviews and the letters I've been collecting from pastors and civic leaders. I must admit I got lucky because none of that was working before. It wasn't until one of the theater promoters, a white man, asked one of his men, a colored man, about you and heard that you all were nothing short of fantastic!" Marcus clapped his hands together. "So, you're in!"

Lucille had never seen Marcus so animated. Although she didn't fully understand, she got caught up in his delight. "What should we sing for the occasion?"

Marcus, Hank and Evelyn looked at each other. Marcus spoke first. "I've got an idea. The Dixie Serenaders show is upbeat with lots of comedy. We can only do one song, so we need to do something different."

Hank interjected, "Well, no one can sing like my girls."

Marcus continued, "Right, so let's start off with the missus and end with the miss. Something new and fresh but will let everyone, 'specially those sitting in the reserved seats—"

"You mean them white folks," Hank added.

Marcus nodded. "We need to let them know that this ain't no minstrel act. If we do this right, the Traveling Loves will get booked up solid from this date forward."

Evelyn cleared her throat. "How about starting with Puccini? *La Bohème*. I saw it performed when I was in New York.

There is a beautiful aria, 'Quando m'en vo.' But what about an accompaniment? Who would have the music?"

"Hmm, can it be sung a capella?" Marcus's eyes widened. "I see something forming in the old noggin'! Yes, classical! That could be glorious. You, Mrs. Love, will sing the aria, big and regal—in Italian. Stage left, in front of the curtain. The beautiful, mystical language will have them stupefied. You'll move across the proscenium as you sing. When you reach stage right, while the crowd is still in amazement, you'll wave Lucille in. We'll add the orchestra for her. It will be like passing the baton to the modern youth. Lucille, I have a special song for you, one that will end strong, perfect to introduce this all-colored revue: 'Lift Every Voice and Sing.' The orchestra will have that music, I'll make sure of that. The first two verses will be your solo, Lucille. The last two you both sing and end loud and strong!"

The theater from the outside was a plain storefront, like many city churches the Traveling Loves played. There was no marquee, just two placards at both sides of the entrance with Matinee Today written in large bold letters. Underneath in smaller lettering was The Colored Sensation the Dixie Serenaders, and printed in smaller typeface, Featuring the Traveling Loves.

Once inside, the theater surprisingly stretched out in row after row of velvet seats. The lights from the high ceiling created a kaleidoscopic pattern across the house floor. The three Loves headed toward the stage, moving quietly down the aisle. Lucille wondered if her mother felt the same chill rising up her spine as she was experiencing. Lucille had never been nervous; she simply sang the song as instructed.

Marcus was already backstage. His voice could be heard floating out from behind the curtain. Lucille peeled it back to see Marcus center stage speaking with two men and a woman encircled by what looked like a treasure trove of musical instruments. There were banjos, guitars, fiddles and violins, trombones, trumpets and cornets. Hank let out a low, slow whistle in amazement. Lucille was sure he was marveling at the stringed instruments and comparing the cache to his own cherished guitar.

"Ah, here is the act that is going to hand you a very pleased, favorable and expectant audience. I'd like you to meet the Traveling Loves: Hank, Evelyn and the Little Girl with the Big Voice, Miss Lucille," Marcus said bursting with pride. "Loves, please meet Mr. Leon Williams, Mr. G. W. Bennett, and Miss Beulah Hill. They are half of the Dixie Serenaders."

The men and woman swiveled slowly in the family's direction. One blurted out jovially, "You two ladies are going to warm up the audience for us? You sure you can handle it? They say you, little lady, are something special. We'll see. Either way, you're helping to save our bacon. They told us we had to change up our act so that we can be here a week. Since we didn't have time to break in a new act and don't have any jugglers or a one-legged aerialist, I'm glad Mr. Marcus brought the Loves onboard to complete our class act. We're professional singers and don't usually use amateurs."

"Hold on, Leon. They may not have the credentials yet, but they definitely have the talent."

"Oh, stop it, Leon," Miss Hill jumped in. "I was a little pup myself—exactly her age, maybe younger—when I got my big break and earned my spot to play with these lugs." She turned to Lucille. "Can you plan an instrument, young lady?"

Lucille, excited to be in the presence of who she felt were royalty, and wanting to match Marcus's exuberance, responded with confidence. "My mother sings and plays piano and my daddy plays the guitar. My instrument is my voice."

"Well, pretty girl, aren't you talking like a vaudeville flyer. Welcome aboard! I'm sure we'll see you on the circuit soon. Until then, break a leg!"

Smiling widely, Mr. Leon added, "Like I said, we'll see. But yes, please do break a leg."

★ ★ ★

When the house lights dimmed, Evelyn Love came onstage to the tune of her tapping heels. She wore her best dress, the one that Lucille always admired. It was a deep dark green satin, lined with rows of frilly black lace from her waist to the hem. Whenever it was brought out of the trunk, Lucille couldn't help running her hands over the smooth fabric and lace appliqué curlicues.

Evelyn stepped slowly out from the shadows. A sheer embroidered overlay fell from metallic threads that softly graced her neck and gathered at her waist. The sheen of the fabric caught the remaining light. Stopping short of center stage, she began the aria. The full house was silent, seemingly mesmerized by the operatic bounty of sound and language. Evelyn's last note hung in the air long after it had left her body. For a moment it reverberated from every high crevice of the theater, hovering before floating down and settling over the audience. Thunderous applause rang out, which was cut short by the strains of piano chords that sounded the start of Lucille's "Lift Every Voice and Sing."

In the wings, Lucille waited for the moment her mother would extend her arm, Lucille's cue to enter onstage. Taking wide steps to the edge of the stage, Lucille found herself bathed in the footlights. She was startled by a sudden flash from the bright white lights at her feet. Her mouth and throat filled with cotton. Even though she couldn't see her audience, she could sense they were different than the usual church crowds. She tried to gulp down air while the sharp, tart sound of the piano stabbed at her. Lucille blinked her eyes to focus. The tops of heads and hats beyond the light shifted in their seats. She squeezed her eyes again to see an image of a sparkling seminude woman with jewels on her fingers rising from the smoke of the footlights.

Lucille blinked again, in disbelief. She snapped her head

toward her mother, who was still on stage, arm outstretched, beckoning her daughter toward her. When Lucille looked back, the bejeweled woman was gone.

Lucille took a deep breath and began. She sang, letting her voice build and fall, lifting it to fullness and light to contrast her depths, just as they rehearsed. When she reached the final verse, her mother joined her. Together their voices rang out, perfectly complementing each other while signifying a contrast of old and young, past and present. When they were finished, the audience roared. There wasn't a call for ovations, as the curtain opened to start of the Dixie Serenaders' first number, which switched the tone to one of lighthearted comedy. The Dixie Serenaders put on stellar musical performances where the sextet played every instrument in their arsenal. The house rewarded the Serenaders with several ovations.

At the end of the show, Mr. Williams called Lucille and Evelyn onstage to take a bow to thunderous applause. Out of the corner of her eye, Lucille spotted her father standing in the wings clapping wildly. His dark skin shone brightly from perspiration and the heat of the lights. She could see he was proud of his two girls who took bow after bow along with the prestigious Dixie Serenaders. After the final curtain, Lucille ran toward her father's open arms, but another man stepped between them.

"Wow! You were just sensational!" The squat, well-dressed man extended his hand to Lucille then turned to her mother. "Ah, *bellissima, signora,*" he added with a small nod.

"Thank you, sir. This is my daughter, sir. And this—" she tugged at her husband's sleeve to pull him from behind the man to her side "—is my husband, Hank Love."

Noise from the audience shuffling out of the theater and the backstage chaos as the crew reassembled the stage for the evening performance rose, swallowing up their introductions and making it difficult to hear.

"And I am their manager," Marcus shouted out as he wriggled through a moving line of stagehands. He had one arm extended and the other stretched out behind him holding the gloved hand of a prim woman who could barely keep up. "Mr. Luebrie, it's an honor," he wheezed out breathlessly. He relinquished the woman's hand and shook Mr. Luebrie's with a noticeably firm two-handed grip. "How'd you like my clients? Great, right? The audience sure did love them. We need to—"

Cutting Marcus off, the man turned to Lucille "Yes, yes, yes. First, I need to shake this young lady's hand." He reached out to enclose Lucille's hand in his, giving it a pat. "Fine singing voice. Really fine…and such stage presence. I need to put you in one of my shows."

Lucille steadied herself and attempted to squeeze out a thank-you, but before anyone could say another word, the man excused himself stating he had to run off to another performance. Over his shoulder, he shot back, "Marcus, let's talk soon."

Giddy with excitement, Marcus slapped Hank on his shoulder. "Do you know who that is? Only the finest producer out there. That's John Leubrie Hill! He's written shows that had even Florenz Ziegfeld standing up and cheering. And here he is in the great state of Tennessee watching my two flowers."

The prim woman Marcus had dragged through the crowd cleared her throat.

"Oh, my apologies. I'd like to introduce you to my wife, Rose."

In unison, the Loves took a step back as the young woman, holding on to the brim of her hat, stepped forward. Hank's, Evelyn's and Lucille's eyes traveled from the bottom of her dainty-heeled shoes, to the tiered hemline of her fashionable dress, to her smiling, cherub-cheeked face. Behind them, a set crashed to the stage floor.

Rose cheerfully shouted over the din. "So lovely to meet you, Mr. and Mrs. Love. And, Lucille…you are such a talent.

I'm so glad my Marcus works with you. I can see why he is so enamored with such talented folks. Especially you, Lucille."

"Rose came in from Chicago and will be in town only a few days. I'm happy that she was able to make it to see you Loves in all your glory."

Lucille stayed silent as the couple stood before her with their hands entwined. A sharp ping zipped through Lucille's chest as she stared up at Rose and Marcus with smiles plastered across their faces. *She has a face like a cherry,* Lucille thought. *A shiny, new cherry just pulled from a tree, right before it turns red.*

Her mother gave her a sharp poke in the side. "Thank the woman, Lucille. She'll think we have no manners at all."

Lucille's mumbled thank-you came out as a cracking squeal. Marcus gave a few more hasty but hearty accolades to the Loves before ushering his wife out of the theater.

"She looks like a cherry, doesn't she? Something about those round cheeks, I think," Lucille said while watching the couple depart.

Her mother added, "That dress and hat is a bit too modern for a married woman. Don't you think, Hank?"

Hank sidestepped the question. "He really must believe we've got the potential to make him a whole lot of money to leave that little filly back in Chicago."

The curiosity of Marcus's mysterious spouse waned as the success of their performance and the warmth of Mr. Luebrie's handshake and attention lingered. Lucille's father and mother became increasingly impressed with Marcus. They nodded in approval when he presented new ideas for performance venues. Despite their show of acceptance, Lucille noticed her father, with arms folded across his chest, still made a practice of voicing his reservations.

"Marcus," her father said haltingly. "The months left on your promise are going to fly by. So far, you've done all right.

Has it been enough to sway me that you can take my daughter away? Well, don't get too comfortable, boy. My mind has yet to be made up."

Lucille guessed her father needed to keep Marcus on his toes. He needed to let Marcus know that Hank Love held the spot of top dog in charge of the Love family. So whenever there was an opening, Hank stated he still was not one hundred percent convinced of Marcus's ability to manage his daughter.

Marcus would counter, "Hank, getting comments from someone like J. Leubrie Hill is nothing to sneeze at. If Mr. Hill says Lucille can be a star, it's gospel. He's created the Colored Vaudeville Exchange to get new talent out there to the big theaters. Yes siree… I'll finish out my year. You wait and see, we'll be on the high road for sure."

9

1916

Lucille peeked into the room her parents shared. Her father, clothed in his good shirt and suit, was lying on the bed. Seeing him on his back with his hands knotted together gave her a quick start, but his light snoring told her he was just deep in dreamland. At that moment her father suddenly looked smaller than usual. Lucille eased herself between the crack in the open door and closed it behind her. In her eyes, her father had always been the mighty warrior laden with battle scars, protecting his family. She stood by his bedside counting his breaths. The exercise assured her he was all right. Her breath began to match his and she relaxed.

Mother was off pulling weeds in the small section of Miss Opal's garden, so Lucille went to the room to find a book to occupy her time. She stood watching her father resting while the house was silent aside from the tick-tock of the grandfather clock that guarded the foyer of the house. She usually loved the heavy sound and anticipated the chimes every hour. Today she was immediately startled by sound, reminding her it was two o'clock. The Loves were to have an early dinner before heading off to a church fete for a newly sworn in minister. Mother was to sing several hymns and play piano. Lucille was relieved that she wasn't included on the program and would just be there to lend support.

Hank stirred, raising his hand to his face before turning toward Lucille. "Hey, princess. Your old daddy was just giving his eyes a rest before going out to tend to the wagon and old Jupiter. You ready for this evening?"

"Yes, Daddy. I'm not singing tonight, right?"

"Naw, it's your mother's turn to shine tonight. But you never know what the Lord may call us to do." Her father spilled out a series of coughs that caused his whole body to shake.

"You all right, Daddy?"

"Yeah, yeah." He cleared his throat. "I'm fine." He fell back onto the pillow. "I just need to rest a bit. I've been seeing shadows for a while. Every time I close my eyes, I'm seeing shadows of men doing some evil things. I got to get them out of my head so I can sleep at night. If I don't, I'm up all night watching you and your mother sleep."

"Like you always tell me, talk to me about them and they'll go away. I don't want my daddy bothered by dreams of bad men." She picked up his hand and raised it to her cheek.

"Don't worry, sweet girl. It's bad dreams about things I don't want to talk about right now. Probably something your mama put in my head to get me to do like I promised."

He eased his body over to the edge of the bed and swung his legs over the side. He then reached over to pull a metal box from underneath the bed. Inside the box was a small brown pouch. "Here, take this." He dropped the pouch into Lucille's palm. Lucille felt the weight of it in her hands. "Fetch me my hat from over there. Let's go outside. I need to talk to you about what's in that pouch and I need to tell you in private. These walls have too many ears and I don't even want you to tell your mother about this conversation. Let's go out by the big tree."

The big tree was in the middle of the field across from the boardinghouse. Lucille nicknamed the tree the Sisters because the single trunk sprang from the ground then divided itself into three distinct sections. It looked like a meeting of sisters, each separate trunk with branches intertwining as they reached for the sky providing comfort and companionship to the others. Its branches spread wide with a few hanging low. Even though the tree could be seen from the road, one could easily hide in the shade and not be seen by anyone. A thick braided rope hung from a branch. It was knotted at the end so a child could grab hold and wrap their legs around it to swing up to heaven and back again.

As Lucille's father stood up, the room heard the pain in his joints through a series of pops and cracks. He winced as he lifted himself up and arched his back.

"Whew! Me and this old body done been through a lot. Gimme a minute. I got to get these ancient limbs working." After a few breaths, he said, "C'mon now. Bring that pouch with you."

They walked out of the house, crossed the road and waded through the tall grass. Lucille had spent a great deal of time running through the field with the girls who came to Miss Opal's classroom. When she was younger, the grass was so high that only the tops of the girls' heads could be seen as they zigzagged through the field to create a perfect maze to play hide-and-seek or stumbled across bird nests and rabbit holes where baby bunnies slept nestled together. Today in the heat of the sun, sixteen-year-old Lucille, who had grown in leaps and bounds in what seemed only months, was now heads above the tallest stalks. She followed her father out to the wide trunk of the big tree. When they reached the clearing, her father leaned his back against the tree and slid to the ground. The walk in the hot sun had tired him out.

"Listen here, girl… I'm gonna convince your mama to let you go ahead with Marcus. From here on Marcus is gonna manage only your career. He's gonna take you on the road without us and get you started on your own singing career. Me and your mama are gonna stay back. I'm thinking we're gonna go on to Oklahoma and get that house we've been talking about. I can't keep doing what we've been doing. Me and your mama are tired."

"You mean it will be just me and Marcus without you and mother? I don't know."

"Oh, you know you want it. Don't you? I know you better'n anybody else. I know you want to be somewhere else rather than riding through town after town living off a collection plate. Plus, my dreams, baby. My dreams be coming fast as of late and I think it's best if we scatter."

"What do your dreams have to do with anything? What do you mean, scatter? Daddy, are you all right? Are you and mother going to be all right?"

"Oh, girl, don't get scared. You're a big girl, a sensible girl capable of making decisions. Besides, you'll have guideposts all along the way. We've practically been in every town and church that peppers the South. Everyone knows you're a Love. Your grandfather got people all over the place that will beat out a message on the drums to let everyone know you're safe, fed and on the right path too.

"You got a chance to do something. I just know it. Every time I hear you sing, my bones start to weep with joy. Marcus has assured me, and proved to me, that he can get you on that big stage in New York, maybe even in the movies. I trust him. Don't you? Wouldn't you like that?"

Lucille smiled broadly. "You know something, Daddy? Yes, I would. That's the kind of dream I've been having."

"Your mama thinks you have talent—you've got a voice that reaches octaves even she can't. You could be the next Black Patti. And if your mother says so, I believe it."

"Do you really think she's going to let me go? Really?"

"She might have a teensy problem with a young girl going off, traveling around on the circuit, but you aren't just any girl. I'm going to assure her that you're in good hands. Me and Marcus have had the man-to-man talk. I told him in no uncertain terms, I'd find him, kill him and skin him if something happened to you—and he knows this broke-down old man would do it too. Marcus ain't going to have you dancing in no dens of iniquity. He's going to get you a real agent, work up a show, hire musicians and get you on the entertainment circuit. You'll have the finest and you'll be showered with gold coins."

A smile spread across Lucille's face. She'd had vivid dreams of standing in front of throngs of people while all eyes were upon her. She could feel soft furs against her skin, heavy jewels pressing against her chest, her hair in marcel waves and pressed into curls against her cheeks like the glamorous ladies in the papers. She could hear the applause and feel the heat from the stage lights. Lucille trusted Marcus too. Besides her parents, she trusted him most of all. She trusted that he would take care of her even though she was nervous and excited about being alone with him on this adventure.

"I know Mother was hoping that I would be able to take the state certification test and then go on to college. I've done well in Miss Opal's science and math lessons. I'm the best out of those other girls."

"You may have to go on and take that test to satisfy your mama. But what's it going to be? College or singing for your supper? You choose. I know what I'd do."

Lucille jumped to answer, but her father interrupted faster. "Wait, first open that pouch I gave you."

Lucille tugged at the leather strings and poured out its contents into her palm. Fifteen gold coins fell into her hand and rolled to the ground at the base of the tree.

"Them coins are real gold. Hold on to them tight no matter where you go. They're worth something. Keep them close and don't use them unless you absolutely have to."

"They're pretty."

"They're more than pretty. They're worth a lot more than they look, but not much. I want you to have them. They'll give you something to fall back on when you need it. Even though it doesn't look like we have much, these coins brought us through some things. They're the reason we are right here on this spot with you singing like you do. I do believe if it wasn't for these little things in the palm of your hand we'd just be scraping up at your granddaddy's little church farm till the day we died. But you've got a chance to be somebody. Them coins came through blood and fire to give you a life."

"You giving them all to me? What about you and Mother? Won't you need something when I leave?"

"Girl, don't worry about your old pappy and your mama. You know I'll make sure we are settled in right nice and all. The Traveling Loves ain't traveling no more, except for you. Besides, these coins grow. This money right here will grow into big dreams. I knew that when I first laid eyes on them. Now, I've got my eye on a piece of land in Oklahoma. Your aunt Sybil, who you never met, lost her husband, brother and son. They were lynched." He paused, gnawing on a stick before spitting on the ground. "She's all right in the body, but in the head... She wrote to your granddaddy for help and through the grapevine I got the news and sent back word that me and your mama would do just that.

"She lives in a town called Greenwood. It's a place where it's just us doing things we could never imagine doing back in Evansville. A whole town full of Negro professionals—teachers, business leaders, doctors and surgeons running things. There are banks, schools, a library, hotels and hospitals that caters to the Negro. It's a shining example of folks coming up from slave times and honoring the broken bones and stolen breath to be the best."

It sounded like a nice place to Lucille. She didn't remember too much about Evansville, but Greenwood seemed like a good town for her parents to finally put down roots.

Her father continued, "We have to go and help your aunt Sybil. They can't win. We can't let evil have the final word. We gonna go help your aunt turn things around to let them know that one thing we do, since the first Africans arrived on these shores, is we keep going. Before and after the freedom proclamation, that's what we do. Just like every season returns."

"I don't know, Daddy. You'll be so far away and I still think Mother might not agree with this."

"I'll tell her you're ready. You're grown and stubborn. I see you've got that spark in your eyes. You're ready to strike out on your own. I really don't want you to stay in one place too long. It seems like bad things tend to happen when we stay in one place. Black folks become a target. Your safety, believe it or not, is that you are going to be a moving target for them evil ofays. You'll always know where to find us and Marcus will make sure we can always find you." Hank reached into the pocket of his overalls and pulled out two more coins. "That's a promise. In fact, gimme a few of them coins."

Lucille complied. Hank started with one finger and progressed to using both hands to claw a hole at the base of the tree. In the well of dirt, he plopped the coins down and covered them.

"Daddy, what are you doing? Now you know Mother will come out screaming like a banshee if she sees you playing around with money like that." Lucille dug her fingers into the rich earth to retrieve the coins. "You'll be wishing and hoping until Judgment Day if you think something gonna spring from that. I'm not a baby anymore. I know you always tell me that money don't grow on trees. Are you trying to tell me that these are some magic beans like they say in the fairy books?"

"Naw, girl. This here is real science. I recognize you've grown into a very talented young lady. You got your mother's good looks and your daddy's smarts. You got all the makings to go far, Lucille Love."

"You and Mother need all the money you can get. Don't you want to buy your wife a house, after she's stuck with you through thick and thin? Take this money and go do that. I'm going to go on to college and become a teacher like Mother wants. Miss Opal says I can be a good teacher."

"Only if you want to, baby. I think you're destined for more." Hank pressed a finger to his cheek and pointed to his eye. "Ya see, God left me with this one eye for a reason. I didn't know it at the time, but He gave me a power. It sharpened all my senses, you see. And I came to recognize that I can see things others can't with just this one eye. And I see you doing something big."

He patted her hand and then tucked the coins back into the ground. "This here marks a promise that these coins will grow alongside this here tree. You watch. The next time you come through here your life will have changed." Hank chuckled. "These coins will shuck off their hard shell, blossom and bear fruit just like everything around here."

10

Lucille had only been on a train once, and she was so young at the time that she could barely remember the details of the trip. Her only memories were of strong, acrid bolts of black smoke filling up the train car that was packed to the gills with black people. She remembered waiting and waiting on the platform and Mother telling her that they couldn't board the train until all the white passengers boarded first. She remembered being herded like cattle onto the only car designated for black travelers, the rustling sound of skirts and petticoats and her face and arms brushing against the rough fabric of strangers' clothing. Woven baskets and carpet bags banged against her head and sharp smells wafted from sacks filled with greasy delights from someone's mama's or granny's kitchen. Lucille's mother had carried a parasol, worn gloves and a hat that she pulled close, pressing her hair to her ears and nape of her neck.

This time, while waiting for the train, Evelyn motioned for Lucille to sit close to her. "Lucille, sit with me a moment while your father checks the train schedule." She took a deep breath as Lucille scooted over. "I know you think I'm hard on you. I am. But I love you and like any mother want the best for you. I've never spoken about my upbringing. You probably think I just sprouted up from a church pew, went to school and did whatever my parents told me, and now I do whatever your daddy tells me to do."

It was true. It was no secret that Lucille favored her father. It wasn't that she loved her father more, just that Lucille found comfort in the warmth of her father's hugs and the softness of his face when he looked upon her. Even in his stern moments, Lucille knew her father would quickly brighten and give her a song, a humorous story and a peck on the cheek. On the other hand, her mother was the one who she'd never challenged—there was always an "or else" that loomed in the air. Evelyn had always been the hard to Hank's soft. On those occasions when her mother did seem to soften a little, it was only because Lucille had done everything her mother asked of her—sang without missing a note, dressed like she was a small child and stayed silent. But despite their differences, Lucille came to re-alize her mother was the one whom she depended on the most.

Evelyn turned to look at Lucille. She took a deep breath before continuing. "You see, I was just a little older than you when I ran away. I ran away from the school that hardworking church folks—in fact the whole town—had paid good money to see me go off to, with the right clothes to represent our en-tire community and to do good. And that was my plan, too—at least it was for a while. It wasn't long before I felt stifled. I was there to uplift the race. And I kept thinking…the entire race? That was way too much for me. But I couldn't say anything to anyone about that. Here I was, the prim and proper minister's daughter. The seed of a man who had taken so many to the water, led them through trials and tribulations from birth to death. And here I am complaining about the pain of carrying some folks from my hometown on my shoulders. I felt guilty because all I wanted to do was sing.

"That very first moment heard Elizabeth Taylor Greenfield, a black woman, sing arias was what did it. I had to sneak in because Negroes weren't allowed to attend her performance. No one said anything to me, I was so young at the time. I couldn't even breathe throughout the entire production. Elizabeth Taylor Greenfield sung so well them white folks were just enamored with her. She went on to sing for Queen Victoria. My Lord, I left that performance with my head high in the clouds! After that, one thing I knew for sure was that I wanted to be on that stage. But for me, I guess it wasn't meant to be."

"Mama, you told me that you sang in church because that was what God called you to do. You weren't happy with that?"

Not done with her tale, Evelyn gripped her daughter's shoulder. "One day, I heard about Sissieretta Jones. They called her Black Patti. Yes, she was one of us and she broke through, not as an oddity but as a star, a real talent. When I heard that she sang as a headliner at Carnegie Hall and at a place called Steinway Hall, I ran. I ran all the way to New York without a plan or anything. I had some money saved. I didn't tell anyone but my mama. She understood, and even gave me a little extra pocket money. But Papa did find out. There were no secrets in our house. He told me not to go. He had said many times that bad things happen to colored girls traveling alone. But your grandmother told me that a woman has to make her own way and she had faith her daughter would do great things with her talents. For the first time ever, I defied my father and chose to heed my mother's advice."

Lucille started to understand. It wasn't unlike the journey she was about to take. She nodded and Evelyn continued.

"When I stepped on that train in Indiana and landed in Manhattan, I had never seen such a big city and such busyness. The sights and sounds—it was all so much, but it excited me.

I wasn't afraid of being lost among the crowd. I found myself staring up at this big monolith of a building that was Carnegie Hall. I didn't have an appointment with anyone. I hadn't even tried to make one."

Her mother chuckled to herself. "I don't know what I was thinking. I was so naive, I really thought that I could just walk in there and convince them to give me an audition. I was *that* sure, *that* confident in my abilities. You see, Sissieretta made the world know that women of our color belonged in the operatic world. That our songs and our voices were the songs and voices suitable to sing even their classics. Our voices carried the same hopes, sorrows, longing and loves. But standing in front of that building that had so many doors lined up, I was suddenly afraid to enter. And that fear had me thinking that I was a foolish girl who came all this way for nothing."

"But you wanted it so badly. You were brave and daring and miles away from home, in a big city on your own." Lucille was so proud of her mother at that moment.

"I never got a chance to go in. My purse was stolen. Snatched right out of my hand. It contained all the money I had. I couldn't go home empty-handed—my pride wouldn't allow it. Luckily, my room was paid for through the week. But how would I eat? I immediately got a job doing laundry at a hotel. This was a dark time for me. When I earned enough money for a train ticket, I took the first one back home. When I showed back up on my daddy's doorstep, he knew I had experienced some deep disappointment and didn't question me about what happened."

"Mother, I understand why you're telling me this… I don't know that things will go my way just because Marcus says they will."

Evelyn shook her head. "Lucille, I'm telling you my story because you are stronger than me. You are the daughter of two people who believe we are all meant to do the work of God. Like my mama told me, a woman must go out and make her own way. So, you go out and do us proud, young lady. All I ask is you stay the course. No drinking, cussing and carousing. Stay close to Marcus. I trust him. Do us proud, my baby."

"I will, Mother. I promise," Lucille said wiping away her tears.

Her belly was filled with so many bubbling sensations, Lucille stood on the platform clutching her stomach to make sure her breakfast and everything else stayed down. When Marcus returned with the tickets, she exploded into hot tears that ran freely down her face. She waved to her parents from the steps of the train platform.

Hank and Evelyn Love, the parents who had never been farther than an arm's length away every minute of her life, looked so small. Both of her parents were always bigger than the life that had surrounded them for the last ten years. In Lucille's mind they stood far above her—no matter how tall she grew—always looking over her. Hank and Evelyn Love stood close together, shoulder to shoulder without an inch of light between them. Maybe it was the first time she'd seen their hair streaked with silver threads and their clothing draped loosely over thin frames. Their wide smiles appeared jubilant but the lines in their faces gave way to a remote sense of sadness. The Loves were separating for the very first time.

11

Cincinnati, Ohio
1917

Church ministers, first ladies, deacons, choir and usher board members and a few ladies' auxiliary club leaders were designated as chaperones to protect Lucille along the way. With a sturdy list comprised of extended family, Lucille felt it was a fresh new first and a fresh new start of her solo career. She still appeared at church functions as she had with the Traveling Loves. She was repeatedly invited to join choirs, quartets and even comedic groups who wanted a big vocalist in their revues. Marcus turned them all down, stating, "We should keep our eyes on the star shining brightly over the horizon." He'd say if she were to join an ensemble troupe now, she would never achieve her destined fame. Lucille trusted his advice. Since leaving her parents, she had come to depend on Marcus for just about everything.

She sang the usual spirituals which brought in the customary honorariums and collections. In most cases, pay was minimal. After paying for travel, lodging and laundry, there was really nothing left for her or to send back to her parents. After each performance where she was lauded with praise, she was surer than ever that she was on her way to the next phase in her singing career—and closer to realizing her dreams of glittery revues, trips across the sea to foreign ports giving sensational performances that those who traveled from one city to the next would talk about for months. So despite the lack of money, Lucille felt a sense of lightness and freedom being on her own and being with Marcus.

She found comfort in the full church dinners from grateful patrons or the hospitality of the boardinghouse owners. Meatless Mondays or Wheatless Wednesdays that everyone observed for the sake of the Great War that was ravaging Europe didn't deter her patrons. Hosts who had gotten a whiff of her growing professional reputation were anxious to impress the Little Girl with the Big Voice who sang the old songs with such relish they felt an energizing spirit sweep across the room. They held nothing back in the way of provisions and stressed dinner tables with ample spreads. Many dishes were gathered from neighbors who wanted to see the local star up close and add a bit of gossip to conversations with envious neighbors. Deep-fried pork chops, baked ham, collards with ham hocks, fresh juicy tomatoes, pinto beans, yams and fluffy biscuits and hotcakes dripping with butter—Lucille never went hungry. There was always an assortment of fruit pies and buttery pound cakes, and sometimes freshly churned vanilla ice cream for desserts. She overheard one of the deacons whisper to another that they liked a girl with meat on their bones, so Lucille continued to satisfy her desire for a plentiful plate. It was a miracle she was able to fit in any of the new dresses her mother had made for her.

Along with her emerging curves came another metamorphosis. It budded and came into full blossom in Cincinnati. It wasn't just a change in her singing, vocal arrangements or in the growing number of venues from churches and church functions to gold-gilded theaters with raised stages and orchestra pits. It wasn't being onstage where there were lights at her feet as well as lights that rained down from the balcony aimed directly at her. It wasn't even following amazing orators, or jaw-dropping acts of eclectic talents, or fanciful jubilee costumed cakewalks that left her amazed.

It was a change in how she began to feel about Marcus, who was leading the charge for every step she took as they traveled toward a destination of fame and stardom.

She had never been shy around Marcus; outside of Miss Opal, he had become one of her most trusted confidants. As he did when he first introduced himself, he asked her what she wanted and why. Even though there were close to ten years between them, she felt she could speak to him about whatever was really going on in her head without judgment, discernment or correction, or worse, being treated like a little girl—the Little Girl with the Big Voice. Warm comfort of nostalgia accompanied her smile and his laughter when they would sit together between performances, talking for hours about their dreams and hopes for the future.

Marcus seemed to be as comfortable with her as she was with him. He spoke freely about the future. He told her what it would look like—what he'd like to have, do or be in the years ahead. He wasn't as animated or amusing as Buster, the world-wandering storyteller at Miss Opal's, but he was just as fascinating.

Lucille and Marcus spent many evenings talking about musicians, dancers and comedians who had been a rousing success and those who received a face full of tomatoes. Show news traveled fast from New York to Chicago and to the larger cities in the South. Marcus told Lucille stories of shady characters who posed as agents to lure acts overseas only to leave them stranded without a ticket to get home. He spoke about ironclad contracts that were actually written in dust and never honored due to some buried loophole written in underhanded ink. He told her he wouldn't hesitate to challenge unscrupulous theater owners in court—in fact, he looked forward to it. Lucille hung on to Marcus's every word, feeling lucky she had been discovered by an honest man, a real agent with an eye for talent and a respect for her craft.

They teased each other like brothers and sisters, giggling at silliness. Then there were times, while sitting on the front porch of a rooming house in Cincinnati while a bright white moonlight settled across fields and rooftops, Lucille fell deeply in love, not only with every word Marcus spoke, but also with his determination. She recognized and admired his commitment to build something from the ground up. In many ways he was so much like her farmer father.

Lucille forgot his age and forgot that he was married. He rarely spoke of his wife, Rose, so it was easy to misplace the fact that he had a wife.

Each note she sang, she began to sing for him. She wanted him to be pleased with every aspect of her performance. Every song that alluded to love, unrequited or not, her heart would swell in her chest, skipping beats uncontrollably. She kept her eyes on him, and imagined him sitting in the audience, longing for her as much as she longed for him. When he hugged her in the excitement of applause at the end of a performance, a favorable review, or a string of bookings, she felt the heat of his breath and the closeness of his heart to hers. She'd hold on to her desire as he slowly released her from his hugs and changed the direction of their conversation. He'd talk about the next show date, the expense of traveling by train, taxi or even by mule-drawn wagon.

When they were alone together, excitement bounced around her chest and ran down her arm, causing the hair on the back of her neck to stand on end. She'd pressed her palms together but the friction of rubbing her fingertips together only resulted in thoughts of Marcus. She noticed his features, the arch of his brow, the curl of hairs of his sideburns, the rough spiky skin around his neck—all minute details that had escaped her over a year ago.

They were staying a few days at an old house in a little village, two inches from the Hamilton County line in Ohio. It was a one-mile-square area the county simply ignored because it was made up of a collection of black homeowners who worked at nearby manufacturing plants. There were no paved roads, no police or fire department; only low wooden houses built to the owner's liking that didn't even have electricity. The small circle of homeowners created a community solely dependent on each other, supporting their dreams of owning their homes since migrating from the South. When a fire or any other disaster struck, they all had a hand in building and rebuilding their homes, as well as their neighbors'. It reminded Lucille of Miss Opal's.

The house was owned by a man they called Old Mister. Marcus said his parents knew Old Mister from the old days when you had to run through bramble thickets for safety. Scars ran from his head to the tips of his fingers and were intertwined with wrinkled skin that made it hard to determine his age.

Marcus asked Lucille to join him to rehearse in a barn behind Old Mister's house, which was a structure of questionable sturdiness held together by slats of wood that appeared as old as its owner. She had been invited as a featured singer for a program at Wilberforce University honoring Bishop Daniel Alexander Payne. He had rallied the African Methodist Episcopal Church as well as white clergy and politicians to reopen the school and bring it to solvency after white Southerners pulled their mixed-race children from the school in support of the war.

Lucille felt they had been doing the same program for what seemed like years; she knew everything from memory and there was no reason to rehearse.

Once inside the barn, Marcus held out his hand and looked Lucille squarely in the eye. "Take my hand."

Without question or hesitation, she clasped her hand around his.

"Now, jump," he commanded.

Without question, Lucille immediately hopped up, while Marcus jumped back. They wobbled and tumbled into each other while still holding hands until Marcus grabbed her shoulders to keep them both from falling.

Laughingly, she shouted, "Hey! You said jump."

"But I didn't say in what direction, did I? You see, my dear Lucille, I've got a plan. If you are going to be the main entertainer, you've got to hold that audience by the hand and lead them in the direction you want. You've got all the right equipment to do that."

"Well, aren't I already the main entertainer?"

"Yes, you are, but the point I'm trying to make is that audiences don't like to be confused. If you're standing in front of them, a beautiful young woman on stage, all by herself, they want to see something so extraordinary, so unexpected that they're so satisfied they followed you down an unfamiliar path and will be happy to do so again."

"What's that got to do with jumping?"

"Well, you got to take the lead. You've got to be in command. Right now, we're working with song after song that has been written and tested time after time. You're walking sheet music. It's nice music, even great music that showcases your ability."

"Marcus, please speak plain English and just spit out what you're trying to say."

Marcus leaned in close. "You've got to titillate me into following you."

Lucille blushed as a chill rose from the base of her spine. "You need me to titillate you?"

"You like that word? Say it again, slowly."

"Stop, Marcus, I will not."

"No, no, no…look me straight in the eyes and say the word slowly."

It was a dare, and she couldn't let him win. This time, she turned to face him, leaned in a few inches from his face. She smiled slyly and repeated the word, letting the tip of her tongue tap out every *t*.

This time he was the one who blushed. "Okay. Ya see, ain't nothing wrong with that word. Nothing at all." He turned away before repeating, "You see, nothing happened when you said it. Did it?"

Lucille recognized she had the upper hand. With a mischievous glance, she responded, "Well, I don't know, Marcus. Did it?"

"Okay, missy, I did that because I want to try something. You've got a big voice. They're already expecting that. The surprise was that you were the Little Girl with the Big Voice. You ain't a little girl no more. So now what? To keep them coming back and build on your skills we got to give them something else. Give them something unexpected. I'm going to make sure we give them folks in the seats something titillating that's what's going to make you a star. You can do it."

Lucille tapped a finger on her cheek. "You know what, Marcus? You're right. I've been singing at these college shows, and I know there's so much more we could be doing. Something a little more fun." Emboldened with a new idea, Lucille gave Marcus a wink. "Or titillating, as you say."

Lucille started pacing. "I've read reviews of other shows and acts out there. Mr. Sherman Dudley's company, the Smart Set, is still performing in theaters along his entertainment circuit all around the South. There are plenty of young pretty girls singing in the Colored Actors Union that are dancing in the Colored Beauty Chorus. And I need to do something else. I'm not talking about revising the Salome 'Dance of the Seven Veils,' like Aida, Queen of the Cakewalk. I think when I'm up on stage, I can talk to the audience more. Lead them with a simple trail of notes, a wink or even a pause. My daddy would understand

doing just a little flirting, but Mother is not going to like anything other than church or classical."

A big, barrel-chested man who looked strong enough to
pull a wagon filled with logs and anvils by his teeth came into
the barn.

Marcus waved a hand in the big man's direction. "Right on
time! Big Bobby, help me out here. Lucille, meet Robert 'Big
Bobby' Wiley."

"You can just call me Big Bobby...everybody does." The
hulking mountain of a man waved a beefy hand and plopped
down on a bale of hay, pulling out a shiny trombone from its
case. The instrument appeared dwarfed as he quickly assembled
his horn. He licked his lips before pressing them to the mouth-
piece to let out a *bap*, then *bop*, then an upward scale.

He stopped, then sang out, "Hey, hey, maestro. Howdy,
ma'am. This the little lady you've been telling me about? I hope
this barn is no indication of where we gonna be playing. That
horse over there don't look like he got the deep pockets I need."

Lucille let out a big hoot. She had never sung with a brass accompaniment. The bold sound of the trombone and Big Bobby
warming up with scales reverberated off the barn's rafters and
filled Lucille with excitement. Even though she wasn't sure
what Marcus had in mind for her new "act" the fine hairs on
her neck prickled with anticipation and she was ready to meet
the new challenge. Lucille was itching to try something new.

"Okay, Marcus. Okay, Mr. Bobby, let's go!"

12

Lucille held her breath. Adding the brash sound of a trombone to a few songs in her repertoire made her feel brave. The call-and-response repartee she developed with Big Bobby was an exercise that left her feeling stronger about her stage presence. But now, here she was with butterflies flittering around her stomach as she stood center stage in an empty, dark theater. Mr. Charles Kenyon Smith—a strange little man who Marcus said made the final decision on which new colored acts made it on the Theater Owners Booking Association circuit—leaned against an old stride piano. The piano player was a man who looked like he would rather be anywhere else. Marcus knew and admired Mr. Charles Kenyon because of his station in the entertainment business.

In silence, the little man—who demanded immediately that they call him Mr. C.K.—wobbled around Lucille as if one leg was shorter than the other. He finally spoke after he swung from one side to the other, circling her about five times. "The church choir hair and that dress—lose it!"

Lucille shifted her eyes to Marcus. She stood frozen to her spot, too frightened to move a muscle.

"Let's try something else," Mr. C.K. said, looking at Marcus. "I got a feeling this little gal can do it. He waved a hand at the piano player. "Sam, play 'Regretful Blues.' Now you." He leaned in even closer to Lucille and shoved the sheet music in her hand. "Follow them notes. This is just the basics. Let's see what you can do with it."

Sam rolled down the keys of his piano with a flourish and begun a bouncy high-stepping tune. Lucille's arms stayed glued to her sides and her hands trembled as she read from the sheet music.

Sam grew frustrated as Lucille misread a few notes. "We can't spoon feed this baby. I'll give it one more shot!"

Mr. C.K. shook his head, then instructed Lucille to repeat after him as he sang the lyrics line by line. She thought she must've sounded like a child parroting the adults to form her first words. Mr. C.K. instructed Sam to start all over again. Lucille took a deep breath and sang from deep in her chest, pushing out the newly learned lyrics so they could travel along with Sam. She held on to the last note until Mr. C.K. held up a hand signaling Sam and Lucille to stop.

He stood, chewing on his cigar. "Whew, saving grace… I see now there ain't nothing little about Little Miss Lucille, except for her demeanor. There's lots of pretty brown gals out there, but I gotta say, not one of them that I know of can hold a candle to a sound like that. Gaaal, you sound like you calling everyone home to a nice big meal and you—" he smacked his lips "—are the dessert."

Mr. C.K. turned his head to spit on the floor. "C'mon, girl… Don't just stand there. You go to toss 'em something they can pick up! That big voice can't do all the work on its own."

Sam kept playing and Lucille kept singing as she took a few

small steps to the left, then a couple of timid steps back to where she started.

Marcus paced over to stand in the wings. He posed with his hands on his knees hoping Lucille would take the hint for her next move. Lucille awkwardly mimicked his movements, adding a little shimmy.

"Girl, what the hell was that? You got to do a whole lot better if you want to get billed anywhere." He turned to Marcus, knowing he was still hidden in the wings. "Marcus, I don't know why you don't just book her into one of the revues that are out there. S. H. Dudley's got about twenty-eight or so theaters in our neighborhood. They're segregated houses but they're itching for a good act."

Lucille shouted back, "I ain't no dancer, Mr. C.K.! Please just let me sing, okay?"

Mr. C.K. shot a squinty-eyed look at Marcus, who finally stepped out of the wings. "Listen, sister, no matter how good you can sing, a mediocre act—and 'specially girls without a pretty enough or light enough face—get corked up to play pickaninny stories. You want that? I know you don't. That ain't you. Don't look so surprised, I'm speaking the truth. But those white theater managers just love a little coon story. We need them to see gold star talent which means money to them. When those white folk see you have the chops to give them something they ain't seen before, if we're lucky, we can shoot up to the top."

Marcus chimed in, "We don't need luck."

"No need for luck? Then you, Little Miss Lucille, better get that body moving like a grown-up gal!"

"Hold on, C.K., don't speak to her like that. Miss Lucille is a young lady. Have some respect!"

"Do you want to make some money? Do you want to see that gal headline? 'Cause from what I heard just now, I see dollars piling up. You just got to loosen up. This is vaudeville.

This is the big show! And I know what it takes to make it in this business right now!" Mr. C.K. looked directly at Lucille. Leaning from one side to the other and pointing at her with the nub of his cigar, he spit out, "Do you want it?" He thrust a pointed finger so that it was inches from her face and shouted again. "Do you?"

Lucille stared right back at him and shouted back, "Yes, sir—I don't mind being the dessert. Desserts are the best part of a meal. I don't mind at all."

"Well then," Mr. C.K. chuckled. "We got some work to do. You go think about what you just said. We can meet back here tomorrow. You gonna be around, Sam? Okay then, be back here tomorrow and bring all that you got."

Marcus and Lucille left the theater in silence, each in their own thoughts about Mr. C.K.'s advisement.

"You know, we don't have to go this route, Lucille."

"The ladies' boardinghouse is only two blocks down and one over."

"No, we don't have to get on the circuit this way. C.K. is a coarse lowbrow. And there's a lot of those types of men all along the way. One thing though, despite his crassness, he does speak the truth. But if you really don't want to..." His voice trailed off. Marcus was unusually solemn. It was rare that he displayed a lack of confidence in his plans.

"Didn't you hear what I said to Mr. C.K.? I told him exactly how I felt. Marcus, I don't want to stop now. I'm not interested in going backward, traveling around from steeple to pulpit. No, that's not for me. And as for Mr. C.K., well, I'm not that naive about show business. I know what it can be for some women—little costumes all sparkling glass beads and feathers here and there." She recalled the burlesque house she peeked into when she was eight years old, the beautiful woman commanding the audience's attention. All flesh, and not an ounce of shame—so raw, so human…yet nothing a respectable young lady was meant to see. "I've seen shows you'd call crass, but if it captures the audience's attention…that's what I want—the audience in the palm of my hand. I know what show business can be—or won't be—for me…unless I go for it."

"So you *do* want it? I need to be perfectly clear with you before we go any further."

"Marcus, I'm not a little girl and don't want to go live with my parents in Oklahoma. I know what I want. Weren't you listening when I said it the first time? I want to be the best part of the meal, the dessert."

Marcus stopped in his tracks. He placed a hand on her shoulder and stared at her as if searching for a stronger conviction. "Really? Is that how you really feel, Lucille? I've sat up at night trying to figure out how I can move you forward and I've avoided this kind of solution on purpose. But your act ain't doing what it needs to be doing. We've got to make some adjustments."

"Marcus, when the Traveling Loves were out on the road, I heard my daddy say a million times that we just gotta push through. Push through to get to the other side. There was always a promise at the end of that. Every time he said it, I knew we were headed somewhere better, brighter…somewhere we could just be the Loves. So, we did what we did because it was what we had to do to reach that better place. Right now, I don't care how I get to the next level. I just want to be there right now."

"Lucille, I made a promise to your daddy. A new direction is good. Are you ready for it?"

"Yes, I am. Ever since I sat at my mother's side at the piano in that boardinghouse in Tennessee, I was singing my way to the other side. Singing and being up there on stage will take me beyond all the bumpy roads, the click of wobbly wheels and the begging for scraps. Yes, begging! That's how I came to see it. I love my parents, but before you came along I was beginning to feel like they were using me, my voice, to beg for food. When I first saw you…when you walked up to me and asked me what I wanted, I knew. For once, I knew there was a way out. And now I've tasted it. I'm not going back. It's glitter and lights from here on in. I'm aiming for the two-thousand-seat houses in front of me and lights so bright that I can bathe in them." Lucille straightened up, determined to show Marcus she meant every word. She was capable and ready, and most of all, she wasn't little anymore, just like Mr. C.K. had said.

Marcus nodded. "Lucille, you have my word. You've had it since I first met you. I'm going to do everything in my power to get you there. I promise."

"And phonograph records!" Lucille continued, her eyes wide with excitement. "I'm going to make a record like they did at the Victor Talking Machine Company. Everyone is going to buy it and dance a shimmy and shake." She tapped her toes to the ground and swung around. "Yeah, even those tightly wound revivalists will be shaking out of their britches."

"Okay, Lucille. Yes, we're going to do it all!" Marcus chuckled. "I know one thing: you got to know the folks who know the somebodies that have the deep pockets. White, black—it don't make no difference. C.K. knows everybody. He's the ticket. You know something else? You're pretty smart. You sure *you* don't want to be a talent manager?"

"I'm not smart, it's just that my daddy taught me. He had to learn to live with one eye. He looks at the world with a wider sense of vision, and that's what I try to do."

The sound of a trumpet wafted through the air. At the corner was a street musician blowing out jazzy refrains for whatever passersby deemed fit to throw into the rumpled hat in front of him. The young, skinny man, firmly planted on bowed legs, his feet pointing east and west, lifted up his trumpet and hit an impressive high note before drifting down into a happy-go-lucky melody.

"Well, Miss Lucille, I've got to say that when I first met you, I wasn't sure you'd come out from underneath your mama's skirt. You were so young. I knew you wanted to sing, but I wasn't sure *how much* you wanted to sing. I guess your passion intensified. You've grown up right before my very eyes."

Lucille felt a warm glow in the pit of her stomach and stepped away from him. Shaken by the sudden rush of emotion and anxious to change the subject, she blurted out, "Now that young man with the trumpet. I'd pay good money to hear him hit that high note again. Wouldn't you?"

13

Lucille pranced back and forth, stopping a few times to give a deep shimmy of her hips. She loved the feel of the smooth fabric underlay and the ripple of threads against her body. The dress was sheer perfection—white silk, drop waist with a gold-beaded overlay. Beads hung down in strands, dripping from the hemline and sweeping against her bare leg.

"This definitely ain't no dress for hymn singing."

"You're right about that, Lucille. We need to build a bigger audience and *this*—" Marcus gestured at Lucille "—is exactly what we agreed on."

"It's been two whole weeks since we heard from Mr. C.K. though. Should I be nervous?"

Marcus lifted his palms to the ceiling. "I'm hoping for good news. If it doesn't come soon, we're back on the road with nothing ahead of us but church benefits that only pay with a basket of pound cakes. I'll have to let Big Bobby go about the business of finding some real payin' work."

Lucille, distracted again by her new dress, disregarded Marcus's gloomy outlook and gave a few twirls. "So, you want to take the lady out of the music I've been singing. This dress is saying there's ain't no lady around."

She swished her hips from side to side. "I think I'll marcel my hair and get it bobbed. Or maybe I'll use all the pomade I can find to wear an Eaton crop with tight, tight curls right in the middle of my forehead. I think that would look quite Parisian, don't you think? With this dress and a new hairstyle, I'll use a bit of eye shadow and darken my eyelashes too. Mother would never, ever let me do anything like that. She'd think it was way too modern…too suggestive. You know, too loose. But it's the modern times, right? And I've got to fit in. I see all those glamour girls shortening hems and dresses hugging everything they were born with. Ooo, with a few finger waves and this dress…" Lucille stopped, placed her hands on her hips and turned slowly around to face Marcus. Delighted she captured his attention, she asked slyly, "You like?"

Marcus gazed at the curves of Lucille's body and her long shapely limbs. He sat wide-eyed as if searching for an answer and the words were slipping through his fingers. Turning a deep red, he slowly rubbed his chin and wiped his mouth. "Yes, I do," finally tumbled out from between his lips. He quickly added, "It's going to fit well with the new music I'm thinking about."

Since going out on the road with Marcus, Lucille had sung in three auditoriums, an outdoor spring festival, revivals—which paid nothing but a meal and an overnight stay at a congregant's home—a couple of college ceremonies and the opening and closing of a lecture series where intellectuals expounded on the plight of the race. Each one garnered thunderous applause for her performance, where she stood stoically alongside a piano dressed in dark colored gowns that used to be her mother's, cinched at the waist with a modest amount of lace around the neck and satin buttons adorning her wrists.

It was clear by the vibrant frock adorned with beads that caught every bit of light in the room that she was not going to sing in those places anymore. She could not be more excited.

"Where did you get this?" Lucille ran her hands lovingly down the dress, admiring the feel and pressing her fingers into the tiniest gold beads.

"I had it made just for you." Marcus paused, then continued, "By Rose. Rose made it. She said if you wear this, you'd be a big sensation and then I can come home to her."

Lucille's smile faded. Aside from the one time his wife came to see the Traveling Loves, Rose never joined in on their adventures. Lucille had fixed an image of Rose in her mind based on their only encounter and what little else she knew of her. Rose was stuffy and prim, not cut out for show business, but she did have a keen eye for flair. That was evident in the costume she tailored to Lucille. Lucille got the impression that Rose was only interested in being comfortably kept at home in Chicago and dealing with her husband from afar. Essentially, she was a mythical creature that lived in a faraway land.

Marcus rarely mentioned Rose, keeping his home life private and his work with Lucille professional. Marcus carried a photograph of her though. In the picture, they stood on the front steps of a house that appeared to have a trellis of flowers with huge blossoms reaching out to them from every step and railing. It was unlike so many other photographs she had seen of couples standing beside each other in an obligatory expressionless pose—Marcus and Rose were apparently enjoying a darling moment, smiling from ear to ear.

No matter how joyous they looked, Lucille chose to dismiss the thought of Marcus having a wife. In fact, the thought of Marcus kissing some other woman made her sick to her stomach.

Lucille collected herself and in a lackluster tone she added, "Well, it needs something else. A headdress maybe?"

Without seeming to notice Lucille's change of tone, Marcus smiled widely. "Yeah, that's it. A headdress with a white feather—that will do it. You'll need some jewelry too. Let me work on getting that."

Lucille sighed. "So where in the world am I gonna wear this?"

A week later, the answer came in the form of two crisp sheets of paper that sat face down on Mr. C.K.'s desk.

Lucille and Marcus sat in Mr. C.K.'s small, two-room office cluttered with stacks of papers, assorted ledger books and handbills piled high in every corner. A dusty upright piano was shoved against the wall. On top of the piano sat a large, garish paper mâché cow's head that had been sitting there long enough to collect a film of dust along its yellowed horns and pink snoot. Mr. C.K.'s desk was cleared of everything except the two sheets of paper. With a grunt and a chomp on the end of his cigar, he slid both in Lucille's direction.

Lucille looked at Marcus before snatching up the papers. Clutched tightly between both her hands, the bold red letterhead announced "Theater Owners Booking Association, the Chattanooga Office: 1212–1213 Volunteer Building" in print so bold it seemed to jump off the page.

Lucille read aloud, her voice threaded with excitement.

"'The Bijou Amusement Company. Operating the biggest and the best colored theaters in the South.' Is that who we're working for now? Listen to this, Marcus—there's the Bijou Theatre in Nashville, the Lenox Theatre in Augusta, and the Lincoln Theatres in South Carolina, Nashville and in North Carolina too."

Mr. C.K. leaned back in his chair looking squarely at Marcus. "Yeah, yeah, yeah, little missy. Mr. Starr runs the Bijou line and he's also president of TOBA. You're about to embark on a whole new journey. Is she ready, son?"

Marcus nodded while Lucille paced the floor continuing to read.

THEATRE OWNERS BOOKING ASSOCIATION
THE CHATTANOOGA OFFICE: 1212–1213 VOLUNTEER BUILDING

BIJOU THEATRE	LENOX THEATRE	LINCOLN THEATRE	ROYAL THEATRE	LINCOLN THEATRE	LINCOLN THEATRE
NASHVILLE, TN	AUGUSTA, GA	CHARLESTON, SC	COLUMBIA, SC	NASHVILLE, TN	NEW BERN, NC

THE BIJOU AMUSEMENT COMPANY
OPERATING THE BIGGEST AND THE BEST COLORED THEATRES IN THE SOUTH

CONTRACT OF AGREEMENT

This agreement made __10th__ day of __Sept. 1917__ between proprietor or manager of __Lenox__ Theatre, City of __Augusta, Georgia__, party of the first, and __Lucille Arnetta Love__ and __Marcus Williams__, parties of the second party. Witness that the party of the second part agrees to produce an act, such as __Vaudeville Musical__ known as __Miss Lucille's Black Troubadours (four people)__, play for __two (2) weeks__ commencing the __1st__ day of __October 1917__, and play a required number of shows each day. The party of the first part agrees to pay the party of the second part for such services rendered. __Seventy-five dollars ($75.00)__ each week.

Charles K. Smith

Party of the First	Party of the Second	Party of the Second

"Whoohoo! A whole seventy-five dollars a week! Marcus, we're rich!"

Mr. C.K. jumped in. "Hold on there, Miss Lucy, you need to understand where all that money—"

"What is this?" Lucille cut him off. "It says Miss Lucille's Black Troubadours? Who in the world came up with that?"

Marcus cleared his throat. "I did! Miss Lucille, doesn't it sound like a good time? I got the idea when we heard Lincoln blow his horn on the street corner. I figured we have Big Bobby backing you up, so I'd been working on adding other musicians—*your* troubadours. I didn't want to say nothing because I might jinx it."

"You hired that trumpet player that we only heard once on the street? What do you know about him? Can he play anything else but the blues for my big-time debut? And who is this fourth person mentioned in the contract?"

"Don't you worry about the fourth member—I've got someone in mind. I felt it in my bones that Lincoln was going to be a good time though. I thought, what better way to draw a crowd? You, Miss Lucille—the one and only, the young woman who can hit notes that can make a man cry—and this wild trumpeter who plays music that will make a man jump for joy. So I hired him."

"You hired him and didn't tell me?"

"It happened so fast, Lucy. I didn't get a chance," Marcus said quickly, avoiding Lucille's stare.

"It looks like you two might need to speak in private." Mr. C.K. pushed himself away from his desk. "Me? All I need is for you to sign on the dotted line of that paper you've got crushed in your hand and then get your black asses to work."

Lucille turned her attention back to the contract and began jumping up and down. The paper in her hand flapped in the air. "I've got to sign?" She flattened out the crinkled papers on the desk. "Don't go anywhere, Mr. C.K. I don't know about being in a band but if Marcus thinks it'll be a hit… Gimme something to write with. I'll sign whatever and wherever you want!"

Marcus pressed his hand over Lucille's. She glanced down at him in his seat. His jaw was fixed tight. She took it as a signal to apply restraint and sat back down. Her foot tapped the floor and her knee bounced impatiently as she tried to contain her excitement. She couldn't wait for the next move in her very first business transaction.

"This is a trial run, understand? You've gigs on the Bijou Amusement tour. They start right away. They won't all be first-rate, large houses, and there will be some small-time venues sprinkled in here and there, but they should be respectable enough. It's three performances a day in a whole string of theaters to play along with other acts. You're being billed as a tab show feature as the Biggest Voice in All the South. You'll have about thirty to forty-five minutes to belt it out."

"I can do that, Mr. C.K. I can belt it out all night long. I ain't never had any problems with my vocal cords. My mother taught me what teas to drink to keep them strong."

Mr. C.K. nodded. "You won't be doing the churches and Sunday school events anymore. No more searching for a clearing in the woods to sing at baptisms by the water. That is, unless you want to."

Mr. C.K. pulled out a fountain pen and held it up between Lucille and Marcus. "Sign and we—I mean, Miss Lucille and her Black Troubadours—are officially on the circuit!"

With a broad smile, Marcus nodded in Lucille's direction. Lucille took the pen and signed her full name on the contract before giving the pen to Marcus, who did the same.

Mr. C.K gnawed on the last bit of his cigar. "Now, don't disappoint me, you two. I'm the middle guy in this situation. Marcus, I'm depending on you. You'll be my eyes and ears, and for that you'll get three percent. Of course, I've got to have a taste for myself. The moment you and your troubadours arrive late, give a subpar performance or blue material where some mother's got to cover their child's ears—or, lord forbid, if you don't show up at all—them white boys of the Theater Association will cut you and me out like we didn't even exist. Do not miss a show, no matter what. Don't try to contact me if you run out of money, miss a train, nothing."

"No, sir, Mr. C.K., Miss Lucille's never missed a show once and she won't start making a habit of it now."

Mr. C.K. grunted in approval. "You better work with what you get. Have your wits about you. Don't put yourself in any unsavory situations. This is a tough, grimy business and you've got to be ready for anything."

"Yes, sir!" Lucille gave a salute. She looked at Marcus then Mr. C.K. "If that's it, we'll be on our way."

Once the door to Mr. C.K.'s office clicked shut behind them, Lucille, unable to contain herself any longer, hopped up and down, clapped her hands and let out a high-pitched squeal that reverberated through the hallways. "We made the circuit! I don't care what size houses we play. I made it to a real, live vaudeville theater circuit! And I'm ready! Been ready ever since I opened my mouth at Miss Opal's boardinghouse. I gotta send my daddy a telegram right away! Oh, how I wish I had some of my daddy's apple-berry wine! We need to celebrate."

Finally giving in to Lucille's enthusiasm, Marcus threw his arms around Lucille to give her a big hug. Laughing, they rocked and hopped together. Marcus whispered in her ear, "There will be plenty of time for that. Right now, we've got to put together a real show."

Lucille pulled away from Marcus, and giddy with excitement, added, "And by the way, the Biggest Voice in *just* the South? C'mon, they can do better than that. I'm the biggest voice, period. Now that I'm on the circuit, I'm going to need more than that one dress."

14

From Augusta, Georgia,
to Charleston, North Carolina
1918

The New Year unfolded with increasing worries and concerns, tears and prayers for those going off to fight the Great War. Still, the entertainment industry flourished with new acts, shows and innovative wonders of talent emerging from hole-in-the-wall towns. People clamored for amusements and distractions to forget about the growing atrocities overseas. Lucille began a tight schedule of dates and destinations, performing with her Black Troubadours three shows a night, three or four times a week. Some theaters were grandiose with plush seating in the orchestra, boxes and two balconies. Always a packed house, no one would guess conscription was snatching up men left and right for the gruesome chore of feeding the European warfront. The audience was a mix of those dressed to the nines or in the standard wools of middle-class workers spending a night on the town to replace sorrows with spirited forgetfulness. All barely sat in their seats. Loud, raucous patrons from the orchestra to the segregated balconies jumped up and down, shouting, dancing and throwing coins on the bare stage.

In every town, Lucille also got a chance to see other colored actors, dancers, troupes and musicians that were bringing in tons of box office money, though they couldn't enter through the front doors of theaters even when they were headliners. With exuberant personalities and all ranges of acts, the performers smiled onstage and laughed offstage while boisterously announcing they were next in line for big money and fame. They told tales of stomping across America trying to get to the next show, the next dinner theater, the next cabaret, the revue. The thought of being a member of this business and the magnificent cast of characters traveling along the entertainment circuit gave Lucille chills.

She wrote her parents, who had settled in Tulsa, Oklahoma, telling them about the well-known tab shows such as the Smart Set and the hilarious and foolishly dressed comedian Butterbeans, who performed with his elegant wife, Susie. There was a lot more Lucille wanted to tell her mother, but she knew she had to choose her words carefully when writing about risqué shows—even her own show.

When she sent a telegram informing them that she landed a spot on the circuit, what came back was a congratulatory response from her father and a lengthy letter from her mother warning her to keep her feet on the ground along with the hems of her dresses. Lucille didn't dare write about the new costumes for fear that her parents would tell her to immediately come home. Lucille tempered her correspondence with details about the nearby churches and who the pastors were, before describing the dazzling theaters, the energetic audiences and other talented acts, actors and musicians with whom she had shared the stage.

Lucille knew Marcus sent his own letters to Hank. Part of the agreement with her father was that he was to be kept apprised of all business arrangements pertaining to his daughter. Her father wanted to hear a detailed accounting of pay, ticket sales, travel, accommodations and even where the troupe was positioned on the playbills. Lucille wasn't sure of all the details Marcus provided but his letters included names of pastors and notable parishioners, and the city's reputable, upstanding citizens who attended performances to assure Hank and Evelyn that their daughter was safe and keeping good moral standards. Marcus and Lucille knew that, to avoid setting off alarms in the Love household, it was best not to mention changes in costumes, music that strayed far from the spiritual or classical path or new venues of questionable reputation that had been added to the roster.

Lucille's first views of the circuit were small dark joints where the crowds were giddy and carelessly downed drinks from shakers, flasks and unmarked bottles magically appeared from under a bar. She watched a panorama of sins play out before her; there seemed to be some degree of scandal being carried right under her satin buckle shoes. Men hustled the unsuspecting and women's arms stretched out from underneath furs. Legs were on display in shiny dresses that rose way above knees to reveal creamy thighs and garters as they flounced in the laps of red-faced men, rubbing a bit of flesh against a man to distract him.

Lucille watched in amusement as long as there was no danger of anyone getting physically hurt from such misbehaving. It was as if everyone was drinking in excess to consume all the alcohol they could before it was banned out of existence. America was about to go dry and her patrons were doing their best to enjoy it till the last drop spilled onto the streets and into the gutters. The government was signaling the public that it was strongly considering amendments to outlaw alcohol as a means to fix what the prohibitionists considered the destruction of America's moral fiber. Even in her young, sheltered life, Lucille was skeptical about that outcome. Having been at more church services along the evangelist trail than anyone could ever imagine, she had seen her fair share of human failures and frailties and there was no alcohol was involved. The decay of all mankind couldn't be attributed solely to the beverage that leads to one's downfall.

Some establishments were so wild that only a flutter of applause would come from those who could lift their heads off the table or the shoulder of a woman long enough to give a wave to Lucille, Big Bobby, and Lincoln, the bow-legged trumpet player. Marcus also found a piano player each night from the union or local church. The piano player was conveniently nicknamed Sam because he would be gone at the end of the show's run and replaced by another who also needed to earn some extra cash for the evening.

Lucille observed the audience from the comfort of center stage as if they were one of Miss Opal's science projects. She followed the call-and-response between the men and women in the audience. She watched their reactions when she led them into song after song that held stories filled with feelings of love and yearning. She sang with a conviction she didn't know intimately. She could only imagine the sensations she sung about, though they were beginning to occupy much of her time on- and offstage. She didn't know what it was, but she knew it more than the sensation of her silk dress as it clung to her thighs, wet from the heat of the footlights.

Every few weeks a new dress appeared, each one more elaborate than the last. She wore beaded turquoise with fringe in Georgia, bright yellow with flowers like fireworks that crossed the bodice to the hem in Charleston and an all-white number with chandelier beads that hung from her sleeves at a stint in Philadelphia. Off the beaten track, in Baltimore she wore gold with a tiered hem and a cape lined with black plumes. The topper was red from head to toe which she wore in Nashville, where she flashed and flickered a scarlet silk fan in front of her face before she sang. She found accessories, ear bobs, gloves and headpieces from various black milliners that made a living creating flamboyant hats and high crowns for deaconesses competing for the hat closest to God at church affairs.

Lucille stopped asking about Rose's handiwork; she didn't want to hear that Marcus's wife created the garments with the purpose of bringing her husband home. Lucille promised herself that to write to Rose thanking her for all her hard work would be the proper etiquette.

With new dresses and costumes and a few techniques she picked up from watching other acts, Lucille began to change her performance. Instead of standing in one spot, Lucille began to move in a catlike sway to match every slide of Big Bobby's trombone. Between each song, she'd talk with the audience while the piano, trumpet and trombone rolled along in the background. She started to tie each number together by improvising a story she made up on the spot. Sometimes they were just re-spun tales that her father had told her when they were traveling by wagon. Or she'd take a theme from some of Pauline Hopkins's serial stories that appeared in *The Colored American Magazine*. She modified the stories depending on her or the audience's mood. Most of her stories were of an innocent woman losing her way in the search for the right man or the trials and tribulations of finding or losing riches and being satisfied by love. She'd never finish telling the story but always ended the act with a song. Lucille left everyone sitting on the edge of their seats, hanging on and wanting more. The audience ate it up! And so did she. Lucille breathed in each ooh and aah of their approval as if it was necessary for her very existence.

White performers that crossed the Troubadours' path loved their sound and Lucille's act so much she'd see them adapt it, adding a bit of dark makeup to make it part of their own in a minstrel revue. With each stolen act, they'd step and shout and give themselves a crown, calling themselves the kings or queens of jazz, the minstrel shows or darkie revues. Lucille viewed the imitators as amusing, even flattering when she first read the reviews and peeked at a performance. It wasn't until she was dismissed as a secondary player by a few theater owners, shouting at her to leave the front of the house until showtime, that it stung. Lucille tamped down her hurt and swallowed the hard rock in her throat when she saw other performers get top billing and a fatter paycheck mimicking her own unique act, the musical selections along with their associated stories.

Lucille chalked it up to being part of the tough business that Mr. C.K. had described; it was just the way of life. She tried to pay those insulting frivolities no mind. She took to heart the advice her mother gave her from the beautiful cakewalk star, Aida Overton Walker: "The profession of performing arts does more toward the alleviation of color prejudice than any other profession among colored people."

The new act brought with it a dizzying wave of sudden attention from such a different crop of folks. No longer was it the genteel folk that gathered at the ceremonial events, but a loud, forward and fast-talking bunch that seemed to be devoid of manners. Lucille vigorously pumped hands of those who seemed over the moon to meet her. She allowed wide-grinning suited gentlemen who sauntered over after a performance to place a light kiss on her hand. She would even pause after such men would extend an invitation to dinner before politely declining.

Maybe it was the flurry of new performances, or the new up-tempo songs with suggestive lyrics that caused a sudden heat to rise from underneath her skin, but whatever it was, Lucille began to see things. As soon as the act before hers ended and a zing of electricity shot through her body as she walked out onstage, before she filled her lungs and fixed her mouth into the perfect shape to caress her first note, a light flickered before her. It started as a sliver of dancing light, like a match struck in the dark. It flitted out from the corner of her eye, then moved to the farthest dark corner in the rear of the house. The first time, she thought it was the illumination from a burning cigar. It wasn't until the spark grew larger and was followed by a woman's voice that she knew this was something more. The voice, a forceful whisper, counted time. *One, two...a one, two, three, four...*

Lucille's eyes widened. She was fully aware of her surroundings. To the audience, prolonged silence heralded a big flop and they'd be ready to pounce on a nervous performer with a flurry of rotten vegetables. She quickly blinked away the light and pushed her focus back to her opening number. It started off as ragtime and slid into a jazzy blues number just as they rehearsed. By the second verse, she forgot about the distraction.

Besides the strange light, something other than show business was taking up her attention. It was as if a match had been struck or a spigot suddenly sprung with cool water and wouldn't turn off; some*one* had grabbed ahold of her senses. Marcus suddenly had her legs quivering and her brain turning to mush. It wasn't like the early days, when she was briefly mesmerized by his every move. She knew back then it was a one-sided infatuation and she pushed those thoughts to the back of her mind. He was busy proving he could be her manager. He was new and different. He represented freedom and adventure.

Again, when they found quiet moments to talk about their dreams and hopes, Lucille digested every word as the nourishment that he only shared with her. Marcus said he was so sure of where he was destined to be that he had staked his life on the road they were traveling. Miss Lucille's Black Troubadours were bound to be a success onstage all across America, which would make Marcus a highly-sought-after agent and talent manager. He also admitted that he had a lot to learn; he was letting Mr. C.K. take the lead and three percent of their earnings after all.

Marcus wanted to be the next big producer like J. Leubrie Hill, Frank Montgomery, Homer Tutt and Salem Tutt Whitney. They were producing machines and making money at all the Negro theaters across the nation with revues and musicals that were generating the biggest stars. Known names were getting the lion's share of the better theaters like the Keith, Orpheum, Paramount, Palace and Hammerstein. Acts like Bert Williams and George Walker and Johnson and Coles opened the doors—albeit the back door—for more black entertainers to play those houses.

For Lucille, the excitement of experiencing life for the first time always came back to her feelings for the man who asked her so long ago, *What do you want?* Even the sensation of the satin and gemstones brushing the backs of her knees reminded her of Marcus. She dreamed about him, hearing him repeat her name in her dreams so much that she awoke bathed in sweat. She'd imagine him reaching for her and telling her he couldn't live without her. His hands would graze the nape of her neck and follow the curves of her back until he would be holding her in an embrace.

As he was telling her about the next appearance, the train schedule, the rehearsal schedule or a change in the music, Lucille would give into a haze of daydreams and imagine him saying to her, *You know* bijou *means* jewel *in French.*

She'd look up into his sable-brown eyes. *Really?*

He'd reply, *That's why he fixed it so we would meet here tonight, at the Bijou Theater. I've never seen anyone as pretty as you around here.*

"Lucille? Lucille! Are you listening to me? Did you hear what I said? You need to give a little speech before you sing. Are you okay with that?"

She looked around to gain her bearings. Startled out of her fantasy, Lucille realized that they were walking in a public park in the bare bright sunlight. She suddenly remembered they were on their way to the minister's parsonage to be introduced at an ice cream social. An event that was the buildup to tonight's formal presentation.

"Wha...? Oh, yeah, I heard you. A speech about the arts,

music and race." Lucille shook her head to dispel the image she had of Marcus holding her while speaking to her in French. "Yeah, yeah, I can do that. I'll just tie some quotes from Aida Overton Walker and Pauline Hopkins. Smart women of the theater, who Mother would also quote when talking about how the arts can help overcome the ill perceptions of the Negro race and show how we can excel beyond the lowly stations where most whites think we belong."

"Good. You looked like you were off in dreamland there for a minute."

Lucille tsk-tsked. "Me? Never. My feet are right here on the ground, next to yours."

On one of the hottest days that had turned into one of the hottest nights, Lucille bounced to Big Bobby's slide trombone slyly giving each musical note its own shine before she jumped in. The light appeared again, starting along the tasseled legs of the curtains. This time it grew into the full image of a smiling woman that Lucille recognized but didn't know. Lucille thought she heard the woman call her by name before instructing her to take a few steps closer to the edge of the stage to pause, smile or even tease. The words stretched out before her. Lucille heard her mother's voice. Not her coloratura soprano voice, but her no-nonsense I'm-about-to-get-a-switch voice pouring out of the woman in front of her dressed in splendor, complete with a choker of amethyst, sapphires and opals.

Listen, Lucille, sing out with grace. And if you can, swing those hips too!

Lucille felt a cool shiver ripple through her body which she shook off as Lincoln splat out a trill of notes, knocking her out of a stupor. Big Bobby joined in with a slide of his trombone. They both took turns in an impromptu chant to get Lucille to start singing and save the act from getting the hook. Even the resident piano player joined in:

"Hey, hey, hey, Miss Lucy!
Hey, hey, hey, Miss Lucille!
C'mon, jump in and join us!
Show the folks just how you feel!"

The chant grew stronger and the woman in the light disappeared in the cloud of frenetic calls as quickly as she appeared. But her words lingered.

Lucille raised her arms, her rhinestone bracelets catching the light. She turned her head to give her band a nod, signaling to them that she was ready to begin. She swung her hips from side to side and began to sing.

15

Baltimore, Maryland

Like clockwork, Marcus received booking notices from the TOBA office with the details of their next performance. Miss Lucille and her Black Troubadours had two-week-long stays at the Booker T. Washington Theatre in St. Louis, Lyceum Theater in Cincinnati, Douglass Theatre in Macon, Georgia, and the Liberty Theatre in Chattanooga, Tennessee. After Cincinnati, Baltimore was added as an impromptu stop as a favor to Mr. C.K. With the schedule neatly in place, Marcus, from time to time, would have to go ahead to not only make sure arrangements were in place, but also to prime the pump—passing out handbills to assure all seats were filled and the theaters would be at or beyond maximum capacity. In those times, Lucille was left alone in a strange town in the care of a pastor's wife, an aunt or a cousin. She was a sensation that easily attracted socialites who would graciously host her at their homes. There was always someone—usually a man—swarming around anxious to show her just the right place to eat or where to catch a good show. And, like men, there were plenty of shows and acts to see.

Young men—clean-shaven, bright and shiny—would smile, bow and give her compliments on her smooth brown skin, delicate hands and the curve of her cheeks. The bolder ones would even compliment the brightness in her eyes. Some in rough cloth suits with tough laborer's hands would invite her for walks around the park. Older men would take her hand and there were some that would sing her a song and request to accompany her onstage. One even gave her a pamphlet to read about God. It became a dance everywhere she went. Someone would be there to introduce her to their cousin or nephew or neighbor's son who was going off to college. Even without much experience with the opposite sex, Lucille easily detected that the whispered caution was probably from a girl who experienced that sway one time or another. But the warnings only intrigued her even more.

They had only planned to stay a few days in Baltimore before climbing onboard a train to Macon, Georgia—one day for the church performance and the other for well-deserved downtime.

The next day after a dinner engagement, Lucille met Wendell—a pastor's son that she had gone on one date with—in the sitting room of the hotel where she was staying. They sat across from one another chuckling at the funny moments from the act they saw together: Butler "String Beans" May, a six-foot-tall comedian who sang and played piano while telling jokes. Wendell even attempted to sing a few measures of String Beans's blues lyrics.

"So sorry to interrupt. Lucille, may I see you for a moment?" Marcus hovered above them as if he had fallen from the sky right in the middle of the room.

"Marcus, I'd like to introduce you to Wendell McLeod. He was gracious enough to keep me company yesterday and we saw the most wonderful entertainment. Wendell, this is my manager, Marcus Williams."

Wendell stood up and extended his hand as if meeting Lucille's father for the first time. Marcus placed his hand on Lucille's shoulder and responded with a curt "Mr. McLeod, please excuse us."

Marcus ushered Lucille out of the room and into a hallway out of Wendell's earshot. He grabbed her by the elbow and pulled her closer to him.

"You can't be showing up onstage with a baby in your belly!"

She peeled her arm away from him. Lucille had never seen Marcus angry. "What? How dare you! He wanted to take me out to dinner, and I enjoy his attention...so there! I don't need you suddenly acting like a jealous beau."

Marcus stopped short and looked at her quizzically. "A beau? Jealous? What are you saying, Lucille?"

They stood silently, at an impasse. Marcus raised his eyebrows, slowly recognizing what Lucille was hinting at. Rubbing the back of his neck, he stepped away from her, thinking the distance would dampen the rising heat between them. He began pacing the floors and threw his hands in the air before shoving them into his pockets as if he'd find answers there. His eyes drifted to the ceiling, then the floor, then from one side of the room to the other until he finally looked at her directly. "I'm sorry, Lucille. Really, I am. I didn't mean for you to..."

On the verge of crying, Lucille blinked hard. "Stop right there, Marcus. Don't say anything else. All I'm going to say is can't you see that I'm... I'm grown now? I can do whatever I want. That means I can want what I want."

"Listen, Lucille, we can forget all about this and I'll send you home to your mama and daddy. You've been getting a lot of attention and it seems it's been going to your head. Hey, I thought you said you want to be a big star. Well, if you changed your mind and you just want to...to...do that..." He flapped his hand in the air while giving her a hard up-and-down look. "You're better off going back to being a Traveling Love."

"Marcus, all I did was—"

Anxious to change the subject, he interrupted. "Listen, I found us a new piano player. Sweet Mitchell Reynolds is the best there is. I've arranged a little meet and greet so you can get to know each other—that is, if you're still serious about performing." He gently nudged her in the direction of the parlor. Wendell, clearly taking Marcus's hint, must have left; the parlor was empty except for one man sitting at the piano.

It was there in the Macombs Hotel in Baltimore where she saw the long, thin arms of a light-skinned, mustachioed man dressed in what looked like an undertaker's black suit, attached to an impeccably shined Baldwin upright piano. He pushed his bowler hat far back on his head and startling blue eyes stared back at Lucille as if she were an annoyance. He sighed, rolling his lips before spitting out, "Young lady, I ain't here to babysit."

With that he began a long ripple along the piano keys. Mitchell banged out one song after another, from hymn to Charleston rag in shotgun fashion. Lucille came in singing loudly enough the curtain tassels shook. Mitchell ran his fingers down the keys and Lucille filled her lungs with air and followed along, matching his fortissimo. When she didn't know the song, she made up words in perfect syncopation with Mitchell's riffs. Soon Mitchell was nodding, challenging her and the piano keys as he pounded out song after song, mixing tempos and criss-crossing genres from jazz to blues to gospel. They both began laughing between the dancing half and quarter notes, watching and anticipating each other's moves until the door slowly creaked open.

Lucille caught a glimpse of Marcus peering in, trying hard not to be noticed. She was quite pleased with Mitchell and enjoyed singing with his accompaniment. But she couldn't help thinking about how Marcus simply disregarded her feelings and embarrassed her in front of Wendell. He never once acknowledged or apologized for insulting her, only shoving her into a rehearsal as if she was as insignificant as a pimento finger sandwich on a tray of cucumber sandwiches. And for reasons beyond reason, she decided to let the anger that was slowly rising within her take over.

How dare he show his face after everything he said to me—and all the things he didn't say, Lucille thought. At once, she sang out lyrics that popped into her head and needed to be released:

"We've been together when dark clouds rolled in
Dreamed of sunshine while the stars hid e'vry sin
I think of you as my personal sweet
My delicious, oh so tasty treat
Just like my mama's fresh berry pie
Oh there's one thing, I won't lie
Your lips are oh so temptin'
And I want to take a fall
But I know I'm just meant ta bein'
Your sunshine baby doll"

Lucille leaned her back against the piano while watching the crack of the door. She hissed out the words while stealing herself for any sharpness Marcus might retaliate with.

"You say you do, but you don't listen
All I want is some kissin'
I know just what I'm missin'
Once and for all
I'm your sunshine baby doll!"

Marcus, stepping cautiously, came into the room with a tray of cookies, his brows deeply knitted together and lips pursed tightly. He stared directly at Lucille. He cleared his throat. "Y'all are sounding hot. I knew this was going to be a duo made in heaven. Mitchell, you and Lucille had people dancing out in the hallways and outside along the sidewalks. Lucille, your friend must have danced his way out the door because I haven't seen hide nor hair of him in the hallway."

Mitchell gave Marcus a once-over. "Marcus, what's this? This ain't no knitting circle. We don't need no milk and cookies. Milk ain't good for the vocal cords and this girl definitely knows how to use hers."

"I told ya! I just thought maybe you and Lucille might want to take a break. You know, give Lucille's voice a rest. I got lemonade in this pitcher and I brought some sweets." Marcus set the treats on a console table across the room, then joined Mitchell and Lucille at the piano.

Mitchell threw down a cigarette butt and smashed it with his toe while pulling out another cigarette from his pocket. "Me? A break? What's that? Do I really need to tell you that lemonade and cookies ain't never been a treat for this old man?"

Sullenly, Lucille pushed herself away from the piano and picked up a cookie from the tray. Marcus had done this before, getting her angry then coming back with a gesture to make amends. It wasn't working this time; he was trying way too hard. The time spent rehearsing with Mitchell hadn't softened Lucille one bit. The fact that Wendell left made her even more angry. She kept her eyes on Marcus as she slowly raised the cookie to her lips. She stopped short of biting.

"Mr. Mitchell…" Lucille said coolly. "Do you think a woman my age can make decisions all by herself, without the help of a man?"

"Miss Lucille, I think exactly what you think."

Delicately holding on to the cookie between her thumb and forefinger, she waved the cookie in the air. "Marcus, these sweets just for me? I think you trying to make me fat!"

Lucille threw the cookie across the room. It ricocheted off the door and rolled over to Marcus's feet.

Marcus angrily kicked it toward Lucille. "There's no need for that. You're not a child, Lucille. You're a professional. Act like one!" Marcus slapped his hands together to brush off the crumbs. "I've had enough, Lucille. My job is to make sure you make it to the top, not to cater to a spoiled child."

"You mean make sure *you* make it to the top." Lucille thumped her hand against her chest. "You've made it clear what you really care about, and it ain't me."

Marcus shot back, "No, what I've made clear, Lucille, is that I'm here to do my job. I'm the eyes and ears of the association. That's how I earn my three percent—by making sure you're where you need to be so that you can get to the big time. Now if you don't want me to do that, just say so. All you got to do is say it, Lucille."

The pause in their spat was filled with heavy breathing. It dared either Marcus or Lucille to move or say what each wanted the other to say. Lucille broke the standoff by backing up to the piano and snatching up Mitchell's smoldering cigarette. She leaned against the piano and, not taking her eyes off Marcus, took a long drag.

"I really can't stand you right now, Lucille." Marcus spit over his shoulder as he turned and left the room.

"Well, you ain't looking too good right now either," Lucille yelled at Marcus's back, returning the cigarette to Mitchell's still-parted fingers.

Thinking it was safe to venture into the private conversation, Mitchell threw his hands on the piano keys and hit a choir of stinging chords. He spoke over the clash of sound. "Whew, you can really sing the hell out of a song, but you got to watch that temper. You got to learn, lil' missy—don't bite the hand that feeds you."

Feeling defeated, Lucille began to cry.

"Miss Lucy, you wipe away those tears. Use that big voice of yours and the obvious brain in your head to concentrate on making memorable music instead."

Mitchell took a long drag of his freshly lit cigarette and then held out his spindly arm in Lucille's direction with what was left of the burning butt. "Here, take another hit of this. Loosen up. Relax."

Lucille took the cigarette, puffed and then took a drag allowing the smoke to roll out from her lips.

"C'mon, girl. Let's do something that will make folks swoon and sway. That's what they want. They'll take that kind of sound and put it on a record for sure. That's where they're going in this business. And if you're planning to be in this business, you got to learn to eat those tears for breakfast, lunch, and dinner. Don't expect no blue ribbon or gold ring at the end of the race either."

"Mitchell, I don't mean to bring you into this, but Marcus and I have been working together since I was a young girl. He refuses to see…"

"Stop right there, missy." Mitchell grumbled almost under his breath. "Damn, I told myself I wasn't gonna get into nobody's business. But sister, if I'm going to play with you, I'm in this." He gave himself a few bars on the piano as an introduction to his forthcoming speech.

"From what I know about you, well, the problem, little gal, is that you grew up with that voice and had all those church-going folks blessing you with roses. You started expecting everyone to give you bouquets. Well, honey, they are out of roses today. You got to earn their love each and every night. And you can if you're smart and pay attention—and if you want it. If you do the work, you can demand it even with the price of admission. You'll earn so much you can finally send some back home to your family so they can rock in their rocking chair and bask in the sun somewhere in the country or wherever you're from."

"Mitchell, all I ever do is work…sing, then sing some more. I want… I want…" She stopped unable to finish.

"Oh, girl, right now all I see is you having a big old tantrum because you can't get what you want."

Lucille plopped down next to Mitchell on the piano bench. "Okay, Mr. Mitchell. I get it. From here on in, I'm keeping my eye on my prize."

"Good! Now, Miss Lucille, quit dropping down on those knees of yours, sobbin', wailin' and cryin'. Loosen up and get to work."

"Can I ask you something?"

"I've given more advice today that I ever have in my life. I don't know much longer I can be a good Samaritan," Mitchell said, but gestured for Lucille to continue.

"You know, I've been singing in front of folks all my life, but now I'm seeing things when I'm up on stage."

"What kind of things?"

"Please don't tell Marcus. He'll start worryin' and trying to manage the situation. But there's a light and a woman who dances…"

"But you just keep on singing right? When that light and strange dancin' woman appears, you keep prancing your fine self all over the stage, right? You keep singin', prancin' and getting paid, right? Does this woman tell you what to do?"

"Yes, how'd you know?"

"Well, welcome to the club. What you got yourself is a muse. You're a real art-teeste now!"

"What do you mean, a muse?"

"Oh, chile…my granny called 'em guardian angels. All of us in this business have 'em. I chased mine away though. The last time I saw him, he was swimming around the bottom of my bourbon one night. I told him he was taking up way too much space and to get the hell outta there. Ain't seen him since."

"Mr. Mitchell, is that true? That sounds like your alcohol talking, not an angel."

Mitchell shrugged, "Alcohol, angel…what's the difference?" He stared back at Lucille with haughty resignation. "Girl, if I said it, it's the God's honest truth." He raised his hand up to the sky, never relinquishing his cigarette, which had almost burned to the nub. "Give them damn sparkly lights or that woman a name. Welcome her onboard with open arms, give her a drink, and let her inspire you. Just stay in control." Mitchell handed her another cigarette. "Now, precious, get out of here. I got to see a man about a horse and after that, this here Black Troubadour got some stars of my own I need to see."

PART III

MISS LUCILLE'S BLACK TROUBADOURS

16

Richmond, Virginia
1923

"I sure hope we ain't following no dog acts this time. My good shoes stunk of shit for three days after our last show on this circuit."

Walking briskly through a dirt alleyway, Lucille stayed close to the sides of the buildings and on the rickety boards they called a walkway between the theater and the boardinghouse.

Marcus, with an armful of feather boas, followed close behind, assuring her, "Naw, nothing like that this time, 'Cille. I told you... I got you booked as the headliner! Slow down. We've got time. You're the star, Lucille. They're all coming to see you!" He continued with warnings about the evils of being too risqué, but his fussing was muffled by the armful of ostrich and peacock feathers.

Lucille was glad it wasn't raining, but a damp cloud of wet mist crept up from the ground. She was soaked by the time they made it to the theater's stage door, where they were met with barking and howling from an assortment of tethered hounds. One mongrel gave them a salute of a leg lifted to pee against the entry wall.

Miss Lucille's Black Troubadours were already onstage and warming up the crowd—no need for their star singer right now. Big Bobby was perched on his lucky stool, sliding the trombone up to the ceiling. Bow-legged Lincoln popped out piercing trills on his trumpet while Sweet Mitchell sat on the edge of his seat making the black-and-white keys of his piano sing out. The musicians, in sync with each other, jumped and arched in unison while spitting out a bouncing tune that gave the audience the feeling that life at this moment was the tonic for good fortune. The band played an updated ragtime tune twisted with a bit of jazz as warm-up. Sweet Mitchell held up his hand, signaling when and who would blend in or stand out. When he saw Lucille and Marcus standing in the wings, he gestured to his two bandmates to power down for Miss Lucille's intro.

Sweet Mitchell was indeed the finest piano player around and everyone Lucille ever met knew it. He had built a name for himself on all the vaudeville circuits. Lucille could see how he earned the nickname "Sweet" from his piano playing; Mitchell hit what most said were unimaginably sweet chords. The crowds roared when the tips of his fingers rode on a wave of sound from the highest to the lowest key and curled all the way back again. It was pure luck that Marcus was able to steal him away from a hole-in-the-wall town in Mississippi to lead Miss Lucille's Black Troubadours. Mitchell's one demand was that he only play *his* piano, which he named Maybelle. Mitchell was such a good musician that Marcus paid a heavy sum of money to cart the old upright everywhere they went. When the band played, Mitchell was in the music, balancing between the loud and soft of his fellow band members to create a mesmerizing sound. When he wasn't playing, he was the most cantankerous person that ever lived.

Lucille grabbed her feathers from Marcus, swung them around her neck and stepped out onstage. When the klieg lights hit, she knew the theater had only one queen—and tonight it was her. She was short and slender but no frail flower by any means. Lucille had a broad back and narrow hips that sat atop long, shapely, muscular legs. She used every inch of her long legs to stride out to the middle of the stage and pause to look at the crowd, giving them time to drink in every curve and angle. They were the same faces she had seen across the South, at least in these types of venues: mostly white men in the choice seats with their mouths open and slapping their knees at the sight of her. There was a sprinkling of well-dressed women who would never admit to anyone they attended such a spectacle as the gentleman's companion for the evening.

Light rippled across her gown and the tiny facets of the beads in her jewelry and headband glittered. Lucille knew from the wide eyes lit by gin that the slightest shimmy would conjure up images of secret music floating through the hills and valleys of the distant dark lands these folks dreamed of conquering. She knew they fantasized about their hands strolling down her back and rubbing her backside while they rocked on the porch under some mysterious cooling breeze. She slowly turned to give the audience a full view of the low cut of her dress and the curve of her back before sashaying up to Mitchell. With her hips still moving, she winked at Marcus, who stood in the wings with his hands folded in prayer, then leaned over to whisper in Mitchell's ear. Lucille opened her show with the raucously up-tempo "Wild Women Don't Have the Blues."

She breathed out the first few lyrics before hitting a full deep-throated vibrato, a surprisingly strong note coming from such a small frame. It was her claim to fame. It was a big mistake to think that because of her slim figure, she was going to hit operatic, birdlike floral notes. She surprised those that didn't know with a sound that most would attribute to a big-busted, seasoned woman with the knowledge of living a life of survival.

Lucille took a few teasing steps forward, right up to the edge of the stage, winked at someone who looked like a George and waved to another she named Henry. She shimmied a little for Horatio and Billy, who was called William Jr. in social circles. Whatever their real names, their eyes bulged at seeing her so close. She brushed her feather boa across the face of Samuel, shook plumes of ostrich at Timothy. She flashed a big this–will–be–a–night–like–no–other smile for all those who stood in the back.

She gave names to the faces she could see to make it feel like she was singing only to someone she knew and loved. In return, they would love her right back. She knew they would love the chocolate brown gal that stood before them. The girl with the shiny skin lit by sequins and the glow of the lights was dancing and singing just for them. And each time she swung her hips, eyes locked on her every move, rolling from side to side. She'd use everything she had to create a story of a life they would never live, or if they had, the memory would either make them profoundly sad or deliriously giddy. She mouthed the words of want and lust, of give and take. And they gulped down her every word along with glass after glass of liquor or, depending on the venue, watermelon whiskey steeped in big jars on someone's dark cellar steps.

Lucille eyed Marcus in the wings, standing at the edge of the curtain. He was so close to being onstage that the audience could probably see the nervous grin on his face and his anxious shifting from one foot to another. He motioned her to pull back. She knew the signal and began to retreat to the band. But the table down front had an empty chair. It was just the place to plant her foot, showing off her satin shoe with the rhinestone buckle. It was just the place to lean into the crowd and sing the final verses.

"I've got a disposition and a way of my own
When my man starts kicking, I let him find another home
I get full of good liquor, walk the streets all night
Go home and put my man out if he don't act right
Wild women don't worry, wild women don't have their blues"

Bathed in the heat of the moment, Lucille closed her eyes, intuitively punctuating just the right words to bring down the house. When she opened her eyes, above the tops of heads bobbing and swirling with every beat of the music, *she saw her*. Up in the right-hand corner of the balcony Lucille saw the crystal white light, growing from a spark to a blazing shining star. She had seen it many times before and she knew no one else could see it. She knew turquoise-blue-and-green peacock feathers would follow and in the center of light, her muse would appear.

Just as Mitchell said, Lucille welcomed her and named her. Aida Overton Walker materialized with a taunting smile. Lucille had gotten used to her spirited presence showing up at any point in her performance. When the real Aida Overton Walker passed in 1914, she had been mourned by thousands. Her renditions of a glorious cakewalk and Salome's "Dance of the Seven Veils" were legendary. Overton Walker left a rich legacy as a performer and Lucille was convinced that Aida had come back to guide her. She knew her Aida and her Aida knew her. Aida whispered words to songs so Lucille couldn't forget.

Tonight, Aida stretched her limbs out from the piercing light to grow as tall as the theater ceiling, dipping in between the specks of dust that floated in the stage lights. Wrapped in purple silks trimmed with gold, Aida tiptoed across the balcony railing while wriggling her body. She stopped to decorate the house with a graceful arabesque before blowing a seductive Salome kiss to Lucille. She was beautiful, shiny deep brown with her black hair, twisted and curled, piled high on her head. Diamonds and pearls graced her slender neck, dripping into her bodice. Lucille dipped and slid her leg to the side to mirror Aida's movements. To the audience, Lucille looked as though she was playing to the last row in the house. But, like many times before, Lucille took her cues from her magnificent inspiration that haunted her onstage and off.

Taking her cue from her Aida, Lucille belted out the rest of the song. When she finished, the audience roared, jumping up from their seats and hollering for more. Aida nodded with approval before evaporating into a cloud of flowers that showered the stage from the balcony. Most of them boys had a plan, and Lucille wasn't going to blame them for wishful thinking as long as they paid the price of admission.

After the hot opening number, Mitchell cooled things down. He rolled down the keys to introduce a song that reminded Lucille of flowing water over smooth stones. Without a word, she casually walked back to the upright piano, fanning herself and dotting her face with her scarf. She knew the audience would wait until she reached her destination. She could feel the whole house buzzing from her opening song.

So what if, just for a moment, my garter peeked out. What harm would it do? I'm sure they've all seen a pretty woman's thigh and have laid down between a few. If not, I'm gonna give 'em an education along with a good time.

She gave them a moment to take a sip of their drinks and anticipate the next song. Lucille leaned against the piano and nodded to Mitchell to begin. She picked a shadowed outline of a man in the back of the room and decided he was going to be the object of her desire for this song. She fixed her gaze on the shape of his head and the slight outline of his features and began.

They were all supposed to fall in love with her. That's what made them come back time and time again. But this man, for just this song, would be her man, her exclusive pet for the rest of the evening. Lucille knew he'd be knocking at her door after the show. They always did.

17

It was almost noon, way too early by her everyday standards, when Lucille was awakened by a rapid succession of knuckles banging on her room's door at the boardinghouse.

Bolting up from a deep sleep, Lucille screamed, "Go away, dammit! We paid for today!"

"Lucille, open up, I got to talk to you!" It was Marcus.

Lucille rolled out of bed, wobbled over to the door and flung it open. Marcus's generally smooth brown complexion was creased with lines, matching his wrinkled jacket and pants. "What? What now?"

"Big Bobby's in jail."

"What you say?" Lucille rubbed her eyes, still heavy with sleep.

"You know, 'Cille, it's them girls. He won't leave them alone. It's all fun when they're teasing each other but now not one of them women is gonna speak up for him. Not one…they're too afraid."

"Damn, and he was the best trombone player we ever had. Where's Sweet Mitchell?"

"I just saw him downstairs. He was half-asleep in a chair and as ornery as ever. He says we should just leave Big Bobby here."

"And Lincoln?"

"Jittery as a bug and a bit slippery about his whereabouts last night. He's the one that told me about Big Bobby."

Marcus pointed at the pile of the sheets melting around the length of a tall man in Lucille's bed. "Who's that?" The man had made no movement despite all the commotion. Marcus deduced there had been a long night of drinking and other homegrown activities that sent him to deep oblivion.

Lucille shrugged and shook her head. "Oh you know…" She then said with a sly, daring smile, "Since I can't have you."

"Stop it. It's too early for that, Lucille. Big Bobby, remember?"

"Well, I told you I always get the stuff I throw out into the crowd back…one way or another."

Lucille looked at her conquest's still body to make sure he was thoroughly asleep before going to the dresser and pulling out a drawer. Underneath the drawer was a worn brown pouch tied with a leather strap. She quickly unraveled it to open the pouch, which was filled with a large roll of dollar bills and a few gold coins.

She thrust a handful of bills toward Marcus. "See what you can do with this. Them deputies might buckle if they see cash. You know how to read 'em. You've had plenty of practice and you're still alive to talk about it. Use them negotiating skills I pay you for. This will at least buy us some time to get beyond the reach of this town."

"I told you to put your money in a bank."

"I don't trust none of those institutions…black or white. But this ain't the time to worry about how I keep my finances. Right now, you've got to hurry. Go see what you can do to get Big Bobby free."

"Yeah, once he's out, we'll have to wipe this town off the

tour because we won't be able to ever come back here," Marcus said while stuffing the money in his jacket pocket and making an attempt to smooth out his clothing to look presentable.

"I don't care. This town is nowhere near where I want to be. There's nothing here for me." Lucille looked over at the long muscular outline in her bed. "He is a fine-looking young fellow, reminds me of the seven hills of Cincinnati. But now that he might know where I keep my money, I may have to kill 'im."

Mitchell and Lincoln were already assembled in the boardinghouse parlor. Both were rumpled from a night of who knows what, but like good troubadours they were ready to get on the road to the next town.

"What we gonna do, 'Cille?" Lincoln asked. "We can't just leave Big Bobby here. He'll die for sure. You know they like to make an example of us when they women involved."

"I sent Marcus to see if he can negotiate."

Mitchell chimed in, "Negotiate? Ain't no negotiating with them. They might have loved you last night, but they will *make* it your last night if they catch one of us messing around with they women. Gal, don't forget where you are. This ain't no big city. We'd need one of them black lawyers to come down here to get Big Bobby out."

Mitchell was right. Money was no guarantee of safety and probably wouldn't matter a bit. The deputy could take the money and still do nothing, or lock up Marcus for attempted bribery. Lucille knew this was dangerous territory.

"Wait a minute, guys. Let me think."

The day's heat was already tremendous. The boardinghouse proprietor, Miss Daisy, offered the trio coffee and sweet biscuits. They all nodded their thanks in silence.

All three jumped when the screen door creaked open and slammed shut with a piercing bang. Big Bobby, with a shining purple bruise around his eye and a sticky deep red gash across his forehead, stood in the doorway. His rumpled shirt and jacket were spotted with blood.

Seeing Big Bobby wasn't the only shock. What was more incredulous was the white girl tagging alongside him with her hand entwined in his.

"Bobby!" Lucille, Mitchell and Lincoln shouted in unison before breaking off into a flurry of questions.

"Where's Marcus?"

"Did Marcus get you out?"

"You didn't see him?"

"How'd you get out?

"Who dis girl, Bobby?"

Bobby held up his hands. "Let's just say Delphina here worked her magic, and the guard just opened the jail cell door. He told me to run. I thought it was a trick and he was gonna shoot me dead in the back, but as you can see that didn't happen. I'm here. Now, I can't stress it enough brothers and sisters, we gotta go, NOW! All of us!"

Marcus ran through the door. "Wasn't no use for your money after all, 'Cille. But we gotta get on our bus and get moving. The piano's loaded up. C'mon, everyone!"

"I've got some good hot coffee, biscuits and jam," chirped Miss Daisy as she entered then took a few steps back when she saw the newcomers and the state of Big Bobby's apparel.

Sweet Mitchell grabbed a cup from Miss Daisy's tray and gulped down its entire contents before swiftly turning on his heels. Lincoln swiped the plate of biscuits and dumped them in a napkin before following behind Mitchell. Big Bobby, looking sadly at Miss Daisy's now-empty tray, grabbed a handful of candy from a nearby crystal dish and bolted out the door with Delphina in tow.

Lucille looked at Marcus then back at Miss Daisy. "I am so sorry. As you can see, some of us don't know how to act. Marcus, give this lady a little extra for any trouble we may have caused."

By the time Lucille and Marcus got to the bus, the Troubadours plus Delphina were standing in the doorway in vigorous debate.

Lincoln, stomping his feet and marching in a circle, shouted up toward the heavens, "Oh, hell naw, man! She ain't going with us."

Glaring at Big Bobby, Mitchell yelled out, "You crazy? Have they done hit you in the head and made you touched?" Looking at the group, he added, "Are we sure he can play tonight, 'cause he gots to be stark raving mad."

Big Bobby pleaded with his bandmates. "C'mon, brothers, I told her we would take her to the next town. She's looking for her brother."

"So what?" Lincoln shrugged. "Boy, all our black asses been searching for our families since slave time. That ain't no excuse to haul some white girl around with us."

Marcus, bouncing on his toes nervously, joined in. "This one time I agree with Mitchell." He turned to Delphina. "Ma'am, thank you for what you did, but you can't go with us. She can't go, Bobby."

"Yeah, she might've saved your ass, but now you 'bout to condemn us all." Mitchell wiggled a pointed finger at Big Bobby and Delphina. "I ain't risking my life for your white piece of ass. We not crossin' the county line with her on the bus. I say we drop her there and leave her fate to God."

"C'mon, man, she helped me get out of that hell hole. They were going to kill me for sure."

Marcus shot back, "We done told you and warned you about where you be dipping that trombone. Shit, they gonna throw our asses off the TOBA—Tough on Black Asses—circuit for sure. Then we won't be able to find jobs anywhere."

Delphina whispered from behind Big Bobby, "I'm sorry for all the trouble."

The group, forced into a silent standoff, looked to Lucille.

She stood quietly off to the side, watching Delphina. Lucille looked over her shoulder for anyone who might be coming to retrieve Big Bobby for some made-up crime, and the rest of them by association. Except for their shouts, the street was quiet.

Thank goodness no one's around. Everyone must be at church. God is giving us this one chance to get clean out of town, Lucille thought to herself.

Without saying a word, Lucille walked up to Delphina, giving her a once-over, determining the girl's character through intuition. Delphina stood her ground while gripping Big Bobby tightly.

Lucille finally spoke. "Okay, stuff her deep in the back. She can go as far as the Chattahoochee, then she got to go find her people on her own."

Mitchell climbed on the bus. "Aw, hell. Man, I thought I was gonna get some sleep on this bus, but now I gotta stay awake the entire hundred miles in case I gotta get a head start running through some cornfields. I ain't about to be on the chain gang again."

18

Outside the city limits, the old motor bus creaked and squealed as it lunged forward over the hard, uneven road. It was a long stretch of road pointed forward between trees and fields. Marcus gripped the steering wheel to navigate the bus over the rugged terrain. Traveling by bus was Marcus's idea of saving a few pennies since now they had to stretch their money between the troupe. It was an old vehicle they inherited from a family friend of Marcus's, a black auto dealer in Oklahoma who perished in the race riots a few years earlier. They had grown accustomed to traveling back roads to avoid anyone who wanted to cause trouble. Life on the road had taught the Troubadours to avoid any confrontation if at all possible. They knew no matter how innocent, someone's black ass was more likely to be carted off to jail or worse, depending on the day and whose god was smiling down on them.

With Delphina in the back, it became a more perilous journey. Despite being stuffed into a crowded vehicle—with a piano in the aisle—everyone leaned against whatever and whomever they could and fell asleep. Delphina, who was looking a little gray and green around the edges, bobbed her head in deep slumber.

"Linc! Pinch down them windows a bit, this bus is smelling a bit fragrant," Marcus shouted. No one moved.

Through a haze of half sleep, Lucille wiped salty beads of sweat away from her chin. Through her burning eyes, she caught flashes of white and yellow butterflies flitting across the tall grass. She saw the heat rising across the dry dirt before them. The sun had taken what was left of the Sunday-morning dew and transformed it from what was once soft and giving earth to cracked red clay as they surged down a road with no other travelers in sight.

She turned her head to watch Marcus as he drove. His handsome face, graced with an early beard, was knotted in determination. He looked as if he had bet all his money on being at their next destination on time. Before fleeing Richmond, Marcus had secured a new gig at a church theater in some small town that was sure to have a black audience. Lucille didn't really mind playing the backwoods joints. She enjoyed the small venues—that's where she felt loved the most.

Marcus caught her staring at him. "Where is your mind, girl?"

Lucille stretched her arms and legs. "Oh, you know what I'm thinking about."

"Okay, I shouldn't have asked. We gonna have to go visit your mama so she can talk some good clean sense into you."

"You thought I was going to say I was thinking about you, didn't you? You thought I was going to say something like 'I love you and I wish we could get married, buy a house' and all that lovey-dovey stuff. Well, not this time, mister. Maybe we should revisit it though."

Marcus gave Lucille a lazy smile. "Yep, you need your mama right now."

Lucille returned his smile with a wide grin. "Oh no, I don't. That's not what I need." Pausing slightly for a reaction, she continued, "Remember when we first started out, Marcus? Mother didn't trust you one bit and Daddy always kept his one good eye on you. You finally won him over, but not Mother."

Marcus laughed. "Yeah, managing the Traveling Loves was the easy part. Facing Hank and Evelyn, on the other hand… let alone letting me take the Little Girl with the Big Voice out on the road without them."

"Oh yeah, Marcus. I remember that first year was rough with everyone fighting over every little thing. The second wasn't much better. I thought at any minute they were going to fire you. I didn't think we'd ever get here. But once the elder Loves saw they didn't have to depend on the kindness of church parishioners for food and lodging—"

Marcus interrupted, "And once they had a little money in their pockets. They just let me be."

Lucille shook her head. "Oh no, it wasn't for money. My mama and daddy never thought about money."

"That's what you think," Marcus quipped.

She scrunched up her face. "No, they let up when you came back with that wife of yours. When you introduced Rose to them and me, that's when they thought you were honorable. It was then Mother and Daddy knew it was all about business. It's because of her they let me go with you. Rose allowed them to settle down for the very first time because they believed you were driven by a real true purpose. They believed you would take care of me and make me a star."

The bus hit a dip in the road and shuddered just enough to rattle the contents of the vehicle, but not enough to rouse the sleeping Troubadours. Lucille slid deeper into her seat, grabbing at the sides to steady herself. She stared at Marcus, who gripped the steering wheel with both hands.

"Remember when them folks gave me my first standing ovation, Marcus? And not just one ovation, but three! I bowed and curtsied, and they loved this here brown gal. The house manager told me they ain't never had folks clap that long for a colored act. I thought that performance in front of all them

white folks would get me a ticket on that steamer, Marcus…
That performance should've got me to Paris."

"Just keep those stars in your eyes, okay?"

"Once I play Paris, there's no telling how much money we
can demand back here. No more bowing down to the Theater Owners Booking Association. Those grubby TOBA fools
won't have a hold on us! I can command top dollar, a recording, a colored revue or play on Broadway. We'll be able to ditch
this broke-down bus and get us a new fine one with fancy gold
writing and my picture on the side." Lucille jostled Marcus's
shoulder.

"Lucille, I've got to keep my eyes on the road or we gonna
end up in a ditch for sure."

"Can you imagine my black face rolling down the highway
looking out over them damn fields and trees that used to snare
us black folks?"

"And a pretty black face it is."

"That's why I love you so much!" Lucille threw her arms
around Marcus, pulling him toward her into a hug that almost
lifted him from the driver's seat.

"Stop, 'Cille… I got to drive this here rickety bus. I got to
keep my foot on the gas or else we ain't gonna make it to the
next venue and you know they gonna deduct if we're late."

They drove for the next few miles in silence. Lucille closed
her eyes, allowing her mind to drift to an innocent Sunday
not yet a year ago when they sat on a porch, laughing until the
breeze cooled their sentences.

He was speaking softly about wants and needs, when the only
music was the chirping birds and the scattering squirrels. They
were so close, lightheaded with the excitement of dreams and
possibilities. He wrapped his arm around her shoulders and the
world went silent when his cheek grazed hers. Only the scent
of their skin separated them. It wasn't until they began breathing in and out again that they parted, retreating only inches
apart, returning to safety.

Lucille opened her eyes, relinquishing her memories. Marcus was staring at her. He remained silent as his eyes went back to the road ahead. She cleared her throat to bring her and Marcus back to reality: sweaty people crammed into a rattling bus.

When Marcus finally spoke, it was evident to her that his mind had drifted in the same direction. He shocked Lucille with his bluntness.

"Luce, I'm only gonna say this once, but I have to get it out. You are a bright light in my life. I do love you, deeper than you'll ever know. But I can never—I will never—leave Rose. I love her too. Before I met you, Rose and I fought everybody just to jump the broom. We could've just lived our lives like our mothers and fathers without getting married the right and proper way, but we got married, as most people do, to officially connect our families and our future children. My grandparents and so many of my kinfolk couldn't do that—you know how they make everything difficult for us. We married and had it documented as an anchor so our children wouldn't be strewn across unknown fields without the knowledge of their roots. We cannot and will not ever let that happen again. Too many of us can't find our roots. So, Rose and I are staying together. We are the trunk of this family tree. I stand with her, and she stands beside me. I won't betray her, no matter what. You understand that, don't you?"

Just then the bus shook violently and ground to a halt, throwing the Troubadours plus one in all directions and out of their sound sleep.

"I've got to get outside." Delphina jumped up and squeezed between the seats and the upright piano, hopping off the bus. She took two steps out the doorway before throwing up on the side of the road.

Marcus shouted from the driver's seat, "You all right, girl?"

"Her name is Delphina," Big Bobby quipped.

"I hope we don't all come down with something 'cause of her," Lincoln added. "Lucille, cover your face."

Mitchell stated calmly, "What we gonna come down with is chain gang fever if we don't get going. What it look like, Marcus? Are we gonna make to Blue's Café tonight? I'm hungry and about to become a fiend if I don't get my fix of something bubbled up in some grease. What's wrong? Can we patch this thing up and move along?"

Lucille rolled her eyes and looked outside to Delphina, giving her a once-over. "We cain't catch what she got."

Delphina was a small-framed young woman with delicate features and pale skin. She held a hand against the bus to steady herself. "I'm okay. I'm fine now. It's just the heat, and the bus, and the smells of everyone crammed up in the bus. I haven't eaten a thing all day." She turned away and threw up again. Big Bobby finally squeezed his way out of the bus to put an arm around her.

Lucille snarled, "Girl, are you pregnant?"

Delphina turned sheepishly to the group.

"Oh lawd!" Mitchell fell against the back seat with his head buried in his hat, giving the impression he was bored with the conversation.

Lincoln leaned far out the window of the bus. Lucille stood on the stairs in the doorway while Marcus, having jumped out from the driver's seat, hovered over the steaming engine. Everyone's eyes met and they looked at each other in a state of stunned amazement as Delphina admitted Lucille was right.

All heads then turned to Big Bobby.

"Oh no, man, it ain't mine! Lawd, I just met this woman two nights ago. I'm good but I ain't that good. She's in a bad way. Now you know why she's got to find her brother."

"Where her man at? I hope he ain't looking for our black asses," Lincoln called out, nervously looking around as if to catch someone following them.

Marcus shook his head. "This is getting worse by the minute. How far are we from the Chattahoochee? I can't say that

I ain't ever thought I'd be so happy to see this side of the river. But we gonna turn her loose there and leave her be."

Delphina spoke up in a thin, high-pitched Southern drawl. "Please, y'all. I'm sorry, but can't I just stay with y'all? At least for a few more miles or so. Around Pittsburgh? Can I ride with y'all to any points around there? Aren't y'all planning to play anywhere near Texas or Arkansas? Y'all headed that way, right? I got a little bit of money but—"

"Texas or Arkansas?" Lincoln snapped. "Who told her we were going all that way! We're not going that way. Are we going that way?"

Delphina pleaded, "It's all the money I got in the world. If it ain't enough, I can do some work. I can take care of your costumes. Miss Lucille, I can iron and sew. You don't have to pay me nothing. I can earn my keep some way. I just need to get close enough to find my brother. He's my only family. He'll take care of me."

Lucille sighed. "Well, Miss Delphina, ain't this a real turn of events. We can't, in all good conscience, leave you here in the middle of nowhere. 'Specially since you're pregnant and all. But I gotta agree, it's too risky for us. Next town, you're out!"

Mitchell, peeking from under his hat, spit out, "I say let's not be so soft. Pregnant or not, we can leave her here. Someone, probably some white folks, will be along this road and she can hitch a ride with them. You know they'll be gunning for our black asses if they see her. If she ain't strong enough to pull this piano off the bus, then we don't need her."

"Now hang on, Mitchell. I'm not so naive. What if we abandoned this girl and she took her white self straight to the authorities and spun some tale about Big Bobby? They'd be after us faster than you can blink," Lucille pointed out.

"No, Miss Lucille, I wouldn't, I mean it!"

"Marcus, are we able to get going?"

Marcus wiped a rag across his forehead. "It looks like we are out of gas, folks. Dammit! Lincoln, I told you to fill it up before we left."

"We left so fast I didn't have time," Lincoln replied sheepishly.

"Well, somebody is going to have to walk on down to the next farm or see if there's a gas station close by. We just need a bit to get to the next town."

"Who going to do that? Not me," shouted Mitchell. "I'm just the piano player. Make Lincoln do it because it's all his fault. Or Big Bobby because we only miles away from a jail cell in either direction."

Marcus slammed down the hood. "Everyone, smarten up. I'll do it. They just might shoot Big Bobby on the spot and who knows what will happen if I send Lincoln. Y'all stay here. If another motorist come by, ask him if we can siphon a bit of gas, okay? I'll add whatever I can get."

Lucille watched Marcus grow smaller and smaller as he walked down the long stretch of road. It reminded her of one of the numerous Pauline Hopkins stories her mother used to tell her where a black American man learns about his blackness while traveling in Ethiopia. A black man alone on the road in the Deep South—she knew so many things could go wrong, but she had no choice but to hope that he would return with a bucket of gas big enough to find their way to the colored side of the next town. Her heart skipped a few beats, and she mindlessly rubbed her chest as a way to rub out the slight grip of fear.

Lincoln, Big Bobby and Delphina moved farther away from the bus to the shade of a clump of wide, tall trees. They were still in clear sight. Lincoln pushed a greasy napkin toward Delphina to offer her one of Miss Daisy's biscuits.

Mitchell stayed in the back corner of the bus, stretched out over the row of seats. His hat dipped low over his eyes and he'd pulled his jacket collar up to his chin even though the air was heavy with heat. Lucille knew he wasn't asleep. She had grown quite fond of the grumpy artiste. He was ill-humored most times but there was always wisdom in his bite. She depended on him not only for his musical prowess but also for his advice even when it was buried in a barrage of sharp comments.

Mitchell positioned his body in such a way that he had a panoramic view of the road in both directions. Like Lucille, something took ahold of Mitchell when he played the piano. Lucille knew the feeling when she sang. It was that something that made her and cantankerous Mitchell kindred spirits. That's why Lucille and Mitchell spent too many days traveling from town to town and too many nights drinking together after a show without even a kiss on the lips.

"Mitchell… Mitchell… I know you ain't asleep. It's too damn hot to be wrapped up like that."

"Woman, no. This here is what I call an *ain't* situation. I *ain't* asleep. I *ain't* going to sleep until I'm in some soft feather bed wrapped in somebody's arms the next three towns over from here. Or maybe I'll sleep when I'm dead. This here *ain't* a good place for us to be in. This *ain't* a good road. We *ain't* near a good, favorable colored town. This *ain't* a good county and the state *ain't* far'n much better. So naw, I *ain't* sleepin' in this no good spot…goddammit!"

"Why are you so sure we in trouble? Look around you. The sun is shining, the sky is blue and all you're doing is being sour."

"Well, because…just look at us. We're stuck in the middle of nowhere. We just sitting here waiting to perform a goddamn cakewalk. The only prize we gonna claim is the rusty shackles of a chain gang if we're lucky."

His eyes shifted over to Big Bobby, Delphina and Lincoln bouncing on a downed tree limb and giggling out loud like children. "Look at those damn fools out there. All out in the open with that damn woman and Marcus is out there on a fool's errand to find some gas. I sure hope he comes back. If I were him, I wouldn't."

19

The roving sun moved slowly across the sky, warming Lucille's face, which was dotted with perspiration. Her dress clung to her wet body. She picked at the fabric, pulling it away from her skin to let whatever available air seep in to cool her off. Lucille pulled her knees up, wrapped her arms around her legs and let the deep dip in the seat cradle her. Marcus spent so many hours in the very same seat driving the band from one stage to another that the cushions were molded to the shape of his backside. The sun, still high in the sky, pierced the window and kept the seat warm.

He had only been gone a couple of hours but the pang of his absence and worry for his safe return bundled itself in Lucille's chest and caught her breath. She closed her eyes while fanning herself, pulling at her dress in the hope of generating a bit of cool air for relief. When she opened her eyes, the first thing she saw was the top of Marcus's hatless head bouncing over the horizon where the road met the sky. He was walking quickly. When she could finally see his whole face, he looked worried. It only took a few seconds to see why.

"Mitchell! Mitchell! Marcus is coming and it looks like he's got company. Wake up! Get the boys and Delphina back here."

Sensing the alarm, Mitchell immediately popped up. "Shiiit! I told you that white girl was going to bring us nothing but trouble."

Mitchell scooted over to the other side of the bus and leaned out the window. The trio had stopped frolicking on the tree branch and were looking toward the road. In a loud whisper, Mitchell commanded, "Bobby, Lincoln, c'mon! Leave that girl out there. There's trouble on the horizon."

He waved his arm, pointing his hand in the direction of the road. From the bus and the field, Miss Lucille's Black Troubadours stayed focused on the flatbed truck slowly following behind Marcus. Two white men were in the front seat, one was riding on the side and two were hanging on in the back. Lincoln pushed Delphina down so she was hidden in the tall grass. He put his fingers to his lips signaling her to stay put and stay quiet. Big Bobby moved quickly to the bus and Lincoln followed.

Marcus kept his eyes on Lucille and Mitchell as he walked up. Without saying a word, he began filling up the tank with gasoline. The truck pulled up alongside the bus.

"So the nigga might be telling the truth. Is this here the big-time singin' group? All I see is a few coons," one of the men snickered to the others.

Another man in the back of the truck jumped down. Someone handed him a gun. "So tell me where y'all off to."

"We're headed to the Academy over in Baltimore. We're playing there tonight."

"The Academy? Yeah, that may be true. That's where all your people go. But how do I know y'all not just trespassing on my property or going over there to stir up trouble with a bunch of race talk?"

Lincoln chimed in. "No…no, mister. We ain't. We're entertainers—musicians. We just ran out of gas and was waiting for Marcus to return with some."

"We're good to go," Marcus said loudly after pouring the last bit of gasoline in the tank without looking at the four men. "We'll be on our way now."

"Now hold on a minute, boy. I got a few more questions to make sure you are who you say you are. These boys don't look like musicians. That one there looks like he stole something. Where did y'all get this bus?"

"I assure you this is our bus. See the sign there in the window? We are Miss Lucille's Black Troubadours. Here is Miss Lucille herself, and we certainly are black. We got a piano back there too."

"Maybe you boys need to play something so I can be sure." One man chuckled out as he spoke over his shoulder to the driver. "What you think, Sonny?"

"Whatever you say, Emmett. Yeah, I can go with some good music. I ain't heard none since Reconstruction," he said, laughing.

Lucille stood still. She let her eyes drift over to the field. If you didn't know she was there, Delphina appeared as a small mound of dirt, as long as she stayed perfectly still. Lucille prayed Delphina would do just that so she would not be noticed.

"Okay." One of the men crossed his arms over the rifle that rested in the crook of his arm. "Before we pass each other by, let's hear a little something. Y'all got to go through my town on your way to Baltimore and we boys won't have the benefit of your performance. So it serves that we should have a show. Sing a little something, girl."

Mitchell squeezed his thin frame between the seats, positioning himself in front of Maybelle. He flipped the piano open and started slowly with the chords of a gospel tune. Lucille knew it well and started humming along. She was determined not to sing a word for these men who would cut them down no matter what they said or did. But she knew she had to do something to protect her troubadours—and the woman and her baby lying out in the open field.

"Naw, this don't sound like something fun. That's it. I know y'all not going to church. I want something a little high-steppin'. Pick it up." The man standing on the flat bed started clapping his hands and stomping his foot. "C'mon, give us something lively."

Lincoln picked up his trumpet and cut through Mitchell's song. He peeled out a riff of notes that could only be attributed to a first line. Mitchell changed chords and followed the trumpet. Big Bobby, with trombone in hand, jumped off the bus and slowly walked over to stand next to Marcus outside. It was a distraction to keep the men's eyes off the field and Delphina's hiding spot.

One of the men shouted to Marcus, "Now what you do? Play an instrument? Dance? Or do you just stand there?"

"I'm the manager and if you like what you hear, we would be more than happy to play for you at a venue of your choice. But for now we've got to get going so we can make our gig."

"I'm told these musicians ain't nothing but a bunch of illicit characters, drinking, gambling, thieving and all sorts of nasty activities. How I know you ain't one of them degenerates? How do I know you all ain't coming to our town bringing devil music?"

The band played louder and louder. The echo rang out across the open field. Marcus shouted over them, "You heard how we started out—with an old Christian tune. You probably sang that in church when you was knee-high."

"You know something, my mama would sing that song just about every single Sunday. C'mon, boys, I've got to get back. The wife's gonna be looking for me and is probably mad as a hen."

One man squinted his eyes and shook his head. "I don't know…"

The truck driver shouted back, "Let 'em go! We ain't got no more time for this shit."

Marcus moved slowly to the bus and in one step, leaped squarely into the driver's seat and started the engine. The bus choked out a loud gasp and rattled.

"Y'all better be outta here. Next time I see you, I want to see a full-fledged revue. For free!" The man with the rifle backed away but kept his line of sight on Big Bobby, who was now on the other side of the road. He raised his hand and another man grabbed his arm to pull him up onto the truck bed. Both men held on to the sides of the truck as the vehicle ambled off down the road, kicking up yellow dust. Big Bobby stayed put while Delphina slowly poked out from the grass and looked about to make sure no one was around.

"Leave her here!" Mitchell spit out in a loud whisper. "We might not be that lucky next time. They will crucify us if they catch that woman riding with us. It won't be anything she can talk us out of. Leave her!"

"We can't do that. Come on. Hurry up, we got to get going fast!"

"Big Bobby's right. No matter what, we can't leave a pregnant woman in the middle of nowhere. Hurry up, girl! They may come back."

The Troubadours bus ambled slowly down the road. Lincoln and Big Bobby pressed their faces against the rear window, their eyes glued to the dark mound in the field—Delphina pressed into the dirt. The truck scooted in the opposite direction and finally disappeared in a cluster of trees. Big Bobby yelled for Marcus to stop as soon as he saw Delphina rise slowly from her hiding place. He scrambled to the front of the bus and leaned out, waving for her to come. Delphina looked behind her and ran at breakneck speed toward the bus. She scrambled up the bus steps out of breath. As soon as her foot landed on the first step, Marcus stepped on the gas and the bus rattled off in the opposite direction of the boys in the truck. If she didn't have a firm grip on the rail, Delphina would've fallen back onto the road. Big Bobby caught her and pulled her close to him before guiding her to a seat next to him.

The group remained silent until Big Bobby chirped, "Marcus, are we going to give them a free concert like you promised?"

Marcus replied, "Negro, please! We ain't never coming this way again! Them boys could've strung us up."

"Not without a fight," Lincoln boldly shouted.

Marcus rolled his eyes at Lincoln's bravado. "And this is the last time I'm going to trust you to get us gassed up!"

20

Cincinnati, Ohio

August 1923
Mr. and Mrs. Hank Love
Tulsa, Oklahoma

To My Dear Parents,

My heart is full of memories today, so I couldn't put off writing you for one more minute. In Baltimore, even though I was racing to get to the theater, I stood for a moment at a church gate and prayed for your good health. I hope everyone is safe. I still fear the terrible race riots that took place two years ago will return. I hope we never see the likes of that ever again.

The Troubadours and I are traveling all the time. Sometimes it feels like I'm bouncing around in that old wagon we used to have. Our bus barely makes it from one destination to another, but Marcus gets us through it. We added another member—a woman who has agreed to help take care of our clothes. It will be good to have a woman's touch.

On the lighter side, I witnessed the audacious Ida Cox singing blues with Lovie Austin on the piano at the Royal Theatre. Both are top-notch. I only hope I can hold an audience like these two women. I hear Mrs. Cox is a top businesswoman who writes her own songs, manages her own band and is recording with Paramount. I plan to do just that someday.

We've just played the Sunnyside Theatre in Virginia, then it's over to the Majestic in Charleston, then we're back in Cincinnati again. This time I hope for many happy returns, and we can get kicked up to more of the big-class theaters!

I am fine and eating well—Marcus is seeing to it. Mother, I am keeping my feet on the ground and promise to come home for a nice long visit when we have time off.

Your beloved daughter,

Lucille

The bustling Cincinnati scene was sure to draw a mixed crowd of swells, belles and working stiffs who gathered up their newly earned coins from the General Motors assembly plant in Norwood. That meant more money for the Troubadours—which they desperately needed to cover the hotel bill and for bringing Mitchell's beloved Maybelle on and off the bus. They were booked for three weeks, so it was an opportune time to get their clothes laundered and pressed. The whole group had been smelling up the joint with sweat-stained clothes. Lucille's costumes—now grown to include an assortment of plumes, feathers, capes, and sashes—needed airing out despite being meticulously taken care of by Delphina.

Delphina did everything she promised and more. She found

and took on tasks to prove herself useful and earn her seat on the bus. Once thing was certain: Delphina was quite handy with a needle and thread, rescuing the troupe's rips and tears, lost buttons and Lucille's rhinestones. Everyone easily and quickly came to depend on her.

When she and Lucille were shopping for dresses in a new town, there were many times that shopkeepers, giving Lucille a hardened stare, would angrily confront Delphina.

"You must be from up North. We don't allow colored in this shop. Have her wait outside." Or they'd say, "You know she's a little too well-dressed to be a domestic. She needs to be in uniform. They get a little uppity and that can cause trouble around here."

Coolly, Delphina would respond, "Lucille, let's go. No need to spend any of your hard-earned money here. And by the way, this is the incredible Miss Lucille who will be singing in front of kings and queens before long. She's my employer."

Any uneasiness Lucille felt about Delphina slipped away. She had become part of the troupe.

Delphina was small but surprisingly commanding and absolute. Her blue-gray eyes were the color of a creek in the early summer, always twinkling as if perpetually smiling and laughing. She spoke in a sweet way that made the mistrustful hesitant and deterred many arguments. Delphina easily charmed every person she met. Her ease in conversation gave the impression of innocence.

She was quite handy and enterprising, chatting freely with everyone from random passersby, handymen, stagehands and theater owners. Within moments of their arrival at a venue, whether black or white, Delphina knew everyone by name, occupation, success and struggle. Her comfortable and comforting demeanor made people give her information and also gifts. Very often she would return to the room she shared with Lucille with stockings, trinkets and jewelry, scented oils or some homemade remedy meant to cure all ills that crept up from drafty places while being on the road.

She chatted freely without divulging her past or how she came to this strange situation. Everyone who spent a few minutes in her company thought, *Isn't she's just as sweet as pie.* It wouldn't be until much later that they realized they had given up some of the most secret accounts of their lives to a woman who they knew nothing about.

What was most curious about her was her scent: a mixture of unearthed mushrooms and sweet sage. No one would ask her directly about the aroma that permeated her clothes. Lincoln mentioned it to Big Bobby once, who revealed that it was her talisman, a good health and good luck remedy—a mixture of herbs that she carried around her neck from her dear friend, Medicine Mary. And, most likely, it was from a pouch filled with herbs she carried that she used to make teas to keep throats lubricated and minds clear from headaches and unsanitary hooch.

Two venues were scheduled in Cincinnati. Each catered to a different audience. Both were sold-out, standing-room-only events. Lucille was on the right path and the chill of excitement before each set was immeasurable.

The first performance was in a small bistro simply called The Spot in an all-colored section of town where a boisterous audience performed right along with the band. The Troubadours were shoved in a corner right next to the bar. The stage was just a section lit by a single light. Marcus said it was the perfect place to showcase new material. Mitchell and Lucille had worked out some songs of their own which Marcus agreed were quite good. The audience easily caught on to the lyrics and sang along to every new and known song. They clapped, stomped and cried, then called out for more. A far departure from the buttoned-up church crowds, uptight dinners and ice cream socials. Lucille loved it—it was so freeing to just sing and move to her body's own choreography along with everyone in the house.

At The Spot, Lucille wore a black shift with little sequined stars at the waist and shoulders with a cascading scarf that hung past her hem. She tucked her thick hair under to create a bob that graced the back of her neck and used pomade to secure a swoop of a side bang to frame her face. Every song that night was about love and temptation, and she coyly flashed her heavily mascaraed lashes at several men she could see in the front row. This was not a performance that Hank and Evelyn Love needed to be informed about; she could hear her mother's gasps from across the miles at the thought of her daughter being so risqué.

The second performance was at the Regal Theater, a coveted gig on any black or white performer's tour roster. Glistening double doors trimmed in gold opened to an elegantly tiled lobby that led to a carpeted aisle and velvet seating. The Troubadours were billed as an intermission act as part of a three-act play, a drama that appeared to have a storyline about a woman's downfall, succumbing to the evils of jazz. It was a tease and Lucille wondered what the playwright was trying to say with having a colored jazz band entertain the audience, but it was money they couldn't turn down. During the intermission, they played in front of the curtain and when they finished, the crowd called out for a legitimate encore. They had no choice but to swing one more number.

Before each performance Marcus gave the same advice: "Give each musician their time to shine. Let Mitchell heat them up and then Lucille, you come back in to tear down the house. We start with the familiar, which you can always go back to if things get slow. The goal is to get 'em dancing in the aisle or at least shaking in their seats. Get them to throw away their cares, to be so reckless they don't care about any losses—money, love or reputation. You've got to do that."

Lucille once asked him, since Marcus wasn't a performer, how he knew what an audience wanted.

"I just do," he replied. "I know what it's like to throw everything away, to take a risk. I've done just that with you. It's like falling when you don't have a net to catch you—the exhilaration is what saves you from being scared. And now my whole future—our future—is riding on you and the Troubadours. You see, my dear, I know we're going to be a hit out there! And once we're through with this circuit we'll conquer the next and the next and the next."

At the Regal Theater, being just an intermission band, they didn't have time for ramping up. They had to hit it hot. For this performance Lucille wore a striking yellow dress with beaded diamond shapes at the hem. The silk dress, deeply cut at the bodice and back, draped her body to keep all eyes on her shining brown skin and long legs. Rose had created an elaborately beaded cape adorned with gold tassels that swung as Lucille shimmied. Lucille chose to wear the cape inside out because once she opened it up, she knew the beads would catch the light and create an aura of stars. When she hit center stage, Lucille slowly opened the cape, and stretched her arms out wide to display a shower of sparkling crystals and dangling yellow tassels falling in an arch from the tips of her fingers like glossy wings.

She paused. A bright light passed before her eyes and she knew what would come next. A voice told her to let her cape go. She released it, and the cape fell into a swirl of yellow silk at her feet. The audience gasped at the dramatic effect. And their reaction gave Lucille a feeling of such sheer exhilaration she knew from that point forward she would do anything to capture that luxurious feeling again. It was the pure sensation of love—just like falling, then floating in a velvet sea.

She could almost see herself walking up the gangway to a ship headed off to ports where she was to be the headliner—just as she had always envisioned. Thoughts raced through her head, exploding into images of possibilities. She had been sing-ing nonstop for her whole lifetime. It was onstage where she felt the most comfortable, felt powerful enough to toy with her audience and hold nothing back. And she was rewarded for her new level of confidence.

She was given her own small dressing room at the theater and when her set was over, like royalty, she sat at her dressing table to receive the adoring public. As usual, a parade of folks lined the hallways backstage waiting to meet her and heap on praise, compliments and invitations. One elderly white gentleman hob-bled briskly through her dressing room door with a cane in one hand, not bothering to knock or wait for an introduction. His cane struck the wooden floor with each step as if command-ing each floorboard to participate in holding him upright. A striking younger gentleman stood closely at his side. The elder tucked his cane underneath his arm and reached out both hands to shake hers. His escort stepped closer to steady him.

His voice crackled. "Beautiful show. I told my nephew that I had to meet the lovely chanteuse. I've been to a lot of colored spectacles and this one was one of the best. Of course, because of you. Beautiful voice, beautiful woman."

Lucille, flattered by all the new attention, smiled and ex-tended her hand to shake his. "Thank you, sir. I'm glad you enjoyed it."

He smiled back. His arm shook as he reached out to take her hand. A veiny web of pink-and-blue skin stretched across the back of his knobby hand, disappearing under the cuff of his sleeve. Staring at her with red-rimmed, watery blue eyes, he slowly shook her hand. He paused while his crooked smile stretched out even wider, revealing several raised patches of shiny skin, deep divots in his cheeks and animated stray wild hairs of a misshapen eyebrow.

"Something strikes me as curious, young lady. Where are you from?"

"Oh, I'm from all over. I grew up in a wagon. But I was born in a small town in Indiana, sir."

The old man's eyes widened. "Evansville?"

Surprised, Lucille stared back. "Why, yes, sir. That's what they tell me. I barely remember the place. How'd you guess?"

"I'll always remember that town. I lost my twin brother in Evansville. I'll never forget." His soft, knotted knuckled hands were still clasped around hers.

"I'm so sorry, sir." Anxious to end the conversation, Lucille slipped her hand out from his and touched her chest as a caring gesture of sincerity. "Well, thank you for coming out to see us tonight. I hope you'll come back to see me and my Troubadours again."

"Oh, I'm sorry. I didn't know you had guests." Delphina stood in the doorway. She was smartly dressed in a rose-colored silk hat that complemented the raspberry-and-tan hues of her tailored light frock jacket and attached scarf, which she tossed over her shoulder. The effect was a very stylish look that framed her face, showcasing her delicate features. Stopping short, Delphina's eyes shifted to the two men and back to Lucille.

"Admirers, young lady. We're simple admirers of Miss Lucille." The younger man took a few steps toward Delphina as if drawn to her by magnets. "And who might you be? Are we expanding our circle of admirers or—" the bold young man paused to reach out his hand to Delphina "—are we expanding our circle of those *to* admire?"

Before Delphina could recover from the overt attention, the older man cleared his throat, signaling the younger man to return his attention to holding him upright.

"Miss Lucille, again, I appreciate your talent and your time. Yes…yes…yes… You are a true treasure." He squinted while tapping at his temples. "Such a pretty girl from Evansville." The elder man's speech petered out to a low hum, but his cold blue eyes never left Lucille's face.

The young man gently guided the old man toward the door. "C'mon, Uncle. We must take our leave."

Lucille watched the men exit. The younger man seemed to intentionally bump against Delphina as he ushered his wobbly uncle out the door. Delphina dropped her glove.

The younger man swooped up the glove before it touched the ground. He held it as if it were a cherished artifact and handed it to Delphina. "I'm terribly sorry. It seems being in such a small room with such beauty has made me clumsy."

Delphina whispered a dainty thank-you through lowered lashes and a shy smile.

Lucille sat at her dressing table watching the interaction and staring at the back of the old man's head. She had been initially excited about the reception, but the old man's words haunted her. How did he know where she was from? She couldn't remember mentioning anything about Evansville in any of her performances. She barely remembered living there.

"You okay, Miss Luce? Who was that, an old friend?" Big Bobby squeezed through the dressing room door while still looking down the hallway. He had become accustomed to checking on Lucille after performances when Marcus had to leave her to conduct the all-important business of collecting their pay.

Lucille waved away Bobby's concern and her nagging curiosity. "He's from my hometown. My granddaddy has a church there. I left when I was a little girl so I don't have many memories about the place. But that old man seemed to recognize me."

"Maybe he knew your folks?"

Lucille shook her head. "I doubt that. From what my daddy told me, no one paid attention to the farmer behind the produce wagon."

21

On the way to Indianapolis,
Indiana
1924

As they headed to Indianapolis, the sky held the threat of rain. The Troubadours were grateful the weather only gave them steel gray clouds and a steady soft crisp breeze that whipped around throughout the day. The bus was quiet. Heads bobbed and mouths dangled open as the Troubadours slept off the previous night's activities. Lucille, wide-awake, was reading a letter she received from the hotel right before they left town.

"What? How can she even think to ask me to come home now?"

A few eyes flipped and fluttered against the light. Lincoln, shaken out of slumber, yelled back, "Who is asking who what? We gettin' more money? What you talkin' about?"

"My mother. She wrote me to say she ran into some man who used to stay with us in Tennessee. She ran into him in Oklahoma of all places! Who'd've ever thought that?" Lucille read the letter aloud:

"Dearest Daughter,

We ran into Mr. Buster Marshall in town yesterday. Remember him from Miss Opal's? You were so young, so I can understand if you don't. He was on his way to California with plans to strike it rich mining gold. He told us he caught your act in Cincinnati. He was really impressed with the songs you chose and how you sang. His exact words were, 'A far cry from the nice church girl music that we sang in Miss Opal's parlor.' He said this with lots of winks, when he described seeing you on stage.

Lucille, I hope you are conducting yourself in a manner that is respectful of a young lady and you are following the advice of that most noble virtuoso and educator, Emma Azalia Smith Hackley. Her books, The Colored Girl Beautiful *and* The Cultured Voice *provide the proper guidance on the etiquette and responsibilities of a young performer. If you can't follow her guidelines, please come home. We now have a very nice place in Oklahoma. Your grandfather is with us now. It would be nice to have all the family at home.*

Forever Yours,

Mother"

"Welp, the only person here doing any type of sinning is Mitchell, staying in those houses of ill repute and all!" Lincoln laughed.

"And your crooked-legged, black ass is right there with me with a handful of you-know-what! That's where all your money is. Ask any one of them girls if they don't know you. Me? I'm just playing the piano, providing entertainment. Picking up some coins by taking up a challenge from the young boys who think they can outplay me. If I get paid with a nice soft bed in a house full of working women...so what?"

"I think you getting a lot more than that, brother."

"And I think you better leave me alone. Don't be talking about where I lay my head, brother. You just worry about that horn of yours."

"All right, boys," Marcus laughed out from the driver's seat. "One thing's for sure, Miss Lucille here ain't been nothing short of a saint. I can't vouch for the rest of you! Lucille, I'll send a note to Hank and Evelyn assuring them that you are walking right, shielded against any improprieties. We're nothing but family fare."

"Thank you, Marcus. They'll believe anything coming from you. It will save me from saying no to them—something I've never done before. But I mean it. I can't go home. Not now when I feel we're so close."

"Del, you're awful quiet. I bet Lucille's mama would be impressed with all these dresses you've mended, wouldn't you say?" Marcus asked.

"I'm sorry, I think I'm busy having a baby right now."

Everyone on the bus whipped their head toward the back seat and shouted in unison, "Whaaaat!"

Delphina's face was twisted and beet red as she pressed herself against the back seat and pulled her knees to her chest.

Mitchell, who had been sitting close to Delphina with his jacket pulled over his head, jumped from his seat. "Is that baby coming out right now?" Mitchell squeezed between seats and Maybelle and hopped over every piece of luggage in the aisle to get to the front of the bus.

"Marcus, stop! You got to pull over!"

Marcus steered the bus to the side of the road, stopping under the shade of a thick oak tree. Once parked, he moved to the back of the bus. "Get back, you knuckleheads. Del, is that baby really coming? Lemme see where we at here."

Mitchell shouted from the front of the bus, "Marcus, do you know your way around those parts?"

"Marcus, what can I do to help?" Lucille asked.

Delphina stretched her legs out in front of her and rolled her head from side to side. "This baby is coming out of me right this minute! Please, this baby is coming faster than I thought."

"I can't believe you're not prepared for this."

"Well, my plan was... Ooo... My plan... I thought I'd be with my brother's family but..." Delphina gripped the edge of her seat. Her already red face turned an even deeper shade of crimson. She pressed her eyes tight and her lips into a thin line until she couldn't help but let out a long winding yell. She shook as the height of the contraction poured through her body. Once the wave subsided, she continued where she left off. "A few things got in the way and here we are. May I have a sip of water, please."

Lucille shouted, "Big Bobby, go get me that jug of water under the seat and grab all the blankets we got! I need something for her to rest her head and back." She spotted a jacket on the seat, grabbed it, rolled it up and placed it behind Delphina.

Lincoln piped up, "Don't you go and use my jacket. I gotta wear that that thing tonight and I haven't paid it off yet!" He looked at Delphina. "Something got in the way, huh? Like Big Bobby?" Lincoln turned to Big Bobby and chided, "Man, you 'bout to be a daddy."

"I told you that ain't mine," Big Bobby whispered back to Lincoln before turning back to Delphina. "Don't worry, Del. You and that baby gonna be all right. People have babies all the time, everywhere."

Delphina looked at Big Bobby. "I bet they ain't never been no white girl having a baby on the back of a bus traveling with a jazz band."

"Naw, I can't say I heard a story like that before." Big Bobby twisted his body, squeezing between the seats to kneel beside Delphina. He put his arm behind her head. "Rest against me."

"Now let me see where we are," Marcus commanded of Delphina. "This ain't no time to be shy. Del...lemme see. Okay, I see the top of the head. Looks like some black curly hair. Lincoln, go light a fire against that knife of yours. We need to make sure it's sterilized. Mitchell, sing us one of your prayers. Can you reach Maybelle?"

Lucille added, "Yeah, maybe we can have a little music to distract and welcome this little one into the world."

Delphina let out a howl. Lincoln covered his ears and made his way off the bus. "I need a smoke. This is getting on my nerves. Damn, how much longer we gonna be here!"

Lucille snapped, "As long as it takes. So stop askin'. That baby don't have no TOBA contract to be anywhere but out of his mama. So we just got to wait until he or she makes their debut."

"Here we go! Mitchell, play something. Maybe if that baby hears some ragtime, he might jump to it."

Between clenched teeth, Delphina squeezed out, "It ain't no boy. I know it."

Lincoln leaped back on the bus. "Man, that sky is getting dark. All we need now is for it to start raining."

A crackle of lightning and a clap of thunder suddenly honored his request and the entire group stopped abruptly, staring wide-eyed at each other.

"Shit, man, why'd you have to go and say that," Big Bobby barked.

Another clap of thunder and rain fell in big fat drops. Lincoln took out his trombone to accompany Mitchell and a little baby girl was welcomed into the world with the sound of ragtime, jazz and the rumble of thunder.

Delphina cradled her baby in her arms. "This little one finally made her entrance and just look at her. She's so shiny and pretty. I think I'll name her Diamond."

Mitchell stopped playing and pulled a flask out of his jacket pocket. He raised it up in the air. "Here's to our newest troubadour, Diamond!" He took a swig and passed it around.

Big Bobby shook his head and blew out a stream of breath

before he squeezed out, "Damn, Mitchell! What the hell is this shit?"

Mitchell cackled, "Shh, Daddy. There's children present."

Lincoln took an extra gulp from Mitchell's flask as the rain picked up speed and turned into a downpour. "I hope it don't be a washout. Baby or no baby, we got to get to the show."

Everyone fawned over the infant and showered little Diamond with gifts. For the next several stops on the tour—shows in Louisville and Lexington, Kentucky—Delphina and Diamond stayed in Lucille's room. After having Delphina and the baby checked out by a local doctor—who refused pay because he was an old family friend of Mitchell's—Lucille wouldn't allow Delphina to help with anything and commanded she stay put to care for her baby within the confines of their boardinghouse, which generally catered to a Negro clientele. No one seemed to mind Delphina and Diamond's presence and went out of their way to make sure mother and daughter had all they needed from clothes to food to money.

The little girl rarely made a fuss, only to eek and gurgle before falling into a serene sleep in her mother's arm, or on Lucille's bed buffeted by quilts and feather-down pillows, or even when nestled in a dresser drawer lined with silk and satin sashes underneath soft blankets. The infant seemed content being held by so many who declared themselves aunts and uncles—not only the Troubadours, but boardinghouse proprietors, maids, cooks and kitchen help, chorus girls, singers, orators, stagehands, jugglers and every other sort of performer that shared billing. All may have wondered but dismissed asking any questions about the two young women, one with a fresh baby snugly wrapped against her chest, and their strange entourage of dusty musicians riding into town in a chugging, dilapidated bus. The life of entertainers on the road made for sometimes eclectic and inventive out-of-necessity bedfellows.

Collecting themselves over an afternoon breakfast at the Supreme Diner as they often did before and after tour stops in the central parts of Kentucky, Marcus brought them together to assess and correct the act and announce the next round of upcoming shows. It was mostly a recovery session from the previous night's reverie and gambling. Everyone mindlessly hummed through Marcus's account of any changes in the show, hotel, boardinghouse or other accommodations, and assignments or union news. This time Marcus included the name of a nurse to check out the baby.

"I think our little Diamond loves this life," Mitchell said in an uncharacteristic manner. "You better watch out—this one might run away to join the circus when she gets older. Before you go, I got something for you." Mitchell handed Delphina a package wrapped in tissue paper and tied with pink ribbons. "It's for our sweet little girl who is already so pretty with them light brown little ringlets."

Delphina unfolded the paper to find two pink crochet blankets and handmade yellow bonnets stitched with the letter *D*. "Why, you little stinker! And I mean you, Mitchell. They're beautiful."

Marcus, Lincoln and Big Bobby gasped as the thin, light-skinned man blushed. "I know a few women who do this sort of thing. Since I guess now we're Miss Lucille's Black Troubadours and Baby Nursery."

Delphina gave Mitchell a kiss on the cheek as a thank-you. It was the first time anyone had seen the man blush. "Well, lil' mama, you gonna need a lot more than that. That baby can't be sleeping in no suitcase."

Marcus scratched his head. "Let's just get to the next town and see what kind of options we have."

Delphina looked up, her eyes wide. "Our options? I can't stay with you guys anymore?"

Lucille chimed in. "Stop worrying, Del. That's not good for

your milk." She stretched out her arms, motioning for Delphina to hand her the baby. "Let me see that baby girl. We're not heartless—not even Mitchell." Lucille stared lovingly into the little cherub's blue eyes. "How much trouble can one little angel named Diamond be? You can stay with me until we figure it out."

At that point, Lincoln, with a big broken-toothed smile, slid up to the group and plopped a paper sack on the table. Inside were baby clothes, blankets, booties and a silver rattle.

"Lincoln, where in the world did you get all this?"

Lincoln tugged on his collar and slid from one side of the table to the other before busting out into verse:

"I'ma tell you a story 'bout a fine little belle
That smiled so pretty that I almost fell
My heart pitter-pattered 'cause she was so fine
Till I seen her two crumb snatchers with three more behind
With all those chillins hanging round her hem
I knew she was the answer to our problem
She took me to her house
Fed me dinner and some stout
When the kids called me daddy
It was time to bow out
So I tipped my hat and I wiped my chin
Said I'd be right back when my ship came in"

Mitchell coughed out a half of a laugh, "Lincoln, you a bow-legged fool!"

The room was holding on to the day's unseasonal heat. Lucille moved around Delphina in their shared room to the open window, hoping a trickle of evening breeze would provide relief. Their only performance that day had been a matinee which was supposed to be a short show sandwiched between an all-female troupe of roller-skating jugglers and a stock company

production of a Dark Town Follies revival. The act ran un-
expectedly longer because the stock company never showed.
The theater owner, desperate for a replacement, pleaded with
Lucille and the Troubadours to give a longer performance, so
they complied and included the scantily clad skaters, who rolled
in circles and figure eights around them as Lucille sang. It was
fun. The theater owner was appreciative because the audience
didn't stomp out clamoring for their money back.

Lucille fanned her face. It was too hot, too moist, and the
room was too small for two women and a baby, trunks and
bric-a-brac. She watched Delphina, who was quietly smiling
at her little baby while tracing her fingers around the infant's
chubby cheeks. Lucille suddenly thought of her mother and father and had an urge to go to them.

"Delphina, you know you're going to have to do something.
The boys are right. It can't be healthy for little Diamond to
travel around like we do. You've got some decisions to make."

Delphina looked up from watching her baby nestle against
her breast. "You know when I met Diamond's father, he decided
he fell in love with me the moment he saw me. I wanted to get
married. He decided, without telling me, he didn't. Then he
decided that he didn't want me anymore. I should have known
better—I did know better. I fell for the oldest trick in the book.
But that little bird fluttered in my stomach and my head. Them
wings was hitting all around my rib cage and elsewhere…mak-
ing a ruckus so I couldn't hear myself think straight." The baby
suckled loudly. "And here we are."

"Yeah, and here you are…you and little Diamond. You don't
think you'll ever see that man again?"

"Not if I can help it. *I* decided that."

"Now, Delphina, are you really sure about the name?"

"Diamond? Yes. She's beautiful and she's gonna shine. I just
know it. She's gonna be just like you, Miss Lucille. She gonna
be out there outshining them all."

"Well, gal, like all women, black or white, we know. We really know. That bird fluttering inside you was trying to tell you something that you already knew. You was digging for the wrong worm."

"Well, Lucille, that's not going to happen no more. Not today, not ever."

"Ooo, you sound so sure about that."

"I have never been more sure. Luce, let me tell you something that I've never told a soul…not even Big Bobby, and I've told him just about everything about me. I woke up one morning—what seems like a million years ago and then sometimes only yesterday—on the street, in the gutter. There was a rotting smell all around me. I threw up from the stench. Then I realized the stench was me. I had been drinking of course—I remembered that much. I didn't remember how I got there or who I had been with. Some man who said I was pretty, probably. I also remember looking down at the broken buckle of one of my shoes and my torn stockings… I don't know why I can't get the sight of my filthy broken shoes out of my mind…but it was then, I knew. I knew I had to change—not only because I woke up in such a pitiful state, but because nobody came to look for me. Nobody cared enough to take me home, clean me up and tuck me in my bed. I knew I couldn't let anyone, not even myself or the pain from my past, ever put me in that position again—on the sidewalk, tossed aside along with the rubbish. I haven't taken a drink since and I decided that from that point I'm not going to wait until some brother, uncle or husband decides my life for me."

"Good for you, Del. Your baby needs you now. This is your family right here. You're one of us now and this little troupe of misfits will help where we can. But this little one needs a—"

Delphina cut her off. "You know what? I don't want anyone else's steps to follow, I just want to feel my own way through. I want a life filled with unexpected surprises, like this little one here."

"Girl, you're talking like you're drinking now. A baby shouldn't be no surprise. Didn't someone tell you about how they come? You fuck, you make babies. That's how it's done. No surprises there. The only surprise I want is the type of flowers thrown at my feet every night."

"Oh, come on, Luce. There's got to be more to life than that. Don't you want to find that special man? Get married? Have a batch of children one day?"

Lucille shook her head from side to side. "I don't..."

"I know about you and Marcus."

"What do you mean?"

"C'mon, ain't no one here lost their sight. We all know. I knew within five minutes of meeting y'all. When you were 'bating on whether or not I should come along with the Troubadours."

"He's been married to Rose for some time now and he ain't letting her go. My dream...it's in someone else's hands."

"For now, sister, but not for long. You keep going. There's an unexpected turn in the road coming."

"I don't have no choice but to go on—I can't believe I'm saying this, but—with or without Marcus. It feels like he's always been there for me,"

Delphina added, "He'll always be there for you. Always. Rose or no Rose, I believe that. See, chin up, girl, that's the bright spot."

Lucille responded. "If nothing else, I have optimism in spades. My daddy is one of the biggest dreamers I know. I got it from him. My mother, not so much. They argued so much I wanted nothing but to get away. Now, don't get me wrong, they fought, but I know they love each other fiercely. When Marcus came into our lives the arguments between my mother and father lessened a bit."

"It was just me, my brother and three sisters. I was the baby," Delphina said wistfully. "My mother died when I was quite young, but what I remember her the most is her smell—her breath smelled like a garden of roses. Me and my sisters would follow her into the woods to 'pick medicine' as she would call it. You know the herbs I always have with me? It's all because of my mother. She taught me how to find leaves, roots and herbs that cure just about anything. She showed me ones to avoid and how to spot fairy circles that surrounded the trees. She'd mark trees with red, blue or yellow ochre, drawing symbols so we wouldn't forget which tree gave what remedy. She told us everything came from the mother and the plants were our brothers and sisters. I didn't understand it then, but I do now. The family will always nourish us if we respect, honor, nurture and treat it kindly. I plan to do that for Diamond. Maybe someday someone will do that for you too."

Lucille smiled. "I've got something for you, Delphina. Well, it's for Diamond, really." She reached into her pocket and pulled out some gold coins. "There's one for twenty and a couple of one-dollar ones that look like they're from the St. Louis World's Fair. It's not a lot, but my daddy gave me a handful of coins for good luck when I first went on the road. I don't know where he got them from—we never had much and were always traveling in a wagon from place to place. But he said to only use them when I was in great need. I guess turn it into a bank for some real paper money. I'm giving you a few now. You got that little girl to take care of and maybe this will help pull you out of some difficulty that may lay ahead… And I appreciate all that you've done for us Troubadours."

"Lucille, I can't take this from you. Y'all took me under your wing when I was at my lowest point. You were there when my little girl made her entrance into the world."

Lucille gently pulled Delphina's arm toward her to push the money into her hand. "Don't be silly. This is what Troubadours do."

22

St. Louis, Missouri

After two weeks of routine and uneventful performances, zig-zagging from Memphis, then back to Louisville and Cincinnati, when the bus pulled up to the stage door of the Booker T. Washington Theatre, the entire troupe filed out with drooping, tired faces of a drunken stupor. It was the first time any of them had played the house. The expectations for the venue were high considering the location near the train station and the big fanfare for its opening from the Colored Knights of Pythias parade a few years ago. There were also glowing reviews of a budding local star, Josephine Baker, who made a splash at the colored revue. Except for a few baby sneezes from Diamond, everyone silently stood leaning against the bus staring up at the theater.

"It looks a bit shabby. Are you sure this is the place?" Lucille wheezed out with a yawn.

"Oh, don't worry," Marcus said assuredly. "It's glamorous enough inside and it will be packed. You'll get an armful of roses for sure."

Mitchell said softly, "Marcus, where are we staying? I need to lay my head on something soft for a second." He couldn't even rustle up enough energy to be his old cantankerous self.

"Let me see, Mitch. I'll go in and speak with the manager. Lucille, you want to come with me?"

Lucille stared into the darkness where the stage manager told them they could find a dressing room. It was a dark corner under a stairwell filled with old sets, warped wooden boards, posts, ropes and sandbags carelessly strewn as if long forgotten. Cool air whispered from underneath a metal door which had been hastily sealed shut with a crooked line of rusty nails protruding dangerously from a cracked two by four.

She looked over at Marcus with raised eyebrows. "Is this our dressing room?"

Marcus stared back sheepishly. The color that burst in his face made it easy to see that he was embarrassed but trying desperately to come up with something to make the best of it. "Well, Lucille, I'm not quite sure. The places that are close by where all the other acts stay is booked solid. I thought we might find something along the way—and I will find something. Until then, the boys can change and rehearse on the bus."

"You know Mitchell ain't going to like that."

"I'll take care of Mitchell. You can stay at Miss Delia's when we're done. It's a little ways from here so we won't be able to go there between acts."

"Dammit! What about food? I'm starving and I got to pee. Did they leave us a colored bucket somewhere?"

"I'll send Delphina out for some sandwiches. Or I can ask one of the boys to get some dinners and bring them back here."

Lucille threw up her arms in frustration. "Marcus, why are we here? TOBA said we would receive top billing wherever we went. We're nothing but chasers here on this bill, a far cry from the top. The only audience we're going to see are the stragglers we have to chase out. Being pushed in the dark corner having to expose all my private parts to anyone who passes by while those damn comedians get their own dressing room... well, that ain't nowhere near the top. In fact, we're going in the opposite direction. I feel like I'm back on that old, rickety wagon. Marcus, I ain't doing this."

"We have to do this. It's in the contract. If we miss one date, they'll drop us for sure. C'mon, Lucille... I fought so hard for us to get here, let's just get it over with. The next stop will be better. Listen, I know it's hard for now. But this is just the beginning. It happens to all the big stars, everyone goes through ups and downs."

Marcus threw off his jacket, rolled up his sleeves and began to move things around. "Look... I can move this set here to make a little space where you have privacy. And wait..." He ran off into the dark and swiftly returned with a lantern. "Now we have light! I'm going to find some more lanterns and I think... Well, it ain't a palace, but we can make it nice." He tried to sound convincing. Lucille stood with her arms crossed, shaking her head as her foot tapped the ground.

"And look at this." He waved his hand toward the nails protruding from the wood door. "You have something to hang your costumes."

"Marcus, this is some shit and nothing is going to make it look or smell pretty."

Delphina arrived moments later. "Oh no, this won't do at all." She handed Diamond, whose eyes were wide as she contently sucked on her fingers, to Lucille. "Let me see what I can do."

Delphina returned with the stage manager. She waved her hand around and without saying a word the manager nodded and left. He then returned and signaled the group to follow. They paraded through a labyrinth of hallways and up back stairwells until they reached a small dusty room in the attic.

"I'm not coming all the way up here to give you your cues,

so you'll need someone stationed to come and get you. You'd have been better off downstairs by the fire door if you ask me. But your mistress said you needed privacy because of your baby. This is the best I can do. If you don't like it, take it up with the union."

Lucille, Marcus and Delphina stood staring at each other as the manager stomped off, his diminishing footsteps echoing against the high rafters. Lucille patted Diamond, who gurgled and blew bubbles, wriggling out of her blanket.

"Where are the other acts on the roster? Even the animal performers have better accommodations," Lucille pointed out.

"Well, we're here through the week. Let's just get these shows over with. I'll talk to Mr. C.K. about this and have him take this place off the roster."

"Don't worry, Lucille. Listen…" Delphina sang out a note. "Great acoustics, right? I'll have one of the guys take your trunk over to the rooming house. You can get dressed over there and we'll use this space just for touch-ups and warm-up. I'll feed Diamond and get a girl to watch her. Then I'll come up here to help. I can be the runner to let you know what's happening onstage."

Mitchell burst into the room, clutching the doorknob for support, huffing and puffing from the long climb up the stairs. "Whew…they told me that you moved to the top. I thought that's great…they moved us to the top of the roster…or the headliner…maybe getting our name on the marquee." He caught his breath. "I didn't know they meant squirreling you away in the attic. Honey chile! If I stretch up a bit, I think me and the good Lord can shake hands. And it's hot as Hades up here!"

"You didn't have to come way up here, Mitch. You just need to make sure they ain't dropping Maybelle in the streets, or else you'll have kindling to play on."

"My pretty little Maybelle is just fine. She done had a protective spirit placed on her years ago. Anyone that does harm to my girl will be cursed for life!" He winked at Delphina, who smiled and winked back.

"Look, everybody!" Marcus threw off a dusty tarp covering an old upright piano. "Mitchell, what do you think?"

"Well, look-ee here!" Mitchell was drawn to the piano as if the instrument called out to him. He ran his hand down the keys, which produced a few twangs and empty notes. Mitchell bounced his finger on one of the silent keys. "It's in pretty bad shape, but I know what to do with this gal here."

"Lucille, you certainly haven't got much to say anymore," Marcus said.

"I'm just thinking. Ain't nobody going anywhere. Del, that baby is still on the tit. She needs to be with her mother. Don't leave her with no strangers. We're all gonna stay right here and have a party till it's time for us get onstage. We'll make the best of this situation for sure. I'll have Lincoln go get us some sandwiches and some cold drinks and we'll celebrate being at the top!"

The group let out various sounds of approval, agreeing to make do with the attic space.

Mitchell tinkered with the piano until Lincoln came back with everyone's dinner. As Big Bobby warmed up, Lucille started into a new song.

"Don't have a spot to call my own
Don't have a pot to call my home
Don't have no window
Don't have no floor
Not even a lover waitin' at the door
Don't have a dime to make a rhyme
Don't have no place to even waste my time
Don't have no shoes
I got the everyday blues
The ain't-nowhere-they-love-me blues

But you won't find me sad
I ain't got nothing to lose
'Cause I'm right here at the top
And gonna sing 'til I pop
While I got the ain't-nowhere-they-love-me blues"

"Yeah, that's sayin' a lot, sister. We gonna put that into the show!"

Even before the final curtain call, the entire cast seemed to be ready to party. The moment the show ended, a flurry of dust fell from the rafters, sprinkling the now-empty stage below as performers, still dressed in costume and plastered in stage makeup, charged up the stairs to the attic for an after-party. What better place to unwind than in the theater, where performers dedicated a chunk of their lives to doing what they craved? Lucille and the Troubadours were the most popular act of the night, playing standing ovation after ovation. The attic, Lucille's dressing room, was now a makeshift cabaret and the place to be.

The attic was hot in so many ways. Two chorus girls clad in flimsy outfits with sequins around their hips found their way into Lincoln's lap and spent the time tickling his chin while he riffed on his trumpet. Delphina returned from taking Diamond to the boardinghouse and sat close to Big Bobby while he walked the small space with his trombone, filling in the impromptu melody. The show's headliner, a white crooner who performed a minstrel number in blackface, sat next to Mitchell while they harmonized familiar tunes at the piano. Even the stage manager stood in the doorway dancing with one of the girls.

With so many people in the space, it was hot as blazes, but the crowd didn't seem to care. Fueled by alcoholic innovations slipped into glasses or flasks, women and men stripped down to the bare necessities as sweat stains blossomed on silk shirts and dresses and plastered hair against their cheeks. They pushed aside crates and opened the windows to let the elevated temperatures flow out into the cool night. They danced in sheer nakedness while Mitchell hammered out tunes by the light of the moon, which shone brightly and winked at the drowsy sun.

In the midst of the ballyhoo, between writhing bodies, Lucille glanced over at Marcus. He was across the room talking with an extremely tall, nattily dressed man she had never seen before. Lucille was amazed at how cool the man looked dressed in a tan-colored jacket, vest and pants with a tightly buttoned shirt collar. The man held a matching bowler and leather gloves in his hands. Lucille felt a rush of heat just looking at him, but nary a drop of sweat escaped from the man's head. Marcus's shirt collar was unbuttoned and his sleeves were rolled up. He leaned against the slanted beam of the ceiling, his body relaxed and his movements animated. It was obvious that he'd had too many sips from the passed-around flasks. Lucille caught his eye. He smiled and then laughed out loud when she mouthed, *So this is the top?*

It might have been the heat, the joyful crowd or the slow burn of the gin, but watching him throw his head back and laugh freely, along with the blare of the music that tugged at her body and bounced along with her heart, despite everything she knew, she couldn't help but be drawn to him. She crossed the room to stand next to him, interrupting a conversation about the state of theater for those in the laugh trade. Comedians who traveled from bar to bistro to theater, borrowing jokes, lines and far-fetched stories to keep a restless, consuming audience interested, ended up resorting to pratfalls and slips so hard on the body that the most talented retired with broken bones and backs. Marcus wrapped an arm around Lucille's shoulders.

"Here's my girl. She can sing any one of those Sophie Tuckers under a table, but sheesh, I can't get her the high-paying gig she deserves. At least, not yet. Lucille, meet Mr. Thomas Mulgrew. He's got his eyes on the prize, just like me."

"She's a looker, all right! How do you do, mademoiselle!"

"Luce, we're both gonna be big-time producers, right, Tommy? 'Cept, I'm going to get there first," Marcus teased. "My Lucille and her troubadours are way above the rest of the talent out there."

Mr. Mulgrew, flashing a wide grin, magically whipped out a business card and handed it to Lucille.

Lucille, more interested in the man who still had nary a bead of perspiration on his face despite the wool bowler perched on top of his head, tapped the card against her fingernail. "Eye on what prize, might I ask?"

Marcus gave a big belly laugh while landing a playful punch to the man's side. "Tommy, you're not trying to steal my talent, are you?"

"Oh brother, you know I wouldn't do that! There's lots of great colored talents out there doing movies, records and shows. You know, like Sissle and Blake, and of course Bert Williams. They been pulling them in with dazzling reviews and making big money. Look at this." The man pulled a folded newspaper from his jacket pocket and pointed to a review. "This local girl was pushing a mop around only a year ago, then all of a sudden she's dancing naked in a chorus and someone spots her among all those other girls. Word is she'll be dancing in Paris any day now. Her success is a mystery to me but that's show business."

"Let me see that." Lucille snatched the paper out of the stranger's hands. "Marcus, read this! This should be me. Not the dancing-naked part, but they should be writing about me… and she's getting reviewed."

Mulgrew interjected, "Now, now, Miss Lucille, jealousy is not a charming trait. Josephine Baker has paid her dues."

"Jealousy? I'm not jealous. How can I be jealous of this skinny gal who can't sing? I'm talking about getting my chance to be onstage in front of thousands and working the big stages in Europe. I'm talking about getting off this Chitlin' Circuit. I didn't spend my life on the back of a wagon with my mama and daddy to keep rolling down the same dirt-covered roads."

Marcus added defensively, "This Chitlin' Circuit has clothed and fed you. And I might I add, got you three ovations tonight!"

"A lot good that does me. Look around, Marcus. We're stuffed in a blazing-hot attic."

"And look at the folks showing you all the love. Right here on Chitlin' Avenue."

"We need to be in New York. We should be in Harlem, now!"

Marcus pulled Lucille away from Mr. Mulgrew. "We'll get there, 'Cille. I keep telling you these smaller shows are important too. What if someone in this very room has the connection we need to spring you into stardom? Just a little more work, a little more patience."

Lucille sulked. "I've been patient, Marcus. I've played every single show with hardly anything to say about it. Or show for it, it seems."

"I thought Paris was your big dream, not New York."

"Well, sure, but knowing I could make it right here and now, *that's* what's going to get me to Paris in grand style. I'll conquer New York first, then it's only a matter of time. I just know it!"

"Remember when I told you showbiz has its ups and downs? This here isn't a down. Look around at this room. All these people are here for *you*. Don't lose sight of that."

"No, Marcus, they're here to tip a few."

"Lucille, I told you we're close. There's always gonna be another act or another star, but there's only one Lucille Love."

Lucille glanced at the swaying crowd, all enjoying themselves to the sounds of her band. Several folks had come up to congratulate her for a great show before the small gathering turned into a full-blown party.

As people started fading out, Lucille and Marcus stayed behind, rehashing her dream, sharing favorite memories of being
on the road. They talked until the sky turned from deep velvet blue to lavender, and cotton walrus clouds floated over the
gray skyline.

Somewhere among the heat and too many sips—Lucille decided to toss aside any restraint and give in. She closed her eyes
and leaned in to kiss Marcus.

To her surprise, he kissed her back.

His kiss was like chugging cool water. A chilling sensation
passed her lips, slid down her throat and exploded in her stomach. One kiss couldn't quench her thirst for more. Her mother's
words rang in her head: *This is a sin.* But Lucille didn't care
what it was. It was Marcus and she had loved him since she was
a little girl, wishing for another place to be. A shinier place far
away from the bumpy back road, the handmade garments and
the silly bows her mother continually tied around her braids
even when her father agreed she had outgrown them. Lucille
loved Marcus the moment he asked her what she wanted. His
kiss was all she wanted. His rough hands gripping her shoulders was all she wanted. His warm chest against hers was all she
wanted. His warm breath against her cheek was all she wanted.
Until she was shaken from her longing.

"No, we can't." Marcus backed away.

"Yes, we can. It's okay. Marcus, I love you."

"I promised your father and mother. I promised…"

She stopped him before he could say her name. "Listen to
me now. You and I know what's going to happen between us."

"Luce, promises were made. I made a promise to your parents. I made a promise to Rose. I made…"

"Stop right there," she said quietly. "Don't you love me?"

"I do, Luce. I love you, but…"

"But? But? There is no but. We love each other so that should
be enough. I'm sorry for Rose. I truly am. She should get a

but, not me. She let you go. I wouldn't have. If you wanted to find fame and fortune, I wouldn't have stayed at home like she did, I would have been on the road with you. *We* would've been finding fame and fortune together. My mother and daddy never left each other's side despite what was going on—that's love. Marcus, that's exactly what you and I have been doing all along, right?"

"There were extenuating circumstances which I can't explain to you. Rose is my wife. We jumped the broom and made it official before God and family. I can't shake that off or take it lightly."

"You told me all that before. I know you love me, Marcus. I can feel it."

"Lucille, you are beautiful. You're clever. And you are so, so remarkably talented. But if we do this, I couldn't be your manager anymore. You've got to know that. I can't manage you… and there is nothing I want to do more."

Lucille sniffed. "I see. You love me but you love being my manager more. I get it."

Marcus looked up to the ceiling and shook his head. He turned to her. "I know I asked you this when we very first met, but I need to hear you right here, right now. What do you want, Lucille?"

Lucille took a deep breath, recognizing Marcus was making a desperate attempt to change the subject. "You mean besides you? The same thing that I told you then. I want to be free— to choose what I sing and how I sing it. I don't want to follow notes that were already written, I want to write my own. I want people to feel the same way I do when I sing. The only way to do that is to fling myself out there in so many directions the crowd must breathe me all in. Every night, every performance, until they are so filled up with me they won't have any choice but to bust out with applause. Besides you, that is love for me. And their love, along with all your hard work, is going to take me across the oceans and back again as a star! I want it even more now."

"I see. You've changed since the Traveling Loves, but maybe not all that much," Marcus teased with a wink.

Lucille added. "Only one thing has changed, and I don't know how this is going to fit into anything I just said. But after seeing Delphina and Diamond, I do want a baby someday. I want a family. Sometimes, I want to get fat so that the dressmakers will have to let out my dresses and I can hold three or four children in my arms."

Marcus's eyes widened. "These dreams keep getting bigger and bigger…"

"But not before I do a picture or two, or a couple of revues. And I want to play the big palaces in Europe. I want folks to talk about me with stars in their eyes. My daddy didn't raise no foolish girl. Until that time comes, I'm being careful, believe me. Careful about everything but you."

"Then listen carefully, Luce. To reach the stars we've got to be everything for each other—including careful."

23

Lucille sat in the last row of the Pekin Theater. It was one of the most luxurious venues that they had ever performed in on the circuit. Dark velvet curtains draped the stage and behind them came the distant sounds of people moving around. They were here for a three-week run. Lucille's heart fluttered at the thought that this venue could mark the start of a higher level of performing. She hadn't seen the dressing rooms but she imagined a more glamorous setting than the cold ramshackle rooms that posed as accommodations.

Lucille and the Troubadours weren't scheduled to go on until later that evening, but it became her custom to get to the theater early to get a feel of the house. She had to see the stage just as the patrons would. It was hot and humid in the auditorium. She could only imagine how hot it would be when folks came filing in, talking and laughing, possibly on their third or fourth sip of gin. She needed to get a sense of the bodies, scented with Verveine and Empress Violette eau de toilette or rosewater. She imagined the whiff of Chanel from the top hats who glided past an unacknowledged class on their way to front-row seats. Sitting in the back of the theater, Lucille imagined the lit footlights, and waves of energy as the audience waited in anticipation of being entertained.

The upstage lights snapped on, illuminating the bare slanted stage with stark white light. Not wanting to be seen, Lucille pushed further back into her seat.

Five men ranging in age and size stepped loudly from the wings. Well-worn tap shoes announced their every move. A barrage of *clickety-clack-clack-clack* filled the belly of the theater. Their jackets and caps flew in all directions as all of the men peeled down to unbuttoned vests and loosely tucked shirts. They floated around the stage, laughing and greeting each other in swift, haughty combinations of turns, flaps, slides and time steps before moving into an inverted V pointing upstage. Lucille knew who they were. They were billed as the Five Top Hats, five handsome and dapper brothers who traveled the circuit as tap dancers and singers. They were known for a smooth act combining acrobatics, juggling and dancing to the most popular upbeat tunes.

At the top of the V was Ginger Reynolds, the youngest of the five brothers. Lucille heard he made a habit of swaying innocents and breaking hearts. Many a dancer swore they were the sole apple of his eye, only to find out that he had tasted the fruits of the whole chorus line.

Lucille couldn't take her eyes off Ginger. From the last row in the theater, she could see the angles of high tan cheekbones dipping into dimples that appeared and disappeared. He was slender but muscular as if he had done plenty of manual labor. As he stood on his mark, mouthing an eight count and tapping out a rhythm combining a flurry of fast and slow beats, he exhibited a cool flexibility and a sense of muscular control. He finessed each step and turn, cutting straight lines with his lean body with precision. He did several quick turns, and each time he landed with a clear double tap on his heels and a quick hop, transferring his weight to his toes.

One of the Top Hats barked out to the group, "C'mon, guys, let's get this number down so we can rest up for tonight. The band will rehearse on their own time once they get here. Cecile, step lively, and Ginger, watch your timing and make sure you stay with the rest of us. We're not following you. Just 'cause you're center, this ain't your showcase!"

Ginger waved his hand and playfully shot back, "Forget you, Lloyd. I've been doing this since the crib. I know what to do."

The Five Top Hats went into vocal warm-ups and after a few scales, Cecile snapped his fingers and counted off to begin singing a cappella until the rest of his brothers joined in:

"Don't you want a man
Don't you want a man
Don't you need a man like me
A man that won't leave you on your doorstep cry'n
Drain your bank account and leave your heart a sigh'n
One who'll wrap you up in diamonds and furs
Keep a smile on your face and make your whole world a blur
A man who holds you close and lights your cigarettes
And provides more fire than all the rest
Don't you want a man
Don't you want a man
Don't you need a man like me"

Holding on to their collars, the Top Hats turned to the side, each striking a dramatic silhouette, their shadows casting long angles across the length of the stage. In unison, they took a deep lean back into a crazy low backbend while Lloyd counted out a long eight count until the tops of their heads were only a few feet from the floor. All this was done while the other Top Hats held a clear note in perfect harmony.

As they moved through the number, Lucille sat up to get a better look at the men onstage. But it didn't matter because the Top Hats stopped midstep when a short burly white man dressed in a lumberjack jacket and trapper cap came running from front of the house.

"Lloyd, you Top Hats got a problem." He ran down the aisle without noticing Lucille in her seat. Standing at the front of the stage, he scratched his head. "You guys ain't got no band! Management just got a telegram sayin' they stuck somewhere between Pittsburgh and God knows where. They might not make it here tonight."

"Damn!" Ginger slammed his foot to the floor with a loud metal clack. "I was counting on them to do this new number to the fullest. I don't want us to be looking like a bunch of fools tonight…not looking good as I do."

One of the Top Hats sneered, "Can you take a moment to stop talkin' 'bout yourself, Ginger? This is the worst news we could hear right now and that's all you thinking about?"

"Did you hear me, fellas? I said you boys don't have no band!" The man waved the stub of his cigar in their direction. He plopped it in his mouth and began chewing on it before continuing, "That's the priority right now, not your swinging dick, man!"

"Maybe my Troubadours can help you out." Lucille strode out of dark, down the aisle and up to the edge of the stage. "If you need a hot band for your—I've got to admit—your neat little number, I might be able to help you."

Lloyd planted his hands on his hips. "Well, if it ain't Miss Lucille. The Little Girl with the Big Voice."

"Yes, the one and only," Lucille shouted back.

"Ooo…she's not so little and I don't see no girl nowhere. I like it when a pretty woman rides in on her horse to save little old me." Ginger grinned down at her.

"Stop it, Ginger, this here is serious business," Sam admonished. "Thank you kindly, Miss Lucille. Is Mitchell playin' to-night?"

"Mitchell is always playing. How much are you paying?"

"The going rate, but we'll pay extra for the last minute."

"Yes, you will."

The burly man clapped his hands. "As theater manager, all I know is you Top Hats have a contract to play tonight. I don't care who you get just as long as you sing and dance for the audience that paying good money to see this all-star coon show."

"What you say, mister?" Ginger charged up toward the man with his fists bared, but Sam held him back and the other brothers formed a semicircle that put them within arm's length of Ginger.

Sam turned to the man. "Listen, ain't no cause for any worry about this at all. We are quite aware of our obligations."

The manager lifted his head and stared at the group of men before taking a step back. He whipped out the cigar squeezed between his lips and rolled his tongue around his mouth. "Well, just make sure all you boys are here, on the dot, and ready. Ain't no dressing rooms for Negroes tonight." He called out to the crew that had been moving around behind stage. "Bob, you ready to lock up?"

An invisible voice floated out from nowhere, "We got a few sets to unload and a scene to block."

The squat little man turned to the Five Top Hats. "I think you all better go now. Your rehearsal time is over." With that, the manager walked up the makeshift ramp over the orchestra pit and straight through the five brothers to disappear behind the stage.

Ginger fumed. "Why you stop me, man! He can't speak to us like that. I want to clobber him."

"We all know what you wanted to do to him," one of the brothers interjected.

Another chimed in, "But you can't, we can't. You know the

score. TOBA can't save us from the chain gang. Just suck it up and we'll be on our way with money in our pockets in no time flat."

Without losing a beat, Lloyd turned to Lucille. "You're welcome to join in too, you know. We'd love to have a big voice like yours."

"I just might." With a sly smile, Lucille added, "I just need to make sure the Five Top Hats are really capable of keeping up with my top-notch boys."

Ginger, who had collected his composure, jumped in. "Whoa, wait a minute...the Five Top Hats always know how to please."

"Do you? That's not what I heard," Lucille chuckled.

"I said wait a damn minute. We've got more than enough time to get a band together. We don't need the Troubadours since Miss Lucille here seems to be raising doubts about our talent."

"Calm down. She's just teasing. Right, Miss Lucille? You're teasing...just pulling our leg." Lloyd, who seemed tired of all the controversy, leaned over to the other Top Hats and said in a loud whisper, "Don't annoy the lady—Mitchell would be as good as it gets."

Lucille smiled. "Oh, I'm sorry. I didn't mean to step on anyone's toes. Of course, I was just teasing. This new number is pretty good—really. You guys look really sharp and oh so debonair. You might want to speed it up, you know, give it some punch, make it a little more lively. I'm sure you can adjust the choreography."

Ginger rolled his eyes. "You gonna let this woman tell us what to do? Besides, we don't have no sheet music."

There was a beat of silence while the guys looked at each other before Lucille set them straight. "First off, Mitchell don't need no sheet music. Just hum a few bars and he'll take care of the rest. The rest of the band will follow his lead like they were born to do. Now, you need my boys or what?"

After a tense silence, Lucille threw her coat over her back and let it fall across her shoulders. "Take it up with my manager when you decide." She glided up the aisle and left the theater through the front of the house.

The street was busy with folks making their way to the rows of stores selling fine clothing, jewelry and linens, between banks and insurance companies. Lucille was smartly dressed with shiny new oxfords, compliments of the string of sold-out performances. Despite her appearance, she knew she would not be allowed into most of the shops without scrutiny. She kept walking while searching the faces of passersby. Marcus was supposed to meet her and take her to lunch, but he was nowhere to be seen. She watched cars speed down the cobblestone and thought, *I want one of those and a driver.*

Out of the corner of her eye, she saw a surprising sight— Delphina, with her arm in the crook of a well-dressed white man's, stepping into one of buildings across the street. Only hours ago, Lucille had just seen her and Diamond at the rooming house on the colored side of town. Now there she was, dressed in Sunday's best with a man that was definitely not Big Bobby.

Lucille ran across the street barely missing a couple of collisions with speeding cars. Delphina disappeared into a restaurant, one Lucille couldn't go into unless they had an entrance around the back—which she knew they didn't. She spotted a policeman coming her way but continued to peer in the window in an attempt to get a glimpse of Delphina. She felt a two-finger tap on her shoulder.

"A penny for your thoughts, ma'am?"

"Marcus! Thank goodness it's you. Did you see Delphina?" She didn't wait for a response. "I just saw that girl, all dressed up in one of my outfits. She's in there with some man I've never seen before."

"Luce, I don't know what you're talking about but whatever it is, it's none of our business. After all this time Delphina has proved herself to be nothing but a good friend to all of us. Let her be."

"Well, she's got some nerve sneaking around like this—"

Marcus interrupted playfully, "Let that woman live her life. As long as she keeps us in clean costumes and Big Bobby out of trouble, Delphina can do whatever she wants to do."

"Marcus, I need to know what's going on with her. She didn't mention—"

"Stop right there. She's a grown woman. Leave it be. You can't be in charge of everything and everybody. You sounding and acting like your mama, Evelyn Love. Let's just go get us some good food so we can be tip-top for tonight. I know just the place."

They made their way over to the side of town where the hustle and bustle quickened as groups of black men and women whipped in and out of banks, insurance companies, restaurants and even an auto dealership that served the city's colored population.

Lucille and Marcus passed a line of horse-drawn wagons loaded with seasonal fruit, pots and pans. They stopped to pick up a few apples and chatted with an elderly man that seemed grateful for their patronage and honored to serve the well-dressed pair. He greeted them with "What a handsome couple. You two look like you just stepped out of a movie screen."

Lucille thought, *I'll sing to all these shop owners! I'll sing to the laborer confined to this stretch of pavement, as well as the patrons that keep this community alive. This here color line traced around our people ain't gonna keep us down.*

They stopped at Peaches Restaurant and had a good helping of chicken and dumplings, steak and potatoes, and for dessert, pound cake and ice cream.

"Okay, Marcus." Lucille slipped her arm in his as they walked down the sidewalk. "What do you know about the Five Top Hats?"

Marcus replied, "Them brothers that dance and do some balancing? Well, I haven't seen them but I hear they're a class act. I do know that one of 'em actually burned a house straight down to the ground with their act. Really! He was juggling some flaming hoops. They make them boys pay the theaters a little extra for insurance now just because of it."

"Oh? Well, I met them this morning. They're in a pinch—they don't have a band for their performance tonight, so I offered the Troubadours. For a price of course."

"Is that right? Are you taking over my job?"

"Marcus, the manager said they'd lose their place if they didn't come up with a band by this evening. Even if that Ginger is asking for trouble, I think we should help them out. Good citizenship, you know."

Marcus rubbed his bottom lip. "Well, it is different. We've never accompanied a variety act before. And the Five Top Hats know how to put on a show."

"But Mitchell and the boys can too. Together, I think that will be one really fine time. Good publicity, right?" Lucille held her breath, hoping she hadn't overplayed her hand.

Marcus scratched his head. "I guess Miss Lucille's Black Troubadours are playing two performances tonight."

24

Lucille watched Delphina as she shook out her dresses and hung them on the dressing room screen. She wasn't sure how to approach the fact that she had seen her and a stranger having lunch at the restaurant downtown. Delphina hadn't said a word about it either, which meant she wanted to keep it under wraps.

"Delphina, the Troubadours have dragged you around all God's creation…"

"There is still more creation out there that we aim to conquer, right?" Delphina continued fiddling with the clothes, clearly nervous.

"I saw you today, Del."

"You saw me?"

"Yes, I saw you as big as the bright light of day. Out there on the street with your arm swinging from some man's. Marcus saw you too. He told me to let you be, so I didn't do what I wanted to do—catch up with you and get a better look at that man and particularly that fetching dress." Lucille sighed. "Listen, I'm not your mama and you can tell me to go mind my beeswax. All I've got to say—besides don't you ever take one of my Paris originals without asking—is you got to think about little Diamond now."

"Luce, there is no one that I think about more. But you know I don't have anything to give my baby girl."

"Well, maybe this life ain't for you right now."

Delphina froze. "What are you saying? Are you sacking me, now?"

"No, Del. I'm saying we got to have another plan for our girl here. Running around with some man isn't the answer. You're her mama, she don't have no other. It's hard, but there's opportunity all around you. Listen, my daddy taught me that you can always find something in your situation that can help you, that can benefit you. God lays it all at our feet."

"Lucille, don't you think I've been thinking about this? We're not in no covered wagon now and no colorful saying is gonna solve my problems. I need something that's gonna help me keep a good life for me and Diamond. And I think I know where to find him."

"Him?"

"Yes, him. I know exactly what to do."

"I hope you not thinking what I think you are. I remember exactly what you said—you weren't going to wait for no husband, uncle or brother to control your life. Delphina, you don't have to do anything right now."

"I've got to be realistic. I've got to—"

"Del, you can stay around the Troubadours as long as you need. Big Bobby certainly won't mind."

"No, he won't mind at all. But I know that as long as I'm here, Robert's gonna be in trouble. And I know what that trouble can lead to—"

Again, Lucille cut her off, "When will you admit that you're sweet on him? Real bad. I can tell because nobody, not even his mama, calls him Robert."

"Luce, I've got a plan. I knew you wouldn't like it because

it's contrary to what I said, but I got to play it out. I'll need that dress of yours and I'll have to leave Diamond here for the night."

"You going out with that white man tonight?"

Delphina flushed. "Oh, Luce, Montgomery—that's his name, but I call him Monte for short. He's an attorney from somewhere in Tennessee and he's rich on his own account. He just wants to have a little fun while he's here. He said he was thunderstruck when he saw me."

"Delphina, they all say that."

"No, it's true. Look." She reached into her pocket and pulled out a necklace with a green gem surrounded by shimmering white stones. "He gave this to me this morning and told me to wear it tonight when we meet for dinner."

"Oh my, that's nice, but that's the sort of thing they give girls who…"

"Lucille, don't ruin it for me, please. I know how it looks, but this is different."

"I don't like it. I don't like where this is going."

Delphina curled her hand around the necklace and angrily spit back, "I can't be waking up every morning just to scrub crumbs off someone else's breakfast plate. I can't."

"Okay, okay… You're certainly pretty enough and your figure done filled out nicely since you had that baby." Lucille sighed, not wanting to give in, but knowing that Delphina was tough. She could handle herself. "Wear that blue dress, the one with the matching cape. If you gonna go down, look good doing it. I'm not happy about it, but you seem to be fixed on doing this. Just know, the Troubadours are here for you if things don't work out."

Delphina wiped tears from her cheek. "It's going to work out. Splendidly. It must."

Later that evening, a very smartly dressed couple walked through Lucille's dressing room door. Delphina, her eyebrows riding high on her forehead, swung on the arm of the shiny white man Lucille saw in the street.

"My dear Miss Lucille, I would like to introduce Mr. Montgomery Garreau," she said with a sweeping gesture. "Monte, this is the incredible Miss Lucille. You'll be hearing more about her as her star is on the rise."

From the time he took her hand, Lucille knew she didn't like him. His face was too smooth. His pink lips too soft. His hair too meticulous and his eyes too blue. He was quite handsome; she had to give Delphina credit for that. And she couldn't shake the chilling jolt up the back of her spine that she had seen him before. Lucille smiled back at Mr. Garreau, knowing that Delphina was looking for her approval.

"Delphina told me what she was doing for you all and from the looks of your act it is money well spent. You're lucky to have such a wonderful patron and beautiful benefactress," Mr. Garreau said.

Lucille's mouth dropped open as she turned to give Delphina a quizzical look. Without acknowledging Lucille, Delphina kept her head up high. Her eyes flitted around the room, avoiding contact with Lucille.

Mr. Garreau, missing the facial exercises occurring between the women, continued, "I like when someone unselfishly gives of themselves to help those in need. It shows this little lady has big character."

Lucille nodded mechanically. "Yes, she is a wonderful—what you say—benefactress. And what about you, Mr. Montgomery Garreau? Do you have big character?"

He threw his head back as he laughed. "You, Miss Lucille, are truly something else. Please call me Monte. It's Lucille Love, isn't it?"

"Why yes, it is. No one ever calls me by my full name. Except for family."

"Oh sure, family. You close with your family, Miss Love?"

"Please, Monte, call me Lucille. Sadly, I haven't seen my family in quite a while. I'm working all the time. I do miss them terribly though."

"Where are you and your family from?"

Annoyed, Lucille sharply changed the subject. "If you'll excuse me, Mr. Garreau, and *Miss* Delphina. I must have a bit of solitude to prepare myself for the next show. *Miss* Delphina, you know these shows take a lot out of you afterward. We have another show tomorrow before we head out." Lucille fanned herself with her hand, feigning exhaustion. "We performers have to be on our toes. Right, *Miss* Delphina? Our benefactors wouldn't have it any other way—it's in our contract. You know about those, right, Monte?"

"Yes, I do. Contracts keep us honest. My daddy used to say men are measured by their honesty." Monte chuckled. "My daddy must have meant measured for a casket, 'cause they say he robbed a bank—how's that for an honest man! I'm not ashamed. I tell everybody about my family's past."

Lucille pretended to straighten her headpiece to hide her nerves. "Sounds like…an interesting tale."

Monte barreled on, "*I'm* honest enough to show I have nothing to hide. I hate family secrets, they get in the way of conducting sound, profitable business. Some of my family made a lot of money being rapscallions and some were saints—probably fewer of those though. Anyway, my daddy, he took a bag full of money from a bank in…in…oh, what was the name of that town? I can't ever remember it. But he never got a chance to spend it because he was found shot dead in an alleyway. They found his body underneath a cart, but they never found the money he stole."

"Oh my, Monte. No need to burden Miss Lucille with such picturesque tales of your family history. She's got to keep her head clear as a bell so she can give her best performance."

Lucille caught Delphina's glance and shot her an eyeful of

daggers before responding with an icy smile, "My benefactress is so right, Mr. Garreau."

Ignoring both women, Monte continued, "All the children in my family heard that story over and over again with a few embellishments as time went by, and my mama, who was delicate like Miss Delphina here, hated that kinfolk kept repeating that horrid story about my daddy. Most of my family thought it was a fitting ending for someone who didn't know anything else but thieving. But my uncle said he always wondered what happened to that money. That has bedeviled him up to this day. He always remembered one of his family members saying that someone must have robbed him in return. Ain't that funny? A robber getting robbed of the money they stole from somebody else."

Monte turned to leave before stopping short as if struck by lightning. "Oh, that's it. It was Evansville! Evansville, Indiana."

25

All the acts in the show were electric that night. The crowd burst out with laugh after laugh from rubbery comics who fell all over the stage between telling jokes and singing nonsensical lyrics. Miss Lucille and the Black Troubadours weren't slated to be onstage until later in the evening. Their reputation had finally reached second billing, which commanded a bigger slice of the door. However, after paying for room and board, pockets were still light, so the Troubadours were glad for the extra money that came with helping out the Five Top Hats, who were head-lining that night's event. The only exception was Mitchell, who cursed for hours about the added show. Despite his swearing, everyone knew he would do it. Anything to be with his darling Maybelle always seemed to turn the little man into a tower of power when he took command of the eighty-eight keys.

Watching the Top Hats and the Troubadours perform from stage left in the wings, Lucille spotted her muse, Aida, with turquoise baubles tucked in her billowing hair. Her brown skin was translucent as she twirled her leg around the ropes and slid down the drapes to land softly on the boards. The Top Hats and Troubadours were working well together, building to a crescendo of movement and jazz music. Aida's slender fingers motioned Lucille to come out from the dark. Lucille shook her head. Averting her eyes from her muse, she moved from tapping her foot to bouncing on the tips of her toes. Onstage, the Top Hats flexed with cheesy grins at the end of every sixteen bars and all, no matter age or physical stature, defied gravity as they leaped over one another outdoing the previous combination in their choreography.

Meanwhile the Troubadours were certainly earning their extra cash tonight. Mitchell, Big Bobby and Lincoln coaxed a flavorful hot sauce from their instruments. Sweat poured from every pore. Lincoln's trumpet blared out the melody, bouncing in his seat, his knees pumped and toes slapped the floor on the downbeat with his heel following suit on the upbeat. Big Bobby's trombone swung around Lincoln's melody while Mitchell's fingers hit chord after chord, dancing along the keys with his signature flare. The Troubadours improvised a rhythm reminiscent of a New Orleans celebration of the departed then rounded down to a Chicago jazz—style riff as if they had rehearsed with the Top Hats for days on end—a true feat for a group where no one besides Mitchell read sheet music. The sound spilled out from the heart and paid homage to their own style while feasting at King Oliver's table too.

As soon as Ginger took center stage, patting the floor with a dance sequence that required an impressive degree of balance and control, Aida returned. A swirling mass of teal silks trimmed in brocade, tempting Lucille with bare legs peeking out playfully. Aida soundlessly stepped with bare feet, gracefully arched her back and swayed her hips, blending with Ginger's chiming paradiddles which the audience rewarded with applause. Aida's moves were the treasures of *In Dahomey* dreams, purely and lusciously African. Together they recalled a multitude of tribes that danced to tell the story of time before ships intent on a manifest of human bondage landed on the African continent.

Aida whispered, *C'mon, make an entrance, girl! Show them folks the Black power of your hips that transcends every limited thought about all of us. Go on, teach 'em a lesson they'll never forget!*

An exhilarating zing went through Lucille's body as she focused her attention on Ginger, impeccably dressed, his sandy red hair gleaming under the light, tapping out a drumbeat.

It was then Aida's taunts from the opposite side of the stage finally hit their mark and lured Lucille out from beyond the velvet curtain.

"Ooo, go on, boys!" Lucille stepped out from the wings. She reached for the edges of her velvet cape and held it out like silvery wings stretching from her fingers. The beaded gold overlay of her yellow dress hit the lights and like tiny sparklers flashed her arrival.

"Hey, Top Hats, can I get a man like you?" Lucille shouted out as she dramatically posed in the circle of bright light. All five of the Top Hats, now standing in their V-shaped formation, whipped their heads in her direction.

"Why yes, ma'am!" Ginger called out and punctuated with a stylish turn, falling to his knees and sliding toward Lucille. He held out his hand. Lucille looked at the audience with a cutesy smile as if to ask their permission before she daintily accepted. The audience cheered and her muse rustled peacock tail feathers, leaped in the air and landed on the balcony rail.

Lloyd stepped forward, tugged on his vest and announced as if he was introducing royalty, "Ladies and gentlemen, the amazing Miss Lucille!" He waved his hand toward Mitchell, Big Bobby and Lincoln. "And the Five Top Hats have the pleasure and honor of accompanying her magnificent cadre of Troubadours to entertain you this evening."

As if rehearsed, four of the Five Top Hats exited the stage. Only Ginger remained. Lucille whispered in Mitchell's ear.

Mitchell nodded and signaled Big Bobby and Lincoln to follow, and her Troubadours broke into their first number, a sly Mamie Smith song that spoke of a good man never being down. Lucille sang directly to Ginger, following him as he smoothly glided through soft grapevine steps that ended with a sophisticated lean against one end of the piano. Not pleased with the dancer's freestyle use of Maybelle, Mitchell gave Ginger an evil eye from under his brim.

As Lucille sang, she moved closer to Ginger, who placed his hand on her hip to gently guide her across the stage. He then twirled around, stopping his spins on the opposite side of the stage. Ginger marched back toward Lucille in a series of teasing moves till he was close enough to give her a peck on the cheek as she sang the last note. He gave the audience a big grin as he received his prize—her kiss—before he bowed gracefully and glided offstage.

In a hail of applause, Lucille bowed for the fifth time while walking sideways to exit the stage where Ginger was waiting.

"Well, Miss Lucille, that was fun." He looked over at the Troubadours. "Thanks, guys! You all were great!"

Lincoln leaned close to Ginger. "Where do we pick up our money?"

"Stop in and see my brother Lloyd. He'll take good care of you."

Ginger turned back to Lucille. "Sugar, I'd like to take you to dinner. You know, to celebrate a successful collaboration."

"Yeah, that was fun, but not tonight, Ginger. This gal is tired."

"Maybe tomorrow then? I won't take no for an answer."

Before Lucille could answer, a chirping gaggle of chorus girls descended around Ginger. One of the women grabbed hold of Ginger's arm. "Hey, mister, you forgot about me? You were supposed to take me out next time you were in town. I haven't heard an invitation yet. What's a girl got to do to get one?"

Ignoring the inquiry, Ginger inched closer to Lucille. "So sorry, Miss Lucille, excuse me. How about tomorrow? I'm cooking. I'm going to find the freshest chicken, one right off the block. I'll give you a meal fit for a Dahomey queen."

Lucille waved a finger in the direction of the woman. "Well right now you've got RSVPs awaiting."

The next night, the Five Top Hats's band finally showed, letting the Troubadours off the hook. After the show, Ginger knocked on Lucille's dressing room door then shouted through the closed door, "I promised I'd cook dinner for you, or take you out for a meal tonight. I'm here to deliver on that promise. Are you decent?"

"Never," Lucille shouted back. "Just wait a minute, I'm changing. I'll be out in a moment."

"I'm hungry and thirsty. In fact, I'm dying out here. Come on, woman, you don't want to see a poor man die on your doorstep."

Lucille finished with the last bit of fresh powder and mascara and wriggled into her dress. She threw on her fox-collared cape and opened the door. Ginger was nowhere to be seen. She walked down the long hallway and spotted him casually leaning with his shoulder against the wall. Facing him was a pretty young thing who seemed so charmed that she had lost her gift of speech and could only giggle at whatever Ginger was proposing.

Lucille loudly cleared her throat and Ginger twisted around to face her. "Yes, yes, yes…this is the fabulous Miss Lucille Love." Ginger swung his arm out wide. "Miss Lucille, meet Lucy Banes, one of the newest chorus members in that knockout S. H. Dudley Smart Set revue traveling up and down the circuit. Isn't that funny? Two Lucys in one night. How lucky am I."

Lucille smiled politely, "Well, Miss Banes, please excuse me as I am starving and must eat. Break a leg!" She turned sharply and walked away.

Ginger followed practically on her heels. "Hold on. Hold on, now. I was just talking with her. She came up to me and asked me questions about the show and…"

"You do not have to explain anything to me, Mr. Reynolds. You're free to do whatever you like."

"What I'd like to do is take you to dinner. Please, Miss Lucille Love." His big hazel eyes were lit with mischief. They caught Lucille off guard, as did his wide smile that called out for a playful pat on his cheek. She could see why he had a reputation from Washington to St. Louis, and why all the girls found Ginger magnetizing.

It was after midnight, but there were a few restaurants open offering a full menu from the kitchen and plenty of impromptu entertainment from any number of performers who hadn't had enough of the stage. Between solos, duets, guitar riffs and even a sand dance from another hoofer that Ginger couldn't help but join in. The convivial atmosphere made up for the home-cooked meal Ginger promised. For hours they traded stories about their upbringing and found similarities as child performers. Ginger learned to dance as a child from his brothers. He had been on the road making money with them since he was seven years old. As children, he and his brothers performed as the Reynolds Rastas, part of an act called Holiday in Dixieland. He learned how to juggle, which was included in the act until a rather unfortunate fiery accident. He told Lucille he couldn't have wished for a better life.

At four o'clock in the morning, Ginger and Lucille walked along the quiet street toward Lucille's rooming house.

Ginger touched her hand. "Come to my place and I'll cook you a breakfast you won't ever forget."

She didn't pull away, but replied barely above a whisper, "Not tonight."

PART IV

**FROM GOLD TO DUST
AND BACK AGAIN**

26

Augusta, Georgia

Tall amber flames licked her fingers. Unable to move her feet, she balled her hands into fists to escape the wall of fire that was now rapidly approaching. Her father's eye patch floated up from the ground, landing on a pile of hay before black smoke rose from the pile. The smoke descended like a whale's mouth intent on swallowing her and her parents, while she slowly evaporated into darkness with a hail of bullets ringing her ears.

Lucille pulled her knees to her chest and tucked her head down as if to protect her heart. When she finally stretched out her bones ached.

"Lucille! Wake up!" Marcus's voice floated over her. "Woman, you're soaked."

"Marcus, wha–what are you doing here?"

"Luce, you were asleep, kicking and screaming. I was laying over there on the settee. You woke me out of the only five minutes of sound sleep I've been able to get. You all right?"

Breathing hard and still looking around to adjust to her surroundings, Lucille wiped the sweat from her forehead. "Oh, sorry. It's always the same dream, but I haven't had it in a long time. I'm in Hell or something. I'm in the middle of a fire but everything is upside down. Daddy and my mother are upside down. It's like they're hanging from the ceiling. They're shouting my name. Then there are gunshots."

Lucille patted her chest as if to jump-start her heart and her lungs. "I was calling for my daddy. I was so scared and the flames just got higher and higher...swallowing up both my parents." She rubbed her eyes. "My daddy is trying to tell me something. I just know it. I need to get word to him and Mother. I got to make sure they're all right. I need to get to a Western Union now."

"Now? It's not even..." Marcus felt his pockets for his watch, which was nowhere to be found. "I don't know what time it is but it ain't time to go to no Western Union. Let's wait for sunlight at least. I promise I'll go and get a message to them. I'm sure they're safe and tucked away in Oklahoma. In fact, I'll go and see them."

Now fully awake, Lucille sat up to face Marcus. "Go see them? What do you mean? Don't we have show dates lined up?"

"Lucy, there's no other way to say this but I've got to go home. Rose is asking me to come home."

Lucille stared back at Marcus. It had been a few peaceful weeks without fighting. They had even sat together, elbows and knees touching, laughing at Lincoln's silly rhymes and melodies. Maybe the memories of sweeter times together lessened the current friction between them. Maybe it was because her mind had been preoccupied with the lithe and acrobatic tap dancing of Mr. Ginger Reynolds. But between awakening from some dark fiery abyss and hearing *Rose*, *husband* and *home*, Lucille could only stare incredulously at Marcus.

"Now your wife wants you to come home from the road? Don't she know that the big house she's living in and the clothes on her back are because of the work you do on the road?"

"Lucille, Rose is all by herself. I've been away for so long. She needs to see me. I need to see her. We are husband and wife."

"Maybe she should come here."

"No. This life ain't good for her."

"But it's good for me? Oh, she's too good for a life of traveling from place to place, but it's okay for this low-life singer, right?"

"Lucille, stop. I didn't want to tell you this way. We've been best of friends up to this point…right? We fell asleep last night counting sheep as dear friends."

Lucille repeated slowly as if something was about to erupt, "Counting sheep as dear friends, huh…"

"Like I said, I can go see Rose in Chicago and take a few more days to go to Tulsa to look in on your parents. I'll send back word on how they are doing so you can rest easy."

Lucille swung her arms around Marcus's neck. "You can't go. I'll be by myself. I'll be lonely."

"C'mon, Lucille, you will never be lonely. You've got the boys and Delphina and Diamond. Besides, not only do I have to see Rose, but I've also got to take care of some business. Business that will guarantee us bigger houses, bigger pay and even some time off so that you can go see your parents too."

"Marcus." Lucille paused and took a deep breath as if gathering steam. "I thought… I really thought you were through with her."

Marcus sighed deeply. "Lucille, we've been through this. I married Rose because I loved her."

"Loved?"

"No…love her. Lucille, you don't understand what it means to be deeply in love with another human being."

"What?" Lucille pounded the bed with her fists. *"I do!"* She screamed, "I do know what it means to be in love with another human being. You're a human being, right?"

Marcus grabbed her wrists. "Listen, I'm not going anywhere

right now. I'm going to stay until we get to Augusta. Then I've got to head up to Chicago to see Rose. She needs me."

"I need you more."

Marcus eased off the bed. Walking backward, he grabbed his jacket and headed toward the door. "Lucille, get some sleep. If you need me, just open the window and call me. I'll sleep out on the porch. I think the night air will help me catch a few winks before sunrise. We'll talk more about this in the morning."

Lucille crossed her arms around her knees and buried her head. Her eyes stung. Marcus talking about leaving hit her like a sledgehammer. For so long, Marcus had done nothing else but cater to her every whim, protect her from unscrupulous advances, from theater owners who wanted her to sing for practically nothing or prance around on stage like a plantation picaninny. She knew he cared about her professionally, and she thought he had come around to caring about her romantically too.

Lucille let the tears fall. Marcus couldn't leave her. Not for his wife—or anybody for that matter. Her skin burned hot, then cold. She pulled the covers over her and, in the dark, felt the heaviness of hurt envelop her. She fell asleep and dreamed again of fire. This time she found herself in her mother's firm grip. Paralyzed and helpless, she was being dragged away from her father, who was calling for her from deep within the flames.

The steel blue light of early morning appeared through the windows and sent a shiver down her spine.

She jumped out of bed, wrapped her coat over her nightgown and pulled her cloche hat low. She pushed back the screen door, expecting to see Marcus asleep on the glider; however, the porch was empty. There was no trace that anyone had spent a sleepless night worried about their love life and career. The fear that she might lose Marcus prickled and stirred her stomach so much so that she couldn't help but throw up in the nearest corner.

★ ★ ★

Throughout the day, little things began to take their toll. The men picking up the piano wanted more money. The dress Lucille had planned to wear that night ripped at the seams. Baby Diamond was stuffy and coughing. Delphina kept disappearing to points left unexplained. And Lucille's fears and frustration with Marcus built up into a huge ball of anger which she felt compelled to hurl at anyone for every slight and irritation.

The previous night's revelation hung around, swirling in her head, reminding her he chose Rose over her. Lucille noticed Marcus took every opportunity to position himself as far away from her as possible. She never thought it was possible that they could be so distant from one another given the cramped bus, small rooms and crowded tables of the local dining spots they had shared over the years.

Everyone within earshot in or outside the theater noticed the rift between them. Eyes rolled from one end of the room to the other. Eyebrows raised waiting for either Marcus or Lucille to explode. Delphina, attempting to melt the frost and distance between the two, tried to push them together. She'd move close to Marcus while holding the sniffling baby then ask Lucille to come look at little Diamond smile. Lucille stayed in her corner. She wasn't falling for Delphina's use of the baby as an olive branch.

Even Mitchell took time out from smoking and grumbling to intervene as the rehearsal went off the rails. "You, m'dear Lucille, are letting your heart lead you around like a donkey. Stop it! I know you love him—we all do! And that's becoming a problem. You've always known who Marcus was and that's why your mammy and paw-paw let you go off with him. He's a man of integrity and, in my very humble opinion, that integrity is not gonna get either of us far in this business. But I've planned to ride this horse for as long as I can before it kicks me off. I suggest you do likewise and stop all this foolishness."

Despite Mitchell's advice, as the rehearsal progressed, Lucille spent more time sulking than singing.

When too many notes rang sour, Mitchell slammed his hands down on the piano, pounding out a stinging string of notes that called everyone to attention. "Enough, already! Y'all coons better make up or drink up so we can get back to making music. I think a little of this gin will put you both in the right space to think of nothing else but getting along." He reached in his jacket for the ever-present flask.

Marcus glared at Lucille and shot out, "That ain't the problem, Mitch, so you can put that bootleg poison away. That doesn't solve anything, it only makes it worse."

"Stop talking about me like I'm not here! Gimme that, Mitchell. Pass it over so I can take a little taste."

Marcus stated flatly, "Will one of you professionals tell her it's not good for her vocal cords, please."

Big Bobby wheezed out between his teeth, "Oh shit, here we go…"

"He's right, Luce. It's not good for you," Delphina said in a small voice.

Lucille grabbed the silver flask, threw her head back and took long gulps until she came up gasping for air. She wiped her lips while averting her eyes from Marcus. Handing the flask back to Mitchell, who took a swig himself, she spit out, "Don't go far with that. I want more."

Marcus watched and shook his head. He pressed his lips into a thin line so that nary a hate-filled word would keep the fight going. The air, filled with a silent, angry heaviness, crackled. Any further comments could lead to one big blowup. "Mitchell, Big Bobby, Lincoln and Del, I need to speak with Lucille alone please. Let's pick this up in about an hour."

Mitchell hopped up from his seat, keeping a beady eye on Lucille as if commanding her to stay put and act right. The others shuffled out behind him. Once the stage was empty and the two were left alone, Marcus and Lucille faced each other, daring the other to cross a line.

Keeping his distance, Marcus started in an even tone. "Lucille, you know how I feel about you. You know how I feel about this…about what we've created here. The Troubadours are deeply rooted in my heart."

"But what about me, Marcus? What about how you *really* feel about me. You can't be with me. You can't kiss me. You can't do anything to show me how you feel about me—not the Troubadours, not this damn tour or fixing all the atrocities we face just trying to entertain people. That's all business anyway."

"From the very beginning I did everything that I promised your parents I would do—including avoiding anything inappropriate."

"You promised my parents that?"

"Well, in so many words… I did. But I did fall in love with you. Who wouldn't? I've seen you grow into this woman who can do anything she puts her mind to, who has no fear of anything at all, who has the biggest voice this side of the Mississippi. I couldn't help but fall in love with you. But I'm married, girl. I'm married to Rose."

"You didn't seem worried about that when you kissed me in the attic that first time."

"I shouldn't have given in then. That was a mistake. I'll admit I'm no saint, but I need to honor my promises again—getting the Troubadours set up for the next leg of the tour and then back to Rose to be the husband I am."

Lucille seethed. "You didn't do what you promised at all. Look at us, Marcus. Yes, we're one step away from a traveling medicine show. It's been almost nine years and we're still playing for pennies, traveling in a damn broken-down bus, still not making enough to ride a train, and I'm still wearing these damn handmade dresses from your wife. How is that anything that you promised?"

"Listen, remember when you were playing the Bijou in Nashville and I was gone for most of the run? I went to the Keiths, the Albees and even those Chicago boys. I thought our string of successes would get us in the door to some of the most prestigious theaters across the nation. They want money and I was sure with our receipts they'd see we could play New York City, Chicago, even San Francisco in white, colored and black-and-tan venues. All we needed was an audition in front of those titans. When I got to the office in Chicago, the hallway was lined with fast-talking agents and managers with acts from Puccini clowns, jugglers, minstrels, dancers in evening wear. All white! Not a tan-colored person to be seen besides me. I was so surprised when they called my name, but I was ready to pitch you and the Troubadours. And you know what happened when I finally got face-to-face with those theater owners? Some bald, underpaid, pencil-neck clerk gave me a once-over then slammed the door shut. But I was determined. I just kept sitting right on that spot in a hard wooden chair in a long dark hallway, right outside the door. I sat for what felt like hours. When the balding man peeked out again, he said, 'Oh, you're still here. Auditions for new acts are downstairs, but they're over.'"

"Marcus, what's the point of telling me all this? I know you go out to get us better work. This wasn't the first time. This sounds like every other disappointment we've had along the way so far," Lucille interrupted.

Marcus held up his hand. "Now hold on. For some reason you think I've been dragging my heels or something. Like I was holding out on the good gigs. So let me assure you I'm not. I've never taken no for an answer if I could help it and this time was no different. A man behind the clerk shouted out to let me in. I had a chance to pitch Miss Lucille and her Black Troubadours. I said I wouldn't leave without a contract."

"So then where's the contract, Marcus? We played Nashville weeks ago. If I ain't seen it by now, that means…"

"Luce, you know they don't just hand out contracts like that. I'm working on it. That's all. The big headline here is they didn't kick me out or ask me to bring them coffee. We spoke like businessmen. Equals across the table, or so it seemed. Those men agreed to meet with me, but made no promises. They had their reservations. There are too many restrictions in the South and the smaller black theaters do make money but they aren't stable enough. I figured if we just kept building our audience or expanded the act—"

"Marcus, please! I've done everything except stand on my head out there. We got them black troupes clamoring for us, for me to join them. But you said I'd get lost in their performances and I wouldn't get much money. Now they're getting spots up in New York and record deals with those bigwigs. And I'm still stuck in Cincinnati, Baltimore and Chattanooga."

"Lucille, I need you to trust me just a little more. You're about to break out. I know it. I can feel it. Just hold on a little bit longer. Now I've got to meet Rose in a few days and—"

Lucille shook her head. "Now I've heard this speech too many times for too many years." Lucille stepped even farther away. They stood on opposite sides of the stage. "Get out, Marcus! Get out and don't come back. Go to your wife. I think we have run our course. I'll take care of everything from here on in. I'll reach out to Mr. C.K. if I need anything. I just want to finish this tour before I decide—did you hear that?—until *I*, Miss Lucille Arnetta Love, decide what's best for me and my Troubadours."

"Lucille, don't say anything else. I'm your manager and I just need you to trust me."

"You're not my manager any longer! I don't need you. I'm tearing up any agreement that we ever had. And if you don't like it, take me to court. Now get the hell out!"

"You can't be serious, Lucille. Not after…"

"I'm as serious as a heart attack. Go back to Chicago. Go back to your precious Rose. I know what to do and I'm taking over from here on in. As of this moment, Marcus, you're fired."

"Lucille, you are being such a child. Now, I've allowed you to threaten and berate me in front of people, but you know what, girl—"

Lucille abruptly shouted over him. "You see that's the problem! You think I'm a girl. I ain't no girl. I'm a woman. A woman who can get whatever she wants and do whatever she wants. And I want you out. I mean it."

Marcus was quiet for a moment. Then nodded. "Okay then, this time you got what you say you want. I'm going back to Chicago for a while. I need to be around people who appreciate me. You go on and be stubborn. But know this, Hank, Evelyn and you are my family whether you like it or not. I'll always look out for you. So let me know when you get stuck somewhere without representation or if you're ever in trouble. Until then, good luck!"

Marcus strode across the stage. Lucille could feel the heat as he passed her. The whole building shook as he slammed the metal stage door behind him.

When the Troubadours returned to the theater Lucille announced Marcus had left.

"What you mean, left?"

"Oh shit, she done did it now."

Lucille, maintaining an even tone, continued, "I'm taking over from here. You all have been with me for a few years now and I trust you beyond measure. Now, I need you to trust me. We still have our connections and contract with TOBA and will continue to receive our instructions from them."

"Marcus ain't coming back?"

"Like I said, trust me, Lincoln. Have you ever not been

paid—by us, I mean? Nothing will change. Absolutely nothing. Now, go get some rest and break a leg tonight, Troubadours."

Mitchell handed over his monogrammed flask. "Here, take this. You're gonna need this over the next few days. Don't worry, I'm watching you. I'm standing right behind you, girl. I gots the faith!" Mitchell waved his hands in the air as if he was in church giving praise before ambling off. He shouted over his shoulder, "And don't let that bow-legged Lincoln get his hands on my flask. He'll just gamble it away. It's got my initials on it and I want it back when you get yourself straight!"

Lucille adjourned rehearsal for the day and returned backstage. She was relieved that she got a tiny dressing room where she could be alone with her thoughts. The alcohol she consumed was working its way through her body. The thumping of her heart banged in her head and her stomach churned. She wished she could forget what had been said between her and Marcus, as far back as when he said kissing her was a mistake and, most importantly, when he said he loved his wife. Rose was getting everything she wanted.

Marcus didn't love her. Her Troubadours loved her, the audiences loved her, and Hank and Evelyn Love loved her the most. She desperately wanted to be with the people who loved her most. She looked around the room. She spotted her brown pouch which she normally hid the moment she arrived at any location. Here it was exposed, its strap undone and a sliver of glittering coins peeking out. She reached for it. The pouch felt lighter than usual. There were only a few coins left and a roll of bills. She looked around the room to see if maybe the coins had fallen among the assortment of other strewn items.

"Damn! I know better than to invite a thief by leaving this lying around...and damn Marcus for distracting me in the first place!"

She absentmindedly wound the strap around to close the pouch. Marcus's words rang in her head. *I will never leave Rose.*

I love her. Rose is my wife. And the most hurtful of all, *I'm your manager* which in her mind meant *I don't care about you.* Lucille wiped her face. The touch of her hand left a searing swipe of hot, salty tears.

"How dare he treat me like some unknowing little girl...like he doesn't know me...like some stupid upstart...some chorus girl...some contract singer he can toss aside at the close of an act. I don't care what he says. I'm fucking fabulous! I'm a fucking sensation! I'm an extraordinary talent and rising star fucking destined for glory!"

In an angry move, her arm swept across the dressing table. Jars, bottles, makeup containers, baubles, bangles, brushes and pins went flying across the room. She shook with tears. "Well, who needs him?"

She should be playing New York City or boarding a ship to Europe by now. The pure grain alcohol that she shared with Mitchell was still making a tour of her head and Lucille shook her head to clear her vision. She plucked through her overturned bottles of perfume and makeup to pick up a folded calling card that read: Mr. Thomas Sullivan Mulgrew. Underneath his name in italicized writing was *At Your Service*.

She fanned the small card before her face, as if it would help cool her anger. "Not yet. Who needs Marcus. It's time I, Miss Lucille Love, make a change."

27

Morton Theatre,
Athens, Georgia
1925

The basement door swung wide open, flooding the room with a tall stream of sunlight. With a resounding crack, the knob hit the back brick wall. Lincoln stood in the doorframe wide-legged with a wide smile to match. "Man, it was hot last night!" He switched on the dim overhead light and the basement lit up, revealing stacks of poster boards, dusty sets, and bric-a-brac piled high around the room.

Big Bobby, who had been sleeping upright in a worn chair that was far too little for his large frame, ran a hand down his face after being startled awake by the sudden bright light and noise. Still dazed and half-asleep, he puffed out, "Whew, yeah… you right about that, brother." He shook his head as if to clear away his confusion. "It's fuck'n hot in here. Lincoln, can you see if you can open that little window over there? How we 'pose to practice down here in all this heat? At least we can get some of that street air coming in here." Big Bobby arched his back to a noticeable symphony of pops and cracks.

"Damn, man, you getting old."

"Yeah, yeah, yeah… I didn't have no room and no money so

I had to sleep down here and as you can see these ain't no luxury accommodations. And anyway, it didn't stop those pretty
brown girls out there giving me the eye all night."

"Well, you should have come with me after the set. But
those exact same girls were looking at me first, Negro. Anyway, that's not what I'm talking about. I'm talking about all
them pretty queens and the rest of the royalty jumping off my
cards at just the right time!"

Lincoln whipped a wad of bills from his pocket, fanned them
out to wave them in the light. "Yeah, them queens were coax-
ing all the rest of them numbers to fall right in line!"

The dollar bills got Big Bobby's attention and he sat straight
up in his seat. "Oh really. Who was playing?"

Lincoln strutted in the circle of light, still waving his prize
in the air. "Oh, you know, the regular hicks. There was only
one smoky at the table that I didn't know and didn't trust. But
after a while it didn't matter 'cause…heh, heh… I took all of
his money too! I'm going back to finish what I started. I told
them I'd give them a chance to win their money back. After
the show, why don't you come with me tonight?"

"Linc, after that last time I went out with you, my money's
been a little funny. I still think some cheating was going on."
Big Bobby fanned himself. "Can you please see if that window opens? Prop that door open too. Anyway, you know we
ain't got paid yet."

"You can borrow it from Lucille. You know, against your
wages."

"Done that twice already. You know she's a lot more tight-
fisted than Marcus. When I asked her, she started talking crazy
because she said she thinks someone has been dipping into her
secret stash. She mentioned horse whipping after that. I took
that as a *no* on the pay advance."

"Well, go and ask Del. I'm sure she either has it or knows where
it is." Lincoln averted his eyes to look at the ground and casually
brushed an imaginary speck of dirt from his shoe. "I know Miss

Delphina would do anything for you, brother. You know that gal has resources, a new well, so to speak...and it's a deep well too. She'd give you whatever you want on loan or exchange."

"Shut up! Del doesn't steal from anybody! If I wasn't still drunk, I'd jump up and punch you right in the mouth for talking about her like that. I ain't asking her for nothing."

"I didn't mean anything by it. Sorry, man. Why don't you ask Mitchell?"

"Hell no! Mitchell will bite my head off. Besides he's paying for his own demons. Also, he'd say something to Lucille and then she'd have to say something to me and the next thing I know, I'll be kicked out, sitting flat on my ass looking for a ride home...wherever that is."

"Lucille won't never kick us out. We're the first of the Troubadours. Now then, c'mon, ask Delphina and we can go double our money. Do it for Diamond."

Big Bobby rubbed his chin. "You know she did show me some coins Lucille gave her. It was over twenty dollars. She might not mind if I borrow it just for a little while and then double or even triple that. That could be good investment money for Diamond. If the table is as hot as you say. Hmm..."

"It is! Or it's gonna be when we get there. I guarantee. You can count on it. Them boys ain't been off the farm. They been playing for fuck'n ears of corn or something. They ain't never played no cards with the likes of us well-traveled gents."

Big Bobby got up and walked over to the window and found it nailed shut. He spotted a shovel by the furnace and using the handle, punched out a pane of glass. Cool air from the sidewalk rolled into the room. He let out a big laugh. "Gents? Since when have you been a gent? Make no mistake—me, I'm just a squirrel trying to get a nut. Mitchell's gonna be here soon to start rehearsal. I'm going to go get my horn. I suggest you do the same. But count me in for later."

28

Clarksville, Tennessee

"Well, if this isn't serendipitous!"

Strands of the old man's gray hair fell across his eyes as he held the coin inches away from his face. He squinted as he twirled the coin between his thumb and index finger. "Where'd you get this from, Zeke?"

"That thing? I was at a game and some fast-talking boy threw it into the pot. He had a few of them. They ain't worth much."

"It's not how much it's worth, it's about where it came from." The man examined the pressed gold coin, imprinted with the profile of a man, bordered with the words United States of America, Columbian Half Dollar, 1893. He flipped it on its back and rubbed his thumb across a ship and the world between the numbers fourteen and ninety-two. World's Columbian Exposition Chicago was imprinted around the perimeter. "You say some colored boy was playing cards with gave you this? Where's he from?"

"I don't know, boss. He was one of those musicians that blew into town. Said he was playing at the Regal. He had some money and wanted a piece of the action. I wanted to take all the money he had. But…but, dammit…that coon got the best of me."

"Musician, you say? What's the name of the band?"

"Miss Lucille's Black Troubadours."

"Ah, okay. Miss Lucille is the singer. This is becoming more and more serendipitous by the minute. That gal's full name is Lucille Love. I heard a bit about these cabaret acts. I believe she started out in Indiana." The old man rubbed the back of his neck, absentmindedly tracing a rough typography of twisted skin, a map of raised scars from an old injury barely hidden by pitiful straggles of gray hair. "I even know about her relative, her father, I think. Some of my kin said he used to have a farm and a vegetable stand back in Indiana. He married the pastor's daughter. Then, poof! They were gone…along with a few other things that were precious to me."

"What? You got all this from spotting a coin I just pulled from my pocket? Here, I got two more from him." He emptied his pockets and slammed the coins on the desk. "It can't be these exposition coins, General. These things ain't worth too much."

"I said it ain't the coin's value I'm concerned with. I know for a fact that coin was one of many. I had lots of them. You know how I got them? Someone had the misfortune of handing them over to some relatives of mine who once visited the only bank in Evansville, Indiana, that stored all those commemorative coins." The old man let the money fall into his lap. His wheelchair creaked and groaned as he pushed himself away from his desk. "Help me to the window. I need some light."

Zeke did as he was told and wheeled the general across the room.

"I just got a piece of news yesterday that I've been waiting to hear for close to twenty years. There was something that we did a long time ago. It was that little job that we—your uncles

Caleb and Justin and me—pulled off that got me in this here chair for the rest of my life."

He went into a trancelike state. "I can still see that damn black boy as he lit that match and watched my skin crackle and blister. He thought I was dead, but here I am and I ain't never gonna forget." He wrapped his hand around the coin. "I ain't ashamed to tell you. You know my past. If I didn't do what I did, somebody else would have. I'm telling you this now because you my flesh and blood, and you know what we do to survive. Plus, I think an opportunity just fell in our laps to retrieve something that we lost here."

"Sure, but what if it's just a coincidence? This might not be what or who you think. You lost that money too many years ago for it to be coming back to you now."

The general smirked. "That's what I thought at first, but something interesting happened not too long ago. Some of my friends were doing a sweep, you know, trying to persuade them remaining Negroes to leave Evansville—it ain't safe to have so many of them around, you see. They were, how you say, lighting a fire under them to move on. One of their churches just happened to burn down during that time and guess what they found in the rubble? A money bag. It was singed a bit around the edges but there it was, clear as day, The Second National Bank stamped right on the front. Are you connecting the dots, boy?" He flicked a coin over to Zeke. "The same bank that these unique coins were held in. Now there wasn't nothing in that bag. I can put the story together. I bet those black folks who been worshipping at that church knew something about that Evansville job all those years ago. On further investigation, I learned the names of the pastor and his family. Reverend Pike had a daughter. Love is her married name."

"Miss Lucille is a Love, all right. But she would have been just a baby back then. How do you think she figures into this?"

"It really don't matter if she knows anything. I'm sure she

loves her pappy, right? She'll know where we can find him to see how his memory holds up. My twin brother died because of that bank robbery. I knowed it was not at the hands of the law, but from someone else—I'm sure of it. I was so obsessed about finding out who did it and took the money he carried." He lifted up his pant leg. "Look at this!" From ankle to knee, it was as if half of his leg had been scraped away. "I almost died for that money and I don't let anything go if it has to do with my family or what's rightfully mine!"

"Still, that was years ago."

"Listen, Zeke, I'm sure this Miss Love don't want nothing to happen to her pappy or mammy. You know what? She might just pay to keep him safe—we'll see. I don't have a problem with shaking down no colored gal. The way I see it, she's doing just a bit too well for my taste." The old man sniffed and wiped his arm across his nose. "I got a feeling all through these dead legs of mine that this pitiful coin right here is going to lead me to whoever killed my brother, burned the skin off my back and took our money."

29

Decked out in a gold plaid jacket and vest and sporting a tan bowler, he was excruciatingly dapper, with thick rings on his fingers visible under his leather gloves. Thomas Sullivan Mulgrew, strutting like the top rooster on any walkway, used every inch of his long legs to glide down the street and take up as much space as possible. Lucille saw him coming from down the block, and watched him stride past the glass window of the restaurant. Within seconds he was standing in front of her table.

"Thomas Sullivan Mulgrew, San Francisco, the gold coast, by way of various patches in Louisiana, at your service, ma'am."

Lucille glanced up from her plate, then picked up her cup of tea to sip while sizing up the long drink of a man. She waved her hand, motioning him to take the seat opposite her. He slid into the chair, sitting wide-legged so his knees poked out noticeably into the aisle on each side of his seat.

He leaned forward, placing his elbows on the table, and proceeded to pull off his tan leather gloves one finger at a time. "I can just feel your name being spoken of and bandied about.

The thought of that is making me tingle. So, you need me to parlay all that small talk into a big spot on the glittering way?"

It had been several months without Marcus, and Lucille realized she needed to turn to someone. Managing and fronting the band was too much work for one person.

"What assurances do I get, Mr. Mulgrew?"

"Assurances? Why, my reputation of course. I've managed some of the biggest groups that are now gaining notoriety on the Great White Way in New York City. I introduced Bert Williams to George Walker. They went on to make fistfuls of money—Bert's still making money even after George and his wife, Aida, died. I didn't get a dime. I learned my lesson and got Flournoy Miller and Aubrey Lyles together to put on that show *Running Wild* up in New York. It's making money hand over fist and everybody is doing that crazy Charleston from the show onstage and in the talkies. Yeah, they're riding high now, taking luxury trips in private cars between gigs in the most prestigious theaters across the country. And what's next for them, you might ask? It's off to golden California to star in films that will be shown to everyone—black and white. I ain't got no time for fighting Jim Crow, but I will do all I can to make some money."

Lucille frowned at his high-toned response. In the years she traveled along the circuit, she witnessed so many big talkers but she wasn't naive—Hank Love didn't raise no fool. "Okay, Mr. Mulgrew, my ears are burning with all the accolades you've laid at this table. What I want to know, truthfully, is what would you do to take me and my Troubadours to the next level of stardom. You see, I'm chasing a star too and I see myself playing the big theaters in Europe. Can you do that?"

His smile grew even wider. "Why, Miss Lucille, that's my specialty. I can get you out of your old contract and into a brand-new one that will put you on that ship sailing the big blue sea before the year is out. But first, what about your current manager, Marcus Williams? Have you parted ways?"

"Yes, you could say that. He went back to Chicago to manage a solo act," Lucille said flatly. She held Thomas's card up to the light as if searching for something embedded in the paper.

"Ain't nothing hidden there, miss. I'm one hundred percent legitimate—everything I say I am. You can trust me on that."

In less than a minute, Lucille ran through her thoughts. Marcus was gone. He had left several times during their journey together, usually returning with an armful of dresses and gowns created by his wife, which Lucille knew Rose had hand sewn with perfection—every meticulously even stitch made to ensure Lucille's success, and in turn fuel her husband so he would come back to her after sending Lucille off to Europe. Marcus had nonchalantly told her so. Marcus and Rose's aim was to build Lucille up then, at an appropriate time, leave her career to the golden fates of success. After all, Marcus had another muse closer to home.

This time, Marcus's departure was different, charged with so much anger. Lucille wondered if firing him was the right thing to do, but then snapped out of it. Time, days and nights of contemplation and numerous letters to and from her parents—who surprisingly cheered her on to manage her own affairs—made her realize hers and Marcus's was simply a mutually beneficial business relationship. Even though she recognized it, she felt empty without him.

Lucille glanced up at Mr. Thomas Mulgrew, who was preening, casually brushing lint from his vest. She thought if he had a mirror, he would be staring at his own image every chance he got within a conversation. Lucille took a deep breath and told herself that she was making a business decision that was best for all her Troubadours. It was not out of spite.

"Okay, Mr. Mulgrew. You're hired! Take me and my Troubadours beyond our present footlights to bigger and better ones.

I only have three demands: no animal acts, no cooning and Mitchell's piano, Maybelle, goes wherever we go. We're pure class and raw talent." She felt good giving out demands and taking control. Her satisfaction of making a decision on her career filled her up. She extended her hand to seal the deal.

Thomas shook her hand vigorously. "You won't regret it, Miss Lucille Love. You won't regret it at all. I've taken the liberty of rounding up a few investors that have taken a keen interest in you and your future. They're white, they know the business and a real money-maker when they see one." He looked around. "It's a shame we can't toast to our new friendship. Damn, tea-totters! This prohibition ain't doing a damn thing about morality, only making those mobsters rich."

"Well, Mr. Mulgrew, we got work to do. C'mon, we have a rehearsal lined up at three o'clock. You need to meet the troupe. You're gonna have to sell 'em a bit. For seasoned performers, they don't take to change easily and are suspicious of everyone. But they'll come around if they believe you can get more money into their pockets."

"I'm not worried about that. I've been told I have a convincing nature."

"Oh, there's also my girl, Delphina, and her daughter, Diamond. They go where I go, first-class. She takes good care of us. Also, we'll need to add a nanny."

"No problem. We're all family now."

Big Bobby slowly opened the three latches on the worn black case. With each click his eyes grew wider and wider as if he was peering into a pot of gold at the end of a rainbow. When he peeled open the case, pieces of a clarinet were tucked deep against blue velvet. Big Bobby sighed like he'd found a woman hiding in there.

"Where'd you find that?" Lincoln asked.

"Once I got my winnings from last night, I knew exactly

what to do with 'em. I got this off one of the guys that's gonna hafta find another job 'cause he ain't playing this no more!"

Mitchell lifted his head off the piano. "Man, you don't know how to play that thing."

"Like hell I don't! I can play just about anything. Give me a few minutes and I'll be sounding like Mr. Sidney Bechet himself. Only better! I might be able to get with King Oliver's Creoles."

Lincoln quipped, "You planning on leaving us, Bobby?"

"I like being a Troubadour. It just ain't no real money. Lucille's belting it out every night and I'm breaking my back to please, but I got to move on."

"Sounds to me like you want out."

"I want more, man. Can I tell you something? You got to promise to keep it secret. Don't tell anyone else. But what I really want is Delphina. I… I love her, man."

Mitchell and Lincoln burst out laughing. Both rolled around while holding their sides.

"Like we didn't know that! You been pining after that gal since you dragged her on the road with us. I'd bet money that she's just as sweet on you too. And Diamond, well, she's a pretty little thing. If you're ready to be a daddy, I know you'd be a good one," Lincoln said.

"But let's be frank. She's a white woman with a child of questionable race. I see your dilemma 'cause the world ain't ready for you or her. My advice, if you love Del, you gotta get another life. You got to get far away from traveling the South. You gotta stay in the big cities or get on that Universal Negro Improvement Association Black Star Line or go to Cuba."

"Mitchell, the Black Star Line? C'mon now, didn't all them ships spring holes and sink? We don't want to send Bobby up the river without a paddle."

"Fellas, you know how I feel about that—don't mock Garvey's vision. He has the right idea. One Aim! One God! One

Destiny! Them UNIA boats and ships make sense to me, no matter how many holes they say they had." Big Bobby caressed the bell of the clarinet before lifting the joints out the case and assembling the instrument. "But playing music is all I've ever wanted to do. I want to play the big houses with the big bands. I don't think I can give that up to do, what, plow fields, work in a grocery, hauling stuff?"

"Well, you better figure something else because you ain't getting younger and this life ain't for everyone. Especially not dragging around a woman with a child. Particularly no white woman. You'll be hanging from a tree for that. Whether she becomes your wife or not, they'll find something to hang you for and call it something else."

"For someone that's never been married, how you know so much about what a woman wants, Mitchell?"

"Look, y'all act like I ain't never been in love before."

This time Bobby and Lincoln spit out their laughter.

"Mitchell, that don't even sound right. The only thing you've been in love with is Maybelle," Bobby said.

"You know what…that's right. Maybelle, with her fine brown wood and sleek black and whites… Yeah, she's the only woman that can satisfy me and I don't have to come off the road to be with her."

"Naw, 'cause we have to carry her heavy ass around with us wherever we go!"

"Ya see, now that's true love!"

Thomas Mulgrew had sneaked into the practice to observe Lucille's boys before introducing himself. He nonchalantly leaned back in his chair, which hit the back wall, and precariously balanced his long frame on its two legs. A gold coin tumbled over his knuckles until he tossed it in the air, caught it and stuffed it back in his pocket. He then struck a match on the bottom of his shoe to light up an already chewed cigar.

The flash of light from the flame illuminated the gold chain that led to a pocket of a violet-colored vest—the assumption of possessing an impressive gold pocket watch.

He sauntered toward the men. "Miss Lucille's Black Troubadours, I'm Thomas Mulgrew. Your new manager."

Bobby, Lincoln and Mitchell all exchanged looks at the sight of the well-dressed man, so slick and different from Marcus's more earthy demeanor.

"Miss Lucille hired me on. She said you all were looking for something more. Am I correct?"

Big Bobby looked Thomas up and down. "A new manager, huh." He extended his hand, introducing himself, Mitchell and Lincoln. "I think I can speak for all of us, Mr. Mulgrew, we all want more."

"Just call me Tommy. We're family now. I know you're hot—I've been following you from Ohio, Missouri and Georgia. Why don't you play a little something before our star arrives? You know, to just get into the mood."

Mitchell gave Lincoln a side eye and whispered, "Linc, this feels like someone died. Let's start with a little going home." He snapped off a count—*a one, a two, a one, two, three*—and instinctually the band knew what to do: "What a Friend We Have in Jesus," a song they had done countless times before. Lincoln and Big Bobby took turns to flourish and then wove themselves in harmony with the pounding melody of the piano. But the music quickly took a turn from sorrowful prayer to a quickening pace as Mitchell transitioned the group into "Down by the Riverside." They played until they sensed that it was time to ramp down and bring the music to a close.

"I tell you what, boys, you've got something here. You can really swing. But we've got to make this ragtag bunch a little more classy," he barked out to Big Bobby, Lincoln and Mitchell. "Your lovely mistress—the real star of the show, Miss Lucille—wants me to recreate your image. Nothing but class and raw talent she said. Well, the talent is evident, but Lincoln and Bobby, you guys look like you still play on the street corners for coins. Them white folks love to see a Negro neat and dressed to the nines. You know, clean, like me. It makes them feel good about themselves."

Big Bobby looked at Lincoln and sucked his teeth. "They feel good about this horn I'm slingin'. That's all that matters, boss."

"You want to make more money? Y'all been wasting your time playing small-time theaters and saloons. First, if you want to make the big time you got to look the part. Everybody needs to be suited down tight, every night. You need to look like you got something, even if you don't. So dress up, gentlemen."

"Where are we supposed to get the money for new suits?" Lincoln gestured at himself. "This is all I got."

"Don't worry about it. I'll take care of that. But you got to shine your shoes, brother. That's how we going to get on that boat."

Lincoln sang out, "We're going to gay Par-eee? Ooo-wee, I hear there's lots of good money on the tables in Europe. Lady luck's gonna smile down on all of us when we're stepping out on the other side of the world."

30

Paradise Theater
Atlanta, Georgia

Lucille tapped her foot in annoyance. Mitchell promised to meet her but after five minutes of standing in the night club's vestibule, he had yet to make an entrance. She had received several invitations to be escorted to a table by very attentive and handsome men, but she chose to wait to make an entrance with Mitchell. Always recognized as the hottest musician of the hour on the entertainment circuit, entering with Mitchell doubled as an advertisement to boost ticket sales for their show.

Lucille blew out a hot breath and pulled back the velvet curtain to peek into the club. As she expected, it was a flurry of revelers throwing back glass after glass of prohibited substances and engaging in act after act of prohibited behaviors. The high energy lifted her spirits and so she decided to step into the room unescorted and unafraid; she, Miss Lucille, the beautiful brown girl with the big voice, was all she needed to call attention to her own show. Her headpiece, adorned with iridescent beads that matched the peacock-blue overlay of her dress, glittered in the glow of low-lit wall sconces. Heads turned in her direction, but despite her dramatic entrance, she didn't hold any-one's attention for long.

Lucille surveyed the room. White-aproned bartenders man-aged requests from swarms of people as two women competed for the crowd's attention—one on top of the bar performed a wobbly Charleston and the other attempted to amble up and join her, but fell into the arms of the men cheering her on. Through the raucous display, Lucille's eyes landed on one table in the middle of the room.

It had been eight weeks since the Top Hats and she and her Troubadours crossed paths. Lucille had been so busy with her own shows that she lost track of theater dates where they would find themselves again on the same billing. But now Georgia once again, Lucille remembered they'd been booked in a string of venues together. Seeing Ginger brought her back to their last encounter, where she was so tempted to leave her senses and spend the night with the man that left a trail of broken hearts along the circuit.

His tie was loose, and a single tendril of his just-about-red hair fell against his forehead. Ginger leaned in and struck a match. The sudden spark jumped to a flame as he lit the woman's cigarette. Her creamy white skin was bathed momentarily in the burst of light. In the glow, she appeared as if she was an il-lustration of the exaggerated modern beauty that defined most of the women who attended theaters, speakeasies, cabarets and saloons. Striking blue eyes peeked from under a fringe of golden hair that skimmed neatly drawn brows and hugged her cheeks with the sleek curl of a trendy bob. A wide swath of rouge crossed her cheeks, and cherry red lips circled the stem of her cigarette holder. She looked unreal, as if she was posing in a magazine stylishly advertising cocaine.

Ginger flashed a smile as he spotted Lucille and waved her over to the table. "Lucille, what a treat to run into you to-night! This here is one of the Five Top Hats' most ardent patrons, Adele. Adele, it's my pleasure to introduce the fabulous chanteuse, Miss Lucille."

"Hello, Lucille. It is such a pleasure to meet you. I've enjoyed your performances with your very talented Troubadours many times. You were here just a month ago at the Royal Arcadeum, or was it the Lenox, right?" She took a long drag of her cigarette. "My father owns a couple of theaters in Chicago and San Francisco. He's always looking for some good colored acts. They always draw a very profitable crowd, where everyone dances like crazy and drinks like fishes." Adele giggled. "My daddy would turn his pockets inside out to pay for a good colored revue."

From the start, Lucille didn't like Adele. She was too perfect and reckless with her casualness; it carried a hidden language. She wondered if Adele was talking about her real father or some sugar daddy. Either way, Lucille knew Adele was angling to stake a claim.

Lucille ignored Adele's crass remark and feigned a smile. "Well, it's certainly my pleasure to meet you, Miss Adele. There are lots of really good colored acts out there. Listen to all the race records out now. And if they're too dark for your taste, there's some white man or woman trying to belt it out, cork it up and copy us colored performers to entertain your crowd."

"Them white boys and girls are entertaining in a pinch but I like the real thing." Adele shot a glance at Ginger before continuing. "I like you, Miss Lucille. There's something fresh and exciting about you. Why aren't you playing in New York or London like that Josephine Baker?"

"I'm close. I'm ready to get off this circuit for sure."

"Really? I plan on taking the Top Hats over to Europe. They'd be a smash and so would you. Those upstarts overseas are creating a stir, you know, the bright young things. The wild artists that always seem to be performing somewhere, famously naked. Of course, they'd find you immensely entertaining. C'mon, sit down and have a drink with us." Adele patted the seat next to hers. "Ginger, go tell Max at the bar to give us the best they can find. We can toast to a profitable future with the both of you, center stage and top billing!" Adele's eyes followed Ginger as he walked to the bar. She then turned to Lucille. "Sweet, isn't he? I can't help myself whenever he's in town, I just have to see him. He's so talented. You know, he talks a lot about you."

"He talks about little ol' me? Now, that's a surprise." Since they last met, Ginger had occupied quite a bit of Lucille's thoughts too. She'd had luscious daydreams of him dancing smoothly across a mirrored stage or his hand lightly touching the small of her back while their hips swayed to a rapturous melody. She had to give herself a vigorous shake to get back to reality.

"Yes, you, Miss Lucille. I was so curious and wanted to see what the fascination was." Adele took a long drag from her cigarette and smoke slowly curled out from between her lips. "Hmm…now I see."

The white woman's voice suddenly sounded harsh. Lucille pressed her lips into a thin line to compose herself, hoping to keep her true feelings from rising to the surface. She wanted to punch Adele in her chiseled face. Lucille knew that this Adele, the smug woman who obviously and openly lusted after Ginger, was indulging in some fantasy, something she would probably deny or boast about in neat little lily-white circles. To hear her casually toss around the fate of black men grated against Lucille's nerves. Adele seemed to be the type of woman who would step over a colored person or anyone she deemed "lesser than," leaving them in the wake of her recklessness without batting an eye.

Ginger ambled over with a bottle under his arm and glasses clutched in his fingers. He filled each glass and then lifted his glass up to give a toast. "To two of the most beautiful women in the club tonight. May you find all the fortune your hearts can hold."

"I'll drink to that!" Adele tacked on, turning up her glass. Ginger immediately refilled it for her.

Lloyd, Ginger's older brother, cruised over to the table. "Miss

Adele, lovely as ever. And Miss Lucille, too. Boy, Ginger, you're the luckiest man in Atlanta tonight."

Between gulps, Adele announced, "Lloyd, darling, one of my favorite Top Hats—next to this one, that is—it's so nice to see you. You were marvelous tonight. I don't know why they haven't already whisked you boys to the big shows in New York. But don't you worry—I'll do all I can to get you there." Adele winked and slid out of her chair. "Now, if you'll excuse me, I see someone I absolutely need to speak to. Someone who can make big things happen. Fingers crossed!"

Lucille took it as her chance to step into the ladies' room to powder her nose, leaving the brothers. When she returned, Ginger and Lloyd had their heads together deep in conversation. She looked around the room and stopped at an empty table, not far from where Ginger and Lloyd were. A slightly inebriated Ginger was speaking a bit too loudly.

"The one thing I've learned is to make no apologies. This is a dog-eat-dog world and I'm a goddamn Top Hat! That means *I'm* the top dog in this business. Isn't that what you always say?"

"Well, it's only a matter of time before one of them little bitches you messin' with bring you down." Lloyd lowered his voice. "And that Miss Lucille, from what I can see, has come waltzing back in the picture and just that quickly put a leash on you, top dog. We all know you are Miss Adele's favorite. I don't care what she says when the booze is talking, I know that white woman ain't gonna like that too much."

"Naw, man," Ginger protested. "It ain't like that."

"Well, that's exactly what it's lookin' like. As much as I hate to say it, Adele is the Top Hats' butter-and-egg man. You find someone with money that wants to blow it on some fine entertainment and we entertainers hold on for the ride—but *she* holds the bank roll. Don't mess it up, man."

"Lloyd, my own flesh and blood, Mama would slap you into next Sunday to hear you talk like that."

"I'll send our dear mother a fur coat. That is if we continue to make enough money. Look, I don't make the rules but that's how it goes in this business. We can't get attached—not doing what we do. The next job, the next gig, is always the one that's gonna take us where we need to go—to the land of mo' money and fame, baby!" Lloyd patted Ginger on his shoulder. "Let that pretty face go. Ginger, listen to your big brother now. Screw whomever—there is plenty of pussy out there for that—but don't fall in love. At least not till we get to Flo Ziegfeld's and we start making that Bert Williams or Bill Robinson money. Now, go get me some ice. Some for my glass and a whole lot for my back. I need a drink or something to make me forget about the pain. Don't tell your brothers, but that last slide across the stage damn near killed me."

Ginger hopped up from the table and bumped into Lucille, who was standing to the side, trying to conceal her eavesdropping.

"I've been wondering where you went." He wasn't tipsy enough to lose his balance, but just enough to need a little fancy footwork to keep from swaying. "Sit with me for a minute, will you?" He dropped into a seat at the empty table. Lucille took a seat beside him.

"You know somethin'?" Ginger began as he pulled out a silver cigarette case. He flipped it open to offer one to Lucille. Lucille shook her head. He shrugged and placed the holder on the table and mindlessly spun it around.

"I've been watching you for some time and I found there's one thing that I really like about you. It's the ways you walk. There's when you're just strolling along the streets window-shopping. But then, how you walk out onstage for that very first set, now, that's a whole different walk… When you hit the lights, everything you got seems to be going in the right direction, shining like the first rays of sunlight bursting out on a summer morning. And, damn, that walk, when the stage lights can't help but follow you, makes my temperature rise."

Lucille chuckled. "How many of them girls have you told that story to?" She rose slowly from her seat and leaned in close to Ginger, intentionally teasing him. Ginger, transfixed, had no-where else to look but at the plump softness of her décolletage. "You see, mister, I know all about you. I've heard all about you."

Although his words made heat rise up from her toes, she turned and sashayed out of the joint. Behind her she heard Ginger humming in his throat, and then smacking his lips as if something sweet just passed them.

They stood side by side on the Paradise Theater stage. The Five Top Hats had a rehearsal and Lucille reluctantly agreed to meet Ginger before going to lunch. Seeing Ginger and meeting the hungry Adele last night put a damper on Lucille's mood. Sharing the bill with the Five Top Hats for the week was ini-tially exciting, but last night extinguished that flame. But then, when Lucille arrived at the theater, all she wanted was to stare at this handsome man: the long straight line of Ginger's nose, his full lips framed by an immaculate mustache and, most allur-ing, his hazel brown eyes. He was only a few inches taller than she, perfectly proportioned with broad shoulders that whittled down to a narrow waist and slender hips. She could see why the ladies flocked to him. It was his dangerous and carefree appeal. He treated his beautiful appearance as if it were noth-ing, but his smooth café-au-lait skin looked as if it was hand-painted by the gods.

He lightly took her hand. "Follow along. I've got something to teach you."

He stepped one foot over the other, starting in front then crossing over to the back. He pulled her along as they stepped from one side of the room then back again.

"Wait a minute. Why is it that men always feel they need to teach a woman something?"

"Oh, I can't teach you nothing. I know you can teach me a

thing or two. Don't worry, sister. I'm a very good student and *love* my lessons."

"Okay, now you're being fresh. If you plan to teach me a few dance steps, you're going to have to sing with me. Or how about sing *for* me?"

Ginger gave a sly laugh. "It's a deal. So, Miss Lucille, let's try it again, soft and gentle now. We call it a grapevine. Easy, right? You got it. Now slap your toe to the floor then quickly draw it back. Like you smacking a baby's bottom. Hop on one foot and stomp. Now do it on the other side, just like this."

Ginger's body barely moved but sharp twangs from the metal taps reverberated as they hit the floorboards. "Everything is better with time. Except when you owe somebody some money." He chuckled.

Lucille was getting giddy moving around the stage. She giggled. "You look so pretty when you dance."

Ginger blushed. "I do, don't I?"

"Look, Ginger, dancing just ain't my forte. It's okay because I don't see it as a flaw. I've learned a bit here and there, but I'm not as smooth as you."

Ginger laughed and threw his arm around Lucille, pulling her close. "Well, of course not, suga'! No one in the world is as smooth as me. I've been dancing since I was a baby. I was hopping barefoot with bottle caps between my toes. It was the only way we knew how to eat."

"I've had some agents say that I'd be as famous as that damn Josephine Baker that keeps getting the plum parts and stealing all the good jobs. I got to admit she's quite pretty, she does dance and, from what I hear, she's not afraid of doing nothing onstage."

"Lucille, you know everywhere we play there's some young upstart trying to move up the ladder, into our spot. You got to have more than just one type of act to continue to get bookings."

"That's what Thomas keeps saying."

Ginger tutted. "I'm just going to say this about that long-neck, puffed-up goose—beware of him. As long as I've been around, I ain't never heard of him, which makes me suspicious. There are some folks out there that can sell snakes with a smile."

Lucille raised an eyebrow, sensing a little streak of green envy in his voice, but didn't want to stay on the topic. As far as she was concerned, with Marcus gone, Thomas was all the Troubadours had between meals.

"Just be careful. That's all I'm saying." He paused, then shyly added, "You know I care about you."

Another surprise. She flashed her eyes and placed her hand daintily on her chest. With a wide smile she chirped, "You care about little old me? Well, I declare, Mr. Ginger Reynolds."

"Let me help you polish up your act a bit. First smile. That's it, show them pearly whites. Now do a little soft shoe to remind folks of the good old days when we didn't have a care."

"Please, when was that?"

Ginger clapped his hands together. "Now, hop on that one gorgeous foot. You know how to do that, don't you? Follow my lead."

Lucille, a bit hesitant, did what she was told and took a little shy hop.

"No, not like that. Hop up high and fast, and land right where you mean to, so your foot makes a sound. Good. Now put your hands on your hips. Now hop up and swivel just a little when you land. That's it."

After a few attempts, Lucille puffed out, "Okay, sir, I'm hopping and swiveling. You know I'm a singer and need my breath."

"Oh, I know," Ginger laughed. "I just wanted to see you hop. I just love to see a pretty gal like you shake."

Lucille laughed and slapped him on his shoulder.

"In honor of the occasion, I'm going to teach you what we call a Cincinnati. It's easy and the sound makes it look like you've been doing this for years. Spank, heel, shuffle, heel, step—we're gonna march backward with this one, okay?"

"I'm not used to all this following stuff, but I'll give it a try since I'm a little partial to Queen City."

"Good. Fall back on your heel and let that be your baseline sound. Now we going to another big city, let's do it to this, St. Louis style."

Lucille waved a hand. "Oh excuse me, honey, I know this one. Let me take it from here my way. What I like to call high fah-lou-tin chitlin' style." She picked up with her own version.

After a few slow tries, Lucille tap-danced a perfect soft Cincinnati in beaded leather T-strap heels in tandem with Ginger.

Breathless, Lucille whispered out, "Not bad. I think I'll get it with a little more practice. My daddy says there are no imperfections, just adjustments to how you look at things. My daddy is a wise man. He says I'll always be his beautiful baby who sings like an angel."

Ginger grabbed Lucille's hand and pulled her close for a kiss. She almost hated to admit how breathless she felt, but at the same time, it was nice to feel so safe and cared for.

Between kisses, he whispered in her ear, "That's what I see too—an angel."

Both jumped when a tinkling of laughter announced the cluster of girls peering from behind the curtain. Lucille pushed herself away from Ginger while Ginger flashed a wide smile at the gaggle of brown-skinned young women.

"Hello, ladies! Oh, there's my beautiful Therese! How are you, dear?"

Lucille noticed one woman whispering in another's ear. She shouted back, "Hello, Ginger. You miss me already, I see."

"Always, doll. Maybe I'll see you for a little two-step over at Club Samson tonight."

"Wait a minute, I thought you said we'd have a bite tonight. Are you standing me up?" another piped in.

"Now, now, Sally," another chimed in. "Can't you see Ginger is busy rehearsing? He no longer has time for us lesser performers. As you can see, he's graduated to the big time."

"Club Samson, huh? You better be glad your new girl's name ain't Delilah—or is it?" The chorine made a scissor motion with her fingers.

All of the women, teetering on their heels, burst out in laughter.

Ginger looked at Lucille sheepishly. "Thems the Chocolate Bon-Bon Revue girls. Well, you know…we're on the same circuit so they're always booked at the same theater so, well you know…we've played with them a lot."

Lucille rolled her eyes, masking the pang in her chest. "I'm sure you have, *darling*…"

The theater was dark that night, so they took advantage of the day off. Ginger and Lucille went to lunch, for a walk in the sunshine and then to see the movie *By Right of Birth,* a film billed as a Negro romance of laughter and tears. Although she was having a lovely day with Ginger, the story hit a bit too close to home for Lucille—a woman searching for her biological parents with the help of a villainous attorney who plots to steal land and oil from freedmen in Oklahoma. Despite the happy ending of love and inheritance, the film sparked a sadness within Lucille she couldn't shake. She hadn't seen her father and mother in so long. She had held Ginger's hand in the dark theater.

"Come home with me, Lucille." Ginger gently looped her arm through his. "Something is gnawing at you. I've got a nice place nearby. You can put your feet up and we can relax."

They stopped in the middle of the sidewalk. People whizzed by carrying packages, or tugging small children by the hand, all in a hurry to get home to make dinner for their families. They became a blur.

"How about you stay with me tonight?" she said.

★ ★ ★

They sat at the edge of her bed. Ginger picked up a coin lying on Lucille's bedside table. He rubbed the coin between his index finger and his thumb before holding it up to the lit candle. Flickering light bounced from the coin and leaped around the room.

"Hmm...treasure," he said in a whisper. He wrapped his hand around the coin before letting it fall through his fingers. It bounced off the pillow and rolled to the floor. "That's nice but what else do you got?"

Lucille smiled and pulled the largest ring off her finger. She tossed it to him. He laughed as he caught it and held the ring's deep garnet up to the candle's flickering flame. The stone's facets poured crimson, blue and purple light across their faces. He balanced it between his thumb and index finger and in a flourishing twist of his hand, the ring disappeared. He brought it out from behind her ear a moment later and Lucille giggled.

"Oh, that's really nice too. But I think this pirate is in search of something else." He let the ring fall on the bedcovers.

"Well, I've given you gold and jewels. I can't possibly imagine what else you wish to possess, sir."

He kissed her softly on the lips. "I think you do."

Lucille's heart raced. Ginger's tongue began to travel across boundaries, slowly climbing and descending the steeples of her body, delivering the unexpected coolness of his breath on her thighs. He pressed his fingers deeply into her skin and, at points where nerves connected, her muscles tightened before giving way to the showering sensation of release.

31

Lucille and Ginger continued their evening at a performance of *Steppin' Lively*. Lucille hated to admit, but the show was nothing short of piss poor. She always tried to be supportive of all entertainers who shared the stage. She'd seen many of the disappointments, largely from disparity of treatment that colored performers were subjected to along the circuits—theater managers who undercut or refused pay for the most insignificant reason, lost contracts, stolen acts and routines and ragged living conditions. Lucille knew artists left standing outside the theater door, far from home with no money and nothing more than a change of clothes in a worn tapestry bag. It was experiences like these that stung and Lucille was forever grateful to her parents and Marcus for sheltering her from so much along her career path.

She remained respectful of the performers; she knew the bravery it took to get up on stage to perform before a crowd. Fruits and vegetables were good for you, but not for the brave entertainer who stood at the edge of the footlights as a target for a whole crop of vegetables when the audience wasn't satisfied.

But tonight, she winced after every garbled line, off-key song and heavy-footed dance number. The show was a steady stream of tired jokes within a retreaded story about a penniless dreamer, vying for the attention of a pretty girl. The choreography needed work; the chorus was made up of girls who looked as though they had been pulled from the producer's down-home family reunion. From her box seat, Lucille could see the seams of their costumes were barely holding together.

Ginger, seated next to her, leaned in close to whisper, "This certainly is a mess. My guess is this show will close before the end of its run, if not tonight. Those thick-ankle farm girls are going to be sent back to tending the cows."

Lucille chuckled. "Oh, you ought to know. You've plucked up so many of those farm girls and now that they got a taste of the Top Hat high life, they're not going back."

Ginger gave her a lopsided smile. "Save all that hilariousness for the stage. I bet you'd get more laughs than the comic they got. Ugh, I hope the entire troupe saved enough for a bus ticket home. Maybe we can duck out of here before the second act. I'm hungry."

"Ginger, you got us these box seats. Everyone will see us if we leave early."

"Everyone should have the magnificent privilege of simply seeing you, Miss Lucille."

Lucille stared back at him, before rolling her eyes and slowly shaking her head, not allowing herself to be so easily charmed— though the intimate tone of his voice gave her goose bumps. Her wrap slid off her bare shoulder. She became acutely aware of the soft fur trim as it fell down her arm. Lucille blushed. She caught an iridescent gold speck in Ginger's brown eyes, and his lips curved into a sly smile. *Dammit*, she thought. As much as she hated to admit it, the rumors were true. What had ensnared so many other women, that bit of tempting magic, that streak of magnetic charm that captured audiences, had gotten to Lucille too. She fought against it, telling herself, *You're playing with fire, girl.*

Ginger grabbed her hand and led her out of the theater just before the curtain fell for intermission.

They stepped into Kit's Kat and Mouse Club, an underground speakeasy where a large man stood guard underneath a barren white light illuminating a metal warehouse door. Inside was a long narrow space with a bar running the length of the room. Eight busy bartenders weaved around each other serving drinks in rapid succession to giddy patrons lined up four heads deep. On a small platform in the corner, four well-dressed band members were setting up to start another set for the evening.

At the far end of the bar, the familiar face of a tall, reed-thin, strikingly dressed woman appeared. She extended a satin-gloved hand. "Ginger, darling! I didn't know you were coming tonight. If I had known, I would have dressed for the occasion."

Ginger took her hand. "You look wonderful as always, Adele." She wore a midnight blue, drop-waist dress with a black netted overlay. Her beaded headband glittered across her forehead like a low-hung tiara.

"Stop it, you are such a scoundrel." Adele flashed her heavily mascaraed eyes at Ginger before her gaze landed on Lucille, looking her up and down. "Oh, hello. It's Miss Lucy, is it not?"

Lucille casually shifted her footing to nestle into the crook of Ginger's arm, giving no indication of being uncomfortable. Lucille flashed a toothy smile. "Oh please, Adele. All my friends call me Lucille."

"Well, Lucille, you came just in time. The band needs a singer tonight. I'm not sure what happened to my other girl, pretty little colored gal too. I think she got entwined with one of our regulars—they can be such savages you know. They get a girl thinking she's something she's not and *poof*, she's no longer fit for the stage."

"Oh. I didn't know this was your club. Are you the Kit of the Kat and Mouse Club?"

Adele chuckled. "Yes, this is my club. My family owns quite a few of these little hideaways. But Kit was the name of a lover of mine—he's no longer around, but he's still making money for me."

Ginger dropped Adele's hand. "Adele, Miss Lucille is off for the night. We just came from *Steppin' Lively*, you know the new show over at the—"

"I heard it was dreadful." The crowd around the bar cheered as the band started playing. Adele stepped closer to Ginger, her lips almost touching his cheek. "Listen, Ginger, darling, I really need to talk to you in private." She glanced at Lucille. "You know, a little Top Hat business." Adele patted Ginger on the chest and glided a finger into the buttonhole on his lapel, giving it a playful tug. Adele waved her fingers at Lucille. "You don't mind, do you, Miss Lucy? You're dressed so pretty. Maybe you can go over to the piano and sing a little something. You can make quite a bit of money here just by singing a few songs."

Ginger politely brushed Adele's hand away from his chest. "Sorry, Adele, I didn't realize the time. It's so late, we must get home to rest for tomorrow's show."

Adele raised an eyebrow. "Really? But you've just arrived." She turned to Lucille. "I've become such a night creature these days. But that's where all the talent—and the money—can be found. I am a modern businesswoman after all."

Lucille gave Ginger a wink. "Well, timing can be a little tricky for all of us in this business. Unlike the rest of us, no early rehearsals for you, right?

Adele turned and waved to one of the bartenders, signaling for service. "No, just counting money and such. And securing acts for all the theaters across America and beyond."

"And Miss Adele is the best in the business—you'll find no man better. Adele, I'll have Lloyd get back to you on any outstanding Top Hat business. *We*—" Ginger looked down at Lucille "—must get home."

Adele seethed. "Well, I suppose Miss Lucy requires her beauty rest." With a sniff, she turned back to the bar.

Lucille giggled, knowing Adele was green with envy.

Ginger angled her toward the door. "We really must be leaving," he said politely.

Lucille, with Ginger's hand at the small of her back, sashayed out, knowing that Adele's eyes were following them.

"Thank you, Mr. Reynolds. You were pretty gallant back there. I'm impressed. Particularly since 'best-in-the-business' Adele holds the purse strings. I don't think she's too happy with you right now. I hope she doesn't take our quick exit out on the Top Hats."

"Don't worry about Adele, my brother will take care of her. As long as we pull in the money, she won't let this personal business interfere with her success. Our contracts are tight and buttoned up, at least for the next few months or so."

"That woman doesn't give two hoots about a paper contract. She's thinking about contact, the kind that still requires a *dip in an inkwell* to seal the deal. By the way, have you dipped…?"

"Nooo dipping here. C'mon, funny lady, I'm still hungry."

Lucille watched the afternoon sunlight dance across the wallpaper as the curtains swayed to the whims of a breeze. Ginger was still asleep. She watched his long lashes quiver against the freckles splashed across his cheeks.

"Stay still," she said softly.

A lazy smile stretched across his face. Dreamily, he whispered back, "You love me already?"

"Absolutely not. Hold still. There's a mosquito buzzing a…" She clapped her hands together above his head and with a satisfactory nod, whipped the blanket off their naked bodies. "Let's go. We need to rehearse. There's plenty of work to do."

Ginger wrestled with the covers, pulling them up to his shoulders. "Aw, c'mere, girl."

He added a wink to punctuate his smile. His eyes followed her, appreciating her shapely body as she walked past the window. The sheer curtains billowing in the wind lapped around her curves.

"No, Ginger," she snapped back. "We have got to get to the theater. The band will surely be red-hot mad, clucking like little hens that I'm late. Don't you have to go over your number with the Top Hats?"

"We've done this so many times. No practice necessary. I know. They know, and for sure my feet know what to do."

"Yeah, right, Mr. Smooth and Fabulous. Mitchell will have my head and threaten to quit for the millionth time if I mess up or miss a cue. Besides it's my name, my band and I got to—"

"Woman, please…get over here! I want to talk to you about something and I need your full attention."

"You do not want to talk."

Lucille walked back to the bed and lay in the crook of his arms, humming a melody. Where it came from, she couldn't remember, but she knew her heart would give her lyrics at the right time.

Ginger gently swept aside a wisp of curls that fell across her cheek and tucked them behind her ear. He leaned in close and repeated the tune as he whispered, "You always have a melody floating around you. Have you always been like that?"

"Yes, for as long as I can remember," Lucille replied. "When I was young, I spent so much time outside, listening to the sounds around me. And my daddy would pull out his homemade, hand-carved guitar and play whatever came to mind. His songs, along with what God set for us underneath the sky, gave me the tunes that I carry with me." She closed her eyes and drew in a long breath, smiling at the memory. "Our years of traveling and sleeping under the stars were just a game until

I suddenly became ashamed of who we were. At that point, it felt like we were strange fugitives who were inches from being on a chain gang. Sure, we started really performing when Marcus started managing us, but I had bigger dreams for the tunes that circled my head."

"Of course you did. You're one of those performers who's been destined for this life from the beginning."

"Every time I sing, I know deep in my bones I'm closer to that dream—the big stage, the major recordings. I can see it more clearly after every performance. I can even taste it. You know, I owe that to Marcus. He gave me that, the freedom to dream. I love…loved him for that."

"But what about me, Luce? You got any room for me in that dream?"

"This is show biz, dah–ling. All the lights pointing at the stage come together to shine on only one star."

"That's a little cold," he said stiffly. "Without the help of others that star is surely gonna fade. And what about last night? You said I was gallant…"

"Oh, I got all the help I need. I got Aida!"

"Who?"

"Aida Overton Walker."

"George Walker's wife? That woman died years ago. How is she helping you?"

"Well, she comes to me."

"What do you mean *comes to you*? Like a ghost?"

"The first time I saw her, she was in a light like no other. It's what they call an aura. Self-contained energy that surrounded everything taking up space before my eyes."

"That sounds like bad hooch to me."

"That's what happens to me when I'm on stage. Mitchell calls her my muse. Don't you have something that makes you want to do better?"

"My empty stomach and pockets are all the muse I need!"

Lucille turned away, embarrassed that she revealed something so personal to Ginger. "You think I've gone a bit nuts, don't you?"

"No, not at all. I do understand what you're talking about. I guess we all have some inspiration like that, or else why do we keep doing the things we do?"

"That's exactly right. You'd think I'd be afraid of some vision that jumps up before my eyes, but I'm not. I welcome Aida. I believe she loves me."

"I love you," Ginger said quietly.

It was too earnest.

Lucille froze, remembering her promise not to get attached. She cleared her throat and steeled herself, knowing she might hurt Ginger with her next words. "Of course you do. *Everyone* loves Miss Lucille Love."

32

Liberty Theatre
Chattanooga, Tennessee

Diamond had begun crawling so fast she was ready to take off and fly. It became more and more evident that the assortment of rooming houses and backstage dressing rooms were no place for an infant. Baby Diamond had quickly become Toddler Diamond and was bouncing all over the place, growing inquisitive. The baby was dressed like a movie star in lace, satin and bows. Someone had even given her a tiara. Still, danger lurked around every corner and finding someone trustworthy to watch her during the oddest times of the day took a bit of juggling. Diamond had collected a trove of clothes and toys from every vaudevillian that crossed their path and either fell in love with her or her mother or both. Lucille, who depended so much on Delphina and had grown to love Diamond, swallowed her feelings and withheld advice. She knew despite her feelings, the best for Diamond would be for Delphina to find a place and settle down.

Opportunities for Lucille to have intimate conversations with Delphina became elusive. Usually between shows they'd laugh and talk, but Delphina began to disappear and had become secretive about her whereabouts. As promised, she'd ask to wear a dress or borrow a pair of gloves or even earbobs and then be off without explanation. Lucille also noticed that Delphina had acquired a few smart and fashionable outfits and accessories of her own. In every city, Delphina suddenly had dates planned. Lucille watched and waited for her friend to tell her who was keeping her company. She didn't ask, because she figured she already knew who was taking up all of Delphina's time: the smooth, greasy-skinned Monte. It wasn't that Lucille was jealous of the man who had come between them, but she just didn't trust him with Delphina or Diamond.

The Troubadours were booked for several venues in Tennessee and would be in the state for over a month. Lucille loved these times when venues were close together. With Marcus, they had zigzagged around like hobos. To Thomas Mulgrew's credit, even though they still traveled by bus, they now had a schedule that gave them a straight shot between cities and made traveling a little easier, at least by allowing them a few days, weeks and hundreds fewer miles between shows.

In a rare moment, Delphina and Lucille found themselves together at a theater. The energy between them felt as awkward and cluttered as the room. Delphina had her sewing kit out, checking for rips and loose threads, hooks and beading on Lucille's costume.

Delphina broke the ice. "So, Luce, how are things going with that handsome Ginger?" Lucille perked up as if a teacher had caught her napping and called upon her to answer a question she didn't know. Delphina's eyes twinkled as she broke out in a laugh. "Boy, that man can move across the floor. All the girls talk about his moves, you know."

"Del, I'm just having a little fun right now. I needed a distraction. I've heard the rumors and I'm sure most are true. But I haven't heard about what's going on in your life, my dear. Spill!"

Delphina turned beet red. "Well, it's just a little attraction. I mean, it's maybe more than a little. It's—"

Lucille jumped in. "I'll say it's more than a little *everything*. We haven't seen much of you lately. Your social calendar and dance card have been quite full." Lucille gave Delphina a wink. "I bet my dresses have been seen all over town."

"Oh, Luce, I don't want to jinx it. Monte is everything I've wanted. He is a gentleman. Look at this bracelet." She shook her wrist at Lucille. "He says he's looking for a wife and is ready to settle down."

"Settle down? Where? He seems to be everywhere we are."

"He's rich. He's got a wealthy uncle who lives here in Tennessee who owns a big farm and horse ranch. So he tells me."

"Del, did he say the actual word *marriage*? I'm just looking out for you and Diamond. I've learned there are plenty of men out there putting on airs of being fine and upstanding who think settling down means having a pretty little lady in an apartment in town while having a doting wife in the big country house."

"No, it's not like that at all. I know there are tricksters out there. I've fallen for a few, thinking that they would be the ones to take care of me. What I've learned is *I'm* the one who must take care of me, and now my sweet Diamond. But Monte feels like the man for me."

Lucille sighed. "Delphina, please be careful. You're playing a big part in this little drama of yours. You've seen enough theater with such plots and schemes. They never work out in the end."

"Lucille Love! I am being as careful as I can, but this will be the stability that me and Diamond need. I see you. I see how you look at me and Diamond—you get that soft look on your face. And I love that look because I love that you want the best for me and my little girl, but it tells me you want us to go…and we should go, but you and the Troubadours make it so hard to leave this family I've come to love."

Delphina rushed into Lucille's open arms and the women rocked in their embrace.

Lucille eked out between tears, "I *do* only want the best for you, Del."

"He asks about you a lot, you know. Monte's always asking about where the Troubadours have been. How you came to sing like that and when you're going to make a recording. I think he's more interested in you than me. Maybe he wants to marry you."

"I'd tell him to get in line, but I really, really, really don't like him," Lucille half joked.

"You've made that clear enough." Delphina leaned down to finish sewing a ripped seam at Lucille's hem. "Everything in me tells me that Monte is different than the others."

Lucille forced a smile, feeling defeated. "I trust you," she said. *It's Monte I don't trust.*

It was one of the best performances of the run. Based on the stomping, whistling and applause, no doubt the Troubadours would move up on the list of performers. The band had gone off to do some late-night carousing and Delphina went directly back to the rooming house to relieve the young woman who was watching Diamond. They deserved the rest.

Thomas, who hadn't been seen for the last few days, saying he was doing some advance work, would hopefully be able to make their rise in the ranks happen. The competition was steep between the barefoot tap dancers and the wildly entertaining balancing act of the slip-and-fall comedians. The Troubadours were at least hoping for second best—unless a place was being saved for a white entertainer. Lucille was going to make sure Thomas heard about the night's last number. From the standing ovation, it would fetch them more money, which was desperately needed.

After the show, the buzz from a rowdy audience still hung in the air, which was already electrified by the Troubadours win for the night. Lucille, dressed in her closing-number costume—an all-white drop-waist gown with the most beautiful matching silver turban—sat backstage at her dressing table, fanning herself. Her chest was still heaving from that last set. *Ooo chile, this was a mighty good night!* She kissed the picture of her parents posted on the mirror, which she did after every performance.

Three short knocks on the door disrupted her thoughts. She sat up straight and gave permission for the late-night visitor to enter. Monte stood in the middle of the doorway, all smiles and white teeth.

"Miss Lucille Love!" He shouted out the greeting like she was an old acquaintance. He was dapper, dressed in coattails. He had his overcoat over his arm and hat in hand as if he was the swellest of swells. Essence of mint or pine wafted around him. "Oh, you were wonderful tonight. I like that last little ditty. 'That snake wrapped; And Daddy snapped; Before he took another sip he cracked that snake with a whip…'" He laughed at his off-key singing. "I won't be able to get that one out of my head for weeks. Have you thought about recording? Or, you know, they have these new coin-operated phonographs that are popping up at all the entertainment arcades. You can charge folks a nickel to hear you sing that one little song all night long. You better look into it, there's a lot of money to be made at the nickelodeons."

With her most polite, businesslike smile, Lucille replied, "Yes, I've heard of them, and my manager is looking into it. Thank you for all the compliments. I'm glad you enjoyed the show. Delphina is off for the night, enjoying a little peace and quiet this evening. And I'd like to join her shortly. Is there something I can relay to her?"

"Oh no, no, no. I just wanted to pop backstage to congratulate you." He then gave her a quizzical look. "What do you mean Delphina is off tonight?"

Lucille realized her error and quickly recovered. "She sometimes comes by to see how we're doing. She's good about that. We colored folks are so fortunate to have such a dedicated patron of the arts like her."

"She certainly has an eye for talented artists, doesn't she? Ever since she introduced us, I can't help thinking about you. I want to know more."

"You want to know more about *me*?"

"Yes. You see, my family likes to take risks, business ventures you might say. We don't normally get into the entertainment field, but Miss Lucille and her Black Troubadours has me thinking… Now this may sound frivolous, but I think here's something that can be fruitful and a bit fun. A little liquor here and a little money there. I think you need me as a partner, a sponsor—or how about a gold patron."

He rubbed his thumb and index finger together before moving closer to Lucille, stopping just inches away from her. "I'm sure you want to cool down from being under the bright lights, Miss Love. And it's so hot back here. I know the theater owner. I'll ask that you be moved to a better dressing room, one with windows."

Surprised by his sudden boldness, Lucille gripped the arms of her chair. Then as sweetly as syrup, she said, "You'd do that just for me?" She was determined not to let Monte know she was suspicious of his offer.

"Of course. You're on the road to being a big star, I know it. Here…" He reached in his pocket to retrieve a handkerchief and waved it in front of Lucille's face. "This is the only thing that should touch that lovely mahogany-brown skin of yours." He let the cloth slip from his fingers and float down to the floor. "Oh sorry, Miss Love." He reached down to retrieve the hankie and as he did, touched Lucille's ankle. Monte's hand lingered there, then he looked up, staring directly at Lucille as if to gauge her reaction.

She held back any response. She wanted to see how far Monte was going to take this. She certainly wasn't planning on giving out any samples to the likes of him.

Monte slowly ran his hand up Lucille's leg as if she was a siren on the rocks tempting him to do so.

With each inch his fingers moved up her skin, Lucille became angrier. When they crawled past her knee, Lucille grabbed the jar of face powder and threw it at him.

Startled, Monte jumped back. White powder covered his face and splattered across his dark suit and shiny shoes. Furiously rubbing his eyes, he yelled and screamed, coughing up swear words. "Damn! You stupid broad! This jacket cost me a lot of cabbage and now you ruined it!"

Lucille couldn't hold back laughing at the sight of him. "Oh, Mr. Montgomery, aren't we ever so clumsy sometimes!"

He lunged at her as if he was about to strike. Lucille didn't cower; it took all she had not to spit in his powder-splattered face. She placed a hand in the open dressing table drawer, suggesting that she had something to pull out to defend herself.

Monte retreated, but not before he hissed out, "Kiss that career of yours goodbye, little chickadee—your wings are about to be clipped. You'll be the biggest black canary singing in the coal mines. Delphina will never support Miss Lucille's Black Troubadours from here on—I'll make sure of that!" He slammed the door behind him.

Lucille laughed out loud at that parting shot, knowing how much "support" their "patron" gave them. She slapped a hand over her mouth a split second later and the room fell silent. *How am I going to tell Delphina?*

The only remnant of Monte's presence and his failed seduction was a wild splash of face powder splayed across the dressing room floor and sprinkled across her toes and stockings.

There was no doubt Monte would make Delphina leave the Troubadours. Lucille knew Monte wouldn't tell Delphina exactly what happened in the dressing room; he would most likely try to persuade Delphina with lies. Maybe he sought Delphina out to tell her right away. Or maybe he retreated to his uncle's veranda in Tennessee for a more convenient time.

"But why would he wait?" Lucille wondered aloud. "I can only hope Delphina won't believe a word he says. I know she loves me, but she might not take the news well coming from me. No one wants to find out they've been a patsy for love."

Over the next few days, Lucille saw even less of Delphina than before. This time, even Big Bobby sadly professed he hadn't spent much time with Delphina, outside of a brief luncheon with her and Diamond. When Lucille and Delphina did find themselves together, they weren't alone. Lucille was perplexed that Delphina hadn't confronted her with any accusations, making her wonder if anything was said. Delphina buzzed around mending costumes, folding clothes, bringing sandwiches and pickles to the boys and doling out instructions to the men carefully moving Maybelle from the bus into the theater. All the things she normally did. But when their paths crossed, their eyes never met. It was as if Delphina wasn't physically present.

Lucille and Delphina were ships passing in the night with hardly a word spoken between them. Lucille eventually concluded that Delphina's avoidance could only mean one thing: Monte had already told her. *But what did he say?*

33

"Them suits he got are so thin you can see the shiny on my black hiney." Big Bobby stretched out his arms and the sleeves of his jacket rose up to his elbows. "Where did you get these from, a mortuary? Somewhere underground, there's some naked old dead men shivering in the cold."

Lucille stepped in with a royal blue velvet cape trimmed with white fur. "Well, boys, how do I look?"

"You look like a queen. But, Luce, look at us! I've heard of undertaker sharp, but in these get-ups we look like some cheap stiffs in a paper casket."

Mitchell chimed in, "What's next? We gotta get corked up and play sambo cotton picaninny? I'll be back to the whore-house before we hafta do that. I'm a goddamn certified musician. He gonna have us back down on the plantation, Lucille. Didn't he say something about getting on some steamboat?"

"C'mon, Mitchell. It ain't that bad." Lincoln smoothed down his suit jacket. "He just wants us to be sophisticated. You know, so we'll be able to ride alongside the big orchestras, you know with James Reese Europe and King Oliver. You look fine, like you're about to play with Mr. Noble Sissle himself."

"Like I can't outplay him," Mitchell muttered under his breath. "Listen, I'm going to wear whatever I want, whenever I want or else me and Maybelle are going back to Basin Street. Lucille, you look as lovely as ever, but you could sing in a sack and still knock 'em for a loop."

Thomas strode into the room. "You got that right! The most talented Miss Lucille looks as yummy as she sounds! Mitchell, you're the man." He reached into his jacket pocket and pulled out a gold flask engraved with his initials and held it out to Mitchell. Mitchell rolled his eyes and pulled out his own.

Thomas retracted his arm and tucked the narrow container back in his pocket. "Mitchell, I only want what's best for the group and my plan is to get you noticed so you can get into the big, splashy colored revues. There's a lot of colored entertainers out there getting noticed and I want the Troubadours to be included. We just got to set ourselves apart from the others—and the way to do it is to listen to me. We need something more than just Lucille's big voice and some bouncy songs. Maybe some dancers. They could sing behind Lucille. How about something sophisticated…an orchestra!"

Lincoln nudged Big Bobby and whispered, "What did I tell you?"

"We need more instruments. We need to sound as big as that Hell fighter, James Reese Europe. That's what's going to get us over to Europe. Once we do that, we can demand time on all the big stages from New York to California. I know a drummer and a clarinetist that can tear the house down."

Mitchell shook his head. "Now, wait a minute. We ain't earning enough money for that! We already cramped inside a bus because we can't afford the train fare."

"That damn spook is talking way too big," Lincoln whispered into Big Bobby's ear. "Mark my words, if he could do all that, he wouldn't be here. We're going to be all dressed up, singing in a poolroom. Just watch and see."

"What's that, Lincoln?" Thomas turned sharply.

Lincoln shook his head. "Never mind. I just want to play."

"Thomas, I don't know about this." Lucille stood with her hands on her hips. "We've done pretty good looking the way we usually look. I'm out front and have to look a certain way to make sure all eyes are on me. The boys, well...you know we create that aura of a low-down speakeasy. People like that. They like that we make them feel like they're doing something rebellious. We punch them in the gut with our music, not dance around all dainty, like in parlors."

"But you would dance in those parlors if the price was right, correct?" Thomas, dressed in a dapper red suit and gold brocade vest, plucked off the fingers of his fine leather gold gloves. He did it with such fanfare, Lucille, Mitchell, Big Bobby and Lincoln stood with their mouths open. "You'd dance for an audience that was willing to pay. That's the audience that's going to get you on the big stage, get you signed to a record label and, most importantly, get you to Europe. What do you think those kings and queens sitting on their thrones want to see, some old grimy street band and singer who croons for pennies, or something fine like I'm trying to create?" He finished plucking off his gloves and slapped them against his palm to emphasize his point. "You hired me to take the band in a new direction—a bigger direction. The old stuff just won't cut it anymore, understand?"

"What is the temperature today?" Big Bobby wheezed out the side of his mouth. "Hot with a tell-me-some-shit down-pour?"

Lincoln nodded. "Yeah, with occasional fuck-you thunder-storms."

Lucille piped in to cool the Troubadours down. "C'mon, boys, we've been doing the same thing for some time now and it's time we tried something new. Right, Mitch? Remember when I was singing like a little church mouse and Marcus got us to pep things up a bit? That got us going in a whole new direction. So maybe it's time."

"Well, I ain't gonna sit up there with a pasted-on house Negro grin while I'm playing."

A scruffy man burst through the doors with a pointed finger aimed straight at Thomas. "Where's my picaninny extravaganza? You promised a revue with all the Southern charm of back home. This all you got? A skinny colored gal and some broken-down musicians? My audience is looking for something that will make them smack their lips like a good home-cooked meal from their very own mammy. If you can't do that, then I can get somebody else."

"Sir, I always deliver," Thomas responded coolly. "Mark my words, your audiences won't be disappointed. I've got an act they'll remember for days after and have them coming back for more. You'll see."

The man stepped closer to Thomas. "Well, I agreed to the billing because I didn't want no snake charm music. No jazz devil music. Nothing that will have them doing anything but a Virginia reel. I better get what I paid for or else *you* don't get paid!" He stormed out, shouting over his shoulder, "And I'm gonna write to the owners to let them know about false representation!"

"Thomas, what in the hell is he talking about? I told you from the very beginning three important things about us Troubadours: Maybelle travels as a Troubadour, we don't work with no animals and we don't do blackface. We are artists and command respect."

"Lucille…come on, doll, they pay you, right? That's how they show respect. It's their theater and their business. The faster you realize you're the puppet on their strings, the better off you'll be in this business. We might not like what they want, but if we don't give it to 'em, we're all out on our high and mighty black asses."

Mitchell jumped up and pointed a finger in Thomas's face. "You motherfuckin' snake-oil hustler, I ain't prancing around for nobody to relive their plantation days."

"Mitchell, from what I've heard, you've danced around for quite a few of them folks, if you know what I mean. Do I have to name names or towns?"

Thomas looked directly at Big Bobby and Lincoln while he continued to address Mitchell. "You and Lucille are who the folks come to see, I know. But we have a contract. Not just with me as manager of the Troubadours, but also with TOBA. The minute they get a whiff of something unpleasant, the only piano playing you'll be doing will be in the back of someone's barn."

"Man, I'll cut you!" Lincoln hopped up reaching for his knife.

Big Bobby held out his arm, catching Lincoln across the chest, preventing him from charging up to Thomas. "You see, I told you this was a mistake! Where's Marcus? If Marcus was here, we wouldn't be going through none of this foolishness."

"*Stop!*" Lucille shouted. "Everyone, calm down! Thomas, no need for insults. You best remember who's the real talent here and it ain't you. I don't give a damn about no contract. I ain't singing in no plantation extravaganza and I ain't having my Troubadours do any such thing."

"Look, you got a show to do. Now you heard what the man wants." Thomas crossed his arms. "Let me remind you the till is on empty. After paying for your suits and that fancy dress and feathered headdress of yours, there's not a dime left. If you want to eat or have a place to shit, you better think about the show you plan to do. Also, Lucille, the owners of the shipping line that's looking for entertainment as they cross the Atlantic will be in the audience. Now, some classic Negro spirituals would be nice. Okay?"

Lucille pinched the bridge of her nose. "Thomas, I think you better leave now before I slug you myself."

Thomas slapped his gloves in his hand and walked briskly to the door, pausing like he had one last thing to say.

Big Bobby lowered his arm a few inches while Lincoln snapped his blade shut and returned it to his pocket. "Lucille, send that snake packing please. He needs to take his sorry-looking scaly face back to San Francisco! If I let Lincoln go, that reptile will be sent back there in pieces."

Thomas laughed humorlessly. "Look, if you can't give me what I want then I have no use for you." Thomas put his gloves on again. "My advice, Lucille? Forget these little side-line activities—these Troubadours, that white trash Delphina and even that weak, sniveling Marcus. I've kept my ear to the ground. He thinks he's still making deals for you all the way from Oklahoma. Ha! He's so confused, he don't know which way his dick is swinging."

"You fuckin' nanny goat! You one dumbass if you think we plan to dance to your tune."

"No...you see, I'm one smart nigga and 'bout to be a rich one with an act that is better'n yours. I got a colored gal with a face like butter and an ass just the right size that leaves mouths watering. She can't sing like you, but her eyes will make you cry if she wants and she'll do anything for a laugh. I'm gonna have no trouble getting her on film, and not just the race talkies or dime arcades."

Lucille sniffed. "Oh right, just like you promised me. You gonna have that pretty little yellow thing corked up and dancing around like a toad? If she believes you're gonna get her on film, I got some beads to trade her. And you know what else? You're fired!"

"I'm not worried, my dear. Guess you and your boys plan to retire because I'll make sure you don't work anywhere else. And I hear there's a bounty on your head. You, Miss Lucille, and all the rest of you by association, better watch out."

Lucille scoffed. "What are you talking about?"

"Why should I care, I'm not your manager now, am I?"

"Get out and stay out of my sight!" Lucille stood up, grabbed her brush and threw it at him. He ducked and the brush narrowly missed his head.

"You'll pay for that," Thomas spit back and slid out the door.

The audience was in a good mood. Clapping, stomping and cheering after each act. They were primed and ready for Miss Lucille's Black Troubadours. The Troubadours were already onstage and as the curtain rose, Mitchell gave his usual roll of the black-and-white keys to signal the band to get going. However, this time, although the roll was as robust as it had been after hundreds of performances, what followed was nothing that the band had ever heard before. There was a jingle of unknown notes in a chaotic key. Big Bobby, sensing something was wrong, slid over to Mitchell while still playing his horn. Lincoln picked up the vibe and went on with a solo to cover.

"Don't touch my liquor!" The glass and bottle that Mitchell sat on the top of the piano rumbled and threatened to tip over as he slammed his fingers down on the keys. He fell forward, stopping short to hover over the piano. His body weaved from side to side like a dry reed blowing in the wind.

Big Bobby stood at Mitchell's side and whispered in his ear. "All right, Mitch. We won't touch anything, but you don't look so good, brother. You all right? Lucille's about to come onstage."

Mitchell looked up at Big Bobby, raising his hands until they were poised in the air above his head. Mitchell's face went limp and his eyes rolled up as he fell backward out of his seat. Big Bobby looked to the wings and signaled to bring the curtain down just as Lucille pranced out on stage. Lincoln stepped out from between the curtains as they hit the ground and motioned with his trumpet for Lucille to follow him across the stage.

Lucille kept singing and took the cue, strutting along as if being called by Lincoln's trumpet. Each step she took forward, he took a step back. By the time they were both center stage, Lincoln stopped. He then bent down to slide his trumpet from the bottom of Lucille's ankle up the long line of her outstretched arm as he reached for the top note of the scale. The audience was enraptured by the simple act. Lucille gave a shimmy as if tickled by the cool gold horn's sensuous climb. The horn's pealing crescendo masked the sounds coming from behind the curtains of Mitchell and Maybelle being dragged from the stage.

When Lucille and Lincoln were done, they rushed off the stage in a hail of applause. The audience stomped and called for an encore, but the Troubadours ignored it. In the corner, Big Bobby sat on the piano seat. A prone Mitchell lay at his feet. Delphina ran in with Diamond on her hip and clasped her hand across Mitchell's forehead. Passing Diamond off to Lucille, she leaned down to press her head against his chest. Mitchell groaned at her touch. He was trying to speak.

"Mitchell must have gotten some poisoned hooch," Big Bobby shouted out as a series of acrobats dressed in red-and-blue tights ran past them to go onstage.

"He's having trouble breathing. Lay him down. Give him some room. Rub Mitchell's chest. I need to breathe for him for a while." Delphina drew a match out of her pocket and what looked like a wrapped cigarette. She swiped the match against the brick wall and lit the cigarette.

The audience in the theater oohed and clapped frantically as the acrobats onstage in front of the curtain created a perfect pyramid while the house band triumphantly played in the orchestra pit.

"Del! What are you doing? Not here. Ain't time for that right now."

"Shh… This is gonna relax him and get him to expel whatever is poisoning him. It'll let him breathe easier." She took a long draw on the cigarette. She leaned close to Mitchell and blew smoke into his face. "Mitchell... Mitchell! Open your eyes and look at me!"

Mitchell groaned. His mouth crinkled and limply relaxed. His eyes flickered.

"Mitchell, look at me!"

Lucille handed Diamond to Lincoln and knelt down beside Mitchell, "Mitch! Mitch! Say something!"

He hummed and squirmed. Delphina took another deep draw on the cigarette and blew a cloud of smoke straight up Mitchell's nostrils. Mitchell's eyes flew open. His lips, regaining color, quivered in his attempt to form words.

Delphina continued, "Mitchell, tell me you love me. Come on, tell me. You know you do."

A small group of performers circled around the tableau of Mitchell lying on the floor, Delphina hovering above him and Lucille on her knees holding the piano player's limp hands. Wisps of pungently sweet smoke rose from the center of the group as if they were circled around a campfire. They all looked quizzically at each other as they simultaneously took a step back upon hearing Delphina's call for love.

Mitchell then sat straight up. His eyes rolled in his head as he whipped his head around to shake off a cloud of confusion. "Hell naw, woman! I ain't in love with nobody. Girl, please don't be shouting them lies."

Delphina took a deep breath and coughed out a giggle. "Oh yes you do, you old goat. You love me."

"Welcome back, Mitchell. Now you better start paying more attention to where you put those lips."

"Not around them old bottles for sure."

Lucille shouted out instructions. "Big Bobby, help him up. Go put Mitchell in my bed. Mitchell, don't you say another word or else your black ass is fired!"

34

Lincoln Theatre
Nashville, Tennessee

"Del, I really need to talk to you."

Delphina stared at Lucille. Pale and expressionless except for wide, clear eyes, Delphina twisted and then pressed her lips into a thin line as if to hold her words back.

They only had a few moments before the show, but it was the perfect time. They were alone in a small stuffy, dressing room with only a shaft of light coming in from a small window that had a view of a brick wall.

Delphina delicately plucked her pin cushion from her sewing kit before she replied softly, "About what, Lucille?"

"Something happened that you need to know about Delphina. First, I am so sorry—"

As if ready to burst, Delphina bounced upright in her seat to interrupt Lucille. "Right! I'm sorry too."

"It's about Monte." Lucille took a deep breath. "You're not going to like this."

Delphina sat back and narrowed her eyes. "What about Monte?"

"You should know he—"

The door flew open and banged against the wall so hard flecks of paint flew. Three men squeezed through the small opening. Two of the men stood shoulder to shoulder blocking the entire entrance, their hats brushing against the top of the doorframe. The third was Lincoln. He was limp, held by the scruff of his neck by one of the huge men and being dragged on bare knees peering through ripped pants.

Lincoln's face was bloody and both eyes were swollen shut. Startled by the sudden entry of the trio, Delphina jumped up. Her sewing basket rolled off her lap, spilling a spray of pins, needles and brightly colored threads to the floor. Lucille sat frozen in her seat.

"I believe this belongs to you." One of the men shoved Lincoln toward Lucille and Delphina. He planted a shoe squarely in Lincoln's back as Lincoln fell straight forward, landing in a crumpled heap at Lucille's feet. Delphina rushed over to him and knelt down to cradle his head in her lap.

Lucille quickly recovered from the sudden appearance of the two shady thugs blocking her doorway and mustered up the courage to shout, "Hey! I don't know who the hell you think you are busting into a lady's dressing room like this, but you need to get the hell out of here! This ain't no barroom brawl." She wasn't waiting for an explanation from the burly men about what happened; she just wanted them gone from her sight.

"That boy owes us money."

"And what does that have to do with me?"

"You his employer, right? If you want to keep this man alive and in your services, you need to cough up the money he owes us."

Lincoln squirmed on the floor, muttering something unintelligible. Delphina leaned close to his face, whispering for him to be still.

"What makes you think I have any money? I'm just a lowly

entertainer, a crooner, not even the main act. Look around. You can see this ain't no palace."

In response, one of the men tossed a handful of gold coins at Lincoln's head, along with a frayed and faded canvas bag marked with faint lettering that read Second National Bank and Trust. One coin rolled along the carpet hitting the tip of Lucille's shoe. With a look of confusion, she slowly bent down to scoop up the coin with one hand and the bag in the other. All while she was digging the point of her satin shoe into Lincoln's side.

Coolly, Lucille stared back at the men. "Again, what the hell does this have to do with me?"

"Your boy here has been engaging in a few little card games with my boys. We travel this circuit providing protective services, you see. Now we feel quite strongly that your boy's been getting' a little creative. You see, he used them coins as collateral. I don't know all the particulars, but these coins sparked the interest of my boss. Is your mama Evelyn Pike, the daughter of Reverend John Pike? And whereabouts is your daddy?"

"Who wants to know?"

"All you need to know is the general is quite interested in your folks."

Lucille took a beat before asking, "What even is this greasy old bag?"

"Look closely at it. It was found at the site of your grandpappy's church."

"The site?" Her heart quickened. She hadn't heard from her parents and until this moment thought they were safely ensconced in their little house in Oklahoma. There had been no word about her grandfather. If something had happened, she would have received a telegram from her mother, or at least Marcus.

"Let me be clear, that bag was found in the rubble of your grandfather's church in Evansville, Indiana. It burnt down to the ground. I can't say if your grandpappy burnt down with it or not, but this bag was picked out of the ashes. So somebody associated with that church must know something about this."

Lucille was nervous, but held on to her resolve. "Not me. I haven't been to Evansville in almost twenty years."

"Ain't that something. Nineteen years ago somebody took this money from my boss's family. A man was killed for this money and my boss will do anything to get it back. Close to two thousand dollars, that's what was in the bag."

"How would I know anything about that? I was just a little girl when you say all that happened."

"Oh, I think you know something, all right. Or else you wouldn't be carrying these around." He pointed to the confetti of coins scattered on the floor. "That boy on the floor there said he got them from you. This is the big-time singer you were referring to, right?" He gave Lincoln a swift kick in his side.

"Stop!" Delphina screamed as she pulled Lincoln closer to her. Lincoln winced.

Lucille squinted and shot out, "My parents and my grandfather are dead."

One of the men took a step back into the hallway and the other took a step forward. "Come on, honey gal. You ain't giving me the bum's rush with that lame excuse. You've got to do better than that."

From the bowels of the theater, the stage manager's five-minute call rang out over the man's ominous threat. Lucille's and Delphina's heads whipped toward the sound. Still, Lucille didn't want to give away the fear that shot through her spine. Her mind hummed with a jumble of images of her parents, her grandparents and even Miss Opal. She had no idea what this meant, but she knew danger when it was staring her in the face. She would do anything to protect all those she loved even if she had to stand firm in an outright lie.

Lucille stood up and took a step closer to the man to position her body between him and Delphina, who was gently patting Lincoln's face as he groaned. Lucille steeled herself for whatever might happen next. Would the thug strike her, pull out a blackjack and beat her and Delphina to a pulp? Her mind shouted to keep them off the scent of her family's whereabouts.

"I don't know how you know my parents' or grandfather's names but let me tell you something. They are in fact dead. They all got headstones up in—" she had to think fast "—in Akron, Ohio." She threw the bank bag down at the man's feet. "You calling my family thieves? How dare you bring up my family in this way."

"I don't care about no nigger sentimentality. All I want is that money. The money that your family took from mine. If you ain't got what I'm looking for then you know how to get it."

Lucille stood firmly on her spot. "I go from job to job. Do you think if I had any kind of money I'd be back here in a room smelling like piss and a thousand field hands?"

The man in the hallway turned his head from left to right, before calmly stating, "Too much talking, Zeke. We got to go. Go on and do it so we can be done with this job."

The front man reached in his pocket and pulled out a gun. "Akron, huh? For that amount of money and payback, we'll dig all of 'em up. If it's not there resting in peace with them, then we'll come after you. Don't believe me?"

The blaring sharp sound of the warm-up band hitting a final crescendo cut through the air at the same time the man standing in the hallway pushed his partner aside, pulled a gun out of his pocket and shot Lincoln in the leg. Lucille fell back into her chair. Both Lincoln and Delphina screamed out as blood poured out of Lincoln's wound.

"We'll come back and finish the job if we can't find our money and if the boss ain't satisfied."

Smoke from the gun curled in the air. Lincoln whimpered on the floor as Lucille and Delphina looked at each other.

Delphina gulped and whispered, "Lucille, I've seen those men before."

The stage manager yelled from the stairwell, "You're on, Miss Lucille!"

The room darkened as gray clouds rolled over the silver sky whipping up a storm. The remaining light grazed on the large violet-red patch on the carpet. The spot was shiny, wet from Lincoln's blood as it dripped through his fingers. Lincoln's shouts of "Oh Lawd! Oh Lawd!" rang through Lucille's head. She winced. Her thumping heart reminded her of the dire circumstances. Hopefully Delphina would be able to patch him up and ease the pain with whatever herbs she had on hand. Delphina left to get her small case of healing tinctures and returned within a few minutes, closing and locking the dressing room door behind her.

The stage manager's voice echoed from the landing once again. "Miss Lucille, it's showtime!"

Delphina's dress was covered in Lincoln's blood. "Hold still and keep your mouth shut for once, Lincoln. It looks like a clean shot. You're lucky. Just keep looking at me, stay quiet and don't go to sleep. I'll bandage you up right."

Lincoln's swollen head bobbled from side to side.

"Luce, I made sure nobody saw me. Lincoln's gonna be all right. I'll tie up his wound real tight and give him something that will make him forget about the pain for a while. I'm sure he didn't know anything about them coins. You know Lincoln, he's got a good heart. If he took that money from you, for sure he was gonna put it back once he hit. But…"

"It don't matter now, Del. Lincoln done brought some devils into our circle and we got to find a way to sweep them out. I swear, Del… I swear before God, I had no idea of any of this. I don't quite believe it, but when I think back, I have to admit there might be a spark of truth in that story they told."

"You think your pappy could've robbed those people? From

the stories you've told me… I say if your daddy did it, them men deserved what they got."

Both Lucille and Delphina jumped when the stage manager belted out from the other side of the closed door, "Miss Lucille, you have to come out, now!"

"I'm fixing her costume!" Delphina yelled to the voice beyond the door. "I'm sewing her up right now. It'll be a few minutes."

The stage manager shouted back, "You better be quick or else. The crowd won't want to wait."

"I'll be right out!" Lucille shouted back. She turned to Delphina. "Thanks, Del. Now the way I see it, this can work out one of two ways. One: it's true. If my daddy killed anyone, somebody is out there trying to settle the score. That means eventually they'll come back to make me pay or kill me. Hell, kill you and Diamond or anyone who gets in their way."

Delphina stopped cleaning Lincoln's wounds and put a hand to her mouth. Lincoln whimpered a string of nonsensical phrases.

Lucille continued, "And that's not going to happen. It sure ain't going to be the result of anything I say or do. Two: let's say it's not true and these goons are just trying to shake this little black girl down 'cause of Linc's sorry ass. It doesn't mean they won't hurt some innocent people just to make a point. I'm going to do everything in my power to keep everyone safe."

"Neither of those are great options, Lucy. What can you even do?"

"Now I could go to the law because the police will be *so* helpful…" Lucille trailed off sarcastically. "Of course, if I was to do that, it would be written up in the papers and we'd all be ruined. No theater would touch us." Lucille shook her head. "Or they'd withhold more of our money, for insurance purposes they'd say. Then we'd be working for free. Them theater owners are just as much thieves as those white boys who busted in here."

Those damn coins. *Oh, Daddy, what did you do?*

This time, the manager pounded on the door. "If you don't come out of there right now, you and your band will forfeit your spot, your pay and never work here again as long as I live! You're on now, Miss Lucille!"

Lucille stepped into the spotlight, as if nothing had transpired only moments ago. When Big Bobby mouthed *Where's Lincoln?* Lucille only smiled broadly and nodded in his direction. She placed a hand on Maybelle to feel the vibrations of each strike of the piano's hammers. Mitchell squinted at her from underneath his bowler, a message that he thought something was amiss. He raised his hands and brought them down on the piano keys, forcing a loud flourish of notes out of Maybelle that told the audience they were starting the set with sounds of the streets of New Orleans.

Lucille lifted her head and turned toward the stage lights. Rows and rows of top hats, caps and chiseled bobbed heads of the boisterous crowd were at her feet. The lights appeared brighter and felt hotter than usual. A smoky haze surrounded each light, creating iridescent halos that grew wider as the heat from the lights blanketed and seared her skin.

Aida, as the regal queen of Dahomey, appeared. Aida's skin glistened with the sheen of oils. She stretched her arm toward Lucille and curled a finger in the air, beckoning Lucille forward. Lucille followed her lead.

Lucille, entranced by her muse, was oblivious to Mitchell and Big Bobby playing behind her. She missed her cue. Her throat tightened and she felt as if she were choking on a gasoline-soaked rag. It had been too much to swallow: Marcus leaving; her failed attempt at replacing him with that buffoon, Thomas; Lincoln getting shot; and the strange threat to her parents.

As she stood center stage, climbing flames leaped up before her eyes and the world turned upside down. Stinging sweat poured down her face. She fanned herself with her hand. *Damn!*

It's so hot! In the blackness between the flames, in the far, far distance, she saw a few heads bobbing and weaving together.

Mitchell whipped his head in Big Bobby's direction, signaling for rescue. In a flash, Big Bobby switched from the trombone to his clarinet and began a winding snake charm. The big man fell to his knees at Lucille's feet and played a sensual, intoxicating mix while aiming the instrument around her ankles. With a long, slow upward motion, he continued his serpentine solo while sliding the clarinet from her ankles to the hem of dress and upward as if to coax her awake.

Lucille heard a sudden loud crack behind her and the sharp sound snapped her out of her dream. As if falling from the sky and landing on a soft pillow, she shook her head and shouted over her shoulder, "Hey, Mitchell, this crowd looks like they want something hot!"

Mitchell, relieved Lucille had come back to her senses, ran his fingers down the piano keys and shouted back, "Yes, ma'am! I got that coming right up!"

Mitchell repeated his pulse-driving introduction and Lucille, fully recovered from her slip into a stupor, stomped a satin heel against the woods in a rhythmic eight count, spun and dipped her way up to the edge of the stage and began to sing.

> "I once met a man who couldn't ride a horse
> So he rode on the back of a tiger of course
> Threaded its tail through a ring in his nose
> And bounced on his back on his tippy toes
> One day that tiger got out on the loose
> So the man went 'n got him a great big noose
> And you know how he got that tiger back?
> He laid out a trap that went snap, snap, snap
> He was happy he caught his big old beast
> 'til that tiger snapped him up and had a delightful feast
> So watch who you catch when you set a trap
> Or you might end up like this unfortunate chap!"

Big Bobby dropped back to his knees and duckwalked across the stage while Lucille kept singing and following him as if under his spell. Big Bobby wound out a long swipe of bubbly notes that traveled up and down the scales. Lucille, remembering the combination Ginger taught her, lightly brushed the floor with a soft shoe, ending with a flurrying crescendo of Cincinnati flap backs to show the audience she fully recovered from Big Bobby's hypnotic runs. And with each jazzy phrase, step and song Miss Lucille's Black Troubadours whipped the audience into a frenzy.

Miss Lucille's Black Troubadours limped onward to the next scheduled tour stop, a three-show dinner theater event on the outskirts of town that required the troupe to be dressed to the nines. Given Thomas Mulgrew's grand retreat and threats, Lucille wasn't sure what to expect from the next string of performance venues but suspected it would be something unsavory—little or no pay or worse, no engagement at all. The show where Thomas promised the theater owner a plantation fantasy had ended with tepid reviews and curses from the owner to never book the troupe again. It was no surprise that offers to perform on a transatlantic ocean liner, like he promised, never materialized. Between dumping their scoundrel of a manager and Lincoln getting shot, the Troubadours were at an all-time low.

Lucille and Big Bobby took turns driving the bus while Delphina tended to Lincoln and Diamond, who was a bundle of boundless energy. Besides Lincoln's snoring and Diamond's whines for being cooped up, the bus was silent. For a long period of time, no one spoke a word even though neither Lucille's nor Big Bobby's driving was steady and the bus lunged from one side of the road to the other. Lucille was driving while Mitchell sat behind her.

"Lucille, I think it's time we cut our losses."

"Mitchell, please. Please don't say that—I don't think I can take it. I know it looks bad."

"Bad? Honey, I don't think it can be any worse." He took out a flask and jerked his head back to take a swig before handing it up to her.

Lucille reached back, put the flask to her lips. "Ooo, that drink is nothing short of fire." She handed it back to him. "Take this stuff before we land upside down."

The bus suffered a flat tire along the way so they arrived at the venue later than expected. The managerless troupe—now a nervous and harried-looking trio plus a battered man patched up to look halfway decent—gave a not-so-stellar performance while a roomful of white patrons danced seemingly without a care in the world. They had to improvise and cut sets short because Lincoln—who had Delphina cover his cuts with makeup and swore he could blow his trumpet as long he stayed seated—was unable to hit some crucial notes due to his busted embouchure.

Once the first show was over, Mitchell left to find a house where he could continue playing, drinking and carousing and lay his head from dawn until they were scheduled to perform. Lucille, Big Bobby and Delphina collectively acted as managers and went to pick up their pay for the night.

"No pay today, folks! At least not for this performance. You didn't finish your act, so by contract, I don't have to pay you."

"What? Didn't you see me blowing my horn, man?" Big Bobby protested. "Didn't you see how they loved me?"

"Don't matter. You tell Mulgrew, that good-for-nothing darkie manager of yours, that he swindled me out my money by promising me top-rate talent. I paid for a whole jazz band and what I heard up there was a far cry from my expectations. If it wasn't for the hopped-up hooch I served my customers, they would've all up and left. No pay today or any day for that matter! Now get out of my office. No pay. And I'm writing this act up."

The Troubadours shuffled out of the office, dejected.

"What we gonna do, Lucille?" Big Bobby asked.

Lucille, simmering, let out a low growl. "Well, we ain't gonna play tomorrow then. Their loss."

"What do you mean, their loss? I need that money, 'cause I got to… Well, don't worry about what I got to do. But queen, listen to me, I really do need that money right now."

"Please, Big Bobby, I can't take any more of these hijinks. Let's just go. We'll make it up at the next town."

"You think that's wise, Lucille? If Marcus was here, he sure wouldn't suggest we leave money on the table like that."

"They are not going to pay us. Can't you see? They're trying to get us to work for nothing. If you let them get away with it now, they ain't ever going to treat us right. I don't care what Marcus would or would not do. This here is my decision. We'll leave and figure the rest out ourselves."

"Who we gonna get to move Maybelle at this late hour? Where we gonna get the money? You know we can't leave without that piano. Mitchell will die for sure."

"I said we'll figure it out!"

35

Even though they didn't have a gig, Lucille decided the Troubadours would stay in Nashville for the next two days. They could use the time off to recuperate. Delphina said she made arrangements to stay at the Lamar House, a big fancy hotel across town. Lucille wondered where she got the money to secure a room but didn't question her. They still hadn't really talked about Monte. At this point, Lucille was afraid to have a full-blown conversation with so much happening. Monte had not shown his face, and Delphina spent her time caring for Lincoln, which Lucille took as a good sign. At least for now, Lucille was happy not to have to share her room with a wriggling baby for once.

Big Bobby, Lincoln and Mitchell were staying at what was sadly the only house standing on the other side of the train tracks. They didn't seem to mind their accommodations. Everyone had seen so much worse while touring in the segregated South. They relished the fact that they could stay in a place where they could be surrounded by all the comforts of their vices.

Lucille and Delphina warned Lincoln to stay off his leg and not get it infected. Lucille didn't want to know about the boys' plans. She wanted nothing more than to lie in bed for the next two days to collect her thoughts and try to piece together a past she never really knew.

However, fate interfered.

She gripped the telegram from Marcus with both hands and read it again. "I knew it! My daddy ain't never been no thief! And he didn't kill anyone!"

Lucille had sent Marcus a telegram after Lincoln's incident, letting him know about the threat against her father. Her stubbornness kept her from communicating with him before, but Marcus and her father had grown quite close and she thought he might know something to verify or disqualify the men's story. She didn't want to ask her parents directly as she thought that might alarm them. She also didn't mention anything about Thomas. Marcus might have gotten wind of it anyway because the entertainment world was small, and with so many performers crisscrossing the nation juicy news traveled swiftly.

"Why would those men tell such lies about my family?" Lucille smoothed out the telegram, which she had inadvertently crumpled in her fisted hand. She read it over and over until the last collection of words jumped out at her: "I'll be there as soon as I can to explain."

Marcus was coming back. But where? When exactly? She didn't know where she was supposed to meet Marcus, but she knew for sure that those men would make good on their threats—the hole they left in Lincoln's leg was proof of that. Who knew what that would mean—beatings, hanging or being shot dead in the street. The goons might have taken the false lead and be halfway to Akron by now, but once they found out what she told them was a lie, if they caught up with her again, it would be a cement block around her neck for sure.

She pulled out letters from her father that she had tied with a ribbon and stuffed into a shoebox, intent on rereading them for any clues. None of her father's letters gave her any insight to her current dilemma, but one wrenched her with such a sense of homesickness that she wanted to immediately run to the arms of her father and mother:

Dearest Daughter,

The Loves nearly died three weeks ago. We thought our bodies would go under the river of bricks, wood and blood in Greenwood...

Once them young men went to the courthouse with guns to protect that shoeshine boy from being lynched, we knew trouble was about to follow. That boy hadn't even had his day in court. It was a shame that he even spent a night in jail or had to wait for a judge, jury, sheriffs, bailiffs, lawyers and a host of paid county employees just for stepping onto an elevator occupied by a white girl. Like they had done so many times before, them local white boys formed a mob around the county jail. The newspapers had gotten them all itched up, prickled with hate and they were ready to scratch. The sight of black men armed with guns—well, you know what was about to happen. I never thought it would be anything like we witnessed over the next two days—a race war, right on our doorsteps.

We almost got burnt up in that little clapboard house just off Archer Street—we moved there to get out of your aunt's hair. She was a mean old woman. It was just what your mother wanted, a white house with window boxes that she filled with big red geraniums and yellow marigolds. But three weeks ago, white men came through town and torched everything up till there wasn't nothing left. No one saw it coming. In fact, we had settled ourselves to believe that things were going to be all right because this time the county sheriff was on our side. By the time we realized it wasn't so, it was too late. Dead men, women and children were scattered along every street. Their blood soaked right into the roads. Our pride, our Greenwood destroyed.

We've got a place on the outskirts of Tulsa now. It's a small farm that was in poor shape, but your old daddy will put it right. You, Lucille Arnetta Love, are the Loves' legacy, our living hopes and dreams. Me and your mama rest assured that the Loves are still standing because of you.

Until we're together again,

Hank and Evelyn Love

Lucille sighed. She never thought it would be the case, but nine years had passed since she laid eyes on her parents. There had been telegrams and letters hand delivered by an aunt or cousin who wasn't really a blood relative but nonetheless family through their extended church connections. Marcus stayed in touch with them as well. He kept his word and visited them in Oklahoma, taking a detour when he had to return to Chicago at Rose's command.

Every night, Lucille got on her knees and prayed for the protection and good health of Hank and Evelyn Love. She would do so with even more fervor now.

She promised herself she would take time off to visit until another tour stop came up. The thought of her parents and the guilt of putting her own desires over them brought tears to her eyes. Lucille wept till she fell asleep on the pile of letters spread out over her bed.

Hours later, she awoke and began gathering her letters and correspondence into a pile. She spotted an unopened envelope she had missed earlier underneath the pile. Her name was printed gracefully across the front. Lucille reached for the envelope. It was light compared to the other letters. She sensed the heaviness of its contents and knew it was news she didn't want to hear. Once opened, there it was, polite words written in black ink against the white paper; Delphina had done what Lucille thought was unthinkable. She had left.

My Dearest Lucille,

So much has happened. He said he loves me and wants to take care of me. Monte and I are getting married. This is the best outcome for me, Diamond and the Troubadours.

I am sorry for writing this, but I am too much of a coward to face you. If I did, I would not be able to leave. I know you all have put your lives on the line for me and Diamond. Mere words cannot express the depth of my gratitude for the kindnesses you have shown me. Please relay to everyone, especially Robert, my heartfelt appreciation.

I love you most of all.

Your sister,
Delphina

Lucille crushed the note against her chest. She couldn't help but feel there was danger ahead in this union. Particularly for Diamond. Did that man—Lucille not only felt in her bones but knew firsthand that he was no good for sure—really want to take care of little Diamond? Worry for the little girl stung Lucille's eyes and pounded in her head and chest. She understood Delphina's reasoning for leaving. In fact, she cheered her on. Lucille had grown fond of the girl that hitched a ride with them nearly two years ago, elbowed her way into their circle, healed and defended and softened even the crustiest of them, creating a band of watchful shepherds and godparents. Lucille had become more fond of Diamond than she had imagined. The child's soft smell, chubby cheeks and toes tugged at her maternal instincts, but also gave her enough satisfaction to nip that desire until her dreams of stardom could materialize.

If a wealthy man made her promises, then Lucille could understand why Delphina would jump at the chance at leaving this uncertain life—moving from town to town where the only bed her little girl had was a dresser drawer or suitcase. Lucille wanted security for Delphina and Diamond, so she prayed that her feelings about Monte were wrong and tried ignore the pang in her chest.

The late-afternoon drizzle softly patted the windowpane. Had Delphina told Big Bobby of her plans? He would be heart-broken.

Lucille folded the letter and slipped it back into the envelope, tying it up with the rest of the stack of mail from her parents. "Well, if there was ever someone who knows how to take care of herself, it's Delphina."

36

"We don't have another tour stop?" Lincoln asked. "I thought for once we might be heading east to Pittsburgh then on to New York."

Mitchell waved the letter in the air. "If you read, boy, the notice says right here that future engagements will be canceled unless we do the bit at the Lincoln Theatre as promised. I hope you don't read like you play cards. You can read, can't you?"

"The tour ain't canceled. But it will be canceled for us," Big Bobby added. "If we don't do it, we'll be all washed up."

Lincoln began pacing. "Oh naw, man. I didn't come this far for this to be over. Lucille, we have a contract, don't we? Doesn't our contract state what kind of act we are? Can't we just refuse to do it?"

Lucille held up her hand. "They don't give a damn about no contract. Thomas got us in this mess. That slick snake made promises thinking we'd eat dirt to get on the high-class two-a-day circuits. He said he'd get back at us for being fired. Now it looks like we've been blue enveloped as if we've been spit-

ting out blue material. If we say or do something nasty, whoever was perched on their moral high horse in the audience
was only offended 'cause they ran out of gin! That's horse shit!
The notice states we cut our act and perform a darkie routine
suitable for family entertainment."

Mitchell, chewing on his cigarette, spit out, "What in the
hell! Our act ain't nowhere close to being blue! We're strictly
family fare! Dammit, our act is clean…at least most times."

"The orders in the envelopes are final. We either do it or quit."
Lucille put a hand on Mitchell to calm him. "We all know who
told the theater owners and the union that we can't be trusted to
be professionals. If we get another infraction, we *will* be washed up
on the circuit we've worked hard to get. Now if we don't put on
blackface paint and give them a happy-go-lucky way-down-South
act, we ain't doing the show—or apparently no other show."

"Them damn minstrel days are over," Lincoln mumbled.
He poked out his lower lip and began shuffling about. "Well,
dem pay'n days are over if we don't honor Tom's deal. What
you think we'uns should do, missum?"

Big Bobby blew out a long, audible stream of air and started
counting on his fingers. "Death comes in threes, man. First
Marcus leaves, then Del and Diamond, and now this."

Lucille stepped between them. "Troubadours! I know how
it looks, but let's think like professionals. We're gonna do the
show, but I got an idea."

Mitchell called out, "I thought you said back when we had
to do it for Marcus, that we weren't going to do that again.
Didn't you say no blackface and no animals?"

"But we've got to get paid and we got to keep working. We
are going to get on that Cunard liner and get overseas. We'll
be international then. We will be top draw and we will be able
to demand whatever we want."

"Welp, for me and Maybelle, its back to playing the whore-
houses. I ain't mad about that. The hours were pretty good and
them girls were always sweet on me for sure."

Big Bobby threw up his hands. He didn't have the fight in him. Since Delphina and Diamond left, he didn't seem to care about anything at all.

Lucille thought her plan was a good one. It would combine a painted face and some plantation or farmyard funnies that would satisfy the theater owner's demands. The Troubadours were set up on the varnished and polished hardwood stage. The venue was a concert hall that was open to this vaudeville show as a special fundraising event. Mitchell, Big Bobby and Lincoln gave her a long, drifting but upbeat introduction. Dressed in a black tuxedo, top hat, white gloves and spats, Lucille grandly slid sideways from the wings and into the spotlight. She struck a pose, tipping her top hat and presenting only a slim profile to the audience. Without singing a note, Lucille swayed forward and back, mimicking one of Ginger's smooth moves. Stepping high and gingerly, she swiveled around until she faced the audience straight on to give the widest, toothiest smile she could stretch across her face—which was painted black on one side and white on the other.

A nervous wave of twittering laughter rippled through the audience. Mitchell, Lincoln and Big Bobby continued playing a bouncing ragtime tune that rang out through the concert hall. Lucille reached in her pocket and tugged a long leash leading from the wings. Out came a tremendous hog. Lucille reeled him close and sat down cross-legged in front of the pig, giving the audience the white-painted side of her face. A hush fell over the auditorium. Lucille sat in a pool of light stroking and tickling the pig's ears and snout. The pig let out a high-pitched squeal and when it plopped on its side, Lucille comically fluttered her eyes while blowing it kisses before she began to sing a number she and Mitchell created only moments ago.

"Down on the ol' plantation
We give you this revue

A show of my true affection
For the one I love to hug and coo
My lil' Petunia is a real fine gal
So much going for her
She's my barnyard pal
Her beauteous frame is something other gals lack
Maybe it's her chops or her fine fat back
She has curls, she has sway
Up for a roll in the hay
Cain't nobody beat my Petunia's soft shapely legs
Unless served on a platter
With some fine scrambled eggs!"

Halfway into the number the first person walked out, followed by a couple marching up the aisle shouting this was ridiculous humor for a coon show. The comments caught fire and row after row of patrons walked out as Mitchell howled with laughter and played louder and louder.

Lucille delivered the song as if she were singing to a paramour. Maybe it was the white greasepaint that made patrons nervous. Maybe it was her sidling up to a puffy faced man, then lifting her leg to dig the pointy tip of her shoe into his thigh. Or it might have been when the dapper chap brightly squealed from the sharp pain and she gracefully bent over to give him a squishy kiss on the cheek, smearing him with greasepaint. Maybe it was when the pig wagged its curly tail and gave the audience a steaming surprise. They wanted a race show and barnyard follies, but maybe it was too much race to handle?

The word moved faster than lightning. After their performance, the rest of the shows were canceled. The theater manager sneered and appeared overjoyed to notify them they were to be cast out as civilians. It was the only time that Thomas, who Mitchell called a dried-up piece of spit, had been true to his word of getting the Troubadours kicked off the tour.

For the first time since Marcus left, Lucille felt truly alone with the weight of her decisions and saddened by the fact she put the lives of the whole troupe in jeopardy with such a careless plan. Now they had no money in their pockets and no chance of another show. Lucille's head ached.

They were on a back road headed north to a town they already knew held no job for them, not unlike the early days on the wagon. She watched the horizon and she prayed for a sign that would give her direction. She thought about her father, a man who could figure himself out of any situation.

"Wait…wait here. Pull over," Lucille asked.

"If I stop, we might not be able to start up again. We don't have much gas and this engine is just about kaput!"

"Mitchell, it will be fine. Stop here. If memory serves me correctly there should be something right over there in that small patch of woods that might save all of our asses."

"Girl, ain't nothing out there but fleas, ticks and probably some black snakes. Let's go before we're stuck out here in the middle of the night. Are we in a sundown town?"

Lucille hopped off the bus and waded through the weeds that lined the side of the road until she reached a small thicket of brush at the base of a tree. She fell to her knees and began digging in the dirt with her bare hands until her fingernails bled from cuts and jagged stones. Never had she thought she'd find herself on all fours, with her knees sinking into the earth and mud saturating her dress, scooping up handfuls of dirt. Determined and breathing heavily, Lucille clawed at the ground until she heard her name echo through the air, followed by the swooshing sound of someone taking long uneasy strides through the field. Big Bobby towered over her.

"Lucille, the boys and I got worried because we couldn't see you no more. Unless you have to relieve yourself, we need to get going. You do know there are snakes out here."

Lucille kept digging around the roots of the tree. "Those snakes don't want me. There is something here, at least I hope it still is. If it is, the Troubadours are going to be all right. For tonight."

The coins her daddy gave her had to be here where they buried them when she was a child. *It needs to be here.* The bend in the road the Traveling Loves had once trekked looked as if nothing had changed over the years and seasons. The notch in the tree where Daddy shaved a branch to whittle was still there even though the grass had grown tall around its roots. She knew people buried things all along these back roads—a message to let weary travelers know help was on the way or that they were not alone in their travels from one point in their lives to another. Even to let them know there were friends and safety ahead.

"Come on, Luce. This is crazy. We need to go before it gets dark," Big Bobby said softly as he gently patted her shoulders.

Lucille ignored him and kept pulling up dirt. She needed a sign to know all was going to be well. Then she saw a string. She tugged it and finally felt the folds of a leather pouch. She pulled it from the dirt and heavy coins fell into her hands. Their coolness burned her palm. "He knew. My daddy knew I'd come back for this one day."

She jumped up and held her treasure up against the fading sunlight. "I found it! I told you I've been this way before. If we can make it to the next town, we can get some gas and have a place to stay tonight." Lucille hopped back toward the bus with Big Bobby marching somberly behind her.

Mitchell shouted, "What you got there, Luce? Magic beans?"

"If you want to sleep somewhere with a roof over your head tonight, you better hush your mouth. I've got enough to take care of all our sorry broke asses, courtesy of my dear pappy!

Now say what you will about prayer, but sweet child o' Jesus, it's working tonight. What you say about that, Mitch?"

Mitchell pulled his hat over his eyes and grumbled a few unintelligible words.

Lucille, giddy with excitement, brushed at the wet dirt stains on the front of her dress. "Yeah, boys, we crisscrossed all over these roads. I didn't recognize it before, but I do remember there were two churches about ten miles apart, sitting in two different states. The church buildings were small and sturdy just like the people who attended service. We sang and prayed with them and they fed, clothed and gave us shelter. I remember someone churned some peach ice cream. I can just taste that confection on my tongue right now. I didn't see those churches on our way here. Maybe they aren't there anymore."

Big Bobby said solemnly, "Some of those fools probably burnt them down a long time ago when they were trying to drive out all the black folks."

"I always wondered why someone would go along with that," Lucille added. "I can't understand how Christians agreed to burning down a place built to worship the Lord."

Mitchell barked out, "Lincoln! Play something for those churches that aren't there no more."

"Prayers aren't going to do nothing," Big Bobby snapped. "But go on and play something for everyone around, Lincoln. I want to hear some music since we out here in the dark with nowhere to lay our heads."

"Oh, stop your complaining." Lincoln shouted while licking his lips. "Everything gonna be all right now. Lucille done went to the rough patch to get us out of a rough patch."

Lincoln pulled out his trumpet. The remaining light of sunset bounced off the instrument as he raised it to the sky.

Big Bobby yawned and stretched out his arms. "Mitchell, are you drinking? Pass that over here."

Lincoln pressed the horn to his lips. Starting slowly and solemnly, he slid his fingers over his trumpet, hitting note after note of a melody that felt like long-lasting love. The music floated on the evening breeze calling for all to remember the seasons of love past.

When he stopped, tears were streaming down his face. "Maybe this is it, folks. This is a sign we should call it quits."

Lucille's eyes widened. "Quit? We can't quit now! Not after everything we've gone through."

"The boy's got a point, y'all. This might be a signal that it's the end of the road." Big Bobby shrugged. "No steady money. No gig. We can't get much lower."

"I told myself I'll be in this business till the money dries up and that looks like where we are now." Lincoln wiped his tears. "But we can't just leave Miss Lucille's Black Troubadours right here in the middle of the road. We got to give her a proper burial."

"What are you talking about?" Lucille stood gripping the back of her seat. "I don't believe what I'm hearing. You pussies are talking crazy. Y'all trying to put me in the ground now? Well, I'm not ready! Now listen, I'm still heading to the top and if you don't want it, including you, Mitchell, you can all get your black asses off this bus right now!"

Silence followed. Big Bobby, Lincoln and Mitchell hung their heads to avoid making eye contact with Lucille or each other. No one wanted to admit their shame, regret and dejection.

Lucille stormed off the bus and began walking down the road.

"Bobby, go after her."

"I'll wait and give her a moment. That was pretty harsh, Lincoln. She's a tough cookie, but you've got to know that had to hurt."

Mitchell whispered, "So, since we're calling it quits, you gonna go back to that big-legged gal you been tell us about?"

"Yeah, deep brown Cecille." Lincoln rubbed his chin. "That

woman can nurse me back to good health all right. I need to be wrapped up in her but first, I'm going back home to New Orleans...to my mama's house."

"Your mama?"

"After all those women you say be pining after you. You gonna go live with your mama?"

"Yeah, I need a good bowl of gumbo before I go any further." He patted his leg. "And I can't really walk nowhere for long periods of time so I don't want to travel much. And guess what—I ain't gambling no more."

Mitchell choked out between gulps from his flask, "What? I know you lying."

"You heard me. No, I think I'd like to keep my limbs and meet St. Peter, with everything God gave me and without any more additional holes in my body. But I don't mean to do that soon."

"Wow, what's next, you gonna be traveling around as one of those evangelists blowing that horn while they're dunking folks in the water?" Mitchell joked.

"Please, man, I'mma stay with my horn. You can't separate me from that. Maybe play with King Oliver or any band Satchmo puts together. I think he'd appreciate a hardscrabble brother like me from back town."

Big Bobby hung his head low and spoke slowly. "So brothers, this is it, right?

"Yeah, it's over, man." Lincoln licked his lips and nodded. His fingers moved in the air as if attached to his horn before he clasped his hands together to let them rest in his lap. "Call the undertaker. The Troubadours are dead."

"I loved working with y'all. We done been through it but now it's time to play ourselves home. We'll all be all right 'cause it's all about this crazy music—them notes ain't ever gonna let us go. It's leading us up to the pearly gates, you know."

Big Bobby looked over at Mitchell, who shook his flask in

the hopes that a few more drops of whatever magic elixir he was carrying would be available for consumption. "Mitch, you go after her. She'll listen to you."

"Yeah," Lincoln piped in. "This ain't good. Tell her we're sorry for everything we ever did."

"You mean what *you* did. You actually got us into this."

"What you mean, Negro? You were right by my side the whole time. You certainly weren't thinking about Lucille or none of the Troubadour business when you were holding that hot hand, were you?"

"Both you imbeciles, shut up!" Mitchell uncurled himself from his seat, squeezed between Maybelle to the front of the bus. "I'll go get her. Then we can talk about making this end official. And by the way, it's all our faults. *We* should have never agreed to that damn jackal's plan in the first place and you fools shouldn't have been out there spreading any of her coins at them gambling parlors. *And* I should have kept my black ass in Chicago and never laid my eyes on the both of you."

Mitchell wobbled off the bus, walking sprightly in Lucille's direction. Each foot in a rhythm all its own, he tottered and weaved as Lucille continued her march into the dark. There was no swing in her arms as she clung to herself, walking in fury.

"Lucille! Lucille, wait!" Mitchell puffed out as he struggled placing one foot in front of the other. Lucille continued on her trek.

"Waaaait!" Mitchell's voice trailed off as he buckled over, placing his hands on his knees to sturdy himself. "Lucille!" The energy it took to call out to her sapped his ability to stand and he fell, lying spread-eagle in the middle of the road.

Lucille heard the strain in his call and whipped around at the sound of a soft thud.

"Mitch! Mitchell! Are you all right?" Lucille ran back to him. His eyes rolled in his head as his arms and legs moved slowly as if he was making snow angels in the yellow dirt.

"Girl, I'm fine. I'm okay," he spit out, slurring his words. "I still ain't used to these country roads. I just took a tumble. Now get your hands off me. I can get up on my own."

It was clear he couldn't get up. Lucille wrapped an arm around Mitchell's shoulders to help him sit up. It was the first time she had noticed he was skin and bones. She could feel his shoulder blades and the curve of his spine through his coat. He was light as a feather.

"Woman, we're sorry for what we said. Me and the boys are sorry for everything we've ever done. But we took a vote and shook on it—it's time for a serious conversation. Now come. Get back on the bus. We'll make to the next town with the teeny bit of fuel we got. Given the situation the Troubadours cain't go on but we're stuck. We cain't get nowhere else just yet."

Big Bobby drove the bus slowly in the dark to reserve fuel. The ragtag lot of troubadours lay draped across the seats. Lincoln's bandaged leg began bleeding. There was no medicine to alleviate his pain or clean rags to rewrap his wound among the belongings they scooped up in their haste to leave. Mitchell's head was tilted back. He breathed loudly through his open mouth. Lucille, her face blank, sat behind Big Bobby, staring into the darkness.

"You okay, Miss Luce?"

"I'm all right. Just worried about Mitchell."

"He'll be okay. He's recovered before. It's just I ain't seen him eat nothing. He's surviving on just that hooch. I'm sure he'll be all right once we get to the next town. Ever since Marcus left—I have to say it, Luce—ever since he left and that god-damn Thomas came and went, good riddance to him, we've been kinda fallin' apart. How'd we get here? I thought we would be in Harlem by now."

"Bobby, you're right—we *should've* been in Harlem by now. Marcus promised us. I don't blame him though, he did what he could as a manager. I think the tide turned when I sold my soul to the devils."

"Devils?"

"Yes. Thomas you know about, and I take full responsibility for that. I was just so angry with Marcus, I thought Thomas would do what Marcus couldn't. And you not going to like this, but I believe one of them devils is the one that ran off with our Delphina."

"Are you telling me Delphina and Diamond are in harm's way?"

"Well, you know Del, she won't get into something she can't get out of. Now, let me tell you, if you ever wanted to know the true name of the devil it's Montgomery Garreau."

Sparing only a few details, Lucille told Big Bobby about Delphina's masquerading as a patron and the incident with Monte.

"I can't believe she suckered him and used us."

"Big Bobby, don't be so hard on her. She was only looking out for Diamond. You couldn't have thought that she would stay in this life, could you? Particularly with those men threatening our lives. She's had it hard—dirt poor and scaping for survival. She's had a lot of challenges like we have."

Big Bobby stayed silent. Lucille could see his face shimmering in the dark. She knew he was deeply hurt that Delphina left him, the one who showed her nothing but sweetness, for someone who might do her and Diamond harm.

As if confirming Lucille's thought, Bobby whispered, "I would never, ever hurt her."

37

The bus wheezed its way on gas fumes and coughed until it rolled silently outside of Bowling Green. Luckily it was on the right side of the town. There was a scattering of people and cars parked along a few ill–lit short blocks of worn–down homes along with a row of storefronts. Coins were pressed into the palm of a rotund woman, Mrs. Golightly, who said her rooming house didn't normally allow actors or musicians, but would give them two rooms and breakfast.

Mrs. Golightly waved a fat finger at the sweaty, sad group. "I'm not promising nothing past tomorrow morning. If there is any trouble, and I mean the slightest, I will toss you all out on your ears."

Lucille didn't understand how Mrs. Golightly could be so high and mighty about her establishment when the building was just north of being a ramshackle heap.

Her room was just a bed and tiny dressing table perched upon a rag rug. Lucille felt small, something that the Little Girl with the Big Voice had never experienced before. Two steps in either direction with outstretched arms, she'd be able to touch both walls. A flame flickering from a lamp set on the bedside table was the only source of light. Despite little scratching sounds from the floorboards indicating the mice were busy at work, this would have to do.

She sighed deeply and blew out the flame of the lamp. With treacherous Thomas ruining their reputation and the threat of goons killing them for something she knew nothing about, Lucille's nerves were not going to let her sleep. She had sent a telegram to her parents to let them know she was in Bowling Green. She omitted details and promised herself only to alert them if she was backed into a corner. From a quick glance around her room, it felt like time was staring her in the face whether she wanted to admit it or not.

Mitchell, Big Bobby and Lincoln had officially thrown in the towel, calling it quits. Everyone had left or was in the process of leaving her. She'd have to figure out what to do next by herself. But like she had done since forever, Lucille would adjust and keep her eye on the prize—though she was no longer certain how to reach her long-sought-after prize.

With no show on the roster, no contract, no scheduled dates and no real money for gas, Lucille thought it best to take some time off before venturing to Cincinnati, where gigs might be more plentiful. Despite the boys unanimously agreeing to disband, they all stayed around picking up one-night gigs nearby— barely enough to keep paying for their respective boardings. Lucille held out hope that it was a sign that something would drop in their laps and bring the Troubadours back to full force.

Mitchell adopted a new regimen, stopping by Mrs. Golightly's to spend time with Lucille. He and the boys were staying a few doors down at Miss Dolly's Place. The sight of Mitchell's thin, bony body, shirt unbuttoned to expose his light, yellow-tinged skin, seemed almost unnatural. But she was comforted by his company. It soothed her nerves and helped her fight the thought of going home to her parents—where she knew she would be celebrated and loved, but was a sure sign of a busted career.

Lucille came to welcome the quiet. It was the first time in years where she could sleep and eat feeling the breeze of the day and night. There was nothing else to do until something jumped up and bit her. That something came in the form of a telegram that arrived a week later. She and Mitchell were sitting on Mrs. Golightly's porch when it was handed to her. Lucille pulled the telegram from the envelope with trembling hands. *It had to be bad news.* Her hands shook so much she ripped the telegram, tearing the post in two. She hadn't written to her parents about the mysterious coins; she hoped that she wouldn't have to put a scare into Mother about the men who were pursuing the dangerous secret that could result in someone's death. The hole in Lincoln's leg reminded Lucille she only bought enough time to delay the thugs from finding her father. Her chest heaving, she caught a long breath when she saw it was from Delphina.

Dear sister,

Beware and be quick. Watch out for General Paul Garreau. I'll meet you in Chattanooga.

Love,

Del

Lucille read the telegram over and over before crumpling it into a ball in her lap.

"I just knew that Monte was bad news—him and his family, it seems."

It had been two months and five shows since Delphina left. Lucille had thought the appearance of two men threatening and shooting Lincoln in Louisville was one of the reasons Delphina ran off and got married. But on the other hand, Delphina had been a hardened trouper and, given her past, Lucille was certain a little gunplay wouldn't have scared her off. Then again, there was Diamond to consider.

Evidently, Delphina was still keeping up with the Troubadours because she knew the next stop on the now-defunct route would have been Chattanooga, Tennessee. She could have never known they would've been stuck in Bowling Green, on the brink of being penniless. Big Bobby must have been keeping her updated—which was dangerous for both Delphina and Bobby. If that husband of hers found out she was corresponding with another man, particularly a colored man, that might be the end of Delphina. Then where would that leave little Diamond?

Lucille slowly sat down, thinking about what could possibly happen next.

"Who do you think she's talking about, Mitchell?"

"I don't know. General Garreau don't sound like no Yankee. So that means there's trouble." Mitchell rolled his eyes and sucked his teeth. "Tsk, I'm glad that girl, after all we did for her, took time out of her busy schedule to spend some of that new rich white money she got now on a telegram for us poor colored folks though."

"This is all about these stupid coins and the money my daddy gave me more than a decade ago. Mitch, I told those guys that shot Lincoln that my parents are dead. And they're going to keep on believing that if I can help it. They're going to try to shake me down for money I don't have. And if we can't come to some agreement, well…" Lucille shrugged. She continued, "And regardless of the facts, the newspapers, both black and white, and the circuit rumor mill will have a field day claiming my daddy robbed a bank while singing in a church choir. Then, even though I was just a baby, they'll treat me like some criminal. Won't nobody hire me to sing. The only job I'll get is picking up after some white family—and I'm not doing that."

"Naw, girl... People will kill for an opportunity to be on-stage. Many of these performers you see night after night, town after town, have dead bodies all piled up behind them. So what? A scandal like that might get you and us center stage, last-act status."

"Until then, we need to figure out what to do now. We need money to get on up to Cincinnati. I only paid Mrs. Golightly through the rest of the week."

"There's another lady's place down the road—I'll ask them if they need a piano player to liven things up around the clip joint and help them johns loosen up their pockets."

Lucille stared at Mitchell. Through her worry, she wondered how she missed noticing that he had become rail thin. His skin was sallow and his blue eyes swam in a pool of yellow. "Mitch, are you okay? You don't look so good. You don't have to do anything. I'll find a way for us."

"No, no, no, queenie. You've done enough, young'n. You can't keep going around taking care of us grown men. You rest. I'll keep my ears open for another quick gig and..."

Mitchell stopped mid-sentence. His mouth hung open as his eyes followed a figure coming up the walkway. "MARCUS!!! Man, you a sight for sore eyes! How'd you find us?"

Marcus was neatly dressed compared to Lucille's limp day dress and Mitchell's shabby appearance. He looked so much like that first moment they met when she was a Traveling Love. Marcus planted a foot on the front step. "Boy, you two look like you've been pulled through a hedge."

"Backward...now, you big palooka, if I wasn't sober, I'd jump up from here and clobber you good," Mitchell said jokingly.

"Hello, Lucille."

Lucille sat motionless. Her greeting was stuck in her throat where it seemed her heart leaped up and got tangled in her vocal cords. She held tight to the arm of the glider to keep from tak-ing one big leap into Marcus's arms.

"Y'all were easy to find." He hesitated. "I heard about what happened and it don't take much to find the whereabouts of an old bus filled with a singer, musicians and a piano."

"Well, what a day. Looks like everybody is finding their way back to the old Troubadours. That's a sign, right, Lucille?" Mitchell nudged Lucille, who was still trying to find her voice.

Marcus cocked an eyebrow. "Everybody?"

Lucille finally stood up, stretched out her arms and ran over to Marcus to give him a hug. "Del and Diamond left us. She ran off and got married to some shady character."

Marcus pulled away from her. "Well then, I've got some bet-ter news! You're going to be bowled over when you hear what I've got lined up."

Marcus's news couldn't have come at a better time: there was an audition for one of the biggest producers who was trying to recreate a musical with an all-colored cast of entertainers. It was just the sort of big production that Marcus and Lucille had dreamed about from the very beginning.

Lucille sat sunk in the middle of the wrought iron bed. She shifted between the yellowed mildewed sheets and ancient quilt. The moonlight filtered into the small room and stretched across Marcus's face. He had aged in the year he'd been away. He had come directly from the train to see her. Since he didn't have a place to stay, Lucille invited him up to her room to rest from his trip. They'd have to keep it hidden from Miss Golightly by being as quiet as possible, which was easy to do since he im-mediately slumped into a chair and fell asleep.

As Lucille covered Marcus with her only quilt, all the previ-ous anger disappeared. All the arguments she had with herself for being so foolish to fall in love with a man who only cared about her career evaporated into thin air. All she could see was the man who approached her when she was a child and asked her what she wanted. She was bone weary from fighting every challenge the Troubadours had faced since he left.

Her heart tripped over itself as she watched his chest rise and fall. She slid out of bed and tiptoed over to him to get a closer look. Lucille lightly touched Marcus's face, feeling the roughness along his chin and running her fingers deep in his coarse hair. She wanted to fall into him and wrap her arms around his shoulders and bury her head into his chest to feel his breathing. Most of all, she wanted to feel the softness of his lips against hers. But her wants were stifled as she caught a glance outside the tall windows.

In the stark moonlight that fell between the only two trees that dared to grow on the street, Lucille spotted two white men. The sight alone was alarming on this side of the tracks. A dark car parked at the curb. Their presence usually meant someone was going to meet a foul end, deservedly or not. One man, who appeared to be elderly, was crooked, stooped over so low that his head hovered at his chest. The other was younger, his posture straight as his hands danced with the motions of explanation.

When the younger man pointed to the boardinghouse, Lucille quickly jumped from the window to hide in the shadows. Her movement failed to disturb Marcus, who only fidgeted in the chair and began to snore. Lucille eased over to the window to see nothing but the guardian trees at their post. She shrugged at the sight of the lonely street. Miss Dolly's, where Mitchell and the boys were staying, was a few blocks down. *Maybe Miss Dolly was about to have some new visitors.*

Lucille crawled back in bed only to toss and turn while the sun rose. Her mind raced thinking of men, money, opportunity and the precariousness of her life and career. Her thoughts were interrupted by a knock on the door. Startled, she collected herself and whispered loudly, "It better be something important. It's too early for visitors and bad news."

She really didn't want to open the door in case it was some-one with the high moral fiber who would take offense to Mar-cus sleeping in the corner or worse. Marcus, however, finally sat straight up, looking around the room as if trying to deter-mine his own whereabouts.

It was Mrs. Golightly delivering a message. "There's a man waiting downstairs for you…a Mr. Robert Wiley. He says it's important."

For Big Bobby to give his full government name, it must be important.

Marcus, fully awake and rubbing his eyes, whispered, "Luce, you go down first and I'll follow you."

Bobby was agitated, shifting his weight from foot to foot. His face was long with worry. "Lucille, it's Mitchell. He ain't doing so good. I gave him a few herbs that Del gave me be-fore she left. She told me it would help with alcohol poison-ing. I told him to hold them under his tongue like she said, but it don't work. He's shaking something awful. He made a fuss about going to the doctor's and when we said we'd take him to the hospital he screamed and turned white as a sheet."

"What happened?"

"I dunno. He was looking pretty raggedy earlier. He was, as usual, hopped up on something and drinking some of that house juice. Then he just collapsed right in front of everybody in the middle of the parlor. He had just finished battling some youngster who came right up to him and challenged him. That boy said he could outplay him and had five dollars to prove it. Mitchell, of course, hammered that boy like like a chop-per squad. And while all them folks were slappin' their thighs and jumpin' to his music, he took a swig and fell straight to the floor. The girls took him to his room, but when I went to check on him, he looked pretty bad. I don't quite know what to do now."

"Let me get some clothes on. Marcus is upstairs. We'll get

over there quick. I'll try to convince him to go to the hospital. We'll drag him there if we have to. Where's Lincoln?"

"He's with Mitchell. I told him to keep trying to give him water or coffee or tea, anything to dilute whatever is torturing him."

Something nagged at the back of Lucille's brain. She'd have to hurry. At this point, she didn't give a damn who saw Marcus leave her room. If Mitchell was sick, she'd do everything humanly possible to save the one man, besides her daddy, that supported her onstage and off for all these years.

In the house where Mitchell was staying, every window of the tall brick building was open. Some were wide open, others just a crack, but all to let in a breeze to cleanse the shadows of the previous night's activities. Inside, a lush circular foyer opened into several lavishly furnished rooms with thick carpets, velvet settees and Tiffany lamps. The dark woodwork was polished to a high gleam. On the left, beyond sliding doors which were slightly open, was a large parlor with two pianos, one on each side of the room. The house was quiet except for the surprising sound of a bleating goat and a wheezing donkey coming from the back.

Big Bobby motioned for Lucille to follow him up the stairs. It was a shock, because as much as the first floor with its luxurious entryway and furnishing had a high-class feel, the long hallway of the second floor looked like it could use several coats of paint. Like the love that was being peddled, it was evident that the classiness was all a sham. But by the time a client had chosen to climb the stairs it didn't matter, for other desires were on the mind.

More shocking was the sight of Mitchell. His small frame was enveloped by the four-poster bed. His shirt was open, revealing sallow yellow skin just barely covering his ribs. His head lay on pillows that were wet and yellow. The room smelled sickly sweet and rancid at the same time, like vomit. Lincoln sat on a chair in the corner, anxiously tapping his knee.

"Mitchell, you…" Lucille stopped short as Mitchell's chest heaved deeply and his eyes rolled back into his head. When he slowly opened his eyes, he stared back at her and clicked his teeth in disgust.

"So what do you want from me, girl? Right now you're bothering me. Let me go. I'm tired—that's all!"

"Take this." She reached in her pocket and withdrew a small silver clutch and pulled out one of her remaining gold coins. She pushed it into his palm and closed his fingers around it. Mitchell weakly tried to jerk away.

"Girl, I don't need your money," he slurred as his head moved from side to side.

"No, but you need this to remember that we're family. You need to be reminded of that. So every time you look at this coin, every time you feel it, you'll know. You've taught me so much. I credit you for giving us Troubadours life. I want you to remember, no matter where you go, that we love you for it." She bent down to kiss his cheek. His skin was cool and clammy. "Eat something. I don't know where you got that stuff you drinking. I don't care…"

He blew out hot breath. "It ain't the hooch. Naw, girl… I'm sick. I'm sick to my bones. The only thing that truly relieves me is Maybelle. Stop talking all that sweet stuff. Sing something. I need to sleep." He rolled over on his side. Lucille could see the bones of his spine poking through his shirt. He mumbled from over his shoulder, "You give that coin to Diamond. That little high-yellow colored girl is gonna need all the help she can get. And who knows if Bobby is gonna be around. I swear that big, black buck got a target on his back. Specially if he keeps chasing Delphina." His whole body shook as he took a deep breath and drifted off to sleep, mumbling, "The world is changing. Crazy, huh…"

Lucille wished she could write Delphina to find out what sort of roots or herbs Medicine Mary might have that could help bring Mitchell back to good health. She watched him as he seemed to wrestle with himself, kicking his feet. Lucille had never seen Mitchell so frail. In the back of her mind she knew what she couldn't ignore. What Mitchell needed was more than whatever Delphina and Medicine Mary had in their little pouches and bottles. He needed a lot more than the earth had to give.

"You both go on downstairs. Bobby, tell one of the girls to go fetch a doctor. Lincoln, can you make it downstairs all by yourself? Tell Marcus I'll be down in a minute. I need to be with my friend, so for now, let's let him sleep."

The floorboards chirped with each step Bobby and Lincoln took as they walked out of the room and headed down the stairs.

Lucille turned her attention back to Mitchell. She wished she could bring Maybelle up to his room or that Mitchell was strong enough to go downstairs and sit at the piano bench that had held and fed him. They had sung books and books of music together. Made up story after story when they ran out of written words. So many times, offstage, Lucille had seen his face soften to the edge of tears when alcohol forced him to talk about his father beating him until his skin was split into shreds. When he spoke through the slits in his eyes about the times his mother hid him from the black man who whipped little Mitchell mercilessly in his rage. He found safety behind the piano until the man disappeared. He then hid in front of the piano, banging out his own rage, confusion and fear on the black-and-white keys that spilled out his life story.

She touched Mitchell's face. His skin held the faintest tinge of warmth, more clammy and stonelike now. She kissed his cheek and heard his voice dissipate into the harsh yell of an older woman who burst into the room.

"Who are all these visitors? What the hell is going on?" She paused when she noticed Mitchell's still body. "Oh…well, he's dead. If you know him, you better take that dead man with you or we'll have to toss him in the street."

"No, he's not dead. He just sleeping."

"Listen, lady, I know a dead man when I see 'em and that man has left this god-forsaken earth. You'll have to pay for an extra day if he stays here any longer."

Lucille turned back around, laid a hand on Mitchell's chest and immediately snatched it away. "Oh, dear God…my dear Lord in heaven…"

Tears fell freely down her cheeks as she kissed his face, where breath no longer escaped between his lips. She was having a hard time catching her own. Lucille managed to go over to the window that looked out to the street. She could see Bobby, Lincoln and Marcus huddled together. Bobby was pointing at three men down the street heading in their direction. Lincoln was backing on to the bus.

She leaned far out from the window, shouting out to Marcus to get his attention. Both groups of men stopped in their tracks and looked up at Lucille as she waved her white hankie out the window. Her face told them all they needed to know. Mitchell was dead.

There was no time for wailing because the men down the street suddenly picked up their pace. Marcus and Big Bobby stood squarely on the sidewalk blocking their entrance to the building. Lucille couldn't hear what they were saying but saw that arms were crossed and fists were tightening. Big Bobby threw the first punch, which knocked off one man's hat, and Marcus jumped in to pin the other to the sidewalk in a flurry of punches. Lincoln yelled from the bus window and had a piece in his hand threatening to shoot. One man broke away from the melee and ran into the house.

Clouded in a veil of tears, Lucille didn't recognize that the men barreling toward the house were the same men who had threatened her in her dressing room, months back. It wasn't until they stood toe to toe with Marcus that she realized the danger. Her heart thumped wildly in her chest. The sound of grunts and fists meeting flesh as bodies hit the pavement could be heard from the second-story window. She pulled away from the window. Her eyes fell on the bed, which was still. It was as if she needed a second heart to grieve for her dear friend, as the heart in her chest was occupied with fear.

I love you, Mitch. I'll be back so we can say goodbye to you and Maybelle. I'll be back to take care of you, baby.

She spun around with indecision until she finally headed out the door to face whatever was happening in open air. She had to get what was left of her Troubadours out of harm's way.

38

Lucille barreled forward, keeping her head down and her eyes watching each step before her. She took the stairs two at a time to stay ahead of the flurry of heavy thuds slamming down on the steps behind her and the cacophony of screaming voices floating up the stairwell. When she reached the fourth-floor landing, the stairs ended. Before her eyes, a cord dangled from the ceiling like a gift from the heavens. She reached up but changed her mind. There was no time to climb up into the attic. Besides, if she did it would leave her trapped. She glanced to the right and stared down a long hallway. The only way out was to run to the other end of the floor and make her way down the back stairs, hoping no one was climbing up.

When Lucille hit the third-floor landing, she crashed into the large chest of the roughneck barreling up the stairs. She tried to reverse, but he snagged the hem of her dress, causing her to trip on the stairs. He then pulled her closer to him, grabbing her by the wrist with his other hand. Lucille tried to jerk away from his grasp, but he gripped her shoulder to push her forward into the hallway. With several thrusts he and Lucille burst through a door to a room where a thin woman with skin the color of infection lay on a bed smoking a cigarette. She made no effort to cover her almost nude body with the thin robe that fell open around her. She stared at Lucille and the man who had stood frozen in their struggle. She blinked slowly, appearing indifferent as if a man shoving a woman into her bedroom was a usual occurrence.

"Get out!" the man growled at the woman.

Moving slowly, she wrapped the thin robe around her bony frame and padded out of the room barefoot.

The man tightened his grip. "You think you can just erase footsteps and a trail just goes cold? You thought no one would ever find you? Naw, greedy people hold on to things."

Lucille struggled to free herself from the man's grip. He squeezed her even tighter when he shoved her against the wall. Lucille felt a burning sensation as her head hit the wall with a resounding thud.

"Greedy people and those who've lost something that means something to them are never satisfied. I'm not ashamed to say that I'm greedy and the people I work for are greedy."

The light in the room flickered and she heard Big Bobby calling out for her, telling her to hurry. The man loomed over her. He grabbed her chin and dug his beefy fingers deep into her cheek. The inside of her mouth pressed sharply against her teeth.

"Answer them! Tell 'em you're coming nicely or else I'll kill you right here! Go on! Tell them!" He loosened his grip only slightly.

Lucille squeezed out, "I'll be right there." It was unconvincing but satisfactory.

"Listen, you mongrel bitch, you got me in real trouble with General Garreau. 'Cause the last time I saw you—when I left my calling card with that damn simpleton trumpet player—you lied to me. We didn't find no Hank or Evelyn Love buried in Ohio. I told you we was gonna come back. So now it's all about you. You owe us some money and the general wants it and answers now!"

"I don't know what you're talking about."

He tightened his hand over her mouth and banged her head against the wall a second time. "Yes, you do! Yes, you do! Or else I wouldn't be chasing you and those other niggers all around town. Plus, your manager told us you and your Troubadours have money hidden all over the place. Now let me tell you what's going to happen next."

The temperature in the room dropped suddenly. The open window carried in the sickening-sweet scent of rotten garbage from the alleyway and a chilling draft wafted in from the doorway, stirring the air between them. From over the man's shoulder, Lucille caught a figure silently slip into the room from the hallway. Her body stiffened at the sight, making it hard to conceal her surprise. Following her gaze, the man broke his grip and whipped his head around to see who was behind him.

Lucille snarled, "Wait. Wait. No, you fucking baboon, now let me tell you what's going to happen…"

In one leap, Delphina jumped on the man's back swinging an arm around his neck, pulling the startled man backward. Lucille pushed him even farther away to get enough space between them to raise her knee and land it in just the right spot. She used enough force cause damage. He whirled around grimacing in pain, trying to grab his injured privates and shake off Delphina, who had knocked his hat off and was ferociously pulling his ear.

Both women took advantage of their momentary upper hand to punch, kick and scratch at his face. He retreated backward, swinging one arm wildly at the ladies, trying to land either a blow to Lucille's jaw or shake Delphina off his back. Scraping his heels against the groaning, uneven wooden floorboards, he struggled to regain his balance. Lucille and Delphina pushed him toward the other side of the room, toward the open window. It was only a brief second in the tussle, but Lucille locked eyes with Delphina. She signaled by tilting her head and Delphina nodded in response. Delphina dug her heel into the man's foot while Lucille gave him another swift and sharp kick to the groin, then both women pushed the man through the window. His head banged against the windowpane, showering the alleyway with shards of glass.

"I'ma kill both you bitches. I'll kill you both," he grunted through clenched teeth. Partially hanging out the window by the seat of his pants, his coattails flew in the breeze. He tried to grab hold of the window frame. Delphina bit down across his knuckles and fingers so hard he had no choice but to let go. He then attempted to grab her face but she was too quick. Gravity took hold and he folded like a crumpled piece of paper, falling out the window as if being flushed down the toilet. It wasn't a long fall but just enough for the big man to land in a series of loud thuds and cracks that ended with him spread-eagle on his back among the garbage bins in the alley.

Lucille and Delphina stared at each other, both trying to catch their breath, their chests heaving from exertion. Their dresses and stockings were torn, hair wildly whipped across their faces and bruises were appearing rapidly. Before saying a word, they reached out to grab hold of each other, hugging tightly and crying in unison.

"Are you all right? Where the hell did you come from? How did you know to find us here?"

"You think he's dead?"

They both looked out the window. The immobile figure, with a crooked line of blood trickling from his mouth, nose and spreading from underneath his head, stared back. A curious goat moseyed up to him and sniffed around his hand.

"If not, I'd say he's on his way."

From their vantage point they could see the police wagon

roll up to the front of the house. Four policemen with batons at the ready filed out and separated. Two entered the alley and the others met a man with a bold mustache and rumpled hair standing at the front of house dressed in a velvet robe.

The thin woman who had been unceremoniously put out returned. She twisted the belt of her robe, then cinched it tight. Squeezing between Lucille and Delphina, she leaned out the window to get a good look and then waved to the cops who had assembled around the dead man.

"You girls know how to handle yourselves. Good work. Oh, don't worry about this little skirmish, it happens every day. Not that a man goes flying out the window—that was dramatic. Didja see that man in the robe down there? That's the police commissioner. He's here so often this is like his place. He'll make sure all them goons disappear. They'll never show their faces here again or anywhere else."

"I still don't understand..." Lucille looked at Delphina in amazement. "Thank God you're here. I still can't fathom..."

Delphina placed her hand on Lucille's shoulder. "Listen, sister, all the pieces started falling into place when I met Monte's family. A nasty bunch if I've ever seen such. All they ever talk about is money, and the freedom to take whatever they want and discard what they don't. Once I met Monte's uncle, the general, and heard him tell that tale of the Evansville robbery many more times in great detail and description, I put it all together. Add to that he had handfuls of the very same coins those men got from Lincoln... That old man was obsessed with them coins and that robbery. I think it was a sickness he had. He blamed all the ills of his life from the burns that covered his body to the weakness in his arms and legs on your daddy, Hank Love. He believed your daddy stole them from him. From what I've seen, I knew their family would stop at nothing to find you again. I couldn't let that happen.

"It wasn't until that old man suggested that they send away my

Diamond…saying she's looking too dark to be around the house. Suddenly that old man took seriously ill. Medicine Mary taught me a lot. He was so sick in the head he couldn't remember his name and was hopping around like a bedbug. You know there are a lot of wonderfully useful herbs out there just growing and sprouting, just waiting to be chopped up finely and brewed into a nice tasting tea. Sweetened just right, it's the cure for everything. When I left, it looked like that old man got old-timer's disease, but just give them herbs a little more time. Monte is so busy trying to grab hold of the old man's estate. That should keep him busy for a while."

Lucille tightened her arms around her sister. "Delphina, I love you! Let's go." She thanked the seminude woman, who had slipped back into bed as if nothing happened. "No need to stay and be questioned by the cops."

"Yeah, sister, I'll tell you more later. For now, Bobby, Lincoln and Ginger are downstairs. We got to get out of here."

"Ginger's here?"

"Yeah, that's how I got here. We went over to the boarding-house, and they said you left in a hurry with Big Bobby. It was a guess that you'd be here. Where's Mitchell?"

The group gathered under a single light that illuminated only a spot in the basement of the Peoria Hotel. It was a place where the owners had once allowed the Troubadours to rehearse in exchange for tickets or charge fifty cents for people to sit in on the session. It was generally a lively spot accommodating about twenty or so people when the Troubadours played. This time, the room felt small, cold and more than ever like a damp basement where jars of preserved fruits and vegetables, fermented wine or discarded items were kept.

Lucille wearily asked, "Where's Maybelle?"

"She's on the bus as usual," Lincoln responded. "I parked it in the driveway of my little honey who lives across town. It's out of sight and she'll take good care of it."

"We need to do something to send Mitchell off right."

"Delphina went to take care of getting the body to the funeral home. Marcus is shadowing her to make sure she's all right and nobody touches her. Them men in the street took a beating. Who knows what shape that other man was in when he went flying out that window. I think he went on to meet his maker right there on top of the trash heap."

"Ugh! I can't think about that." Lucille slapped her hands over her ears. "I can't take much more of this! I need something to calm my nerves."

"Hold on to this." Lincoln handed her a smoke. "No need getting into no stiff drink—not after what we seen with Mitchell. Man, are we in sorry shape. I thought it might be easier once Marcus, and now Delphina, had returned. I thought we'd be on easy street and making our way up there in Manhattan. I can't believe…" Lincoln covered this face.

Marcus and Delphina entered the room. Although both had hats pulled low, it was easy to see their faces were ashen and eyes were red-rimmed from weariness. Delphina made a beeline over to Big Bobby, who embraced her tiny frame, rocking her back and forth. He whispered into her ear. She looked up into his face and nodded. They backed away to a dark corner without releasing their embrace and the room suddenly became warmer.

Marcus broke the silence. "Delphina took care of everything. Mitchell will be buried tomorrow. I hope we can hold out until then. I don't think we were spotted but I can't be sure. Those men are going to be hopping mad."

Lincoln picked up his trumpet and put it to his lips. Short staccato notes shattered the air. "I just have to do this. I have to do this for Mitchell."

39

New York City

Marcus arranged for the Troubadours to take the train from Chattanooga to New York, leaving behind everything that had held them together for so many years—a bus, a piano and Mitchell. They all had been the definition of home for Miss Lucille and her Black Troubadours.

All the signs were there. Lucille knew the moment they entered the big sprawling city and watched the spectacle of Harlem's wide busy streets filled with black people from windows to stoops to sidewalks that she was meant to be here. It was the breeze she felt as she walked down Lenox Avenue. She knew in her bones she was meant to be right here in New York City.

From the time she read the post that Pauline Hopkins was presenting a lecture at the YWCA for the Colored Women's Association, nothing would delay her New York residency any longer. And when she actually saw the woman who had given her mother sage advice that she quoted her time and time again as encouragement, it was as if fiction had come to life. Lucille wanted to tell Mrs. Hopkins that it was her words, her directives, that kept Evelyn Love—and by extension, her daughter—from drowning. Lucille wanted Mrs. Hopkins to know that she had modeled her life and had taken up the mantel of leadership after learning about her command as editor-in-chief of *The Colored American Magazine*. She wanted her to know that she had her own version of the Hopkins' Colored Troubadours; Lucille Love and the Black Troubadours lived a wild life, entertaining while spreading the message of the richness and history of music.

"The Black Troubadours, huh? Are you any good?" Pauline Hopkins smiled as she took Lucille's hand.

"Oh yes, ma'am. We're really good. We've got an audition downtown this afternoon, singing everything from classical to jazz."

"Well, let me thank you for your contribution to uplifting our race, young lady."

Lucille was so honored she curtsied. It was as if the world was telling her that her mother was sending her approval.

She had telegrammed her parents to let them know where she was staying. They knew Marcus had returned so Lucille was assured they knew she was safe. She received a message from them telling her they were safe as well and were planning a move to California to start a new life once again.

It was a new life for the Troubadours too. It was an invitation they had all dreamed of receiving. It was an invitation that kept each of them going against all odds in an industry they couldn't refuse. For Lucille, it was an invitation that came with a price: losing their most cherished Troubadour.

Lucille pulled the fox collar closer around her neck as she headed to the theater. The crisp, cool breeze that whipped around the buildings and nipped at her ankles carried a hint of excitement.

Ballyhoo, a brand-new show with music composed by the best around and backed by a boatload of money, was to be mounted as one of the biggest shows featuring a cast of the most talented entertainers on this side of the Atlantic. It was to test its wings in Europe before being on New York's Great White Way. It was the biggest stage Lucille would ever play, a cavernous box that felt like it went for miles and miles into black corners that made her even more nervous. She had never been nervous like this before. Jittery bugs fluttered around her stomach every now and then before a performance, but then Aida would take over and they'd melt away. In the past she could always count on her trusted Troubadours to save her and bring her back to life. She could always depend on Mitchell to pull a song along. He had been her sturdy tugboat and she relied on his ability to read her like no one else. He knew when she was straying off course and would bring her back. But now Mitchell was gone. The heaviness of his absence hung over and filled up the stage. This new piano player, a stranger Marcus found, sat at the piano biting his nails and looked as though he couldn't care less what happened beyond the next few minutes.

Lincoln and Big Bobby were both sweaty, their shirts rumpled and pants dusty at the knees. They had both stayed at a rooming house in Harlem; they too were fascinated by the bustling city. Lincoln marched around in circles, slightly hopping as though his leg was giving him trouble. A child wailed in the background. Although Lucille couldn't see her, it only meant Delphina and Diamond were somewhere in the theater.

The theater manager looked each of them up and down. "This better be good. We've seen enough singers and none of them bopped like we wanted. Where'd you find this worn little group? This ain't no playing-on-the-corner-for-pennies show—this is the big time. I need to see some polish."

"We're as polished as they come," Lucille shouted out into the house. "We wouldn't be standing here if we didn't have what it takes. I'm Miss Lucille and these are my Black Troubadours. We swing and shine like nobody else!"

"We'll be the judge of that."

Lucille turned slowly to face Big Bobby and Lincoln. They had been together and so close for so long they silently gave a four count to start. Big Bobby slid his trombone into a slow climb as Lincoln placed his trumpet to his lips, puffed out his cheeks to herald in a fusion of triplets to introduce Lucille's number. Only thing missing was the piano pickup to usher in the melody. He came in late, in the wrong key and with an ill sense of timing that sent a clash of notes braking through the air. Big Bobby and Lincoln were usually able to bounce off each other, taking a hint from one and then carrying out an embellished melody. But the sound created a muddy mix several times in the intro. Diamond's high-pitched squeal topped off the jarring concoction as she broke into loud protests that echoed out from the recesses of the theater.

"Stop!" Lucille shouted to halt the trio of musicians. Turning back to the men, she said, "Excuse me...so sorry. We need to start over. This here is a new member of our group. Give me one minute, please, and let us start over."

The manager sighed. "Smitty, will ya go find that child and its mother and kindly escort them out. Okay, okay, sugar. Get it together and let's get started. We don't have much time."

Lucille stood onstage, breathing deeply to gain the strength to sing. The air began to fill her up, stretching every inch of her lungs. Each breath she took felt like hot grit sweeping through her body. She held on to the sensation until she had no other choice but to release it. She shot a creased brow at the piano player before giving a count for them to start again. It only took a second for the trombone, trumpet and piano to regain their footing and Lucille took the plunge and dove in. At first, each note fell and rolled softly over her skin, caressing her before falling to earth. She heard each one hit the wood planks, soaking into a stage floor scarred from singers, hoofers, musicians, comedians, jugglers, choirs and every other body that had graced the lights and been associated with the trade.

And with each breath she grew stronger. Fueled by the need to tell the story that painted a different picture for the small audience of people who loved Mitchell and for those who didn't even know him. She fell to her knees. The beads gracing the hem of her dress splayed out before her. Suddenly the piano reminded her of home, where Mitchell would have played a solo between the verses. Not the apartment with the plush green carpets and silk tasseled and beaded lampshades, but the buckboard wagon where the lush branches of tree after tree passed overhead as they traveled down dusty roads. Where Miss Opal schooled her in math and the sciences. Where Daddy and Mommy silently loved each other, vowing in whispers to stay together and fight whatever demons stood before them. Home wasn't one place anymore—it had always been the music and the memories born from blues.

By the time the piano player hit the last stark note, Lucille's face was wet with tears. She saw three or four men in suits stand up in the row of deep cherry-colored seats and the small frame of a woman walking hurriedly toward the stage. One of the men shouted angrily, "So early in the morning? I don't want no drugged-up Negro singer! Get her off the stage!"

"No wait! Wait a minute, Sal," the woman shouted back. Without hesitation, she tiptoed across the makeshift board that crossed the orchestra pit to the stage. She leaned down and placed a hand on Lucille's back. "Miss Lucille… Miss Lucille, are you all right?"

Lucille shook with all the loss and abandonment that she had felt all her life. She roared, crying loudly in the crook of her lap. After a few long minutes, she was able to turn her head away from the wet tears that stained her dress to see the woman still kneeling beside her. The theater was silent. The men in the velvet seats were mute.

"I'm so sorry, ma'am. But he's gone. He left me here alone and I can't…"

The woman whispered. "Listen, you gonna have to do something because if you don't, those men out there are going to sweep you aside like yesterday's news. I've heard you sing and I've heard the Troubadours perform. You deserve to be here. I'm sorry for your loss, Miss Lucille, but you know the saying, 'The show must...'"

Lucille didn't give the slight woman a chance to finish. She rose to her feet, took a deep breath and swung her arms in the direction of the band. "I know where the show has to go and it has to go on. C'mon, Troubadours, let's finish this number. Let's do this for Mitchell."

As the band struck its opening chord, the woman jauntily returned to the audience, shouting to the men, "It's all right. No drugs, just a broken heart. See...see, she's all right now. I give you, Miss Lucille's Black Troubadours!"

Lucille shook herself out of her sadness, gave a nod and a big smile to the little white woman who had just pulled her from the brink.

"Sorry for the moment, folks. I'm gonna sing a little ditty I wrote myself. Something that I call 'The Fruit Man's Blues.' Come on, Big Bobby and Lincoln. Join in when you can and swing it for me, Charlie!"

Lucille couldn't hear anything else that was being said. There was a cacophony of voices surrounding her. She thought she could hear Mitchell calling her name as she belted out lyrics that popped into her head complemented by her steadfast troubadours and a piano player who miraculously improvised a driving jazzy vamp. It was then that Lucille spotted Aida dressed in a turquoise blue wrap. Her bare feet, adorned with toe rings and jewels around her ankles, swung over the edge of the balcony as she waved goodbye.

40

They stood closely together, shielding each other from the wind that blew the waves of the ocean to a violent end against the docks. Everyone had left, sprouting out in different directions. All with the hope their travels and plans would yield fruits of happiness.

Lucille pulled her fox collar tightly against her neck to block the cool air and shuffled her feet, hoping that the movement would circulate the blood to stand against the cold. "They're not giving me a break, I've got to sing tonight. A girl's got to sing for her supper. I don't want to catch a cold. They might drop me in the middle of the Atlantic if I can't."

"You'll be fine, Lucille. In fact, you'll be more than fine. You'll always be a Traveling Love. Hardscrabble and fighting all obstacles. God is on your side, my dear darling. Love is your namesake and it pulls through no matter what."

She lightly patted Marcus's chest, lingering just enough to feel the quick pulse of his heart. The flush of heat reached the surface of her skin and she fought back tears. Looking into the eyes of the man who had seen her grow from the Little Girl with the Big Voice who would do anything to please her parents to a woman with a big voice and even bigger determination to succeed. A woman who knew exactly what she wanted and would exhaust every means to do what it took to be onstage and sing in front of the world. However, this time, words could not find the sound of her voice. Her mouth was dry and she could only mouth the words *I'm sorry.*

Lucille finally broke down upon the realization that this time it was real. This time Marcus was leaving her, and she might never see him again. Marcus had given his last words of advice, encouraging her to sign the agreement for her—only her and not her Troubadours—to go under the *Ballyhoo* management team for two years, which would give her time to test her wings onstage, then venture out to other things, such as recordings or films. He was going home to Chicago to be with Rose; Delphina and Big Bobby made plans to stay together, going to New Jersey to stay on a commune to raise bees; Lincoln decided to stay in New York to play for anyone who could use a bow-legged trumpet player.

And Lucille was heading out on a ship sailing off to her destiny, a land where she would be able to do the things she had only dreamed. She was going home too. No picket fence, only the boards and footlights. She leaned into Marcus and sobbed a wave of tears. He had done so much for her, and they had been through so much together.

"I'll watch over Hank and Evelyn. Don't worry. I'll write you to let you know how they're doing. I'm going to work at the Pantheon, promoting acts and maybe get involved with the motion pictures. It's a growing industry."

"Marcus, please let me know you won't be far away. I need to know that."

"You're going all the way across the ocean and then who knows where."

"But I need to know."

"I won't, Lucille. I won't be far away."

Marcus gave her a kiss on the cheek before backing away, then turned and walked briskly toward the street. Lucille watched him until he was no longer visible in the crowd. Walking up the gangway, Lucille paused to look at the elevated view of the city behind her. Gray buildings sprouted from the ground, each competing with the other for being the tallest structure to touch the sky. Cars barreled around trucks piled high with cargo destined to foreign points on the globe. She took a few more steps up the steep incline, boarding the ship that would carry her to her dreams. She stretched her arms across the rail, took in the view and inhaled the sea air.

Lucille was suddenly drawn away from the city's horizon. She turned to the tall, slender man standing next to her with his coat collar turned up against his ears. He would keep her company and act as her partner onstage and in the next leg of her journey. Silently, as if in prayer, they both leaned against the railing and looked down. Far below, the white foam of the waves curled against the sides of the ship, daring them to lean even farther over the railing. The waves rhythmically taunted them as they slapped the ship in an enticing beat, teasing them to come greet their ancestors on the ocean floor whose origins and destinations crossed and double crossed the seas.

The man jumped back, pulling Lucille with him. Throwing his arms around her shoulders, he smiled and kissed her on the cheek. With a wink, he said, "Well, Miss Lucille, are you ready to conquer the world?"

Cheeks warmed by a blush that defeated the cool ocean breeze, Lucille replied, "Ginger, this world is getting smaller and smaller. Let's go sing and dance before it catches up to us."

CAKEWALK

Sometimes a cake
Ain't quite civilized
'Cause stirred in the batter is a cup full of lies
Sometimes a cake
Is made out of smiles
Hidin' cuts and bruises mile after mile
Sometimes a cake
Ain't nothing but crumbs
Tryin' to silence my voice and keep me mum
Sometimes a cake
Just ain't no prize
But I'll keep on steppin' 'cause I'm destined to rise
Sometimes a cake
Has slices like wings
And until I get mine I'm just gonna sing

★ ★ ★ ★ ★

Acknowledgments

As long as humans have searched the sky for the brightest star to provide guidance, comfort, hope and wonder, so has there been the desire to acquire fame. Staring at the sky, one wonders: How can I grasp and capture a star's beauty, its ethereal light?

On the ground, we attempt to recreate the marvel of that far-off star. We set up platforms that elevate and distance; illuminate those stages with mechanisms to replicate and capture our brightest talents to perform before us. And we are amazed by the ones that dazzle us.

This fictional story is my song for women during the vaudeville era and turn of the century who dared to navigate an industry that was insistent on racial caricatures. Stars such as American soprano Sissieretta Jones; the "Queen of the Blues" Mamie Smith; "Empress of the Blues" Bessie Smith; Aida Overton Walker, the "Queen of the Cakewalk" and so many others—only a fragment of their lives appear in faded yellow newsprint, yet they changed the course of the entertainment industry by chasing their dreams to mercurial heights. Singing, dancing, acting and using theatrical platforms to tell stories that gave us strength, emboldened our dreams or made us laugh or cry, these women took control of their careers and opened opportunities for African Americans all over the world.

The fairy dust of their talents fell to earth to dispel old ways of thinking and spark remarkable change—inspiring new genres and art forms. Thank you to the myriad of entertainers who overcame obstacles to obtain equal representation in the entertainment industry during the period.

There have been so many individuals who have inspired me to write and particularly focus on strong women who learned to take on the mantle of leadership. I would like to extend deep-hearted appreciation to Ms. Lucille Hubbard. Although she is no longer with us, she was a fearless pioneer and advocate for women accessing opportunities in the media and entertainment industries in front of and behind the camera. She gave me my first taste of working as an on-camera host and interviewer. The experience ignited my curiosity and creativity. Ms. Lucille, the tremors from the wake of your fabulousness are still felt today.

Thank you to my amazing editor, Lynn Raposo, for your patience, astute eye and creative contributions that helped shape characters and craft this story. Without you, The Traveling Loves would have been lost in the weeds. You are a jewel.

Another gem I can't thank enough is my fabulous agent, Kevan Lyon of Marsal Lyon Literary Agency. I am forever grateful for your guidance and support.

A big thank-you to Leah Morse, my publicist. I appreciate everything you've done to get the word out. You are a treasure. And to the entire marketing and publicity team, thank you for placing this story in front of as many eyes possible.

I'd also like to extend a hardy thank-you to copy editors Stephanie Van de Vooren and Greg Stephenson. Without you, the story would be about wayward time travelers.

A tremendous thank-you to reference librarians at the local libraries who directed me in my search for material on the business of vaudeville. Without libraries, librarians and those who protect the flow of information, we would all be lost. I am so indebted to your commitment to the art of acquiring knowledge.

I am so grateful for my immediate and extended family for rooting for me, particularly when I was feeling out of my depths for even attempting to write a second novel. Your encouragement throughout my publishing journey kept me going.

And thank you to my forever loves—John, Omari and Chloe, the best "hype team" ever! And my mother, Olivia, whose light continues to shine down on me. She taught me that true love really does conquer all and there is no such word as impossible.

THE
JEWEL
OF THE
BLUES

MONICA
CHENAULT-KILGORE

Reader's Guide

1. Discuss the various characters in *The Jewel of the Blues*. What did each character sacrifice to obtain their perceived goal?

2. Do you think Hank Love made the right decision to leave Evansville?

3. Marcus and Lucille had a complicated relationship—both professionally and personally. Did Marcus truly acknowledge Lucille's feelings for him? Did he lead her on, or did he just use her to advance his career?

4. How did Aida Overton Walker help Lucille's career?

5. The Troubadours provided the melody and background music to Lucille's singing. How else did these characters contribute to the story?

6. What were the dangers in having Delphina travel with the Troubadours?

7. As leader of the Troubadours, Lucille made some difficult and questionable decisions. How did they set her and the troupe back? Conversely, how did those decisions propel her and the troupe forward?

8. Do you think Delphina should be forgiven for leaving the Troubadours and marrying Monte?

9. Do you think Ginger was truly in love with Lucille? Are you happy about Lucille and Ginger ending up together by the end of the story?

10. Have you ever held a grudge? For how long? Have you ever sought revenge?

Music plays a large part in the storytelling of The Jewel of the Blues. This collection of songs was selected as a small representation of the larger jazz era and artists that inspired the story.

"O mio babbino caro"—Kathleen Battle, 2014*
"Missouri Blues"—James Reese Europe and the 369th U. S. Infantry (Hell Fighters) Band, 1919
"Crazy Blues"—Mamie Smith & Her Jazz Hounds, 1920
"You Got Ev'ry Thing a Sweet Mama Needs but Me"—Sara Martin, 1922
"My Way's Cloudy"—Marian Anderson, 1923
"Down Hearted Blues"—Bessie Smith, 1923
"Down Home Blues"—Ethel Waters and Her Ebony Four, 1923
"Lift Ev'ry Voice and Sing"—Manhattan Harmony Four, 1923
"I'm Going Through with Jesus"—Emma E. Beacham, 1924
"Wild Women Don't Have the Blues"—Ida Cox with Lovie Austin and her Blues Serenaders, 1924
"Black Bottom Stomp"—Jelly Roll Morton and his Red Hot Peppers, 1925
"Heebie Jeebies"—Louis Armstrong and his Hot Five, 1926

Scan to listen to The Jewel of the Blues *playlist!*

---

* Inspired by this modern version of the soprano aria from the opera Gianni Schicchi performed by Ohio-born, coloratura soprano Kathleen Battle.

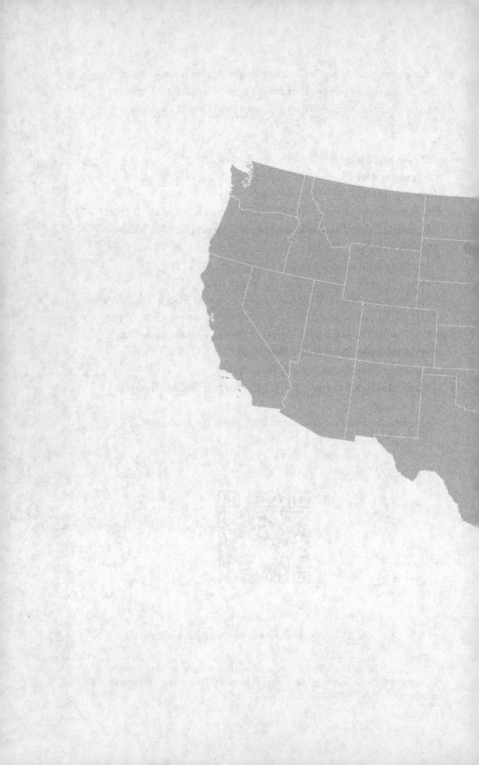

TOUR MAP & THEATER NOTES

Theaters operated under the Southern Consolidated Circuit, which merged with Dudley's Theatrical Circuit, which then merged with Theater Owners Booking Association (TOBA). Some operated under the Keith Southern Circuit.

Chapter 16

The Academy of Music
Location: Richmond, VA
Misc. Theater Notes: Academy-balcony and gallery were reserved for Colored patrons. Mamie Smith, phonograph star and singer of "Crazy Blues" and other popular hits, appeared in very notable, elaborate and expensive gowns.

Chapter 18

Douglass/Royal Theatre
Location: Baltimore, MD
Misc. Theater Notes: The Douglass Theatre (renamed in 1925 as the Royal Theatre) was part of a circuit of theaters for Black entertainment. Sits 1,349 for vaudeville and movies.

Chapter 20

Sunnyside Theatre
Location: Staunton, VA
Misc. Theater Notes: Opened by Mrs. R.L. Pannel. Also served as a dance hall for African American patrons.

Casino/Regal Theater; Lincoln Theatre; Roosevelt Theater; Pekin Theatre; Victoria Theater
Location: Cincinnati, OH
Misc. Theater Notes: Casino Theater—Sits 1500; combination vaudeville, dramatic and photoplay house.
   Lincoln Theatre—"Prettiest little playhouse in the city," catered to an African American audience.
   Roosevelt Theater—Operated by the Lincoln Amusement

Company, ran African American road shows, high-grade motion pictures and vaudeville.

Pekin Theatre—One of the first nickelodeons owned and operated by an African American, Ollie Dempsey.

Chapter 21

Washington Theater; Fountain Airdome Theater
Location: *Indianapolis, IN*
Misc. Theater Notes: *Washington Theater—Advertised entertainment under "Theaters for Colored People" in the Indianapolis News.*

Fountain Airdome—Was an outdoor theater.

Chapter 22

Booker T. Washington Theater
Location: *St. Louis, MO*
Misc. Theater Notes: *Owned by C.H. Turpin, an original member of TOBA. Large turnout for film tests by the Colored Motion Picture Company searching for the "perfect lover" for two-reel African American comedies. Big parade for vaudeville/phonograph stars Butterbeans and Susie, who rode up in a limousine in 1926. It was deemed the best parade since the Colored Knights of Pythias turned out for the theater's grand opening.*

Chapter 23

Pekin (Majestic) Theater
Location: *Jackson, TN*
Misc. Theater Notes: *Vaudeville and first-run movie house. Its Wurlitzer organ accompanied silent films.*

Chapter 24

Liberty Theatre
Location: *Nashville, TN*
Misc. Theater Notes: *Operated between 1921 and 1928.*

Chapter 26

Lenox Theater
Location: *Augusta, GA*
Misc. Theater Notes: *Built in 1921 by four prominent African American businessmen, the Lenox Theater was the only theater where African Americans could sit anywhere in the theater and not be relegated to the balconies of other houses.*

Chapter 28

Morton Theatre
Location: *Athens, GA*
Misc. Theater Notes: *Built in 1910 by Monroe Bowers ("Pink") Morton. One of the first vaudeville theatres built, owned and operated by an African American. In 1914, the Black Patti Musical Comedy Company and Shark's and Tolliver's Smart Set Companies appeared.*

Chapter 31

Paradise Theater
Location: *Atlanta, GA*
Misc. Theater Notes: *Vaudeville house owned by Elijah Davis.*

Chapter 32

Dunbar Theatre
Location: *Savannah, GA*
Misc. Theater Notes: *Vaudeville/photoplay house owned by Savannah Motion Picture Company. First film shown was African American filmmaker Oscar Micheaux's Symbol of the Unconquered.*

Chapter 33

Liberty Theatre
Location: *Chattanooga, TN*
Misc. Theater Notes: *Owned by Sam E. Reevin, an original*

member of TOBA. Managed dancers, acrobats and shows such as Mae Wilson's Brown Skin Beauties. Miss Lucille and her Black Troubadours are billed at the Liberty with sister act Sweetie May and Bonnie Bell Drew, two shows nightly, 7:00 and 9:15.

Chapter 35

Bijou Theater
Location: Nashville, TN
Misc. Theater Notes: Sits 1,642 in orchestra, two balconies and boxes. Managed by Michael and Milton Starr, who built a chain of forty-five to fifty theaters under the name Bijou Amusement Company. Bessie Smith and Susie Sutton Company appeared regularly.

Chapter 40

63rd Street Music Hall/Daly's 63rd Street Theatre
Location: New York, NY
Misc. Theater Notes: Miss Lucille's audition was in the same theater where the landmark African American musical Shuffle Along premiered, inspiring the Harlem Renaissance on Broadway.